"Palmer writes terrific medical suspense, and he has thrown political intrigue into the mix . . . fans won't be disappointed."
—Associated Press

"Michael Palmer once again delivers an adrenaline-pumped political and medical action thriller . . . Palmer fans will not be disappointed in this suspenseful and realistic, fast-paced whodunit."
—*Jewish Journal*

"A must-read for fans of political intrigue."
—*Fort-Worth Star Telegram*

"The military conspiracy is frightening, while Lou's interactions with his daughter and his blossoming romantic interest in a tough attorney provide some breaks from the merciless pace of the investigation. Suspend disbelief that an ER doctor can, or should, attempt some of these actions and enjoy the ride."
—*RT Book Reviews*

"Michael Palmer mixes politics, medical science, and the military to create another suspenseful medical thriller."
—Examiner.com

OATH OF OFFICE

"One of the most exciting thrillers of the year."
—*Huffington Post*

"This is Palmer at his most terrifying, most plausible and, worst of all, most realistic."
—*RT Book Reviews* (4.5 stars)

"Perfect."

"Michael Palmer anchors his thrillers in high concept and steeps them in medicine. *A Heartbeat Away* opens with a prologue, and from the opening line, the reader knows things are not going to go well . . . This is the book for readers who wholeheartedly believe politicians are capable of anything."

THE LAST SURGEON

"Prepare to burn some serious midnight oil."

"Highly suspenseful and compelling."

"Palmer has always been a good writer but he has never crafted a story as suspenseful as this one . . . This is the kind of book you read with a bright light on and all the doors locked . . . Franz Koller is one of the most deadly villains to grace the pages of a novel since the introduction of Hannibal Lecter."

"Should please . . . all those who enjoy their suspense mixed with medical characters and settings."

"The thrill of the non-kill . . . [is] chilling."

"More twists and turns than a sociopath's psyche . . . inventive and effective, an entertaining and engaging read."

THE SECOND OPINION

"A heart-pounding medical thriller . . . satisfying, expertly paced [with] enough suspense to keep readers happily turning the pages."   —*Boston Globe*

"The novel is not merely a thriller but also an exploration of its central character's unique gifts and her determination to communicate with her comatose father despite overwhelming odds. Another winner from a consistently fine writer."   —*Booklist*

"A splendid novel."   —*Globe and Mail* (Canada)

THE FIRST PATIENT

"An exciting thriller that is full of surprises and captures the intense atmosphere of the White House, how the medical system works, and how the 25th Amendment could be brought into play. I thoroughly enjoyed it."
—President Bill Clinton

"An incredibly realistic, frightening thriller that is every White House doctor's nightmare."
—Dr. E. Connie Mariano,
White House Physician 1992–2001

"Endlessly entertaining . . . the roller-coaster ride of a plot builds to an undeniably shocking conclusion."
—*Publishers Weekly*

ALSO BY MICHAEL PALMER

MICHAEL PALMER

RESISTANT

St. Martin's Paperbacks

This is a work of fiction. All of the characters, organizations, and events portrayed in this novel are either products of the author's imagination or are used fictitiously.

RESISTANT

For information address St. Martin's Press, 175 Fifth Avenue, New York, NY 10010.

ISBN: 978-1-250-03091-7

Printed in the United States of America

St. Martin's Press hardcover edition / May 2014
St. Martin's Paperbacks edition / May 2015

St. Martin's Paperbacks are published by St. Martin's Press, 175 Fifth Avenue, New York, NY 10010.

10 9 8 7 6 5 4 3 2 1

Dedicated with love
to my sons, Matthew, Daniel, and Luke

One of the duties of the State is that of caring for those of its citizens who find themselves the victims of such adverse circumstances as makes them unable to obtain even the necessities for mere existence without the aid of others. That responsibility is recognized by every civilized nation. . . . To these unfortunate citizens, aid must be extended by government—not as a matter of charity, but a matter of social duty.

—FRANKLIN D. ROOSEVELT, FIRESIDE CHAT, 1933

Throughout the course of human history people have endured uncertainties brought on by illness, poverty, disability, and aging. Economists and sociologists take delight in labeling these inevitabilities as threats to one's economic security, when in truth they are the price each individual must pay to fund their existence.

—LANCASTER R. HILL, *100 Neighbors*,
SAWYER RIVER BOOKS, 1939

PROLOGUE

A heavy pall had settled over Boston's White Memorial Hospital.

Becca Seabury's condition was deteriorating.

The hospital grapevine was operating at warp speed, sending the latest rumors through the wards and offices of the iconic institution, chosen two years in a row as the number-one general hospital in the country. This morning, in all likelihood, the decision would be made—a decision that almost everyone associated with White Memorial, from housekeeping to the laboratories to the administration, was taking personally.

Before long, the team of specialists—orthopedic, medical, and infectious disease, would either choose to continue battling the bacteria that the press and others had begun calling the Doomsday Germ, or they would opt to capitulate and amputate the teen's right arm just below the shoulder.

In room 837 of the Landrew Building, a group of carefully selected physicians and nurses had been assembled. At the doorway to the room, as well as at every elevator and stairway, security was keeping the media at bay, along with any but essential personnel.

From the day, more than two weeks ago, when Becca was operated on to clean out infection from the site of her elbow repair, she had been front-page news.

Flesh-Eating Bacteria Complicating
Cheerleader's Healing

The seventeen-year-old, captain of her school's championship team, had shattered her elbow in a spectacular fall during the state finals. The violent injury was chronicled on YouTube and immediately went viral, making Becca something of a household name around the globe. A successful reconstruction by Dr. Chandler Beebe, the chief of orthopedics, followed by several days of IV antibiotics, and the conservative decision was made to wait one more day and discharge.

That was when Becca Seabury's fevers began.

The Landrew Building, less than two years old, was the latest jewel in the expanding crown of White Memorial. The eighth floor featured four negative pressure isolation rooms—airtight spaces except for a gap beneath the door, with a ventilation system that brought more air into the room than it allowed out. By the time a nurse escorted Becca's family to the waiting area, there were seven in gloves, gowns, and hoods in the spacious room.

Chandler Beebe, six-foot-six, towered over the rest.

Nearly lost among them, motionless on her back, was a pale, fair-skinned young woman, with hair the color of spun gold. Her lips were dry and cracked and the flush in her cheeks looked anything but healthy. An

IV with a piggybacked plastic bag of meds was draining into her good arm. The temperature reading on her chart was 102.5 degrees. It had been as high as 104. Her blood pressure was 85/50.

Chandler Beebe, once a guard for the Harvard University basketball team, was generally unflappable. Now, beneath his mask and hood, he was nearly as pale as his patient. It was the smell, he knew, that was getting to him. Despite his years operating in war zones and medical missions to third-world countries, he had never been fully able to accustom himself to the odor of pus and of rotting flesh. Glancing at the monitor, with a nurse holding up Becca's arm, he began unwrapping the gauze he had placed around it eight hours before. Beebe had two teenagers himself, a boy and a girl, both athletes and excellent students, and as brave and well-adjusted as this girl. But he couldn't get his mind around the image of either of them being at the crossroads of decisions like this one.

The progressive layers of bandage as they were removed were first damp with bloody drainage, then soaked. The ooze, from eight inches of filleted incision, reeked of untreated bacterial growth. The color of the flesh darkened. Twelve days before, Beebe and a surgical colleague had reopened the incision he had made when he did the initial, meticulous reconstruction. The infection had come on with the speed and ferocity of a Panzer attack. Fever, shaking chills, new swelling, intense pain, dehydration, blood pressure drop. Signs of infection in an enclosed space. There was no choice that day. The incision had to be opened, debrided, irrigated, and drained.

Now, it was time for another decision.

Becca Seabury's antecubital space—the inside of her elbow—looked like ground beef that had been left in the sun. Muscle fibers, tendons, ligaments, all basted in thick, greenish purulence, glinted beneath the portable saucer light overhead. Beebe heard his brilliant chief resident inhale sharply, and vowed to reprimand her for the audible reaction as soon as it was appropriate. In the next moment, he decided not to mention it.

"Becca, it's Dr. Beebe. Can you hear me?"

There was little response except a fitful moan. Beebe, his jaw set, looked across the bed at the chief of infectious disease.

"Sid?" he asked

Sidney Fleishman shrugged and shook his head. "As you can see, she's still toxic. No change in the bug, and no effect from every antibiotic in our arsenal. Her white count has dipped a bit, but there are no other signs that we're winning. We've gotten permission to try one of the most promising experimental drugs that is being tested on strep and MRSA, but this Doomsday G—this *bacteria*—is like nothing we've seen. Strep, but not really strep, resistant to methicillin and vancomycin, and carbapenem."

"Conclusion?"

"I think we have some time. Not much, but some— especially with the infection still limited to her elbow."

Beebe inhaled deeply and exhaled slowly. Fleishman, as bright as anyone at White Memorial, was advocating a continued conservative approach with the addition of a new, experimental drug, which was showing effectiveness against methicillin-resistent staph aureus.

How much time do you think? Beebe was about to ask when Jennifer Lowe, Becca's nurse, standing at the foot of the bed, cleared her throat by way of interruption. She had been massaging lotion onto Becca's left foot and now had turned her attention to the right one.

"Dr. Beebe, I think you'd better have a look at this," she said. "I didn't see anything here an hour ago."

She gently folded back the sheet and gestured to the foot. All five toes were reddened, and swelling extended two inches toward the ankle.

Beebe stepped to his right and inspected this new development—first with his eyes, then with his gloved hands.

"Sid?"

Fleishman studied the foot, then checked for swollen lymph nodes in their patient's right groin—often a sign of expanding infection.

"Nothing yet," he said, "but this is clearly new infection, probably seeded from her arm."

Chandler Beebe ran his tongue across his lips and took one more breath.

"Jennifer, is the OR ready?" he asked.

"It is."

"Call to tell them we're bringing Rebecca Seabury down for removal of a septic right arm. I'll speak to her family. Thank you for your efforts, everyone. My team, go ahead. I'll meet you in the OR. Oh, and Jennifer, call pathology, please, and tell them we'll be sending down a specimen."

The room emptied quickly and silently. These were medical professionals—the best of the best. But every one of them was badly shaken.

Jennifer Lowe, thirty, and a veteran of half a dozen missions to villages in the Congo, bent over her patient. Lowe's marriage to a physical therapist was just six months away. She was a spark plug of a woman, the daughter and granddaughter of nurses.

"Be strong, baby," she whispered. "We're going to get through this. Just be strong."

It was at that moment she felt an irritation—an itch— between the middle and ring fingers of her left hand. While she was at work, her modest engagement ring hung on a sturdy chain around her neck. She had eczema, but never bad and never in that particular spot.

Not all that concerned, she moved over to the sink and stripped off her latex gloves. The skin between the fingers was reddened and cracked.

CHAPTER 1

Liberty is worth more than every pearl in the ocean, every ounce of gold ever mined. It is as precious to man as air, as necessary to survival as a beating heart.

—LANCASTER R. HILL, *A Secret Worth Keeping*, SAWYER RIVER BOOKS, 1937, P. 12

"Two-oh-six . . . two-oh-seven . . . two-oh-eight . . ."

"Come on, Big Lou. It hurts so good. Say it!"

"Okay, okay," Lou Welcome groaned. "Two-oh-nine . . . It hurts so good . . . Two-ten . . . It hurts so good . . . Oh, it just frigging hurts! My . . . stomach's . . . gonna . . . tear . . . open . . . Two-twelve . . ."

Lou was doing sit-ups on the carpet between the beds in room 177 of what had to be one of the bargain rooms at the venerable Chattahoochee Lodge. Cap Duncan, shirtless and already in his running shorts, was kneeling by Lou's feet, holding down his ankles. Cap's shaved pate was glistening. His grin, as usual, was like a star going nova. He had done three hundred crunches before Lou was even out of the sack, and looked like he could easily have ripped off three hundred more.

Every inch a man's man.

Lou's best friend, and for ten years his AA sponsor, was a fifty-two-year-old Bahamian, with a physique that looked like it had been chiseled by one of

Michelangelo's descendants. He had earned his nickname, Cap'n Crunch, from his days as a professional boxer, specifically from the sound noses made when he hit them.

It was April 14—a Thursday. Lou's trip to Georgia had been ordered by Walter Filstrup, the bombastic head of the Washington, D.C., Physician Wellness Office (PWO), a position that made the psychiatrist Lou's boss.

Filstrup's sweet wife, Marjory, a polar opposite of her husband, was in the ICU of a Maryland hospital with an irregular heartbeat that had not responded to electrical cardioversion. But as one of two candidates for the presidency of the National Federation of Physician Health Programs, Filstrup was scheduled to address the annual meeting, being held this year at the lodge in the mountains north of Atlanta.

Wife in ICU versus speech in Georgia. *Let . . . me . . . think.*

Not surprisingly to Lou, Filstrup had actually wrestled mightily with the choice. It wasn't until Marjory had an allergic reaction to one of the cardiac meds that the man turned his speech over to Lou along with his conference registration, and an expense account that would cover all Lou's meals, providing he only ate one a day.

Whoopee.

"You're slowing down, Welcome," Cap said. "You're not going to get to three hundred that way."

"I'm not going to get . . . to three hundred *any* way."

Cap, his competitive fire seldom dimmed, delighted in saying that most people's workout was his warm-up. Lou, nine years younger, and at six feet, an inch or so taller, never had any problem believing that. Their connection began the day Lou was checked into Harbor House, a sober halfway house in one of the grittier sections of D.C. Cap, given name Hank, was working as a group leader there while he cajoled one bank after another trying to scrape together enough bread for his own training center. Twelve months after that, Lou was living on his own, the Stick and Move Gym had become a reality, and the two friends, one black as a moonless night, and the other a blue-eyed rock jaw with the determination of a Rottweiler and roots that may have gone back to the Pilgrims, were sparring three times a week.

A year or so after that, following a zillion recovery meetings and the development of a new, infinitely mellower philosophy of living, the suspension of Lou's medical license was lifted, and he was back in the game.

"Okay, then," Cap said, "do what you can. It's no crime to lower your expectations. Only not too far."

"Does everything . . . we do together . . . have to be . . . some sort of competition? Two-twenty . . . two-twenty-one . . ."

"I assume we're going to have breakfast after our run and I don't believe in competitive eating, if that helps any."

"Of course. It would be the one area I could kick your butt."

The Chattahoochee Lodge had been built in the twenties for hunters and had been enlarged and renovated in 1957, the same year Elvis purchased Graceland. A sprawling, rustic complex, the main building was perched in the mountainous forest, high above the banks of the fast-flowing Chattahoochee River. As ecotourism boomed in the early 1990s, the place became a major destination for leisure travelers, birders, hikers, and convention goers, with rooms often booked a year in advance.

Lou, board-certified in both internal and emergency medicine, had never particularly enjoyed medical conferences of any kind, so it was a godsend when he whined about the impending trip to Cap and learned that his friend's only living relative was an aging aunt, living just outside of Atlanta. Working full-time in the ER at Eisenhower Memorial Hospital, and part-time with the PWO, Lou had more than enough in his small war chest for another ticket south. The quite reasonable rent for his second-floor, two-bedroom apartment down the street from the gym and just above Dimitri's Pizza helped make a loan to his sponsor even more painless.

Proof that the idea was a solid one was that Cap haggled surprisingly little over the bartering agreement Lou proposed—two months of weekly sessions in the ring for him, plus an additional four lessons for his precocious fourteen-year-old daughter, Emily. Cap would get the window seat.

Having to put up with Filstrup notwithstanding, Lou loved his job at the PWO. The pay was lousy, but for him the irony of going from being a client to being an associate director was huge. The organization provided support and monitoring services for doctors with mental illness, physical illness, substance abuse, sexual boundary violations, and behavioral problems. Most new PWO contracts required the troubled physician to enter some sort of treatment program or inpatient rehab, followed by regular meetings with their assigned

PWO associate director, along with frequent random urine screens for alcohol and other drugs of abuse.

Lou was hardly averse to counseling and psychotherapy for certain docs, but he strongly believed that, physician or not, addiction was a medical illness and not a moral issue. Walter Filstrup disagreed.

When Filstrup finally handed over his carefully typed speech and the conference program, the trip got even better. Not only would Lou and Cap have time for some training runs together in the mountains, but while Cap was visiting his aunt, Lou would be able to take a conference-sponsored guided tour of the Centers for Disease Control—the CDC.

More irony.

Lou had spent nearly ten months of his life in Atlanta and had never even been close to the world-renowned institute. The last time he was in the city, nine years before, was for the one-year reunion of his treatment group at the Templeton Drug Rehab Center.

It was time to complete some circles.

CHAPTER 2

One man can dream, a handful can plan,
thousands can strike, but just a hundred,
properly placed and effectively utilized, can
reshape the world.

—LANCASTER HILL, *100 Neighbors*, SAWYER
RIVER BOOKS, 1939, P. III

His name was Douglas Charles Bacon, but to the seven others participating in the videoconference, he was N-38. *N* for *Neighbor*.

The Society of One Hundred Neighbors, conceived in secret during the early 1940s, arose from political philosopher Lancaster Hill's treatise, *100 Neighbors*. Hill's masterpiece, and several volumes that followed it, were written in response to Franklin Roosevelt's economic and social legislations known collectively as the New Deal. Initially, there were only a dozen Neighbors, strategically placed throughout the country. But within a year, the one-hundred-member limit prescribed by Hill had been reached. One hundred neighbors. No more, and no less.

Bacon was a jovial, round-bellied Southerner, with a mind for numbers and an encyclopedic knowledge of Scotch. He was still a crack shot with a Remington, even after the hunting accident that had left him with a permanent limp and only two toes on his left foot. As the chosen director of the society, he was an ex-

officio member of all seven of their current APs—
Action Projects. From what he had been told just two
days ago, AP-Janus, the most ambitious, far-reaching
undertaking in the group's history, was in trouble.
Bacon took a sip of Macallan 18, one of his favorites,
and smiled thinly. No one who knew him had ever seen
him lose his cool. Perhaps Scotch was the reason.

N-80, Dr. Carlton Reeves, was a professor of surgery
at Michigan. When Bacon first learned of the Janus
bacteria, he had assigned Reeves to look into it further.
Later, when the stunning possibilities had become
clear, he had made the physician the coordinator of the
AP and helped him to form his team. It was Reeves
who had convened this advisory committee videoconference.

The members of the Society of One Hundred Neighbors blended with those around them as effectively as
chameleons in a jungle. They wore business suits and
ties to work, flannel shirts or uniforms or lab coats, and
often carried briefcases. They lived in cities or towns
in nearly every state, and whatever their talents, were
uniformly respected for the quiet skill they brought to
their jobs. But beneath their varied positions and appearances, the members of One Hundred Neighbors
were joined by a singleness of purpose.

They were all, by the most widely accepted definitions, terrorists.

The goal of the organization, a straight line from
Lancaster Hill, was quite simple. By any means, they
were pledged to eliminate the suffocating government
programs of entitlement that had brought America
lurching to the brink of bankruptcy.

Bacon took the brief oath as director in 1993, taking

over from the woman whose failing health had led her to relinquish leadership of the society. It was the year Bill Clinton had begun his first term as president, and also the year Islamic fundamentalists bombed the World Trade Center. Bacon, a registered Democrat and universally revered investment banker, had squelched efforts to put him on a short list for a post in the Clinton cabinet. Too much visibility and too little mobility.

His office was in the North Tower of the WTC. However, he was away at the time of the lethal bombing. His vacation was hardly a coincidence, given that he had financed mastermind Ramzi Yousef and had chosen the day of the truck bomb explosion. The goal of the Neighbors at that time was the erosion of the public's confidence in the head of the House Armed Services Committee that would lead to his resignation.

"Are we ready, Eighty?" Bacon asked. "I'm certain Nine will be here shortly, so we might as well begin."

Bacon's face, like those of the others, was electronically distorted. The bottom of the massive screen displayed small boxes containing the encrypted video feed of each attendee, while the center area was reserved for a larger display of whoever was speaking. Bacon's feed was the only one to run in the upper-left corner of everyone's display.

The director held fiat over all board decisions. The advisory committee was there to help plan a new AP or to deal with decisions involving a member. Bacon would be a Neighbor until he could no longer do the job, after which his number would be given over to his replacement. Lancaster Hill had wisely laid out the blueprint of succession seventy-five years before:

Any Neighbor who no longer serves the cause
because of an illness, shall be retired by the
board, and their number reassigned to their re-
placement.

Except for health issues, no one ever left the society
of their own volition. Members were sometimes dismissed when they lost their positions, or their influence otherwise waned, but they were always quickly
replaced. Rarely, a member insisted on disengaging
himself, or was found to be a security risk. In those in-
stances, there were specialists in elimination who
were kept on retainer at the advisory committee's
discretion.

The final screen lit up as Selma Morrow, N-9, activated her camera. She was chief of strategy and operations for Phelps and Snowdon, considered one of the
strongest hedge funds in the country. She held the same
position on the society advisory committee, and as such
was a consultant to every AP. A personal favorite of
Bacon's, Nine would be his nominee to succeed him
when the time came. For the moment, though, succession was not the issue.

The Janus strain was.

"Good to see you all," Eighty said, "at least as much
as I *can* see you. I wouldn't call you all together unless
you needed to hear this update regarding AP-Janus. To
review, the Janus bacteria came to our attention some
time ago thanks to N-Seventy-one, who stumbled on
the germ accidentally while investigating another bacteria. The complete microbiology of Janus is too complex to go into here, but basically, most bacteria are

divided into two major groups depending on whether or not their cell walls accept Gram staining—a process invented in the late nineteenth century, and still widely used today. Gram positive bacteria appear purple under a microscope, and Gram negative, once they are counterstained with the red dye safranin, appear pink."

"Excuse me," Twenty-six, a specialist in mass psychology, asked, "but you said most bacteria are either Gram positive or Gram negative. Most but not all?"

"Precisely."

"But the Janus bacteria is neither?"

"Right again. Even though nearly all bacteria are either Gram positive or Gram negative, a very few, relative to the probably tens of millions of different species, are Gram intermediate—neither purple nor pink. There are even some that are Gram variable, staining either positive or negative depending on the age of the germ at the time it is removed from its culture medium for staining. But Janus is different. Janus has the genetic makeup that enables it to change from positive to negative and back again. Other properties of the germ are constantly in flux as well."

"Like a shape-shifter," Ninety-seven said. "That's why it's resistant to all antibiotics."

Ninety-seven was a mechanical engineer and mathematician, just six years past earning a dual Ph.D. at MIT. The youngest of the Neighbors, her adult-adjusted IQ had been measured at 182.

"Actually," Eighty replied, "it seems the Gram positive form is sensitive to some antibiotics, but the Gram negative is totally resistant to all—all, that is, except one—a sequence, actually. Almost by accident, Seventy-one stumbled on a combination of chemicals that, administered in a particular order, completely eradicated the Janus strain. It was tried on infections induced in pigs, then monkeys, and finally in several humans. The sequence eradicated every one of their infections—like magic."

"No side effects?"

"None in the past three years that we can see. But now a problem has arisen."

"You mean a challenge," Bacon corrected.

"Of course. A challenge. The Janus strain is working as we hoped. In that regard, it is clear to everyone in the government that we are capable of delivering on our threat."

The name of the demon germ had been carefully chosen. Janus, the two-faced Roman god of duality—beginning and end; comedy and tragedy; birth and death; health and sickness. There was something unsettling about the name, which was just what the advisory committee wanted. Something creepy.

Bacon approved of the way the head of AP-Janus was going about his explanation. Unfortunately, the director knew what was coming next.

"But the situation has changed," he said, completing Eighty's thread. "Our treatment is no longer effective."

Taking another sip of Scotch, Bacon worked to keep his emotions in check. After years of probing and experimenting, of whittling away at obstacles and taking baby steps toward the ultimate goal—specifically a threat Congress and the president could not dismiss—they finally had the technology to complete the mission, to fulfill the dream. There had to be a way to overcome this setback.

"Precisely," Eighty said. "The *challenge,* as you so aptly put it, is that the Janus strain is simply too good."

"Too good?" Forty-four asked.

Forty-four was a highly decorated retired admiral, now a U.S. senator from Rhode Island. His responsibility was to keep his identity a secret, while brokering the bargain with the government that was at the heart of the Janus project. Nine was assisting him, and until this unexpected development, they had been close—extremely close—to pulling it off. The spawn of Roosevelt's New Deal was on the verge of being erased, and Lancaster Hill's vision was about to become reality.

America would no longer be held hostage by its government, and the country would begin to flourish, freed at last from the financial shackles of entitlements. Social Security, Medicare, and Medicaid would become anachronistic symbols of America's parasitic, destructive social welfare policies. The staggering national debt would shrink like a bank of spring snow. Only those who could afford it would ever be admitted to a hospital.

"First of all," Eighty said, "the spread of infection has gone beyond our predications. Then, when we tried to pull back while the powers in Washington were considering our offer, we discovered that Janus had become resistant to our treatment."

"Explain yourself," Forty-four said.

"Nine is keeping track of all of the reported cases of infection."

"I'll patch it onto the screen," the head of strategy and logistics said.

A map of America appeared on the screen. There were red dots in most of the states—each dot, according to the map's key, representing an infection with the media-dubbed Doomsday Germ.

"This map is from twenty months ago," Nine said. "Every one of these infections were placed by one of the people we enlisted to assist us with this aspect of AP-Janus. They are all reliable, and fully support our philosophy and goals. Now, here is a map from nine months ago. We expected some contagion, and that is what we are seeing here. At this point, Health and Human Services Secretary Goodings asked us to pull back and have our people treat the infection with our system of antibiotics until she could meet with the president. That's when the trouble began."

A new map replaced the old and immediately Bacon felt his chest tighten. Instead of seeing red dots in fifteen states, there were dots in every state, and the numbers in the original states had quadrupled.

"I thought the bacteria needed a deep wound to spread," he said.

"That was what we thought as well," Eighty replied. "Not only has Janus become resistant to our treatment, but it is spreading in unexpected ways. It's quite remarkable, in fact. Our scientists have never seen so profound an adaptation take place so quickly."

"Forty-four, what is the current status of our negotiations with the secretary?" Bacon asked the senator.

"They're panicked about the fact that word is leaking out. We knew they were stalling until their microbiologists could come up with an effective treatment, but as far as we can tell, they haven't gotten there. The deadline we gave them is almost up, but of course with this new resistance, as soon as the government realizes what's happened, we will have lost our leverage."

"The rapid adaptation has taken us all by surprise," Eighty said. "Initially, as you alluded, it took a significant inoculum of bacteria for infection to take hold—a deep wound. Now, any sized cut, even a gap from a hangnail, might be enough to cause an infection. Doctors would need to be using extreme bio-safety protocols to properly protect themselves and other patients from the germ."

Bacon felt his cheeks flush. He dreaded the answer to the question he needed to ask.

"What does your model show in a year's time?"

"This is just a projection," Nine said, "but I'm afraid you're not going to like what it shows."

Again, one map faded from the conference screen, soon replaced by another. Bacon steeled himself. The red dots made the country appear to have suffered a severe case of the measles. Thousands of cases, involving even the less populated states.

"Good lord, what's the death toll projection?"

"Unless we can find a way to treat the infection, the death toll will just continue to rise. In addition, of course, AP-Janus will be finished. Our bargaining chip will have vanished, and the hunt for the identities of every one of us will intensify. Sooner rather than later, the FBI will offer enough for someone to crack."

Bacon cringed and leaned back in his plush leather chair, feeling the coldness of the damp stone floor soak into his bones. Instead of rescuing America, the Society of One Hundred Neighbors was about to destroy it.

"We are not mass murderers," he said. "We have a purpose here. . . . Ideas?"

After a silent minute, Ninety-seven, the mathematician/engineer, spoke up.

"If we launch a containment strategy, we believe we can limit the loss of life to less than a thousand individuals. But remember, that's only a projection. At the moment, the cart is very much dragging the horse."

"What sort of containment strategy do you have in mind?"

"We would need to kill all infected individuals," she said without emotion, "and stop infecting new ones. Even then, to stretch my equine analogy, the horse may already be out of the barn."

Bacon grimaced. "We are so close. The president and the secretary know what Janus can do to public confidence in our hospital system. They are close to caving in. We absolutely cannot stop now. Eighty?"

"I believe we need to take a more active role in developing an effective treatment for the germ. Seventy-one, who made the initial discovery that started AP-Janus, is working intensively at modifying the treatment protocol. And, of course, from the moment we first contacted them with our offer, the government has been working on a solution."

"How close are they?"

"They have a microbiologist leading a secret task force," Eighty said. "Our ability to intercept his communication with his team is frequently compromised by the NSA, but we have reason to believe progress is being made."

"So then, we put this scientist to work for us," Bacon

said. "We must possess both the cause and the cure or all is lost. Can we get to him?"

"Thanks to Nine's foresight, we have had a contingency plan for this very scenario in place from the moment we activated AP-Janus. Forty-five is our inside man. He should be able to obtain the asset."

At last, Bacon had a reason to smile.

He took a more relaxed sip of his Scotch, and said, "Then you will proceed."

CHAPTER 3

As for man, the biological laws make no exception for intelligence or wealth. The laws of God only demand that we do what we can in what time we have, to make the world a place where laziness and sloth are never rewarded.

—LANCASTER R. HILL, *Climbing the Mountain*, SAWYER RIVER BOOKS, 1938, P. 111

Lou had fallen twice while traversing the rain-slicked rocks and roots. Lou and Cap finished at a slower pace, turning some heads as they dragged across the rustic lobby of the lodge, muddied and scraped.

"I think we'll bag our run today," someone called after them. "Too much of a contact sport."

Still shaken from his falls, Lou headed for the shower while Cap checked the highway map for the best route to his aunt's house in Buford. Twenty minutes later, Lou emerged from a cloud of steam, ready to take on the forest again.

"Looks like I might be back after dinner, so you'll have to eat without me," Cap said.

"Not a problem. I should probably do some schmoozing for Filstrup anyway."

"How do you think the election is going to go?"

"Honestly? . . . The speech lacks passion," Lou said. "Abraham Lincoln could give it and it would still fall flat."

"Ouch."

"Many of the docs involved in physician wellness organizations are in recovery themselves. Filstrup's views, well, they're clinical at best. Long on pomposity, short on grit."

"Why is he running for this office, anyway?"

"You're talking about a guy who has called me for progress reports on the election several times since we got here, while his wife is still in the ICU. Clearly his ego was bought in a plus-sized store."

"Well, I'm sure you'll give it your all."

"Believe me, pal, I care a lot more about Marjory Filstrup's irregular heart rhythm than I do about Walter's election. Besides, even though I've got another day to read it over, Filstrup would gut me if I so much as changed a word, so what there is is what they're gonna get."

"After our run tomorrow, I'll listen to you read it if you want."

"You're going to hate it."

"Nah, man. It's cool. I haven't had a vacation in ages, and I'm really happy being here, so helping you and your boss out is the least I can do."

"I'm glad the trip's working out, thanks in large part to that touchdown catch you made out there."

"Aw, shucks."

Lou left while Cap was showering. The van hired to shuttle folks to the tour of the CDC was idling near the entrance to the lodge. Lou doubted he would be on time to snag a window seat, but to his surprise there were only two other passengers. According to their name tags, they were Dr. Brenda Greene, an internist from Oregon, and Dr. Harvey Plimpton from Connecticut, who had lost interest in his specialty of gastroenterology somewhere in his late fifties and had become certified by the American Board of Addiction Medicine.

Greene, a garrulous and gregarious redhead, was utterly dismayed with the small turnout.

"I don't think people understand what an unusual experience this is going to be. The Centers for Disease Control doesn't even offer tours, except of their museum. My ex, Roger, is in the public relations office and pulled strings to arrange this for us. A guided tour of the CDC is a once-in-a-lifetime opportunity."

"Physician health people can be a little narrow," Plimpton said. "What made you sign up, Lou?"

"I've never been. I had no idea they didn't give tours. I have always thought of the place as sort of a Disney World of microbiology, featuring Bugland and Epidemiologyland and AndromedaStrainland and the like."

The Templeton Rehabilitation Center was believed by many to provide the most effective treatment for chemically dependent health professionals in the world. Lou's addiction, primarily to amphetamines, had evolved as he moonlighted more and more hours in an effort to help his father, Dennis, a union laborer then on disability, meet the college tuition expenses of Lou's younger brother, Graham. The deal was that Graham was never to be told. Lou feared that the fragile relationship between the two headstrong brothers would shatter. As things were, they had never grown close.

The last time Lou had been in Atlanta, the anniversary of his arrival at Templeton, was the last time he had been in the city. By then, many of those from his "class" had been lost to follow-up, and too many others were dead.

Bad disease.

The memories, tempered by the years and the recovery meetings, roiled in Lou's mind as the van rolled through the streets of the city where the turnaround in his life had begun.

Druid Hills, home to the CDC as well as some of Atlanta's most elegant mansions, was some five miles from downtown. The van and its three passengers cruised to the main entrance past the agency logo— white rays on blue, beneath the block letters CDC. The driver pulled to a stop in front of the main building and informed the trio of the pickup time for the return trip to the lodge.

"I could stay here for days," Greene gushed.

"Is your ex coming to greet us?" Lou asked.

"Doubtful. Roger and I are on decent terms, but we split because I told him he wasn't motivated enough to amount to anything."

Lou shielded his eyes against the glare of the morning sun. The air, free of the scent of lab chemicals, smelled instead of flowering plants and trees. He gestured at a towering brick smokestack rising up from behind a mirrored-glass building. The sprawling complex seemed perfect for incubating secrets as well as specimens.

"I wouldn't be a bit surprised to learn they're taking volunteers for human experimentation, if you want to extend your stay," he said.

"I assume you're joking."

"Alas, people are always making that assumption."

Lou followed the others into the tastefully appor-
tioned lobby, chilled enough to raise goose bumps. He
wondered about the negative pressure rooms, HEPA air
purifiers, and other bio-safety protocols employed at
various areas in the facility to keep lethal pathogens
contained.

"If you've ever wondered what a bioterrorist's candy
store looks like," Greene said as if reading his thoughts,
"well, this is it."

A brunette dressed in a sharply tailored navy blue
suit approached. The tag pinned to her ample lapel said
that her name was Heidi, and that she was with public
relations. She glanced briefly at her clipboard, perhaps
making sure she had the correct number of visitor
badges to hand out.

"Hello and welcome," she said with the slightest hint
of an accent. "My name is Heidi Johnson, and I'll be
your guide for your visit today. I assume you are Dr.
Greene?"

"Brenda Greene, that's right."

"I have a message for you from Roger Greene.
He regrets that he has meetings all day and won't be
here to escort you personally, but he welcomes you to
the foremost facility of its kind in the world, and
knows I will fill in admirably for him. Now, unless
there are questions, I guess I should make sure I have
the right people before we head off."

"I assume you know that we're from the Physician
Wellness conference," Greene said.

"Chattahoochee Lodge. We don't generally offer
tours, but Mr. Greene, who's my boss, arranged your
visit personally."

Lou glanced over at Brenda and felt certain he could

read her mind about the relationship between her ex and Heidi.

"I had expected a larger group, but the smaller numbers only mean we will be able to see more," Heidi said.

From the gardens outside to the sparkling interior to Heidi's perfect smile, Lou sensed that the CDC did its very best to downplay its important and often dangerous work. However, Heidi's demeanor dimmed slightly after she finished handing out name badges.

"I'm afraid Dr. Chopra, the director of our Division of Bacterial Diseases, has been called away on business, so we're not going to be able to visit her lab before our tour of the grounds and the museum. We have two alternatives. We could visit the Division of Viral Diseases or take a tour of our Antibacterial Resistance Unit."

Viral diseases . . . Antibacterial resistance . . . A candy store for terrorists. The phrases reverberated in Lou's thoughts.

Harvey Plimpton, who had been taciturn in contrast to Brenda Greene, came alive at the option.

"Antibacterial resistance. Before I changed specialties, I did research on E. coli mutation. Can we go there?"

"If you both agree," Heidi said.

Lou and Greene made brief eye contact and nodded.

"Great, we'll start your visit there," Heidi said. "I'll call and let Dr. Scupman know that we're coming. I think you'll find him . . . well, quite interesting."

"What do you mean by 'interesting'?" Lou asked.

Heidi returned an enigmatic smile, but not an answer.

CHAPTER 4

The government exists to provide order to the people while 100 Neighbors exists to define what that order shall be.

—LANCASTER R. HILL, *100 Neighbors*, SAWYER RIVER BOOKS, 1939, P. 17

It was three tenths of a mile from the main building to the CDC's recently constructed Antibiotic Resistance Unit. Led by Heidi Johnson, the small group trooped there through a muggy, seventy-five-degree morning. The ARU, an expansive, single-story blockhouse-like rectangle, was constructed of gray cinder block. Dense low shrubbery surrounded it, but there was little in the way of artistic landscaping. Lou wondered if the designer had been intimidated by the notion of the germs the building was to contain or had simply been instructed not to make the place too inviting.

As if validating his suspicions, security protocols commenced upon entry. An armed guard, young and fit and not the least bit engaging, came out from behind a small, unadorned desk in an equally undecluttered lobby. He took IDs and registered fingerprints using a biometric scanner. Moments later, another armed guard appeared from behind a locked steel door, this one secured by a keypad entry system. Escorted by the second guard, Lou followed the others into a long,

windowless corridor, with unframed, foot-square photos
lining the wall on each side—unlabeled, unappealing,
colored microscopic and electron microscopic images
of germs, mostly bacteria.

The air, possibly filtered through some sort of recir-
culation system, tasted stale. Passing in front of a glass
interior door, Lou spied a trio of scientists dressed in
white knee-length lab coats at the far end of a hallway
to their right. He glimpsed them just before they vanished through a side door into what might have been
yet another corridor . . . or a stairway.

Creepy.

The mystery of what lay beyond that passage tugged
at Lou's curiosity and had him suspecting that there
was more to the facility belowground than above. The
labs housed germs that were resistant to treatment.
The battles that must be raging within those unappealing walls were intriguing. How many lethal forms
of microscopic life were being cultured and studied?
Could the scientists he had seen be working on something other than antibiotic resistance—weapons of
mass destruction, perhaps? He kept pace with the others but let his imagination run on high.

Following a maze of shorter corridors, the group
passed through an open doorway and entered into a
space with no scientific equipment inside—a conference room and library, with floor-to-ceiling bookshelves. Tomes and bound periodicals, neatly arranged
and labeled, occupied the entirety of two walls, and
there were half a dozen bridge chairs set in front of a
large flat-screen television positioned at the front of the
room.

Awaiting their arrival were two people, a man, mid-to-late fifties, and a woman, perhaps two decades his junior, both wearing knee-length lab coats. There was no identifying information—their names or the name of the unit—stitched above the breast pocket. The man had a broad, flat nose, heavy-lidded green eyes, and unruly gray-brown hair, carelessly parted on the right. His pallid complexion hinted to Lou at unbalanced hours spent indoors, probably in this vitamin D–deficient sarcophagus. The blue oxford shirt beneath his open lab coat would never pass anyone's wrinkle-free test. His associate, her raven hair pulled into a tight bun, had an academic look, enhanced by heavy-framed glasses. Petite and quite cute in a mousy sort of way, she, at first take seemed reserved and uneasy around the arrivals.

"Hello and welcome," the man said, his speech, purposefully or not, delivered in a sepulchral tone. "My name is Scupman—Dr. Samuel Scupman. I am the head of the Antibiotic Resistance Unit here at the CDC. My associate is Dr. Vicki Banks. She will be assisting with today's presentation. Mr. Greene in public relations tells me you are all physicians."

"Except me," Heidi said. "I work with Mr. Greene."

Lou again saw Brenda's eyes flash.

"I'm Dr. Brenda Greene," she said. "Mr. Greene and I are—were—married. This is Dr. Harvey Plimpton and this is Dr. Lou Welcome. We're attending the national physician health organization meeting, and we're all thrilled to be here."

Scupman, looking as if he could not care less who they were, nodded but made no attempt to shake hands.

His eyes narrowed, possibly at the notion of having to interact with a species composed of more than one cell. A cloud of sorts passed in front of his face.

"I confess I was surprised that your husband would offer up our unit this way," he said. "Much of the work we do here is top secret. To guide you into the heart of our lab would be profoundly irresponsible. You see, within the confines of this facility exist more than ten thousand different species of bacterium—"

"Actually, at last count, we have more than twenty thousand," Vicki Banks interjected.

"Yes, of course, thank you," Scupman said. "Twenty thousand different strains of germs, many of which are so lethal that even for people highly trained in biorisk management, including the most advanced biosafety and laboratory security protocols, the dangers are still quite pronounced. I know you'll want more, but for your own protection, today's tour will be confined to the safety of a slide show."

"We understand," Brenda said, her disappointment obvious.

"Please, if you'll take your seats," Banks instructed. "Dr. Scupman has another commitment, so we'll need to begin right away."

As soon as everyone was settled, the lights dimmed and the first slide—bright colors, high definition— appeared on screen. It depicted a series of pink, rod-shaped bacteria, housed within a pink culture medium.

"What you are seeing here," Scupman said, "is a Gram negative motile bacterium called *Burkholderia pseudomallei*. This impressive little creature is the root cause of the infectious disease melioidosis. Without proper treatment, mortality rate for infected organisms exceeds ninety percent. Vomiting, high fever, cough, and profound chest pain combine to deliver a mercilessly slow and agonizing death. This bacterium, endemic in parts of Asia, Australia, and Africa, is currently classified as a category B biological weapon agent. It is sturdy, easily obtained, easily cultured, and stable enough to be weaponized. Impressive, yes?"

Scupman flashed through a series of slides depicting different germs while speaking of the miraculous properties of each of them as if they were his brilliant, accomplished children. The more he rhapsodized, the more uneasy Lou became. It was one thing for Scupman to love his work, but another altogether to idolize the very beasties he was trying to defeat.

"Humans possess a vast array of defense systems to guard against such foreign intruders," the entomologist went on, "and yet, despite all our impressive advances in science and medicine, we still have not unlocked the secret to the body's abilities to defend itself. The step from genetic response to antibacterial effect remains as mysterious to us now as the origins of life itself. You may be impressed with our body's capabilities, but I am here to tell you that frightening as it may seem, there are very few battles that bacteria are not equipped to win.

"How can an organism like *B. pseudomallei* remain hidden inside the human body for years, *undetected* by the immune system, as though a prowler has taken up residency within a burgled home, and then suddenly and without warning, become active and spread throughout the body until the victim's life-giving blood turns to poison? This"—Scupman held up a single finger—"is but one of the questions our researchers are working to answer. For the very fate of our planet, our ultimate survival, depends on gaining access to this knowledge—of separating out the bacteria essential to our well-being from those bent by their genetics on destroying us. We are at war each and every day against an armada of microscopic enemies—enemies without consciences, whose only purpose is to multiply and metabolize; enemies genetically determined to achieve complete and total victory, even at the expense of the life of their hosts."

In the dimly lit room, Lou could almost see Scupman perspiring from his own enthusiasm. A weighty silence ensued, nobody sure of how to respond to the man's rant. It was Brenda who eventually broke the tension.

"Dr. Scupman, is there a genetic component that could explain why the bacteria remain dormant in some people?"

Scupman appeared pleasantly surprised, perhaps by the literateness of her question. He turned up the lights.

"Dr. Banks, would you like to handle this one?"

Scupman's associate looked as if she would prefer to listen. But when she did speak, her answer was delivered with confidence, and with none of the bravado of her boss.

"You're all familiar with Toll-like receptors?" she asked.

The three physicians nodded.

"Then you know these proteins are what initiate the fight against deadly bacteria. TLRs are like ten-digit alarm codes. For any pathogen that comes into contact with an immune cell, a code is entered, and if the germ is not benign, an alarm gets triggered, activating the body's defenses. And yet, *B. pseudomallei,* like a microscopic magician, tricks the system by entering the code of a harmless bacterium, leaving the body unaware of the intruder's presence. So to answer your question, yes, we believe there is a genetic reason why some people become infected but never get ill. Still, we are far from using that knowledge to develop an effective vaccine or antibiotic."

"Thank you, Vicki," Scupman said.

Banks smiled demurely, and looked to Lou even more attractive than on first impression. In spite of himself, he noticed that she wore no wedding ring— no jewelry of any kind, in fact.

"This is for either of you," Lou said. "Do scientists believe that bacteria like *B. pseudomallei* normally mutate after infecting the host or do their properties stay fairly constant?"

"And you are?" Scupman asked.

"Welcome. Lou Welcome. I'm an ER doc from Eisenhower Memorial in D.C., but I have my boards in internal medicine as well."

"Good question, Dr. Welcome. One thing I have learned during the course of my twenty-five-year career studying bacteria is that nature is constantly grooming and furbishing them to be the ultimate warriors. As I said, these are soldiers going to war without a conscience and without fear. In the battle for species survival, they are the most powerful threat mankind will ever face. Trying to account for and combat the in-host mutations of bacteria is like pitting a child's soccer team against a Manchester United team that is not only more powerful at the opening whistle, but ever-changing during the game, and playing by different rules. Put another way, bacteria are much better at surviving than we are at developing effective vaccines or antibiotics."

Lou pulled his eyes from Vicki.

"Thank you for underscoring my point," Scupman was saying. "Humans are messy, whereas microbes are perfect—a perfect society largely invisible to our eyes and yet existing all around and within us. As I said, there is no reasoning in a microbe, no hesitation, nothing to delay the inevitable attack. When threatened, these mindless killing machines transform, mutating seemingly at will into something that cannot be defeated. They act instantaneously without regret or regard for others.

"You see, Dr. Welcome, a single bacterium contains all the necessary components for growth and multiplication. They do not contemplate their existence. They are neither impaired nor well. The simple state of being is their life's sole purpose. With a blind, singular ambition to produce more of themselves, these magnificent organisms exist unburdened by man's frivolities. In many cases, we are helpless to defend against their might."

The room took on the oppressive atmosphere of a midsummer day, weighty and dense. Even Vicki Banks looked a bit ill at ease. Scupman broke the mood with a wan smile.

"Let's continue with our slide show, shall we?" Vicki said.

For the next twenty minutes, she ran through a series of slides depicting the functions of the laboratory and the work being done to develop effective antibacterial treatments. Several minutes were dedicated to an explanation of the different types of agents that had been declared by the government as having the potential to pose a severe threat to public safety.

The two scientists made quite a pair. Vicki was calm and academic, Scupman utterly passionate.

If Filstrup's speech conveyed even a tenth of the fervor Scupman demonstrated for his work, Lou was thinking, the man would have more than a decent shot at winning the election. But that simply wasn't the case. Lou risked another glance at Vicki Banks, and just caught her looking at him.

Easy, buddy, he said to himself. *Easy.*

"I have a question," Harvey Plimpton said when Scupman had finished.

"Yes, of course, then I really must be off."

"You've shown us a number of frightening bacteria. Is there one species in particular that you are most terrified of contracting?"

"That's an easy one," Scupman said, his hands now clasped together beatifically. "Many of my colleagues might argue that any of several virulent strains of carbapenem-resistant enterobacter are the most lethal of all. It's true that these are certainly terribly powerful bugs. For me personally, though, without question, to contract the newest strain of *Streptococcus pyogenes,* cause of the condition known as necrotizing fasciitis; to be eaten alive from the inside out; to go from one limb amputation to another, would far and away be the worst death imaginable."

CHAPTER 5

It takes discipline to confront the most horrible truths.

—LANCASTER R. HILL, *A Secret Worth Keeping*, SAWYER RIVER BOOKS, 1941, P. 110

This was it.

For the foreseeable future, Jennifer Lowe vowed, this was the last time she was going into an operating room. It had been eight days since Becca Seabury's right arm had been amputated. Now, the teen was back in the OR. This time it was going to be her right leg.

Becca was toxic. Really toxic. In addition to her leg, there was evidence of infection in her core—her lungs and heart, and the structures surrounding them. It had been horrible to watch. Jennifer had been at her side every day—ten- or twelve-hour shifts. No days off. Jennifer's supervisor at White Memorial had warned her against making any other schedule changes with the other nurses, but she went ahead and did it anyhow. She had been on two- or even three-week medical missions to the Congo where she essentially worked twenty-four-seven.

"I have an apartment and a new mattress waiting at home," she would tell anyone who wanted her to take a break. "What do *these* people have?"

It wasn't the hours surrounding Becca's care that were getting to her, it was the helplessness and frustration. It was the waiting. She shifted where she was standing on a riser in order to get a better view over the surgeon's right shoulder. This case had been incredibly draining on the entire team since the original, triumphant repair of Becca's arm, but the development of infection had been toughest on Dr. Beebe. He seemed to have aged significantly since the first call from the ortho floor that something was going wrong with their star patient.

"Scalpel . . . suction . . . clamp . . . another clamp . . . scalpel . . . retract more, please . . ."

To Jennifer, Dr. Beebe's words were like white noise. The only thing she felt the least bit relieved about was that Becca was deeply anesthetized.

"Hemostat . . . more suction, please . . . right here . . . suck right here, please. Bart, her blood's looking a little dusky. Is everything okay?"

"Oh-two sat is down some. I'm working on it."

Beneath her surgical mask, Jennifer felt her own respirations increase. Subconsciously, she rubbed at the V between the third and fourth fingers of her left hand. The eczema, for that is what she was certain it was, seemed to be getting a bit more intense—a bit more itchy. Given the disease that was ravishing her patient, it would have been foolish for her not to consider the possibility that she was incubating the same thing. But if it looked like a duck and quacked, it was a duck. And this rash looked like eczema.

Just in case, Jennifer had done some reading about the bacteria infecting Becca's incision and surgical repair—the bacteria some in the press had dubbed the

Doomsday Germ. The medical world, and the patients themselves, had been asking for trouble since the invention of penicillin, and more and more, the bacterial world had been delivering in the form of resistance.

There were effective treatments for some viral illnesses, such as herpes and influenza, but no antibiotics that worked for bronchitis, most middle ear infections, or a common cold. First-year medical students were warned not to use antibiotics unless a specimen had been obtained and a bacteria cultured from it. Ideally, the specimen should also be sent for antibiotic sensitivities. Yet each year, over and over again, thousands of times, millions, tens of millions, antibiotics were prescribed by physicians who wanted to keep their patients satisfied, and to keep them from bolting to another doctor.

It hadn't been that long since the first reports of this new strain of bacteria had surfaced. Although the name some reporter had given it was frightening and catchy, it still wasn't even the stuff of front-page headlines. A case here, another case there. Just another antibiotic-resistant microbe. No one really seemed that worried about it. In fact, Becca Seabury was only the fifth documented case in Boston, only two of them at White Memorial, one of the busiest hospitals in the world. In addition, all the cases Jennifer read about, in Boston and other places, were like Becca's—large, open fractures or post-op wounds.

The MRSA bacteria—methicillin-resistant staph aureus—was much more prevalent, and from all she could tell, was gradually coming under control. She had the sense that the Doomsday Germ, a coccus with peculiar staining patterns, was an aberrancy—the sort of infectious agent like chicken pox that caused a minor illness in most, but went absolutely, lethally berserk in a few others.

Eczema. That was what was itching her hand. Nothing more, nothing less.

Please God. Let Becca make it through this. Let her get better and lead her life with what limbs she has left, and what the prosthetics people can make for her.

"Bart, how are we doing?" Beebe was asking in a soft voice. "Bleeding's stopped here, but I'm not completely happy with her color."

"Working on it, Chandler. Pressures down a bit. I've started some dopamine."

"I'm ready with the oscillator, Bart. Go or no?"

There was a break in the exchange.

Prolonged silence, penetrated only by the beep of the oxygen saturation monitor.

"Go," the anesthesiologist said finally.

Please, Jennifer pleaded once more. . . . *Please.*

At that moment, Beebe looked back at Jennifer.

"Jennifer, you holding up okay?"

"As well as can be expected, I guess," she answered through her mask.

"Given Becca's overall condition things are going as well as can be expected, but this is the hardest part now. I'm going to use the oscillating saw to separate Becca from this infection. After the infection is gone she'll start getting better. I know you probably know all this, but given how much you have invested in her care, I wanted to be sure."

"I've seen an oscillating saw used before."

Jennifer purposely didn't add that it had been an incredibly stressful, unpleasant experience for her.

"Okay, so you know the kind of noise it makes—sort of like a dentist's drill."

Like a hundred dentists' drills.

"I know," she said.

Jennifer's jaws clenched at the first screech of the powerful oscillating saw, an instrument whose blade cut by rapid back-and-forth movements rather than by rotation. She had never done well in dentists' offices. She was a brave—some had even said fearless—nurse, but the noise and knowing what was going on beneath the huge saucer-shaped lights caused her to avert her eyes. Limiting the sterile field with drapes depersonalized things a bit, but this was a person who had come to be like a younger sister to her.

The amputation of Becca's leg at a spot just below her hip was almost complete when trouble began. Jennifer looked up just in time to see it develop on the monitor screen—extra heartbeats, almost certainly ventricular premature beats. First one, then a pair, then a burst of four together. Her own pulse leaped.

"Bart?" Beebe asked in his surgical voice. "What's the deal?"

"We've got sudden VPBs and a pressure drop. I'm giving her amiodarone." Jennifer tensed even more. Amiodarone was used to suppress the irritability of Becca's heart, and to stabilize her suddenly unstable rhythm. The VPBs could just go away, or they could be the beginning of something very bad.

"Janet, call cardiology," the anesthesiologist said to the circulating nurse.

By the time Jennifer Lowe checked the monitor screen again, the pressure was forty. Becca was crashing—

complete cardiovascular collapse. Her heart, compromised by infection, had gone as far as it could go.

"Looks like she's about to code, Chandler. You're going to have to close as fast as possible."

Oxygen saturation plunging.

Pressure thirty.

Extra heartbeats increasing, then suddenly changing into a rapid, totally irregular sawtooth rhythm.

"V. fib," the anesthesiologist called out. "Call a code blue now. Start chest compressions, get the code cart, and get ready to defibrillate."

Like a video put into fast forward, the action in the OR increased immediately. From her place on the riser, Jennifer watched transfixed. She was skilled at all aspects of resuscitation, but she was there as an observer, not part of the code team. Much as she desperately wanted to help, she knew that there were more than enough hands. Too many people in a code was asking for trouble. The best thing she could do at this point was to stay out of the way.

But she knew from the moment they called a code blue, that Becca was doomed. In essence, the resuscitation had begun as she was put to sleep and intubated. There was not much to be done that would get at the reason her heart was giving up.

"I don't see any end tidal carbon dioxide, Danielle. Chest compressions need to be deeper and faster."

"We're almost closed, Bart. How's she doing?"

"Horrible. Ready to defibrillate, Mary."

"Pads on. What settings?"

"Two hundred joules. Everybody ready? I'm clear, everybody clear. Shock."

Jennifer saw Becca's body jolt. The monitor remained unchanged.

V. fib.

"Restart chest compressions," the anesthesiologist called out. "Give her one milligram of epinephrine and continue compressions for two minutes."

Jennifer knew there was no way the team was going to give up without a fight, especially with a teenager's life at stake. Another twenty minutes would be conservative.

From where she stood, she could see Becca's face. Her eyes had been taped shut through the entire case, but even with that and the breathing tube, and the compressions and the action swirling around her, Jennifer thought there was a serenity there.

She stood motionless as the violent compressions continued, punctuated by more drugs and shocks. Then finally, after what seemed an eternity, it was over. The anesthesiologist, clearly shaken, checked the clock, thanked the team, and stated the precise time.

Beneath her mask, Jennifer finally felt the flood of tears begin. Still, she stood there, unaware that she was rubbing at the odd rash between her fingers.

CHAPTER 6

Should a person offer to plow a farmer's field for
no fee, the farmer would be a fool to plow it for
himself.

—LANCASTER R. HILL, *100 Neighbors*, SAWYER
RIVER BOOKS, 1939, P. 24

"I'm afraid I've not progressed as far as I had hoped."

Dr. Andrew Pollack's voice came through the speakers with perfect clarity, not at all distorted this time. The latency from the last encryption program had made conversation almost inaudible. At least, Kazimi thought glumly, this was one thing going right.

"Just send me what you have," he said.

"You're going to be disappointed, Kaz."

Kazimi hesitated. Three years into all this, and he still had not grown accustomed to being called by that name, even though he was—at least according to his driver's license, passport, birth certificate, social security number, and those associated with him personally or online—the person called Ahmed Kazimi. Those perfect documents were not the product of some fly-by-night backroom forger, but came courtesy of the federal government of the United States of America. As for the Stanford microbiologist who had been born with another name, that man was simply missing—vanished one day into thin air, and presumed by the police, the university, and all those who knew him, to be dead, drowned while sailing in his small sloop.

"Lately, I've come to expect disappointments," Kazimi replied finally.

"Well, at least we're not dealing with a real crisis."

Kazimi fought the urge to correct Pollack, who was convinced that he was part of an online task force made up of military men, scientists, and even bestselling writers of fictional suspense. Their mission, conceived and orchestrated by the president himself, was to create scenarios involving bioterrorism and then to devise ways to counter the danger. Kazimi skillfully bounced a soccer ball on one foot while awaiting the brilliant Northwestern University entomologist's data transmission. It had taken years of constant effort, but finally Kazimi and his virtual team of experts were making real progress in developing a macrolide/beta lactam antibiotic to treat the Gram-positive fluctuation of the bacterium dubbed the Doomsday Germ. To his continued dismay, coming up with an effective treatment for the Gram-negative fluctuation continued to elude them.

At least Kazimi had the endless resources of the federal government at his disposal. The lab where he worked was located in the basement of a brownstone in Brightwood, a quiet Washington neighborhood near the District's northern tip. To ensure secrecy, the government, at his suggestion, agreed to hide the lab in plain sight. Nobody, not even the resourceful One Hundred Neighbors, would presume to look for a government-run microbiology laboratory in a residential neighborhood.

Before he vanished, the lab had been built to Kazimi's exacting specifications. He had incubators, freezers, an electron microscope, biological safety cabinets, plus several computers. What he did not have—at least not yet—was a viable treatment for the Doomsday Germ.

"Have you received my transmission?" Pollack asked.

Kazimi thought he heard a slight phase shift in Pollack's voice—the equivalent of a digital quaver. Perhaps it was just his ears playing tricks again. Fourteen hours working with few breaks in a basement lab, with no access to sunlight, and rare direct human contact, could do that to a man. Yes, it was just his ears playing tricks, he decided. The data Pollack sent came through the decryption program just fine.

"I've received it," Kazimi said.

"You'll see that my latest approach does appear to inhibit bacterial protein synthesis, and that I'm also inhibiting ribosomal translocation. The main problem continues to be speed—killing the little beasties fast enough to overwhelm their ability to mutate and gain resistance. If we can accomplish that, the very elements that have been working against us will be working for us."

"Very good," Kazimi responded. "Give me a minute to review the findings in more detail."

He saw the problem in a matter of seconds. Another scientist may have needed a day or two to spot the glitch, like finding a needle in a haystack of data, but not Kazimi.

"The bacteriostatic agent you have been using is getting in the way," he said.

"Perhaps . . . No, wait. I see what you mean. I see exactly what you mean. Let me test the drug with a different one."

"And with none at all."

Again Kazimi thought he heard something in Pollack's transmission—an electronic shimmer that briefly distorted his voice.

Had they been compromised?

The architects of the Doomsday Germ were not to be underestimated. They had created an organism more sophisticated than anything he had ever seen. He would not have been all that surprised if they had somehow gained access to these secure transmissions. If so, it might result in an acceleration of the timetable they'd issued.

Kazimi shuddered at the thought and debated whether to include this new suspicion in his daily report. A false alarm could raise concerns about his mental state. He's hearing things, they might say, becoming paranoid. Every person, even someone with his penchant for solitude, has a breaking point. He feared tipping the scales in a way that could risk his involvement with the project. He had come too far, given up too much, not to see this to the end.

"Nothing to be disappointed about," he said, rubbing at the grit stinging his eyes. "You've done well, Dr. Pollack."

"And how about the other players in the game?"

The game.

Again Kazimi felt a pang of guilt for the ongoing deception, but it was a necessary precaution. Nobody could know about the very real threat facing America. The only people, as far as he was aware, who knew the specifics of his research were the president, the vice president, and a few select members of the president's cabinet. The CIA and FBI, each investigating things from different angles, had to have amassed vast amounts about One Hundred Neighbors, but the inner circle with full knowledge of the threat the terrorists were presenting was limited to the most essential personnel. Even the smallest leak about the threat facing the nation would likely cause panic on an epic scale.

"Do you have another piece of the problem for me to try, or would you prefer I keep working on this one?" Pollack went on.

"Yes, keep working. The others will have a look at these data as well. We're doing great."

Another lie. Kazimi had been dishing them out like Halloween candy ever since he gave up his life to go underground. The truth was they were fast running out of time.

"You know, I'm really enjoying this little exercise of ours," Pollack said. "Much more so than I thought when you first approached me. I'm glad I decided to come aboard."

There it was again—an audible phase shift in Pollack's voice. Kazimi decided this was definitely something to go on his report. He might be wrong, but it was worth the risk. Even if it turned out to be nothing, NSA experts would probably have a new encryption program installed by morning.

Kazimi checked the time on the wall-mounted digital clock. Five-thirty. Soon he would need to recite the Isha, the fifth of the daily prayers offered by practicing Muslims. He always prayed alone in his bedroom upstairs, never in congregation, as was his communal obligation. It was, however, a forgivable offense given his unique situation.

After the Isha and dinner, and possibly a short nap, he would head back to the lab. Completely spent, and feeling almost ill with fatigue, Kazimi ambled up the spiral metal stairs to the lab's only exit, his head bent, his arms dangling limply at his sides. He was a handsome, brown-skinned man in his late thirties, fit but not muscular, with slender shoulders and a narrow waist. But the stress of his work, coupled with the lack of sunlight and exercise, had aged him. Kazimi wondered if his former colleagues back at Stanford would even recognize him now.

At the top of the stairs, he pressed his forehead against the visor of the dual iris capture scanner. The red light on the wall-mounted keypad turned to green. From his pants pocket, he withdrew a small contraption, a code creator the size of a credit card. He pressed a button on the creator and the LED screen produced a one-time-only five-digit number, which he entered on the keypad. Almost immediately, he heard the titanium rods securing the door disengage. Getting out of the lab was just as tightly controlled as getting in.

Waiting for him on the other side were two men and a woman—three special agents from the FBI. In addition to his guards, the brownstone was secured with window and door alarms, along with motion-activated security cameras placed throughout. Kazimi never grew too close to his security detail. The agents tasked with his protection rotated every three weeks or so to keep them sharp and focused, and every three or four months they were replaced. It had to be dull protecting a man who toiled alone and worked almost continuously when he wasn't sleeping or praying.

Kazimi had a remarkably facile memory. By the second time he met them, he knew the names of each agent detailed to him. They exchanged pleasantries and truncated conversations, but as far as he knew, none of the men or women knew about the work he was doing in his basement lab. Three guards was a typical number for his security detail. Some days there were two. On days when he went food or clothes shopping there might even be four. But he could not recall ever having been guarded by just a single person.

The agents were expecting him.

Each day he posted the times when he would be saying his prayers. Alexander Burke, fairly new to the team, led the way upstairs to Kazimi's third-story bedroom. Burke was a lanky man, with corn-colored hair and gray eyes. He was followed by Maria Rodriguez, then Kazimi, and finally Timothy Vaill. Vaill and Rodriguez, always professional but likeable and open, were husband and wife. Mocha-skinned and kinetic, Rodriguez was a pert five foot two, which was to say a foot or so shorter than Vaill, a solidly built, laconic fellow, who was constantly squeezing handgrips or doing exercises using a set of adjustable dumbbells.

"Going back to work after you pray?" Burke asked as they climbed the narrow wooden staircase leading up to the top floor.

Vaill and Rodriguez grinned.

"Dr. Kaz always goes back to work," Vaill said.

Burke smiled sheepishly. "Yeah, I should have figured that. Don't you ever get out, Dr. Kaz?"

"My work is too crucial to leave it for any extended length of time," Kazimi said.

"How about women? Do you ever want to—you know—date? I mean, you've been cooped up here for a long time now."

Kazimi stopped climbing. His expression was hard.

"I am a Muslim first and an American second," he said, allowing his withering look to linger. "My beliefs prohibit carnal pleasure outside of marriage. And Agent Burke, I would prefer if we keep our conversations professional."

"The new boy's learning," Rodriguez said with a chuckle.

Burke held up his hands.

"My bad. Just getting the hang of things, I guess." At the top of the stairs, he opened Kazimi's bedroom door. "Just a quick check before we leave you alone, Dr. Kaz."

"No need to explain. I've been through this so many times before, that it is routine."

With the exception of a twin mattress, end table with a digital alarm clock, gooseneck lamp, copy of the Koran and several microbiology journals on it, and a prayer rug rolled up in a corner, the master bedroom was virtually bare. There were no pictures, no plants, nothing to warm the space. This was where Ahmed Kazimi slept and prayed and nothing more. It took only a minute for Burke to check the bathroom and closet, and beneath the bed, and to wave him up the final few stairs. Rodriguez and Vaill followed but stopped in the doorway.

Usually, as soon as the room was deemed safe, the

detail retreated to the living area on the second floor. This time, though, Burke remained by the edge of the window, looking down below.

"Dr. Kaz," he asked, "is that truck frequently parked in the alley?" Burke's voice was tinged with concern.

Rodriguez and Vaill took several steps into the room.

Just as Kazimi reached Burke, and peered down below, the agent spun around impossibly quick, his weapon drawn. The gunshots—two of them—were deafening. Kazimi cried out and reflexively dropped to his knees, covering his ears. The stench of gunpowder filled the room and burned his nostrils. Just ten or so feet away, Maria Rodriguez's head exploded as the bullet tore through the front of her skull.

Tim Vaill was reaching for his gun when Burke fired twice more. Kazimi was on the ground now, shaking violently, his hands still clutching his ears. He saw Vaill driven backward by a bullet to the front of his chest. His horrified expression at the sight of his wife would live in Kazimi's mind as long as the terrible images of her corpse. Vaill was teetering on the top step when the second shot hit. His head snapped to the right, blood spurting from just above his left temple. He flew backward, tumbling down the stairs.

Kazimi was pulled to his feet by Burke and held there while the agent opened the window.

"It's actually *our* dump truck parked in your alley," Burke said. "Don't worry, Doc, we put in plenty of padding."

Before Kazimi could respond, he was falling. Three stories below, he landed softly in a pile of foam rubber. Before Kazimi could even move to get out of the bin, Burke landed beside him. The engine roared and the dump truck backed up onto the street. Kazimi felt a stinging jab at the base of his neck and saw Burke withdraw the syringe, then pin his arms to his sides.

In less than a minute, everything went dark.

CHAPTER 7

What one should expect from unemployment
benefits is added unemployment and nothing
more.

—LANCASTER R. HILL, *100 Neighbors*, SAWYER
RIVER BOOKS, 1939, P. 111

The conference officially began the day following
Lou's trip to the CDC. While Cap stayed over at his
aunt's house until late afternoon, Lou spent the day attending workshops and lectures dealing with changes
in the board of registration policies in various states,
research studies on the success rate of physician
monitoring, medical ethics, addiction treatment, and
sadly, suicide prevention. His work for the PWO may
have been emotionally taxing and frustrating at times,
but as long as Walter Filstrup kept his distance, it was
always fascinating.

The keynote address, from the man Filstrup was
hoping to replace, dealt with the question of whether a
physician health program should limit itself solely to
reporting that a suspended doc had adhered to the pro-
visions of their monitoring agreement. At the other
end of the spectrum was allowing the director to step
up and offer the licensing board a thoughtful, subjec-
tive evaluation of the physician's recovery, and the likelihood of relapse, reminding the board that no matter

what or who or where, whether it was a doc or a teacher, a quarterback or an airline pilot, there was never any sure thing.

Never.

Fortunately, Lou's therapist and the program head at Templeton Treatment Center had gone to bat for him, and the people at Eisenhower Memorial had listened. Otherwise, thousands of hours of studying and years of training would have been trashed.

By the time Cap returned to the hotel at nine, Lou was conferenced out, and grateful that the day to come would begin with another run through the mountains.

Cap had other ideas.

"Are you still thinking about a run tomorrow?" he asked as they headed to their room. "Before I left for my aunt's I checked out the health club down in the basement. Pretty fine. We could go there and do some lifting instead of slogging out on the trail."

"They have any punching bags?"

"Not that I saw."

"Hotel gyms never have boxing stuff. I opt for the run. The concierge suggested a new trail for us to try. He said it'll take us up even higher into the hills, with great views of the Chattahoochee."

"You know, the weather report posted in the lobby said it's going to be a misty, rainy morning tomorrow. I was thinking I might just sleep in. I did a lot of driving today."

Lou was disappointed and, he realized, still somewhat embarrassed by his two tumbles the previous morning. The sooner he got back on the trail, the better he would be feeling about it.

"You know the rules of safe trail running," he heard

himself saying before he could swallow back the manipulative words. "Can't go without a partner, partner. I've got a big speech to deliver tomorrow, and it'll be flatter than roadkill if I don't get in a run beforehand."

"You said it was going to be flat no matter what you did."

"Maybe so, but Filstrup is going to order a copy of the recording of the damn thing. No way he won't believe I cost him the election if he loses."

"Which you say he will."

"It's just a strong suspicion, but yes. Come on, pal, don't leave me hanging."

Cap relented, but not with any of his typical enthusiasm.

The early morning air woke Lou more completely than any cup of coffee ever could. From the lodge's front porch, he scanned the thick band of mist that blanketed the forest. The forecast, posted in the lobby, called for the drizzle and fog to dissipate over the next few hours, then give way to sunshine.

It was just twenty or so minutes past dawn. The drizzle wasn't much, but it was more than enough to dampen the ground and make the rocks slick. They would have to be extra careful. Despite the conditions, Lou could hardly wait to immerse himself in these woods once again. The serenity and natural beauty of the place was food for his soul, and he vowed to find a way to make trail running a more regular part of his life—maybe join a club of some sort.

Cap was stretching his hamstrings on the lawn, looking only a little more awake than when Lou had roused him a half hour before. He had crawled out of bed mumbling about the predicted fog, drizzle, and rain. But typical of the man, he was rallying.

"Okay, buddy, I'm warmed up," Cap announced, looking again like the determined athlete he was. "Which way are we headed?"

Lou unfolded the contour map.

"We're going to wind our way up the Blue Ridge Trail, right here. It looks like we'll be pretty high up, so we might get a bit winded."

"You got the GPS?"

"Right here in my pack," Lou said, holding up the bag. "Snacks and water, too."

Lou had checked both Trail Runner backpacks after his slips. Moleskin, two four-inch ACE bandages, rope, knife, mini flashlight, the map, Band-Aids, gauze, and a finger splint. He also had a special hemostatic bandage he had appropriated from the ER that would help to clot any bleeding from a scrape to a more serious laceration. He was betting the kit would see some use.

"How far are we going?" Cap asked.

"Hour out and an hour back, is what the concierge said."

"Then let's hit it."

Lou started at a brisk jog, and behind him, Cap kept pace. By the time they left the hotel property, Lou's sneakers were soaked. They continued running single file, following signs to the Blue Ridge Trail, which quickly diverged from the one they had taken two days before. This one initially rose sharply through dense forest, then leveled, then rose again. Beautiful. Absolutely magnificent. The overcast brightened as the canopy thinned. The drizzle seemed to be letting up.

Lou quickly came in tune with his body. His legs felt strong, and the slope was presenting no breathing difficulties—at least not yet.

"Still thinking about my bed," Cap said from behind.

"We'll run that thought right out of your head," Lou called back.

In his mind, a trail qualified as a technical run if it had substantial terrain variation, challenging rock formations, maybe large cracks and exposed roots, and quick changes in elevation. In other words, if it could answer "absolutely" to the question: Can I end up in the hospital if I'm not careful? Lou slowed his pace. The Blue Ridge Trail, especially given the weather, was fitting his definition of technical with the equivalent of a summa cum laude GPA from Yale.

Thirty minutes into the run his lungs began to burn. His nostrils flared as he worked harder to get in air. From behind and slightly to his left, he heard Cap's footfalls landing against a garden of loose rocks, embedded in lightly packed, muddy soil. Except for a few short stretches, the pitch continued to rise. The run back, largely downhill, was going to be interesting. Lou was feeling it in his legs now, and wondering what level of runner the hotel concierge might be. This was turning into one hell of a trail.

"Follow my line," Lou called over his shoulder. "I've got a good read on this section."

"I'm with you, bro."

It didn't sound as if Cap was even breathing hard. No big surprise.

Awhile later, distracted by a nasty stitch that had developed in his side, Lou slipped on a gnarled root and stumbled. Before he could go down, Cap's hand clamped on his arm and steadied him.

"Come on, buddy, we got this," Cap said.

"Nice grab."

They had to be nearly an hour out—the turnaround point. Lou's body was beginning to settle down again, but the next stretch proved the most challenging yet. He sensed the lactic acid building in his muscles, and resolved to make time to do more cardio after they returned home. Around a sharp bend, they came to a series of large boulders covered in slick wet moss. Lou stopped, breathing heavily now. Even Cap seemed relieved at the brief respite.

"We climb over?" Cap asked, surveying the obstacles.

Lou checked his watch. Fifty-three minutes. He wondered if they had bitten off too much, and for the first time, thought about walking.

"Unless you want to head back," he said. "We're just about to where we had planned on turning."

"We finish what we started. Just be careful."

Using their hands, they scrambled up and over the rocks, landing in a shallow puddle at the other side that turned out to be an inch or so of mud.

First just slow down a bit, Lou thought. *Just a bit.*

The pitch elevated once again. Lou's heart rate jacked up until he felt it beating in his throat. A jumble of thick, slick roots. No problem. A gauntlet of large rocks. Piece of cake. Risking a glance behind him, Lou saw that Cap was keeping pace, still running loose and within himself.

"You're killing it!" Lou called out.

"You too, amigo."

At that moment, Lou realized his breathing was coming more easily. The nagging stitch in his side vanished. It was a second wind—as much mental as physical. He had experienced what he assumed was the involuntary flood of endorphins on runs before. His mind began to calm and his senses heightened. With the lightening sky, the wet woods hummed with energy and the sounds of the forest. Birdcalls. Insects. Raindrops tapping against leaves. The counterpoint of their footfalls. And from somewhere far down the steep hillside to his left, the white noise rush of the Chattahoochee.

They were out in the boondocks, now, far from civilization, the connection to the forest growing with every stride.

Meanwhile the pitch continued to rise higher and higher. Lou was aware and alert, but also relaxed. His mind and body were wonderfully in tune. He was still on a high when they hit the one-hour mark and made the one-eighty.

"From the contour map, this looks like the highest we're gonna get," Lou said. "You want to take the lead?"

"No, no. I'm fine searching for things to stare at that ain't your butt."

"You're whacked. The pace getting to you?"

"We should have brought our gloves so we could stop and go a couple of rounds right here."

There was no sign of the nearly ten years' difference in their ages.

"That would be a gas," he said. "Rather than having my block knocked off by you in the gym, I can have it knocked off at altitude."

"It should fly farther. . . . And Lou?"

"Yeah?"

"I'm glad you talked me into making this run."

Lou grinned and started up again. The second-wind euphoria was gone, but he sensed he had enough in the tank to make it back.

Keep pushing . . . keep it going.

Cap followed Lou's lines, staying in single file until the path widened. Pulling alongside, he was breathing harder than before as he ran shoulder-to-shoulder on Lou's right, just a couple of feet from the edge of the drop-off. From time to time, far down in the valley below the trees and rock-strewn hillside, they caught glimpses of the river—a thin gray snake slithering through the endless shades of spring green.

"Pretty stuff, eh, bro?" Cap said.

"Like Dorothy said: I don't think we're in Kansas anymore."

Lou tried to gauge the slope to Cap's right, but here the drop-off was too sharp to see anything straight down. During one stretch, he did catch a good look. He had always had a touch of vertigo staring down from anything higher than a third-floor porch. Now his stomach tightened at the height and the steepness of the grade. He hadn't really appreciated it on the run out, but the trail sat atop a fifty- or sixty-degree cliff face with a slope that paused in a rock-strewn wooded ravine before dropping off again. *Pass the Dramamine, please.*

Lou was about to suggest that the two of them return to a single file, when there was a sound from his right. Cap lurched past him somewhat awkwardly. A glance at the ground showed that he had slipped on a nearly invisible, flat, wet rock. Initially, Lou was surprised and even a bit amused. But then the situation registered. Cap's arms were extended, waving wildly, sweeping the air for balance. There was a glint of panic in his eyes. Clearly, the man was in trouble. Big trouble.

Trying to stop short, Lou skidded and stumbled, but managed to stay on his feet. Cap, who had incomparable footwork and balance in the ring, was out of control, twisting in what seemed like slow motion, and staring down at the drop beneath him. Lou pivoted and reached out. His fingers caught hold of Cap's backpack strap. But his grip was poor. Cap's upper body was already over the edge, and his weight tore the strap free. He twisted and reached back, clawing for Lou's outstretched hand. At the last possible moment, their palms met and their fingers locked.

Please hold . . . please! Cap's eyes pleaded.

His fingers closed on Lou's, but it was a tease, not a grip. In an instant, gravity snatched his hands away. He pawed at the air like a novice backstroker. Then he slammed against the cliff face, and was gone. Stunned beyond understanding, Lou sank to his knees. For a moment, there was only silence. Then he heard a cry and the snap of branches breaking, followed by more silence. Lou crawled closer to the edge, hardly aware that the muddy ground was falling away from beneath his knees. Shaking viciously, nearly unable to stand, he pushed to his feet. Finally, almost inaudibly at first, then a bit louder, he heard Cap cry out.

Lou's heart stopped. Then it began hammering.

"Cap, it's me! I'm here! I'm coming! I'm coming for you! Hang on, brother! Hang on!"

He raced to his right, as close to the crumbling

precipice as he dared, peering over for a way down. It took twenty-five feet or so before he saw a slope he felt he could handle. On his belly, clawing to maintain contact with the dirt and stones, grabbing at roots and bushes, he worked his way down, pausing to listen for Cap's voice, and each time believing he was hearing it.

Five feet . . . ten . . .

In the ER, Lou prided himself on staying cool even when faced with the most dire medical emergencies, or the most horrible crunches. Now he felt frantic and utterly out of control.

Five more feet . . . another five.

His slide loosened rocks, mud, and pebbles that rained down on him, getting in his mouth, and eyes. From his right, he felt certain he could hear Cap's groans.

"Hang on, buddy! I'm almost there!"

Breathe in . . . breathe out. For God's sake, Welcome, get it together. Whatever has happened over there, he needs you. The best friend you've ever had needs you!

The steep drop had begun to lessen. Lou stopped himself and peered through the trees. Nothing. The sounds were close, though. Very close. He pushed to his feet and thrashed to the right. A dozen more feet and he spotted Cap, spread-eagle on his back on a fairly level piece of rocky ground. He was continuing to moan, but was otherwise motionless. There was blood smeared across his face and shaved scalp from a cut across his forehead.

Then, as Lou hurried across the last ten feet, it registered that Cap's right leg was bent at an odd angle. It took a moment to make sense of what he was seeing. When he did, his stomach instantly knotted. Protruding from a gash at the midpoint of Cap's thigh, was a jagged, bloodied spear of white bone—the fractured mid-shaft of Cap's femur.

CHAPTER 8

It is the obligation of the family, not the government, to provide for those who cannot provide for themselves.

—LANCASTER R. HILL, *100 Neighbors*, SAWYER RIVER BOOKS, 1939, P. 167

For Lou, filthy and soaked, the scene was surreal.

Cap was moaning piteously. The jagged mid-shaft of his right femur, surrounded by spaghetti-like strands of muscle, protruded garishly from a four-inch gash—easily the worst compound fracture Lou had ever seen. A tree? A boulder? Whatever caused the break really didn't matter. The femur was perhaps the strongest bone in the body, and the force that shattered it had to have been enormous. The leg, itself, was shortened and rotated.

Lou knelt beside the man more responsible for his recovery than anyone else beside himself. The two-inch laceration above his right brow was bleeding briskly, blood pooling in his eye socket and running down the center and side of his face. There were no other obvious injuries. Lou felt sick—nauseous and shaky. But he knew what he had to do.

Process.

At the center of treating multiple people with trauma,

or one person with any number of injuries, was process—the step-by-step approach to evaluation, triage, and treatment. That this was his best friend and a virtual saint to all who knew him needed somehow to be put aside. Whatever had to be done to save his life, however dangerous or painful, had to be done.

As Lou checked Cap's mouth, tongue, and airway, he flashed on a story the man had shared from when he was in his early teens and a group of thugs, all older than he was, kept beating and harassing him. In that neighborhood, there was never any way to avoid them. No place to hide for long. Cap's solution was, no matter how bad the pummeling, to never let any of them know he was hurt. Before long, they lost interest and left him alone. Cap Duncan was tough then, and he had grown even tougher over the years.

Heart rate one hundred ten. Rib cage and sternum intact to palpation. Carotid, radial, and left femoral pulses all present, although not very strong. The right groin, where the femoral pulse could usually be felt, was already swelling, probably from blood working up from the fracture site.

Airway, breathing, and circulation. All check.

He gingerly worked Cap's backpack off and opened it on the ground next to his. The man's muted cries echoed forlornly off the trees, and momentarily reminded Lou of the remoteness of their location.

Stay focused!

Neck seems uninjured.

Just in case, Lou used one of the ACE bandages and an empty backpack to improvise a stabilizing cervical collar.

Time to stop the bleeding.

"Cap, it's me. It's Lou. Hang in there, buddy. Hang in. I'm going to press on your forehead. Here, squeeze my hand if you can hear me. . . . Cap?"

Lou took half the gauze pads to wipe the blood out of Cap's eye and off much of his face. Then he used the same gauze to apply heavy pressure to the laceration.

"Cap, it's me. It's Lou. Squeeze my hand if you can hear me." Perhaps a flicker. "That's it, buddy. Squeeze again."

Lou kept up a steady stream of patter as he maintained pressure with his right hand. With his left, he soaked another gauze square with water from his backpack and wiped Cap's face clean. Comfort. Every bit of comfort he could produce for the patient and the doctor was a help. He worked some water between Cap's lips and then squeezed a few drops into his mouth. Cap swallowed. As Lou moved through the process he had mastered over the years of training and ER work, the need to extend his examination and to improvise treatment became increasingly important.

"That's it, big guy. Hang on. Just hang on."

The forehead hemorrhage had largely abated. Lou set a square of hi-tech hemostatic bandage over the laceration. There would be time for a dressing later. Another small squeeze of water between Cap's lips. Again, he swallowed.

Pulses slightly stronger. Abdomen non-tender and flat. Arms and hands intact.

"Cap, it's me, Lou. Open your eyes if you can. You're doing better. Better and better and better."

The leg was truly scary. Obscene to many. To a seasoned ER doc, it was just dangerous. The heavily muscled thigh was capable of holding literally quarts of blood—more than enough for someone to bleed out. The pain and internal bleeding had Cap hovering near shock. Lou had decided not to risk missing something potentially lethal by getting immersed too soon in the most obvious, spectacular injury. Now it was time to get to work on that.

He glanced back the way he'd come, wondering if he could possibly climb back up the cliff face to the trail. No chance. Besides, leaving Cap alone was something he could only bring himself to do after all other options had evaporated. For a half minute, while he collected his thoughts about the leg, he tried hollering for help. His cries were instantly swallowed by the dense forest. What about the river? If he could get Cap down there, perhaps he could fashion some sort of raft. But the woods were still shrouded in mist, and he could not even see the river from where they were.

Focus, Welcome. Focus!

The bleeding from the mid-shaft was continuing, and, if anything, seemed to be worsening. Lou checked for pulses behind each ankle and on the top of each foot. Left side, no problem. Right side, none. The femoral artery had almost certainly been torn. Big trouble.

It was then Lou realized Cap's groans had stopped entirely. Again he went through the process—the A, B, Cs.

Pulse rate one fifteen. Pulse strength down from four to three on a ten scale.

"Come on, pal! Stay with me. Stay with me."

Time was becoming even more of an enemy. He had to put on a tourniquet near the groin. Cap was still moving air effectively. His pupils were midsize and equal. Was there hemorrhage between his skull and brain? It didn't look like it, but if there was, Lou knew there was little he could do about it. It had to be first things first. He had to continue to stem the blood loss.

"Cap, it's Lou. I'm here."

The moaning began again—barely audible, then louder. Lou got to work on the fractured leg.

"Cap, you're bleeding badly," he said, uncertain if his words were registering. "I'm going to have to apply a tourniquet to stop the bleeding. It's going to hurt. I need you to brace yourself. I've got to move your leg."

From within his pack he removed the nylon rope and his Spyderco knife. He measured off an arm's length of cord and was readying to cut it off when something made him stop.

Again, the process. He had to remain focused, but at the same time stay cognizant of what might lie ahead.

If things went as he hoped, the rope and the other ACE bandages would be needed intact for something else entirely—getting out. Setting the cord aside, he pulled off his sodden shirt and, using the knife, cut and tore off two strips. Next, as gingerly as he could manage, he knotted them together, slid them around Cap's thigh inches below the groin, and tied the ends tightly at the skin.

At the first movement of his leg, Cap screamed. Then he screamed again, and thrashed his head from side to side as much as the makeshift collar would allow.

Lou hated the way his friend came to, but was ecstatic that he had. The odds of pulling things off and saving his life had just improved. For one thing, the man was light—awake or at least responsive to deep pain. For another, the cervical spine was almost certainly intact. If Lou needed the ACE bandage for what he had in mind, he would use it. He took what remained of his shirt, and blotted the perspiration that had suddenly materialized on Cap's face and bald pate.

"Sorry to hurt you, pal. Your leg is broken, and I have to stabilize it. Do you understand?"

Silence.

"Cap, can you hear me?"

Suddenly a faint nod, followed by a coarse whisper.

"I . . . hear you."

Yes!

"Squeeze my hand, big guy. That's it. That's it. Now the other hand . . . Perfect. Cap, try to just lie still and concentrate on your breathing. Deeply, now. In and out. I'll explain everything in a few minutes. For now, I need to tighten this thing on your thigh. It's gonna hurt."

"Go . . . for . . . it."

The hemorrhaging was starting to slow, but only marginally. The tourniquet, arterial spasm, or diminishing volume? It was impossible to tell. He had to add torque. Lou crawled in an arc until he found a hefty stick, two feet or so long. He slipped it under the makeshift tourniquet and slowly rotated it clockwise. Cap cried out, but he didn't scream. Instead he grabbed a fistful of soil and squeezed it tightly.

"Fuck," he groaned. ". . . Oh, fuck."

His breathing remained steady.

After two full turns, the bleeding was reduced to a slow ooze. Lou used the hi-tech hemostatic bandage to finish the job.

"Cap, stay with me. Stay strong."

From his pack, Lou retrieved his cell phone, not at all surprised to see there was no signal.

"Help!" he hollered. "Someone please help!"

It felt as if his voice had traveled only a few feet through the heavy air.

Another check of Cap's pulses. Still palpable, but down to a two.

Lou sat back and wrapped his arms around his knees.

Either he figured out something to do, and soon, or Cap was going to die.

It was as simple as that.

CHAPTER 9

To place economic security in the hands of the government is quite literally a return to our medieval ancestry where feudal lords took responsibility for the economic survival of the serfs working their estates.

—LANCASTER R. HILL, *Climbing the Mountain*, SAWYER RIVER BOOKS, 1941, P. 18

Lou estimated they were five miles from the lodge, assuming they had averaged ten minutes per mile over the uneven terrain. The concierge had warned him that cell phone signal strength in the mountains was spotty at best. After failing to get a dial tone, Lou checked the time. He had a new concern. It could take two hours to get back to the lodge and return with help—probably not much less even with an ATV. By that time there could be severe tissue damage caused by the tourniquet. The other potential danger was one he could not shake from his mind—severe shock and cardiac arrest.

Despite what Cap had said right before he stumbled and fell, he was never hot about making this run. Lou had talked him into it. Now there was no way he could allow him to die. The tourniquet had to be loosened as soon as hemorrhaging had clearly been stopped. Somehow, someway, Lou would get the man out of these woods without leaving his side.

"Listen, buddy," he said, his voice managing to stay even. "This is going to be the tough part."

"Do . . . what has . . . to be . . . done," Cap answered, stopping between words to breathe.

With a few decent sips of water, and the bleeding slowed to an ooze, the physical evidence of shock had begun to ebb. As Lou had done with the tourniquet, most of the tools he needed to complete the next phase of the process would have to be improvised. Most medical schools and hospitals, Eisenhower Memorial included, offered a variety of continuing education classes on a regular basis. Six months back, Lou had taken a two-day wilderness emergency medicine course. Ironically, his decision to do so was inspired by his newfound passion for trail running. The class, taught almost exclusively by incredibly competent paramedics and specially trained EMTs, with a few ER docs sprinkled in, was well organized and terrifically informative. With two jobs and a kid, courses and lectures were often triggers for him to catch up on sleep. But fortunately, not that one.

Lou performed a quick, repeat physical. Cap was going to need all of his will and his strength just to survive the pain of what was about to be done to him. The exam offered Lou a whisper of confidence that his friend could endure what lay in store for him without slipping back into shock. Looking over the leg, the ugly bent angle, twisted like a wrung-out dish towel, the bone splintered and frayed at the edges, Lou questioned his own ability to inflict the required amount of pain. But the leg had to be straightened or the chances of saving it were negligible.

No matter how hard he tried to reason away the

guilt, it kept gnawing at him. If only he had been less insistent. If only he could have been less exuberant.

If only . . .

Lou forced those thoughts to the back of his mind. For Cap's sake, he had to stay in the moment, fully focused and committed to the process.

"I've got to straighten out your leg so I can splint it," Lou heard himself say, his voice actually breaking between words.

Cap's gaze seemed to sharpen. He eyes locked with Lou's. There was no trace of doubt or fear on his handsome, bloodied face.

"You do what has to be done, Doc," he managed.

"Actually, Cap, to do what has to be done, I'm going to need your help."

Cap brushed the back of his hand across the damp bandage on his forehead.

"Tell me," he said.

The misty rain had largely let up, but the world was still slippery and cool. To make matters more difficult, bugs had reappeared and were beginning to attack Lou's face and naked back.

"Straightening and splinting your leg is a two-person production. Unfortunately, you've got to be one of those people. I'm going to get a couple of thick branches to be the splint. Then I'm going to tie the rope around your right ankle and loop it around that tree by your foot. When I say push, I'm going to need you to push your left foot against the tree with all your strength."

"And you're going to pull the rope."

It was a statement, not a question.

Lou nodded. "If together we have the strength to do this, we're going to pull the two segments apart and line them up the way they should be. Then I'll keep the tension on by wrapping the rope around the tree, and you keep the tension on by pushing. Got it?"

"Sounds like fun."

"When I get the rope tied around the tree, I'll use our bandages and maybe your shirt to hold the splint in place. The setup will make sure those sharp bone ends don't cut anything they haven't cut already."

"Got it."

It sounded straightforward enough, but the truth was, Lou had serious doubts whether or not the two of them could pull it off. They had to overcome the tight spasm of the quadriceps group, the strongest muscle in the body. Just how strong Cap's quad was would become clear in a few minutes.

Splint 'em where they lie, Lou thought, recalling one of the lessons from the course. *Splint 'em where they lie.*

It took five minutes of tromping through mud and old sodden leaves before Lou found a suitable pair of branches, each about a foot longer than Cap's leg. One of them had a fork at the end, which was going to be helpful. Lou did not have enough ACE bandage to secure the splint in place, so he cut the backpacks and Cap's shirt into strips that, along with some excess rope, would do the job.

But first, they had to straighten out his leg.

Lou glanced over at his AA sponsor, who mercifully appeared to have drifted off.

"Buddy, you got to get ready," Lou said, gingerly securing the rope around Cap's right ankle. Even the slightest movement of the leg induced a groan. This was going to be bad.

"I'm ready," Cap said.

Lou released the rope and felt around the ground for a sturdy stick, which he gently slipped between Cap's teeth.

"Here you go, pal. Just pretend you're on a Civil War battlefield and bite down on this anesthesia machine when it hurts."

"It already hurts."

"I mean *really* hurts," Lou said.

"Swell."

"I got no whiskey like they had at Gettysburg, but I promise that if I did, I'd let you have as many swigs of it as you wanted."

"Just do what you need to do."

"Okay, this is it. Five . . . four . . ."

The rope tightened around Lou's wrist as Cap preempted the countdown by jamming his foot against the tree. Lou gave the rope another wrap around his own wrist and wedged his foot against a boulder to help with leverage.

"Three . . ."

"This wasn't your fault," Cap said through the stick. "I wanted to come on this run."

"Two . . ."

"Let's do this!"

"One! Push, Cap, push!"

His gaze fixed on the fracture site, using all the strength he could summon, Lou pushed against the boulder and pulled on the rope. Cap cried out as he forced his good leg against the tree. After a few seconds, he spit the stick out and bellowed, the sound echoing off the canopy of damp spring leaves. Then, like a fast passing train, his screams stopped. His eyes were narrowed and utterly determined, as if he had crossed a threshold of pain tolerance. He was hyperventilating rapidly through his nose.

Lou felt his friend's intensity, and called upon his own legs for more power. Finally, millimeter-by-millimeter, the jagged, bloodied bones began to slide apart. The spasm in Cap's quad was lessening. Lou's teeth were clenched as he ignored the nylon rope cutting into his wrists and demanded still more from his legs, which were themselves beginning to spasm.

The femur ends moved past one another and disappeared into the gash.

"More pressure, Cap. We're doing it! We're doing it! Force that left leg out straight."

The man responded, and Lou sensed another few millimeters of movement. With the tourniquet still tight, there was essentially no bleeding. Maintaining maximum tension, he wrapped the cord several times around the tree. The femur fragments held.

"That's it, baby! Keep the tension on. I'm going to set the splint now. You're going to make it. You're going to make it off the battlefield and we're going to win the war. Then you're going to go home and get elected the first black governor of Virginia."

There was no response. Wide-eyed, Cap was staring straight up, awake and unconscious at the same time, but still maintaining the force necessary to keep his leg extended.

It took Lou several minutes to wrap the ACE bandages and nylon straps from what remained of his backpack around the sturdy branches he had placed alongside Cap's leg. He then created another wrap around Cap's foot with the remaining strips of back-pack fabric.

"Looking good . . . looking good," he said.

But there was more to be done. Undoing his shoe-laces and knotting them together, he secured one end to the fork in the branch at the bottom of the splint, and pushed the other end up and underneath the nylon strips around Cap's foot. This would hold the traction on the leg.

Cap's eyes had closed, and for the briefest moment, Lou thought he might not be breathing. In fact, that was an issue. He had at last surrendered to the pain. His breathing was shallow, and his pulse, still without much force, had slowed to ninety. But he was no longer con-scious.

"Nice going," Lou whispered. "Damn, but you are tough."

The rain had stopped completely now, and the sky had begun to brighten. Lou lay what few bandages he had across the wound, rocked back on his haunches, and examined the splint. Given the circumstances, it was about as good as it could get.

For several minutes, he caught his breath and de-bated between trying to claw his way back up the steep hillside to the trail, or building some sort of A-frame litter and heading down toward the river. It would be hard going—a few feet at a time over nasty terrain, but in the end, the thought of leaving Cap was unacceptable, and he opted for the litter, provided he had enough rope.

Naked from the waist up, and now starting to shiver, Lou stood, stretched, picked up the knife, and began casting around for some branches he could lash together—hopefully ones still on the ground.

It was at that moment he heard loud rustling coming from the dense woods downhill from them.

There was no chance it was the wind.

CHAPTER 10

As for man, the biological laws make no exceptions for intelligence and his fate is the same as
all lesser creatures. Death.

—LANCASTER R. HILL, *100 Neighbors*, SAWYER
RIVER BOOKS, 1939, P. 212

Bear? . . . Wild boar? . . . Coyote? . . . Mountain lion? . . .

Lou listened, frozen, as the rustling grew louder. He
was no expert at such things, but this was nothing
small. In deciding not to leave Cap alone while he
scaled the steep dirt and rock cliff and ran back to the
lodge, abandoning him to the jaws of a carnivorous animal had never even been a consideration. Perhaps it
was just a deer. Whatever was moving through the
dense net of brush was closing on them fast.

A pit opened in Lou's gut. Beside him on the ground
was a thick, barkless branch he had rejected for the
splint, but was keeping near in case he needed it for the
litter. It was longer than his arm and capped at one end
with a series of short spiked branches, giving it the heft
and feel of a medieval mace.

Shirtless and shivering, scraped and bruised, Lou
crouched in an attack stance, holding his weapon like
a baseball bat. Cap lay on the ground nearby, eyes
closed, breathing shallow and grunting, unaware of this

newest danger. From the beginning, he had been going in and out of shock due to diminished blood volume and dilated vessels caused by pain. Cap was a fanatic about working out. Now, every minute spent toning his muscles and strengthening his cardiac status was going to be brought into play. But, as with everything biological, the ability to resist shock had its limits. Renal shutdown . . . cardiac arrhythmia . . . brain cell death. The window to getting Cap medical attention, especially fluid replacement, was closing fast.

Lou was uncertain whether to remain absolutely quiet or get noisy. *No half measures.*

"Who's out there?" he suddenly heard himself shouting. "Anybody out there?"

No answer.

The sound of rustling bushes grew louder. Now Lou could see movement of the topmost branches. He gritted his teeth, tightened his grip on the rain-slicked club, and eased closer to Cap as the muscles in his arms, back, and neck tensed. His gaze was riveted on the spot where whatever was approaching would soon emerge. With a steadying breath, he raised his weapon.

Bear? . . . Wild boar? . . . Coyote? . . . Mountain lion? . . . Deer? . . .

To Lou's astonishment, it was none of the above. The creature who entered the small clearing was human—a ragged, weathered man, tall and lanky, with a craggy face that was, for the most part, buried beneath a billowing, gnarled gray beard. His hair was tucked inside a hat made from the pelt of some black and tan animal.

There was nothing about the man's stance or bright hazel eyes that said he was a threat. He could have claimed to be fifty or eighty, and Lou would have believed him. He wore a fringed, oil-stained buckskin jacket, spotted with what might have been dried blood. Dangling around his neck was a leather thong, heavy with bear claws. Strapped to his narrow waist, sheathed within a beaded leather scabbard, was one of the largest knives Lou had ever seen. It made his efficient Spyderco blade look like a toy.

Perhaps, Lou mused, as he and the intruder sized each other up, the woodsman had used the knife to kill the rabbit lashed to his belt. Or maybe he had used the double-barreled shotgun he held loosely at his side. The man's gun came up just a fraction as he checked out the weapon in Lou's hand.

"You don't throw that log at me and I won't shoot you," the man said in a thick Southern drawl as languid as his movements.

Lou needed no additional coaxing. He set the stick on the ground and raised his hands.

"No need to go puttin' yer hands up, neither," the man said, setting the butt of his shotgun on the ground. "I ain't gonna shoot you. I just didn't want you gettin' clever with that there bat."

The man took several steps forward and extended a grimy hand to Lou.

"Name's Floyd. I live and hunt in these here woods. Heard lots of screamin' and figured someone might be in need of some help."

Lou's hand vanished inside Floyd's calloused grip.

"My friend Cap fell down that ridge. He's badly injured. Broken bone was sticking out through his leg, but we were able to get it back in place and splinted. He needs water, though. Needs it bad."

Floyd removed a thin leather flask from his belt and handed it over.

"Not what it looks like," he said. "*Well* water. I jes filled it this mornin'."

Lou cradled Cap's head and allowed him to take several grateful sips. He aspirated the fourth or fifth one and went into a spasm of coughing, cringing in pain with every one. His carotid and radial pulses were one-ten and thin. The fluid volume he was down was barely going to be touched by what he could get in by mouth.

His skin was cool and clammy. His lips and fingernail beds were disturbingly blue. Continued oozing into the thigh was quite possible despite the tourniquet. There was room in and around the heavy muscles for a couple of quarts, and Lou had once seen a woman bleed out into her thigh from what looked like a simple fractured hip.

"This man looks to be in pretty bad shape," Floyd said. "I'd say he needs a doctor."

"I'd say you're right."

"The way you done that splint tells me yer either one yerself, or you was an eagle scout."

"Both," Lou said, a kaleidoscope of images of the highs and lows of his life flashing through his mind.

Cap's next few swallows were deeper than before, but ended the same way. It was like they were shooting a rampaging elephant with a BB gun.

"We need to get him to a hospital, and fast," Lou said. "How far away do you live? Do you have a phone or . . . or a car? Better still, a truck. Is there a road out to your place? How far to the nearest town?"

Floyd brushed his palms across the front of his pants.

"Easy now, Doc. Easy. You kin pepper me with as many questions as you like, but I'm only equipped to answer one of 'em at a time. I stopped gettin' educated a little short of medical school, but I'd like to say somethin' before I wade into that bog of questions a yers."

"Okay, but quickly."

"If we don't get this fella outta here, none of those other questions are going to matter."

First things first.

Countless AA meetings over the years, many of them with a blue-and-gold-fringed banner on the wall saying precisely that, and here Lou was getting a one-sentence seminar on the subject from a woodsman, who had probably figured out the simple philosophy on his own.

"Sorry," Lou said, calming himself with a deep breath, checking Cap's pulses once more, and continuing to hold his cool hand when he was done. "How far from here do you live?"

"Half mile, thereabouts."

"Half a mile?" Lou looked surprised. "There's no town anywhere near here," he said, recalling what he had seen on his trail map.

"Me 'n the missus live right here in these woods. Her family land, not state owned, so we ain't poachin'. We grow our own food and I catch whatever else we eat. We got no phone 'n no reason to have one."

"I can't get a signal up here."

"Maybe out in our field you will."

"You have a truck?"

"We got a road . . . if you kin call it that. No car, though, 'n no truck. We got a canoe with a five-horse outboard that we use to bring stuff we grow 'n make to Hadley, 'bout five miles downriver. Not sure we can get yer friend here in it, though. It's only sixteen feet."

First things first.

"Okay, okay. We'll worry about that when we get there. Let's build some sort of drag litter that we can also lift, and see if we can get him down to your place."

"I wanted to tell you we needed to do that before you started firin' questions at me," Floyd said. "A drag litter'll be a job, but I'm sure ol' bucky here kin get us the branches we need." He patted his enormous knife. "He's got enough sawteeth to do the job, 'n you got rope. Negotiatin' yer friend down this hill may be another matter, but I would say we got a chance. We should get goin', though. He's lookin' weaker by the second."

Twenty minutes later, the two of them eased Cap onto a low-tech stretcher—A-shaped, with a hefty stick lashed across the head to use for lifting when dragging was too impractical or painful. For a time, pain prodded Cap into intermittent consciousness, but soon, he drifted off someplace Lou hoped was pleasant and peaceful, and stayed there. Almost six feet of solid muscle, Cap was heavy enough. But the added weight of the splint and the litter, combined with the difficult terrain, made transporting him a Herculean task. If they were going over level ground and not downhill, the task might have been close to impossible. But foot by foot, at times inch by inch, they kept moving, Lou slipping and stumbling until he thought to borrow Cap's shoelaces, Floyd moving with surprising agility. Even though there was really nothing further he could do, Lou paused every few minutes or so for assurance that the most important man in his life had a pulse and was still breathing.

Floyd, whose last name, Lou learned, was Weems, was a beast—wiry, and at least equal to him in strength. For most of the trek, he remained silent. When hoisting the head of the litter he'd whistle softly—a tune that might have been a birdcall. A simple life, led simply. Even after just a short time, Lou sensed this gift of a man was the embodiment of the sort of serenity he had been working toward for ten years.

Lessons . . . everywhere lessons.

"Not far now," Floyd said, hoisting the litter to his chest in order to negotiate a fallen tree.

Lou occupied his mind during the tough parts of the descent by wondering how he might thank him.

What do you give a man who wants for nothing?

Time was running out. Despite the rugged work, Lou was shivering uncontrollably. His strength was going. His best friend's miserable situation had already driven him across an invisible line of stamina. Now it felt as if there were no place further to go. He was about to beg Floyd for an update, when the forest began to thin.

"Yer doin' fine, Doc," Floyd said, the first time he had felt the need to voice such encouragement. "Almost there."

The man's words were an elixir. Lou lifted his end of the litter just a little higher, and began losing himself in what they might do next, with or without a cell phone signal.

"Floyd?"

"Yassir?"

"You mentioned you had a field by your place where you grow things."

"I did mention that, yes."

"Well, tell me, does that field of yours have enough space in it to land a helicopter?"

CHAPTER 11

On the heels of the Social Security Act, the work of Dr. Ray Lyman Wilbur and his Committee on the Costs of Medical Care lies in wait, readying to unleash a flurry of new legislation with a bite far bigger than its bark.

—LANCASTER R. HILL, *Climbing the Mountain*, SAWYER RIVER BOOKS, 1941, P. 72

The pounding inside Special Agent Tim Vaill's head showed no signs of letting up. If anything, it might have been getting worse. The rhythmic beating against his temples made him think of The Who's Keith Moon, fanatically pounding away on his bass drum. *Bam! Bam! Bam!* Vaill squinted, trying to block out the light, but that only seemed to make his headache worse.

Where in the hell am I?

What happened to me?

Feeling dizzy now, Vaill struggled to get oriented. In fits and starts, like free-floating pieces of a jigsaw puzzle, his thoughts began drifting into place. He remembered falling—falling backward.

Where?

Stairs . . . he had fallen backward down a flight of stairs.

But why?

Had he been pushed? Bit by bit, his memory returned,

bringing with it a different sort of pain, this one spiked with anger.

Burke. I was shot by fucking Alexander Burke.

That thought quickly led into another—an image vivid and powerful enough to tighten around his throat like a python.

Maria!

His heart stopped. Maria had been there right beside him. Vaill concentrated, trying to wrangle more pieces of those shrouded events from his aching and battered brain. He winced from the effort. Out of desperation, he bit down on his tongue, trying to redirect some discomfort from the amplified thumping in his skull. The spike in pain did little to jar loose his memory of her. No matter how hard he concentrated, he had no clue as to her fate. But somewhere at the edge of his awareness he sensed it was bad.

Vaill pawed the grit from his eyes and forced them open.

How long have I been asleep?

He took some time to assess his surroundings. He was lying on a comfortable bed.

What bed? Where?

Glancing down, he saw that his left hand was wrapped in some sort of gauze bandage. An IV line had been attached to a vein alongside the wrist of his right arm. A nearby purple bruise suggested it had not been an easy vessel to nail. There were a pair of windows in the wall to his left. The blinds were open, allowing bright sunlight to spill into the room. It had been late in the day when he'd been shot. Prayer time for Dr. Kazimi.

How long? . . . How long have I been here? . . . Maria. What happened to Maria?

He was seized by an image of her—a distorted mental picture, woefully out of focus, swirling like smoke. She was falling—melting like the witch in *The Wizard of Oz*. Moments later, faces intruded on the unsettling picture.

Who are they? When will the pain in my head go away? Where's Maria? What happened to her?

"Tim, are you with us? Can you hear me? . . . Will he be able to speak?"

The words dragged Vaill out of his fog. He recognized the steely, authoritative voice immediately. It belonged to Beth Snyder, FBI director of Special Operations—his boss. Snyder, whose notion of time off was a Sunday afternoon nap in the office, rarely went to see an agent in person unless it was to attend their funeral or visit them in the hospital. Barring some great cosmic joke, the hard-boiled woman was far from Vaill's idea of heaven, so he assumed he was in a hospital somewhere.

"Give him time," a man with an accent said. "His wound was not life-threatening, but it was a serious injury."

Wanting to change positions, Vaill pushed back on his elbows to prop himself up. Even that slight movement sent lightning bolts crackling through his head. Clenching his teeth, his vision having gone white, he forced himself to move past the pain. He needed to look Snyder in the eyes and ask the question he could not seem to answer for himself.

"Maria," he managed. His voice was a strangled

croak, with barely enough power to escape his parched throat. He tried again, digging deeper, ignoring the pain the way he had been taught at Quantico. "Maria . . . where is she?" Even though Vaill wanted water more than air, all he could do was keep asking for her. Each time he spoke her name he expected a sliver of memory to return, but nothing came.

"Agent Vaill, you should try to keep your movements to a minimum."

The stranger's accented voice again—a doctor of some sort, Vaill now believed.

"Who . . . are you . . . Where is Maria?"

Vaill inched his head around to face the man—an Indian or Pakistani, wearing turquoise hospital scrubs beneath a long white coat with his name stitched in blue script above the breast pocket. Beth stood beside him, her expression grave.

"Agent Vaill, my name is Dr. Nayan Gunter. I'm a neurosurgeon here at Eisenhower Memorial Hospital—*your* neurosurgeon. You were shot while on duty. You've suffered a fairly significant injury to your left temporal lobe, but the bullet was easy to remove, and you seem to be recovering nicely."

The gunshot.

Vaill's memory began to solidify. A bullet had struck him mid-chest, impacting his Kevlar vest hard enough to knock him off balance. He was falling backward when a second bullet hit. The fall prevented what most certainly would have been a kill shot to the head.

"Maria . . . where is she?"

Beth spoke now. "Tim, you're doing well, but it's going to take some time for you to recover. It's a miracle that you're alive."

Then why don't I feel like a miracle? What's gnawing at my guts? Why do I feel like I've been handed some sort of death sentence—something that would leave me crippled for the rest of my life? . . . Maria . . .

Beth took hold of his hand—not a normal gesture for her. Her heart had been calcified from years of wading waist-deep in human misery.

"Tim, you need to brace yourself," he heard her say.

Then it came to him, like a tsunami crashing down, drowning him in despair. He swallowed back a jet of bile. What was a hazy recollection gave way to vivid detail. Maria's head snapping back . . . The hole in her forehead . . . Blood exploding out from her ruptured skull . . . The gruesome crimson spray on the wall behind her . . . Her body going limp as though she'd been unplugged from some life-giving machinery . . . Her horribly vacant eyes.

Vaill remembered now. He remembered his programming kicking in with knee-jerk speed. He remembered going for his gun, obsessed only with shooting Alexander Burke dead. But either the man was simply faster, or seeing Maria crumple had cost Vaill a split second. Now, he was imprisoned in a hospital room, about to be told by his boss that his wife was dead.

Tears stung the corners of his eyes as Snyder talked on, but he battled them back. He would cry for Maria later. He would cry rivers. But first, there was a promise to be made—a commitment to vengeance. Vaill had always been cautious when it came to making promises. But not this time.

He and Maria had dated for two years after they met at Quantico and fell instantly in love. More than once over those two years, she laughed at the irony that he was afraid of nothing except commitment. His response was that he had been raised never to break a promise, and the promise of marriage was a commitment unlike any other. A month after that, she gave him a final chance to step up or lose her, and he proposed on the spot. He had never once regretted making that pledge, nor had he ever had any problem keeping it. Now, as Beth Snyder talked on, Vaill made another promise. He would find Special Agent Alexander Burke and kill him . . . or die.

"Tim, I'm so sorry," Snyder was saying. "Every agent at the Bureau is working nonstop to find the bastard. We're going to get him, Tim. I promise we're going to nail him."

"How long have I been here?"

"Two days now."

Vaill's throat tightened. Each breath was an effort. Maria had been dead for two days and until this moment, he did not even know it. What was her family doing? Who had been notified? Where was her body? When was her funeral? He should have been with her family, grieving alongside them, not lying helpless in a hospital bed. In twelve years of marriage, he had grown as close to Maria's family as he was to his own. He and Maria had not been blessed with children of their own, but they had plans. Now, in a burst of noise and smoke, those plans had all been blown away.

"I need to talk to you alone," Vaill said to Snyder, his whisper stronger than it had been.

Snyder looked to the doctor. Reluctantly, it seemed, Gunter nodded.

"He needs rest," the surgeon said. "Given the nature

of his injury, his recovery is quite remarkable, but the damage to his temporal lobe might be significant."

"I'm sure a few minutes alone with me won't do him harm," Snyder said. "Thank you, doctor. Thank you for understanding."

Vaill waited until he heard the door close. His parched throat begged for water. Snyder, sensing his need, gave him some ice chips on a spoon, followed by a small sip through a plastic straw. She was as tough as anyone Vaill had ever worked with, but her compassion was genuine. Vaill knew she was sick with guilt at having been taken in by a dirty agent.

"What is it?" she asked. "Trust me, Tim, you're safe. We've got guards out there around the clock hoping that Burke tries to finish what he started."

"I need to get him, Beth," Vaill said. "I need to hurt him, and then I need to kill him."

"Tim, you know we don't operate that way. I want you to go on medical leave for a while. The agents, and me especially, want him almost as badly as you do. We'll take care of it."

"That's what I knew you'd say. But I'm not going on any medical leave. I'm going back on duty and you've got to put me on the case to get him."

"I'm sorry, Tim. I know you're hurting, but I can't do that."

"Can't or won't?"

"Does it matter?"

Vaill took another few sips of water. This time he held the plastic cup himself.

"Beth," he said, "you know how close Maria and I were. We were getting ready to adopt a kid. The forms have all been filled out. I can show them to you. It could have happened any day. That fucker killed her. He killed the only woman I've ever loved. You're the one who put us together with Burke on the Kazimi detail. *Please.* You owe it to me to let me find him."

Snyder took a step back from the bed.

"I'm not sure," she said.

"But you're not saying no?"

"I'll talk it over with your doctor, and give the situation some serious thought, okay?"

Vaill nodded.

"She was my world, Beth. She was everything to me and I watched her head get blown apart."

"You stay strong, Tim," Snyder said, squeezing his hand. "I'll speak with Dr. Gunter, then I'll be back tomorrow morning."

Vaill dismissed her with a wave. Slowly, his eyes closed. He began to drift off wondering whether he had the strength to stand up, incapacitate his guard, and simply walk out of the hospital. If he had no other choice, it would happen.

Unable to sleep, he rolled onto his side and for a time, stared out the window. He was lost in a montage of lurid, bloody fantasies, when Dr. Gunter appeared at his bedside.

"Good news to share," the neurosurgeon said, checking something in Vaill's bedside chart.

"Yeah, what's that?"

"I had a long conversation with your chief, Agent Snyder. She told us of the discussion she had with you—specifically your desire to return to work as soon as possible and resume your investigative duties. I sent for the head of my department, Dr. Weitz. We reviewed your remarkable progress so far, and ended up assuring Agent Snyder that, barring any unforeseen complications, there is no medical reason why you would not be able to continue in the capacity to which you are accustomed. You are in fact one of the luckiest gunshot survivors I have ever encountered."

Tell that to my wife, Vaill thought savagely.

"Thanks, doc," he said instead, turning back to the window.

The pounding in his head had intensified, and with it came an overpowering confusion. It was as if the passive neurologic process of thinking was a ball-peen hammer smashing down on his brain. He barely heard Gunter excuse himself and leave the room.

CHAPTER 12

A true Neighbor must be pure of heart to take the Oath of Secrecy and in doing so, swear to uphold the ideals of the society before God.

—LANCASTER R. HILL, *100 Neighbors*, SAWYER RIVER BOOKS, 1939, P. 167

The powerful rotors of the twin-engine helicopter flattened the young crops and tall grasses of the field beside Floyd's cabin. Lou had been unable to pick up a cell phone signal until they were in sight of the cabin's fieldstone chimney and the river. At that point he and Floyd still hadn't settled on a method of getting Cap to a hospital that wouldn't further shorten his already dwindling odds of survival.

The sparkling red-and-white paint job emblazoned on the cockpit doors showcased the company name— North Georgia Air Ambulance. It had taken forty minutes following Lou's call for the chopper to arrive. Were it not for the GPS on his phone, it could have taken considerably longer. Lou had described the landing area to the pilot prior to take off. She required a hundred-by-hundred-foot minimum to land, more if there were surrounding trees or wires, of which there were none provided she made her approach from the south. Blessedly, the weather cooperated.

Floyd's wife, Rebecca, an ample, rosy-cheeked

woman, wearing a gingham housedress, shielded her eyes against the swirling dust and debris. The pilot of the impressive-looking aircraft took advantage of the low foliage along the river to make an angled approach, and made a picture-perfect touchdown on the improvised landing pad. Lou noticed that Floyd, tugging on his beard, was watching the landing with a reverent expression, as though he'd been transported from his simple frontier life into the distant future.

Two crew members in red-and-white jumpsuits emerged from the aircraft and raced to Cap's side as the rotors were still slowing. They were followed by the pilot a minute later. Lou had provided them with details of the accident they would be dealing with, and what they could expect to find. The trauma nurse, Julie Bellet, sounded skeptical of the description of Cap's injury, and what had been accomplished by doctor and patient in the forest. Lou didn't blame her. He was still having trouble believing it himself.

He quickly exchanged names with the team. Daniel, a paramedic, was a muscular man in his twenties with the grip of a bear trap. He hauled a trunk-sized mobile crash cart over to where Cap lay, carrying it as if it were a toy. Julie Bellet carried a much smaller case, which Lou assumed held instruments. She was an attractive woman, perhaps in her early fifties, silver-haired, fit and intense. She made a brief survey of their patient, focusing for a few extra seconds on the splint and tourniquet. Then, straight-lipped, she looked over at Lou and minutely nodded her approval.

The pilot, Captain Dorothy Tompkins according to her name tag, was a slender five-six or -seven, maybe thirty-five, with short chestnut hair, and an EMT patch on her sleeve. She and Daniel removed a stretcher from the back of the aircraft, carrying it still folded over the damp, soft soil before snapping it open. For Lou, watching the team work was like immersing himself in the music of a top-notch jazz trio.

"Stay close, Dr. Welcome," Bellet said, "in case we need another set of hands."

Doubtful, Lou thought, realizing at the same time that if they needed him, there was serious trouble.

Floyd's wife had supplied him with a tattered flannel work shirt and a pair of hand-sewn cotton pants that fit him just fine. She and Floyd stood well off to one side, reminding Lou of the stoic farm couple in *American Gothic.* Just another typical day in the forest.

"Squeeze my hand if you can hear me, Mr. Duncan," Bellet was saying, her voice calm and unhurried. "You're going to be okay, my friend. We just have to get you stabilized and then over to the chopper. If I do anything that hurts you, just signal me."

"Lou . . . comes . . . too . . . ," Cap managed.

"We got room for one patient and one passenger, Mr. Duncan," Daniel said, fixing oxygen prongs and a cervical collar in place. "You want this one, you got him. Besides, after seeing that splint and that litter, we'll be making him an honorary member of the team anyway."

"Me, too," Cap said, smiling around nearly clenched teeth. "I . . . helped."

"We'll get you a set of wings when you're settled in the ER at Arbor General. Okay, a little stick, now."

The IV, hooked to a large-bore catheter, was in and taped down faster than a Cap Duncan jab.

"You make these?" Daniel asked Lou, gesturing to

the makeshift contraptions as he took down the dressing.

"All three of us," Lou said as if apologizing for the workmanship. "We were pretty desperate."

"Yeah, well, I've been doing this job for five years and I've never seen anything like it."

"I was taught by paramedics."

Bellet completed her evaluation with Cap still drifting in and out of consciousness. Even beyond his leg, his rock-hard body seemed somehow compromised, and for the first time in Lou's memory, his best friend looked his birth certificate age.

"We go as soon as we pour some antiseptic into that wound and get it redressed," Bellet said. "Moving him isn't going to be that easy. I think we should lift the drag litter as is. Daniel and Dr. Welcome, that's your job. Sir, you and our pilot can get our stretcher set up in the chopper."

"Everyone just stay low at all times," Captain Tompkins warned. "You don't get a second chance to make up for forgetting that one."

Daniel gave Cap some more morphine.

"How tough is this guy?" he asked Lou.

"They don't come much tougher."

"How long on the tourniquet, Dr. Welcome?" Bellet asked.

"An hour forty."

"Mr. Duncan, I'm going to loosen this tourniquet. Sorry if I hurt you."

The trauma nurse waited until Daniel had redressed Cap's gash, then gingerly removed the stick and set it aside, leaving the band of cloth in place. For a minute or two, the group waited in silence. No oozing. Julie looked over at Lou and again nodded. This time she was smiling.

"You must be a hell of an ER doc when you've got some real equipment around you, and not just a bunch of sticks and ropes."

"As long as the nurses are as sharp as you are, I'm pretty good," Lou replied.

"I believe you are. Okay, let's get your friend to a real bed."

Thanks to morphine and Cap's advertised toughness, the transport and transfer went off with just a few moans of pain. As soon as the cardiac monitoring equipment was in place, Daniel gave Tompkins the thumbs-up sign for liftoff. Lou took Cap's hand in his and held it.

It was time to leave the woods.

Sound-dampening earphones in place, Lou knew he would remain on edge for the entire seventy-five-mile flight from the field beside Floyd and Rebecca Weems's cabin to the Arbor General Hospital helipad. He was actually ready to climb into the chopper before he managed to wrangle a post office box number in the river town of Sledge Crossing.

Weems felt certain he would have no trouble replanting the damaged part of their field. He had offered it up as a landing pad even before he learned that he would be saving Cap the pain of having to be hoisted up using a winch and basket. As he settled into his seat, Lou vowed that it was not the last time he would see the eccentric woodsman and his wife. He also knew that whatever material thanks he passed on to them would be insulting if not rejected altogether, unless it were carefully thought out.

"We're ready to lift off," Tompkins yelled back over her shoulder. "Put on your helmets."

"Thank you again, Floyd!" Lou shouted out the open hatch.

"Tain't nothin' I did. You two are good people. Jes get him healthy. Come back and visit Rebecca and me anytime. My woods are your woods."

The helicopter's rotors sped up as the burly paramedic pulled the hatch closed and latched it. Through the porthole, Lou could see Floyd using his arm to cover his eyes as he backed away. The chopper wobbled a bit as it gained lift, and then settled down. Moments later, they were on an angled ascent, steadily gaining speed.

Lou watched as the couple, standing shoulder-to-shoulder, became enfolded in their world, and silently thanked the vast forest that had somehow been small enough to deliver Lou and Cap a savior.

CHAPTER 13

> The true means to provide sound and adequate protection against the vicissitudes of modern life may be found in self-reliance, a return to family values, embracing the pioneering spirit of our forefathers, and the shared belief that God, not government, is the determinant of life and death.
>
> —LANCASTER R. HILL, *100 Neighbors*, SAWYER RIVER BOOKS, 1939, P.50

He could not believe he was alive. As consciousness returned, Ahmed Kazimi moved his arm, expecting to find it restrained—chained to a wall, perhaps. To his surprise, he could move both his arms and legs freely, although his whole body felt stiff and achy, as if he'd been passed out in the same position for hours. Instead of his familiar work attire, he was clad in shimmery red silk pajamas.

He imagined, as he opened his eyes, that he would be awakening in a barren, concrete room, the floor covered in damp straw reeking of urine—the sort of prison he'd come to expect from television shows and movies. Instead, he sat upright on a firm, king-size mattress, underneath black silk sheets of the highest possible thread count. He was cocooned within diaphanous white draperies that hung down from a beautifully ornate mahogany canopy frame.

Massaging his throbbing temples, Kazimi tried to clear his blurred vision, but without much success. Where was he? Why had he been taken in such a way? The questions swirled in his mind like windblown sand. Who was Burke? How had he infiltrated the FBI? Kazimi had been forced to the floor beside the window of his bedroom, so his image of Burke killing the two other agents protecting him was indistinct. The rest of what happened was even more hazy. He had been shoved out his third-story window into . . . into what? An open-bed truck filled with foam padding. The last thing he remembered was Burke injecting him with a drug that quickly made him feel like someone had poured concrete into his ears.

Gradually, Kazimi's vision came into focus. He crawled out from the canopy and found himself in a richly appointed room adorned with magnificent oriental carpeting, laid on an exquisite fieldstone floor. The same stone covered the lower half of the walls, leading him to think of a medieval castle. The upper half was an ornate fleur-de-lis design done in crimson velvet.

The air was scented from three massive bouquets of fresh-cut flowers arranged in crystal vases. Directly across from him stood a black lacquer bureau, inlaid with mother of pearl, and above it hung an ultra-modern plasma television, currently powered off, but with a remote attached to it by Velcro strips. In addition to a well-volumed bookcase, there were five beautifully framed and lit paintings that Kazimi, hardly an expert at such things, believed were a Degas, a Picasso, a Monet, and possibly two of the Dutch masters—almost certainly all original.

Kazimi took a few tentative steps. He was wobbly and weak at first, but gradually regained his balance. Standing in the center of the room, he made a more extensive survey of his posh accommodations, and was both amazed and repulsed by the decadence surrounding him. He had always been a man of simple values, for whom material possessions had meant nothing. Perhaps, he mused, knowledge of that philosophy is why his captors elected to imprison him inside such opulence.

Moving to the corner of the room next to the bookcase, Kazimi scanned the bar, stocked with the finest spirits and bottles of wine, most likely from the very best vintages. Though alcohol would never pass his lips, he knew the value of wine bottled decades ago. In front of the bar was a glistening ebony table with four Louis XIV chairs, also most likely not reproductions. As a frequent guest of international conferences on bacteriology, he had been put up in hotel suites before. This room made even the most luxurious of those look like some of the concrete homes of his native Pakistan.

Automatic lights came on as he stepped into a cavernous bathroom tiled in spectacular white marble flecked with gold, and featuring a shower, steam room, and Jacuzzi tub cast in what appeared to be pure copper.

Glancing at his reflection in the oversized mirror, he winced at his raccoon eyes and sickly pallor. Again, the questions:

What drug did Burke give me?

Where am I?

What do they want with me?

How can I fight them?

How can I escape?

He rested his hands on the granite countertop until he felt steadier on his feet. Then he left the bathroom and crossed to the shuttered, black-lacquered double doors, which he assumed exited the garish room.

Locked.

He examined the walls and even under the carpet, searching for another way out. Only then did it register that the space had no windows. A velvet and silk dungeon.

At that instant, a sharp knock on the door startled him.

"Come in," he managed. His voice, hoarse from disuse and possibly from his having been drugged, sounded foreign.

A key turned in the lock. The double doors swung open on soundless hinges and in walked a stoop-shouldered man with graying hair, neatly parted on the right. He was impeccably dressed in a butler's uniform, and was wheeling a food cart bearing several trays. The pungent aromas were as familiar to Kazimi as they were pleasing.

"Good evening, sir. My name is Harris. I'm the head butler here. Welcome to Red Cliff."

"Where is this place? What is it?"

"I have been instructed to tell you that all of the food products and ingredients meet with the dietary restrictions of your religion. I hope you find the preparation to your liking."

"You've been instructed by whom? Who told you to bring me this food?"

"If you'll excuse me, sir. My orders are to deposit

the food cart and then be on my way, and I have maintained my position here at Red Cliff over the years because I always follow orders. Your host will be joining you shortly. Would you like me to set the food out for you, or would you prefer to do it yourself? The utensils you will need are right here."

Harris pointed to a rolled-up cloth napkin. Kazimi immediately noticed the pointed end of a knife poking out the top. His eyes narrowed as he began thinking of ways he could use the knife to aid in an escape, but he knew the timing was bad. He wanted answers. Who had taken him and why? Who had orchestrated the murders of two FBI agents? First he needed to meet his host. Then he would consider escape.

"Just set the food out," he ordered disdainfully.

Harris closed the door with his foot.

"I'm sorry, sir, but it locks automatically. If you wish, I'll stay with you until your host arrives."

For the next several minutes, Kazimi paced the silk and velvet dungeon while the butler identified, then set out dishes of food on the ebony table—lamb in a turmeric gravy, white potatoes in a rich red sauce, gogji beans with turnip in black pepper gravy, sweet green tea with cardamom—food from the Kashmir region of Pakistan, Kazimi's home during his early years. Another knock on the door. Harris immediately stopped what he was doing and stood beside Kazimi like a trained dog.

"Come in," Kazimi called out.

A key sounded in the lock. The double doors swung open, and in walked a moderately overweight, suave-looking man, fifty or so, who stood there as calmly as if he were assessing a pair of ballroom dancers. His right hand was wrapped around a walking stick capped with the tennis-ball-sized head of a lion, either bronze or, more likely given the opulence of Red Cliff, gold. His other hand comfortably grasped a tumbler of whiskey. Kazimi, who had lived his life in relative self-denial, disliked the man at once. He had a broad and flat nose and the coal-dark eyes of a predator. The impressive cane was more than decoration. The new arrival walked with a modest limp, favoring his right leg. Kazimi's thought of overpowering him lasted only until two beefy men—one white, one black—materialized behind the man, filling the doorway.

"Thank you Harris," the fat cat said. "You did well, as usual."

"Dr. Kazimi," Harris said, "may I present to you the master of this house, Mr. Douglas Bacon."

CHAPTER 14

The only entitlement guaranteed should be the fruits of one's own labor.

—LANCASTER R, HILL, *A Secret Worth Keeping*, SAWYER RIVER BOOKS, 1937, P. 199

"Pleased to meet you, doctor," Bacon said, gracefully maneuvering his tumbler of whiskey to the hand holding the cane so he could offer his free hand to Kazimi. Eyeing Bacon's hand with contempt, Kazimi kept his arms tightly folded across his chest. It was a small display of defiance, but at this moment even the smallest victories mattered. "Very well," Bacon said, returning the tumbler to his right hand and indulging in a sip. "As you wish."

"I wish to leave here now!" Kazimi snapped.

"That, I am afraid, is not possible. We need your help."

"Exactly who are 'we,' Mr. Bacon?" Kazimi asked.

"Please, call me Doug. And all answers in good time, doctor. All in good time."

No one disagrees with or even questions him, Kazimi thought. *Ever. Keep the pressure on. Someone is going to crack. If not Bacon, one of the others I will be asked to deal with at Red Cliff. Someone is going to show me the way out of here.*

"What do you want with me? What is this all about?" Kazimi's demands came out without nearly the force he had intended. Most likely, the drugs in his system still lingered. "Who are you?"

"I am not your enemy, Dr. Kazimi," Bacon said with the hint of a Southern accent. "That is the first thing you need to know. Or would you prefer I call you Dr. Farooq, the name you abandoned when you left Stanford and went to work for the FBI?"

"Whatever you want from me, you're not going to get it."

"That remains to be seen."

"Where are my clothes?"

Kazimi tugged at his silk pajamas as though they were burning his skin.

"While you are my guest, you may have anything you wish. Whatever clothes you desire; whatever food; a prayer rug and a place to pray; a place to exercise. Simply ask and it is yours. But I remind you, time is of the essence. Lives are at stake. Many, many lives."

For all Doug Bacon's cultured charm and geniality, Kazimi sensed a ferocity in him—a dark intensity and commitment to . . . to what? How was Bacon connected to the Doomsday Germ? It was clear from his bearing and the way he had orchestrated Kazimi's kidnapping and imprisonment he was a powerful, utterly determined force. And for the first time in Kazimi's life, his faith in Allah could not ablate his fear.

"I want the clothes I was wearing when you brought me here," Kazimi said. It felt good to issue a command.

"As you wish," Bacon said. "They are washed and folded. I'll have Harris bring them to your room right away."

"And then I demand to be escorted from these premises," Kazimi said. "I will not assist you in any capacity. You will get nothing from me. Not one bit of my cooperation."

Bacon returned an oddly inscrutable look that made Kazimi feel exposed and penetrated. It was as if the master of Red Cliff was surgically dissecting his personality, computing at lightning speed every thrust, and preparing a parry for it in advance. Controlling people was a game to him, Kazimi concluded, and one he played very well.

"I need your cooperation, so how about I offer you a deal," Bacon said, breaking a pregnant silence. "If you agree to my terms you will be permitted to leave Red Cliff, I will even assist with your departure."

"Go on."

"As those who know me are aware, I am a betting man. I enjoy the rush of a good gamble. All that is required here is for you to best me in a battle of wits."

"What is the subject matter of this battle?" Kazimi asked. "I am smart, but not in every area."

Bacon's face brightened. "Ah, doctor, that is part of the fun of this wager." His drawl seemed to have become somewhat more pronounced. "You must agree to participate without knowing."

"And if I refuse once the subject of our battle is known to me?"

"Then our wishes will become demands and you will simply comply with them. You will swear to accept this wager in Allah's name."

"I won't do it."

"I'm giving you a chance to walk away from here, Dr. Kazimi. The people I work with would not like this.

Not one bit. Can you outsmart me in a game of wits? Naturally, I believe the answer is no. But will you not take a chance?"

Kazimi considered his options while eyeing the two powerful guards. It would be impossible to force his way out. His options were limited at best.

"I accept," Kazimi said finally. He trusted his intellect. He could match wits with any Mensa member. Bacon might get a rush from betting, a sin for true Muslims, but he'd regret ever making this challenge.

"Very well," Bacon said. "Let us begin."

Crossing the room, using his cane for leverage, he went over to the ebony table, deposited his whiskey tumbler, and retrieved from the place setting the serrated steak knife Kazimi had noticed earlier. Then he took up his previous spot in front of the open door, symbolically positioning himself between Kazimi and his freedom.

"Now then," Kazimi said. "Ask your question. Test me. I am not afraid."

"In Allah's name."

"In Allah's name."

Bacon leaned forward and held out the knife, ebony handle first.

"It is not a question," he said, "but a deed you must perform. Take the knife."

Kazimi hesitated. Bacon waved the handle of the blade, encouraging him.

"If you refuse you will lose without even having tried," he said, a sardonic smile teasing the corners of his mouth.

Kazimi wavered, then grasped the knife by its handle, point facing out.

"Very good," Bacon said, smirking. "Well done. Now then, to win our little game, I ask you to kill me."

The guards moved instinctively toward the man, but he held them back with a raised palm.

"Take the knife and kill me," he repeated. "If you do, I give my word that you may walk out of here without any interference." He swiveled to face his guards. "Is that understood?" The men nodded. The reluctance Kazimi detected in both their eyes and mannerisms made him feel certain Bacon's offer was for real. Bacon took a step forward until the tip of the blade, quavering in Kazimi's outstretched hand pressed up against his ample abdomen.

"Go ahead, Dr. Kazimi. Do it. Kill me and then walk away."

Kazimi pushed with the blade, but not hard enough to puncture the fabric of Bacon's white shirt, or worse the skin underneath.

"I give you three seconds to comply. Plunge the blade and walk away. Three . . ."

Kazimi pressed a little harder.

"Two . . ."

Harder still.

"One."

Kazimi let the knife drop to the floor.

"How did you know?" Kazimi asked with his head bowed, keeping his gaze fixated on the blade, his one possible means of escape.

"Take not life, which Allah has made sacred—except by way of justice or law. Thus doth He command you, that ye may learn wisdom. Chapter six, verse one-fifty-one. Murder in self-defense is permissible, but here I was unarmed. Taking a life this way is forbidden by your religion. It would be considered a *haraam*—a truly detestable act that would anger Allah. Am I not correct?"

"You are," Kazimi said.

"I hereby declare our battle of wits—or should I say, battle of *wills*—over. And now I ask that we begin anew. Allow me to introduce myself once more. My name is Doug Bacon and for the foreseeable future you are to remain a guest in my home."

Bacon did not bother extending his hand this time.

"Not guest," Kazimi said. *"Prisoner."*

"I need to learn more about you, Dr. Kazimi, such as your reaction to stress, and I need to learn these things quickly. Your brilliance in infectious diseases is very important to us. Crucial would be a better word. Believe me, whatever happens here at Red Cliff happens for a carefully designed purpose. The stakes are high. Frighteningly high. And we have no intention of failing."

Before he agreed to leave Stanford and go undercover, Kazimi had been thoroughly briefed by his FBI handler, Beth Snyder, on the highly clandestine extremist group named the Society of One Hundred Neighbors. He had no doubt now that Doug Bacon was one of the higher-ups, if not the leader, of that organization. It did not seem the man was using an alias, and the fact that he was purposely so free with his name was not a good sign. Either he had plans on holding him indefinitely, or Kazimi was a dead man walking.

"I presume you've found the accommodations to your liking," Bacon said, returning to the lacquered table to retrieve his whiskey tumbler.

"You can skip the civility and the small talk, Bacon.

Where is Burke? Why would you authorize the cold-blooded murder of two people like that? Burke was a coward. A pathetic coward."

"Mr. Burke is no concern of yours," Bacon said. "For now, you need nourishment. There is work to be done."

He motioned to the food Harris had set out.

"Wager or no wager, I'll die before I do any work for you."

"That is a problem we have considered and rejected."

"No! I do not need to eat. I need to get out of here. I absolutely refuse to help you murderers in any way."

Doug Bacon's smile turned menacing.

"I assure you, Dr. Kazimi, you will eat when we say, and you will rest when we say, and most important, you will work when we say. The only thing in your life we will not control are your prayers. A new prayer rug is beneath the bed. Right beside those two vases of flowers, facing toward the wall, is Mecca."

CHAPTER 15

A government exists to provide order to the people while 100 Neighbors exists to define what that order shall be.

—LANCASTER R. HILL, *100 Neighbors*, SAWYER RIVER BOOKS, 1939, P. 27

On the stretcher beside Lou, covered with a heating blanket, Cap was in a drug-induced sleep. Lou had come away from his wilderness trauma course convinced that in any situation outside the hospital, he would go with a paramedic, EMT, or trauma nurse over most M.D.s any day. The North Georgia medevac team had done nothing to dispel that notion. Their biggest decision after Cap was stabilized was whether or not to do anything with the splint. After sending photos to the orthopedist covering the Arbor General ER, it was decided to leave that as it was and to start immediate antibiotics.

Even though Cap was on IV fluids and pressors to raise his blood pressure, it remained a disconcerting 85/55. Residual shock from blood loss into his thigh was a possibility, although there was no sign of continued bleeding. Internal hemorrhaging from a ruptured bowel or lacerated spleen remained lurking on Lou's list of possibilities like an alligator in the marsh.

Cap would need to be worked up carefully before being taken to the OR for repair of his shattered femur.

In addition to his low pressure, Cap's other vital signs were also shaky. His body temp was still ninety-four degrees Fahrenheit. Hopefully the hypothermia was due to exposure and not early shutdown of his kidneys or liver, or anything going on in the regulatory centers of his brain. Given his vitals, including a pulse rate hovering at 110, and a respiratory rate of twenty-four breaths a minute, Lou knew they had a long way to go before he'd take a relieved breath himself.

He was just about to ask for an ETA, when the jagged cityscape of Atlanta appeared in the distance.

"Almost there, pal," he said, mustering just enough enthusiasm to get a thumbs-up sign from Cap.

"What are they injecting into me?" Cap asked, his voice not much louder than the flap of a butterfly wing.

"Morphine," Lou replied, electing to ignore the fact that the question had been asked and answered before.

"Ah, the good stuff. I thought so."

"You worried?"

"You worked on my leg back there, doc. You tell me."

"Your blood pressure is still a little low, but you're not getting that much morphine. I can ask to have you get a little more."

"Don't worry, it won't send me down the slippery slope."

Lou knew he and Cap were in complete agreement when it came to prescribed painkillers and other mood-altering drugs. Just because a person had been addicted to drugs or alcohol did not mean they were barred from receiving medically controlled pharmaceuticals, so long as the doctor who wrote the script, or ordered the meds in a hospital, was fully aware of their history.

During a pickup touch football game five years into his recovery, Lou did a number on the cartilage and a ligament in his right knee that required extensive arthroscopy. He still clearly recalled the first days following his surgery: *The instructions for the Percocet says one or two every four to six hours. Is this one pain I'm having, or a two? . . . It's been three and a half hours. What if I take two now and wait an extra hour for the next dose? . . .*

Obsession.

His dormant addiction was making him crazy. The pain of having the narcotics around quickly became worse than the pain in his knee. After a day and a half, he talked things over with Cap, then poured the pills in the toilet, and broke out the Tylenol and Motrin.

Cap had been there for him throughout that struggle. Now, with their roles reversed, he would be there for the man for as long as he was needed. At the moment, though, Lou was worried a lot more about Cap's sagging blood pressure then he was about reigniting Cap's addiction.

The chopper circled twice before making a feather-soft touchdown on the helipad atop a glass-and-steel sixteen-story building. The empty landing area, built in the shape of a cross, looked vast enough to accommodate four med flight helicopters. Within seconds of wheels down, a three-person team in aqua Arbor General scrubs began the unloading process. Lou exchanged hugs and handshakes with the crew from the

North Georgia Air Rescue and caught up with Cap and the Arbor staff just as the doors to the express elevator opened. Cap and his splint made it inside by an inch.

"There's an ER team waiting for him," the nurse said to Lou on their way down. "Everyone is ready."

Cap was slipping in and out of consciousness again. Surgery could not happen soon enough. Two minutes later they were headed down a long corridor, walking briskly under a phalanx of fluorescent lights. It had only been a few days since he was last in a hospital, but it felt much longer, and just the smell of the place filled him with relief. At times during the hours just past, Lou had serious doubts, but now he felt certain Cap Duncan was going to survive this ordeal.

As if in warning against overconfidence, Cap's respirations became shallower and slower.

Come on, everyone . . . Come on!

The scene as the electronic doors to the ER swung open was as familiar to Lou as his bedroom, only now he was on the fringes of the action looking in. He managed a thank-you to the team for their professionalism and kindness, just as nurses converged on the stretcher, and with quiet efficiency began the hookup to monitoring equipment, oxygen, and IV poles. Cap woke up moaning as four of them, using the sheet beneath him, transferred him to a bed with a stretcher lashed to the end of it to accommodate his splint.

Good stuff.

A stout, hard-looking ER nurse asked Lou to wait off to one side while the team went to work. It seemed as if everyone knew he was an ER doc, but how good an ER doc was anyone's guess, and this wasn't the time to find out. Clearly, Floyd Weems's clothes did nothing to enhance their confidence in him.

He thought through how the team at Eisenhower would handle things if he were in charge. He'd order labs including a six-unit cross-match, recheck Cap's vitals and, ready to intubate him if his respiratory rate fell, administer enough pain medication to perform a decent exam before positioning him for x-rays. Arbor General was a top-notch academic hospital, and everyone here was speaking the same language as at Eisenhower—the language of competence and caring.

On a scale of ten, activity in the massive ER seemed to be perking along at about a four. Lou had heard enough to know that the place was abuzz over the ingenious in-field reduction of Cap's compound fracture, and the fact that the patient himself had assisted in the procedure. Soon the hospital grapevine, assuming it was as efficient as the supersonic one at Eisenhower, would have carried the news to the remotest corners of the place.

Lou waited until the initial commotion had settled down, and moved over to the doc in charge, a handsome, broad-shouldered man with a Hollywood jaw and coppery skin, who looked as if his teenage years were not that far behind him. They moved out to the hallway, exchanged introductions, and agreed to use first names. Cap's life was, for the moment, in the hands of Dr. Hal Garvey and his staff.

If Lou's unusual attire registered, Hal Garvey didn't show it. There wasn't much any ER doc or nurse hadn't seen in one form or another.

"You look like you could use some medical attention,

yourself," Garvey said, pointing to the gouge running down the side of Lou's bruised and dirty face.

"I'm okay," he said. "For the moment, all I'm worried about is my friend. His real name is Hank. Cap is something from his career as a prizefighter. Not many people call him anything other than that."

"Cap it is. I'll tell the staff. I'm the chief resident down here. This is my fifth year counting a year of research. I don't know if you've heard much about AGH, but this is a good place—the best in the South, we think. We're going to take excellent care of your friend."

"That's terrific to hear. I sensed good things as soon as we got here. Cap's very special to a lot of people in D.C., including me. I'd do anything for him."

"From what I've heard, you were quite the miracle worker out in the woods."

"Believe it or not, Cap did a lot of the work. He actually was the one who reduced the fracture by pulling on a rope and pushing against a tree with his good leg. I just splinted the pieces in place."

"Impressive. Your friend sounds tough."

"No one who knows him thinks otherwise. Hal, I don't want to sound pushy, but I want him to have the best orthopedist in the hospital. Can you help me out there?"

Garvey checked his smartphone.

"Ortho is possibly the strongest department in this hospital. They have a rotation for handling referrals from us, but if a patient requests a specific surgeon, I can call and see if they're available. Dr. Lichter would be scheduled to take this case. He's more than competent. Trust me, Cap will be well cared for on every level—especially when word gets around that he reduced his own compound fracture. A little like that guy who cut off his own arm to free himself in that canyon in Utah. Listen, let me finish going over him, and I'll put a call into Dr. Lichter. Why don't you wait in the doctor's lounge down that hall on the left. There's a restroom with a shower in it where you can get cleaned up. And also some scrubs. I'll come and get you when we've got a plan in place."

They shook hands and headed in opposite directions, Garvey back into Cap's room and Lou to the doctor's lounge.

Before he reached the corridor, Lou heard a soft, somewhat distorted voice say, "I wouldn't let Lichter do the surgery."

CHAPTER 16

Great change is brought about not by desire, but
by perseverance. Where once there lay an empty
parcel of land, you see now a city, built brick by
brick by the steady hands representative of
determined wills.

—LANCASTER R. HILL, *100 Neighbors*, SAWYER
RIVER BOOKS, 1939, P. 6

Lou turned to locate the source of the voice and needed
a moment to realize the speaker was below his eye
level, a frail, tousled, bespectacled man, nearly lost behind the complex console of his motorized wheelchair.
It didn't take a diagnostic wizard to see that he had
severe spastic cerebral palsy.

"I'm sorry," Lou said. "What did you say?"

"Don't be sorry," the man replied, enunciating as de-
liberately as he was able. "Lots of people ask me to
repeat myself. Others should, but don't. The truth is,
most people can't be bothered. Sorting out what I'm
saying is simply too much work for them. Long sentences can be tiring for me, too. Sometimes leave out
words that aren't important. Sometimes use screen and
joystick."

His speech was articulated with effort, and some
words were distorted by involuntary grimacing and
grunting. But in general, his physical limitations were

more prominent than those affecting talking. The man was probably around forty, and his disability was impressive—spastic quadriplegia, one of the most disabling manifestations of CP. His facial muscles and limbs were in nearly constant motion, and his lips were often distorted. Straps on his wrists helped keep his limbs in proper alignment.

Lou had the impression he had never walked, and at the very least, had help dressing and undressing himself each day. But despite his condition, he was able to manipulate a very complex wheelchair console, and to make his speech legible by shortening his sentences if his listener was willing to make the effort to concentrate. Perhaps his most appealing feature, though by no means his only one, were his dark brown eyes—wide and intelligent, even behind the thick lenses of his tortoiseshell glasses.

Lou's experiences with CP were largely limited to a girl in his high school and to patients in the ER. But over the last decade, he felt connected to those people on a very special level—one that unfortunately not all physicians shared. Based solely on outward appearances—poor motor control and thick, difficult speech—too many doctors assumed that CP was a global neurologic disorder affecting not only movement and speech, but intellect as well. In truth, with exceptions, a CP person's intelligence was fully engaged.

Lou was sensitive to any form of generalization or stereotyping—especially medical stereotyping. As a doctor who had past troubles with drugs and alcohol, he had encountered too many colleagues who judged his condition to be a moral deficiency, or who lumped him in with others afflicted with his disease.

The wiry man in the wheelchair appeared simply to be hanging around the ER, and nobody working there seemed to care. It was Lou's nature to listen to people—especially those with information that might be useful to him. He pulled over a chair so they could be at the same level.

"You said Dr. Lichter is not the right doctor for Cap?"

"That's what I said," the man replied.

"How'd you hear our conversation anyway? You were at least fifteen feet away from us and we weren't speaking that loudly."

The man pointed to a tiny microphone affixed to his wheelchair and then to the small plastic hearing aid in his right ear.

"As if CP wasn't enough, also a little hard of hearing. Don't want to pick up other's conversations, but it's that or miss a lot. Name's Miller. Humphrey Miller."

"Nice to meet you, Humphrey Miller. Do you work here?"

"I do. Pharmacy tech ten years. Pharmacists fill rolling cart and attach to front of chair. I transport to floors. Just brought white coat laundry. Spares at my apartment. Often here after my shift when there's action."

"I certainly guess you could call this action."

"Hospital buzzing 'bout you and friend even before you landed."

"I'm Lou Welcome, an ER doc from Washington, D.C." They shook hands, albeit with some difficulty. "Humphrey's not a very common name."

"Neither is Welcome."

"I have a feeling someone in my lineage—maybe someone with a sense of humor—changed it from something else somewhere along the line. My father doesn't seem to want to tell me who, or else maybe he doesn't know."

"As might guess, mom huge Bogart fan. Naming me Humphrey in addition to my CP was double whammy."

Even with his shorthand speech, it took Humphrey most of a minute to get some sentences out.

"Let's hear it for parents," Lou said, immediately drawn to the man.

"You didn't fidget," Humphrey said.

"Excuse me?"

"Usually when I talk any length of time, people fidget or stare off into space. You didn't do either."

"That's because you do require some concentration," Lou said with a chuckle, "and I never fidget when I'm concentrating."

Humphrey's bass laugh at his own expense was joyous, and fun to watch. He was the school nerd all grown up. His ears were large for his head, but somehow fit his personality, as if anything smaller would be a disservice to his character.

"So, what's this about Lichter?" Lou asked.

"You seem like nice guy. Here's tip. Don't let Ed Lichter do operation."

"Why not?"

"Lichter decent enough but not best we have. Loses interest after case is done. Turns things over to residents soon as can."

"Go on, but please forgive me in advance if I ask you to repeat."

"Sure. If complications, Dr. Len Standish follows up better. Man is wizard. Did my ankles to stabilize them."

Lou quickly pushed back and stood up, anxious to return to Garvey.

"I believe you, Humphrey," he said, "and I thank you. I owe you lunch."

"I heard compound femur fracture. You may be around awhile."

"I'll be around as long as my friend needs me. First, though, I've got to go and get him assigned to Dr. Standish."

"Won't be disappointed. I'm here. Let know how make out."

"Promise."

"Then decide dinner. Maybe later tonight. But forget lunch. That time passed hours ago."

Lou felt his throat tighten. He checked the time and pounded his forehead with the heel of his palm. It was five in the afternoon.

He had missed giving Filstrup's speech by two hours.

CHAPTER 17

Until such time when government entitlements threaten our liberty and the pioneering spirit of our founding fathers, the Neighbors shall hide in plain sight and will be in appearance what their name suggests: neighborly. Each Neighbor shall remain committed to the overriding ideals of blending in with their community and enjoying the fruits of life, while sharing in the glory of God.

—LANCASTER R. HILL, *100 Neighbors*, SAWYER RIVER BOOKS, 1939, PP. 10—11

Cap was awake and actually watching television when Lou entered his hospital room bearing a large box of chocolates, a paperback thriller, and a couple of glossy magazines. He immediately brightened.

"Hey, buddy," Cap said, "long time no see."

"Yeah, like two hours ago while they were getting ready to discharge you from the recovery room. I hope those drugs are feeling as good as they're acting."

"Man, I get so out of it from them, Stevie Wonder could be singing at the foot of my bed and I wouldn't remember. How you doing?"

"Let's just say if we were allowed to trade in days, I would have done it for the last couple."

"Same here, amigo. Don't know if I ever properly

thanked you for what you did for me out in the woods. That was a pretty dumb, clumsy thing for me to do."

Lou made a face suggesting that the mea culpa was totally inappropriate.

Cap's airy room, on the eighth floor, was a double, but at least for the moment he was without a roommate. His bed was the one by the window.

"The docs said the surgery was a big success," Lou said, setting down the stuff he had brought.

Cap's face was puffy from all the fluids he'd been given. He gestured at his elevated leg, suspended above his bed by an elaborate contraption of ropes and pulleys, and held in place by a steel external fixation frame.

"Guess I'm going to have to take a pass on trail running for a little while," he said.

"Day at a time, bro. Now, who could have taught me that?"

Most of the pins, plates, and screws Leonard Standish inserted into Cap's leg to hold the fragments of bone aligned were now a permanent part of his anatomy. A test for the TSA people at the airports.

Even though the surgery was a success, the risk of problems post-op remained high. There were those who believed that simply being a hospitalized patient, especially one needing assistance for almost everything, carried a serious risk of complications. In addition, blood clots from immobilization were a constant danger, and the hardware penetrating skin and bone were an invitation to infection. This was going to be a long, long haul. But Lou was determined to be there for the man every step of the way.

"So what's your professional assessment, doc?"

"I think we're lucky we weren't running in the

Okefenokee Swamp, that's what I think," Lou said. "We'd both be gator meat. The nurses showed me your post-op films. You have what we call a comminuted compound fracture. Nasty but totally fixable. Things are really lined up well. I'm not sure there's any doc out there who could have done a better job than Leonard Standish did. You deserved the best and you got it. And we can thank a pharmacy tech named Humphrey for that."

"Did someone call my name?"

As if on cue, Humphrey came motoring in, maneuvering the heavy chair by joystick. Once again, Lou was impressed by the deftness with which he worked the controls.

"Right hand a little better than left," Humphrey said as if reading Lou's thoughts. "You must be famous Cap."

"I'm sorry, I didn't quite catch all that," Cap said.

"He said you must be the famous Cap," Lou answered. "Think of listening to Humphrey like me getting the first boxing lesson at your gym. I had to concentrate or I was going to miss something."

Humphrey was dressed in a plaid, collared shirt and khakis. HUMPHREY MILLER, PHARMACY TECHNICIAN was stitched in blue script above the pocket of his short clinic coat. He motored closer to Cap's bedside.

"What are you, my interpreter?" Humphrey said to Lou, filling the room with his rich laugh.

He reached out a shaky, wildly spastic hand, and Cap took it in his and held it for several beats. Connection made.

"Thanks for your recommendation," Cap said. "Seems you done me good."

"Glad to do it. Met Lou in ER. Saw him leaving gift shop with huge box of chocolates. I'm serious choco-holic."

He laughed again.

"Here you go," Lou said, opening the box and hold-ing up the guide.

Humphrey pointed and Lou fished out the piece and handed it to him. It took some doing, but he got it into his mouth.

"Well, I'm glad you helped," Cap said. "My leg thanks you as well."

"Looks like you'll be taking lots of painkillers," Humphrey said. "I'll rush meds up here."

"Thanks."

"And you'll be sure to take them," Lou said. "Right, Cap'n Crunch? Sometimes this guy's too tough for his own good."

"Me, too," Humphrey said, laughing. "You really look out for each other."

"He's my brother from another mother," Cap said.

"Must be nice," Humphrey replied, a faraway look in his eyes. "Don't have brothers or sisters. One of me was too much. Listen, dropped off meds. You want nurse bring you some? Nurses on ortho like me."

"You da man, Humphrey," Cap replied. "Thanks. If they have something in addition to the IV pump, I'll take 'em. The leg is starting to really throb."

Humphrey motored out while Lou pulled up a chair to replace him at Cap's eye level.

"So what's my future looking like, boss?" Cap asked. "How long will I be here?"

"Not sure. This was big-time surgery you had. It may be too early for them to know, but I promise, Cap, in time you'll be bouncing around the ring again. Speaking of ring, is there anybody you want me to call? Anybody at Stick and Move we should notify?"

Cap bit at his lip and looked away.

"I have Eddie Foster watching it for me, but I really can't afford to pay him for long. Fact is, I been operating right on the edge of red for a while. I only decided to take this trip because it was you and I hadn't been out of D.C in like forever."

Lou felt himself shrink inside. He remembered the cold, misty rain and Cap's suggestion that they do the gym instead of a trail run. Then he realized Cap had turned back from the window and was studying him.

"You're blaming yourself for this, aren't you, Welcome?"

"It was my idea to run."

"Yeah? Well, get that notion right out of your head. I'm a big boy, bro. I make my own big-boy decisions and I own the outcomes of my actions. This ain't on you or on me. This was an accident, a crappy, rotten, nothing but damn bad-luck accident, and nothing more. So if I catch you on the pity potty, I'm gonna break your leg just so you can feel better about yourself. *Comprende*?"

Lou managed a half smile.

"Loud and clear," he said.

They talked some about managing Stick and Move in Cap's absence. All of his good work in the community over the years had earned him the loyalty of everyone who knew him. But these were not people who could afford to work very long without being paid. Still, this was enough of a tragedy already without losing the gym. There would be a way.

"So what's happened since I've been decommis-
sioned?" Cap asked.

"Let's see . . ." Lou pretended he had to think hard
to come up with the biggest developments. "Um . . .
Filstrup lost the election."

Cap made an "aw shucks" clicking sound with his
mouth.

"That's too bad, but expected. Was it close?"

"I don't know," Lou said. "I sort of missed the whole
thing."

It took a moment for the implication to set in.

"Oh, man, Welcome. You missed the speech. You
never gave your speech?"

"Believe me, it wouldn't have helped," Lou said.
"Like I told you, he was doomed from the start."

"But you know how Filstrup thinks. He's going to
blame you for the loss."

"I'm sure he already has. I called him while you
were in the OR. If his wife wasn't in the ICU, I think
he would have flown down here to bellow at me in
person."

Lou stood up and went over to the blinds, adjusting
them to let in a little more sunlight.

"Your job gonna be in jeopardy?" Cap asked.

"No way. He's headstrong, but not *that* headstrong."

"Why am I not hearing that in your voice? Which
job handles your health insurance?"

"The Eisenhower one."

"Maybe you can get me a job there, then. I don't
have any insurance, you know."

"I know that. I have an appointment in a few minutes with the financial services office."

Humphrey cruised back into the room.

"Who's job is in jeopardy?" he asked.

Lou gestured at the small parabolic receiver on the wheelchair console.

"No one's job is in jeopardy. What's the range of that damn thing, anyway?"

"I was at good angle. Wasn't that far. Hope you keep job."

"Thanks, Humphrey." Lou checked the time on his Mickey Mouse watch and turned back to Cap. "Listen, pal, I'll stop by later. My flight home is first thing in the morning. I'll catch up on work and settle things down with Filstrup, but I'll be back on the weekend or before. Do you think you'll be okay without me for a little while?"

"What did I say about me being a big boy?"

"Well, just in case, I may get in touch with Atlanta Central Service and see if some of our brothers and sisters in the storm can stop by for an impromptu meeting."

"Fine by me. Now, you go take care of what you've got to take care of. I'll put in a call to my aunt Dorothy if I get lonely for company. Besides, ol' Humphrey here will come and visit me. Right?"

"Right."

Lou bent over between the IV tubing and hugged his friend.

"I'm so sorry, buddy," Lou whispered.

"Nonsense. Go do what you need to do."

At that moment, surrounded by the ropes and pulleys and fixation hardware and pillows and IV infusers, the former unbeatable prizefighter looked extremely small.

Lou paused at the door.

"I got your direct room line," Lou said. "I'll give you a call before I come back and then tomorrow when I land."

Cap returned a thumbs-up and then pointed to the door, giving Lou his permission to leave without any guilt.

With Humphrey not far behind, Lou headed into the hallway. But he found it impossible to disconnect from his sense of responsibility. It was just that way with him. It had been for as long as he could remember. Stopping at the nurses' station, he made several introductions and was charming enough to make sure Cap got every bit of attention he might need. Humphrey pulled next to Lou as they headed down the hall toward the elevators.

"You guys really care for each other," Humphrey said. "I can tell."

Lou had to stop walking so he could focus on Humphrey's lips and speech.

"You got that right, my friend," he replied.

"Do you mind if I ask what you are doing about the insurance?"

Lou tried to mask his concern, but suspected the effort was futile.

"We have friends," Lou said. "Lots of them. We'll do whatever it takes."

As before, Humphrey looked a little forlorn.

"That's what I figured you'd say."

Without another word, the man motored himself toward the elevator.

Lou fell into step behind.

CHAPTER 18

A country's strong military will lose to its weak economy every single time.

—LANCASTER R. HILL, LECTURE AT PRINCETON UNIVERSITY, NOVEMBER 12, 1938

The three days Tim Vaill spent in the hospital had passed like months. All he thought about was getting out, getting back to work, and starting the hunt. Now, five days after his discharge, he was finally right where he needed to be—in Franklin, Tennessee.

He was seated in his agency-issued Chevy Impala, parked across the street from the blue clapboard colonial home of the man who murdered his wife. The photo, in a white envelope, was tucked into the inside breast pocket of his suit jacket. It would be a weapon of last resort, but he would use it if he had to.

Seated beside Vaill was his new partner, Charles McCall, a handsome African American man in his late twenties. Vaill was impressed by McCall, but more because of his street smarts than his Ivy League diploma from Penn. There were a lot of smart folks who joined the FBI. Most were idealistic and came into the Bureau with a strong belief they'd get back in action and adventure what they'd be giving up in private sector pay.

Most of those young recruits were wrong. The Bureau was a lot of paperwork, a lot of waiting around, and, true to its name, a lot of bureaucracy.

"How long are we going to sit here and wait?" McCall asked.

Those were the first words either man had spoken in twenty minutes. Initially, Vaill had asked to go on this assignment alone, but his boss, Beth Snyder, immediately denied the request. He felt bad for giving McCall the cold shoulder, but he was still in deep mourning, and all a new partner did was remind him of the partner he'd never have again.

Then there were the headaches—blinding, distracting pain, mostly above his right ear, where the bullet had been removed, but also behind his eyes. There was nothing predictable about what brought them on, and nothing reliable to make them go away. They usually lasted just three or four minutes, maybe two or three times a day, but the duration had been getting longer, and the pain worse. Yesterday's attack had lasted nearly a half hour. Thankfully, he was alone in his hospital room at the time.

Tylenol and Motrin were no help, and he didn't dare mention them to his boss or his doctor. If he did, he would be out of the field in a blink, and in all likelihood, back in the hospital. Some sort of migraine, he convinced himself. Half the people he knew had them. A few of them every day. Until Alexander Burke was behind bars or roasting on a spit in hell, he would do his best to get through them and control his irritability toward McCall.

Vaill checked the house using high-powered binoculars just as Lola Burke entered her living room. She was a slender, pretty woman with shoulder-length blond hair, wearing a blue knit sweater and formfitting jeans. Her face was fresh and innocent, almost cherubic. It would have been tough to pick her out of a lineup as the wife of the FBI's most-wanted man in America. Vaill kept watching as she passed out of the living room, then returned. Having aced all his psychological profiling and behavioral analysis classes at Quantico, he could sense the woman was nervous—maybe waiting for something.

"I think we're clear, Chuck," Vaill said. "Let's go have ourselves a little chat."

Vaill never dreamed he'd be doing fieldwork so soon after being discharged from the hospital. Against his wishes, Beth Snyder had tried to give him a cushy desk job with the task force assigned to monitor the Doomsday Germ. He was to work with the huge team trying, so far unsuccessfully, to pin down any of the Society of One Hundred Neighbors. Finally, with his doctor's go-ahead and his own burning passion to avenge Maria, Snyder had relented, but only after extracting from him a pledge of objectivity.

At the start of the Doomsday Germ crisis, a top-secret communications pipeline had been established involving every hospital. The goal of the pipeline was to record each documented case of the Doomsday Germ. The FBI put hospital administrators on notice that information leaks would not be tolerated. Any such leak could result in obstruction charges and even impact JCAHO accreditation, vital for a hospital's federal funding.

The containment strategy was necessary to subvert the panic that would follow should news of the germ, and more specifically the plans of the terrorist group calling itself One Hundred Neighbors, spread to the public. Not surprisingly, there were some leaks, but mostly the media chose to act responsibly, reporting the story as an emerging strain of *streptococcus pyogenes* and nothing more.

For now, the extent and deadly potential of the Doomsday Germ was a well-guarded secret. But with their deadline growing ever closer, the One Hundred Neighbors would not keep it a secret much longer. And when word got out, and the mutilation and death rates began to soar, confidence in our hospital system and health care in general would quickly collapse under the strain.

Vaill had studied the files on Alexander Burke and sensed the man's wife knew more than she had shared with the agents who had questioned her. He wanted a crack at her himself.

"She's already been interviewed by three other agents more experienced at interrogation than you," Snyder said. "She doesn't know anything. She and Alexander have been on the outs, and she hasn't heard from him in months. What makes you think you're going to find out anything different?"

"Because she hasn't spoken to the man whose wife her husband murdered," Vaill had replied.

The next day he had a plane ticket and a new partner.

The flagstone walkway was bordered by neatly tended shrubs. Vaill led the way up three steps to the front door. He brushed a hand across the breast of his suit coat for reassurance the envelope was still there, and rang the doorbell. Lola Burke checked them out through her sidelight window. Her expression went from curious to saturnine in the time it took her to open the door. She did not bother asking who these latest suits were, or what they wanted. According to her file, well before her husband became first an agent, then a fugitive, she knew what a G-man looked like, and also that they seldom brought anything but trouble.

"I guess there's no shortage of Feds," she said. "You people just keep rolling in like Old Man River. I haven't heard from him if that's what you're here to ask."

Vaill and McCall flashed their badges—protocol. Lola sighed and made a face as if they were her least favorite vegetable. She kept her arm against the door frame, as a barrier.

"Mrs. Burke, I'm Special Agent Tim Vaill and this is my partner, Special Agent Charles McCall. I know we're not the first agents to come here to speak with you, but it's very important that we find your husband. We were wondering if we could try again."

Lola rolled her eyes and lowered her arm.

I've been through this all before and I've got nothing more to tell you, but go ahead if you really need to.

They followed her into a bright and airy kitchen. Light spilled into the room from a bank of mullioned windows that looked onto a lush lawn. The home, from Vaill's quick inspection, was well appointed—nice furniture throughout, granite countertops in the kitchen, new appliances, too, but nothing that looked unaffordable on an agent's salary. If Burke's motive for murder was money, it certainly wasn't ending up here.

"Want something to drink. Water?"

"No thank you, we're fine," Vaill said, speaking for

both himself and McCall. If Maria were here, she'd be the one speaking for Vaill.

Lola shrugged. "Suit yourself," she said. She took a seat at the kitchen table, with her back to the windows, leaned back, and waited. Vaill sat where he had a full-on look at her face. Either she was an expert with makeup, or her smooth, porcelain skin showed none of the strain he'd seen on other people who's loved ones had gone missing.

She doesn't think he's gone forever.

"Before you get going," Lola said, a slip of venom in her voice, "let me save you both some trouble. I haven't seen him. I haven't heard from him. I have no idea where he is, or where he might have gone. I don't know why he did what he allegedly did. All I know is that he's gone and you're here to harass me some more, as if my life isn't already enough of a shit mess, because you think my husband murdered two of your own. Does that about sum it up?"

Just prior to leaving on this trip, Vaill had spent several hours with the brightest minds from the FBI's Behavioral Analysis Unit (BAU), getting a crash course on some of their techniques. In the span of her short and embittered speech, Lola Burke had given away four glaring tells confirming she was a liar. She was fidgeting with her hands, acting nervous. She was also uncooperative, making negative statements and complaints, saying nothing to support the search. In addition, he'd get more eye contact from a blind person, but when she did look at him, her pupils were the size of two nickels, possibly the result of a pheromone found more commonly in liars than truth tellers.

Thank you, BAU.

It was going to take patience and finesse to get her to come clean—and perhaps the picture.

"We apologize for adding any strain to what is most certainly a difficult time, Mrs. Burke," McCall said. "If you don't mind, could you tell us about the last time you spoke to your husband?"

Good, Vaill thought. *Let McCall get all the bullshit out of the way. He's smart to keep it nonconfrontational—good cop, bad cop.*

Lola sighed heavily. She then went through a long and passionless diatribe about the day her husband left for his latest assignment. She shared what he ate for breakfast that morning, how he kissed her good-bye and said he'd call her soon, same as he always did when he left on an assignment. She was adamant that he did nothing at all out of the ordinary—no indication that he was planning on going rogue.

McCall dutifully took notes, even though Lola had already provided the same information to the agents who had been there before.

"So there's nothing else?" McCall said. "No explanation for your husband's actions? No idea where he might be?"

Lola shot McCall an angry sideways glance. "I don't have any information, Agent McCall. I'd be more interested to know what you all have come up with."

Jackpot.

This was the opening Vaill had been waiting for.

"You want our theories?" he asked.

"I'd like to think the massive manpower of the FBI could come up with something, so yes."

More anger. More negativity. More lies.

"I can't speak for the Bureau," Vaill said, his eyes

fixed on her, "but I'll tell you what *I* think. There are three possible reasons why someone would betray their country: money, sex, or ideology. Now, you're a good-looking woman, Lola. If you don't mind my saying so, any man would be a fool to betray you in that way. That doesn't mean anything, though. As they say, love is blind and it can be blinding. But you don't seem like a woman scorned, and if your husband had left you for another woman, if he'd been seduced into this betrayal, you'd have had at least some suspicion along the way. You seem angry with us for intruding, but not angry at Alexander. So let's take sex off the table for the moment."

"Whatever."

"How about money? Did he get paid to murder two agents? If he did, it had to be a hell of a lot of money, which would make me think again about sex . . . or drugs, I suppose. But when I look around this house, and from what I could tell of Alexander, I don't see a man obsessed with money, or on drugs. Just my opinion, maybe I'm wrong."

"You're not," Lola said flatly.

"So, that leaves ideology—a belief so profound, so consuming, it could make a person commit an unspeakable act. It would need to be something at their core—a powerful, misguided sense of justice. Maybe you share that belief. Maybe that's why you're angry with us instead of outraged and sickened by your husband's actions. Is that your husband, Lola? Was he a misguided individual? Is that why you've lost him?"

"Misguided is your word," Lola said, looking away.

"Well, I lost something, too," Vaill said. "Mrs. Burke, I'm not speaking to you as an agent. I'm not even here to vilify your husband. I'm here because of this scar."

He pushed aside his hair to give Lola a look at the track left by the bullet that had torn through his scalp and into his brain.

"Why are you showing this to me?" Lola asked, looking away quickly.

"Because that's where your husband shot me," Vaill said. "I was standing next to my wife, my partner, a beautiful woman named Maria, when he shot her dead at point-blank range. Right here, just above the bridge of her nose. Then he shot me—twice."

"Please stop."

"I didn't see evil in Alexander's eyes. I saw fervor— a belief. And I don't see any evil in you, Mrs. Burke. I see a woman who loves her husband very much, the way I loved my wife. And I think he made a promise to you. I think he told you he'd come back for you when he could, when it was safe. But I'm here to tell you that he's never going to come. He's never going to come because sooner or later we're going to get him—and because the belief that led him to kill my wife is stronger than his love for you. Like me, the person you love more than anything, is never coming back."

This time, Lola's quivering lip and the tears welling in her eyes seemed genuine.

"I . . . I want you to leave," she managed.

"We can do what's right, Mrs. Burke," Vaill went on, ignoring her plea. "We can do what's right and not turn our back. Please, Mrs. Burke, you're not in any trouble. You won't be in trouble. You have my word on that. But please stop lying for him. Tell me everything you know that might help us and we'll be gone."

Lola bit her lower lip.

"Please go," she said. But there was no force behind her words.

Vaill forged ahead.

"Do it for my wife."

He withdrew the envelope with the crime scene photos inside and spread the three of them on the table. It had ripped at his guts to keep it so near to his heart, but Lola Burke was close to cracking. This was a beautiful woman's flesh and blood and bone. Lola gasped at the gruesome photographs. Even McCall looked disturbed. Vaill kept his eyes fixed on her, in part to keep himself from looking at the pictures again.

A tear broke loose from the corner of Lola's right eye and wound down her cheek. She flipped the photo facedown on the table.

Then, without a word, she stood, walked through the kitchen entranceway, and disappeared down the hall. McCall was reaching for his gun, but Vaill raised a hand to hold him back.

"Don't, Chuck," he said. "We're okay."

A moment later, Lola returned with a small plastic baggie. She passed it over to Vaill.

"This is the DVD my husband sent me after he disappeared," she said. "It's the last time I heard from him. It contains everything I know. I'm sorry about your wife. I'm so sorry."

She walked McCall and Vaill to the door.

"We're going to have this handled by our evidence-processing people. You know the drill. There're almost sure to be more questions once we've gone over this," McCall said.

"I'll be here," Lola said. "I'm not going anyplace for the time being."

"It goes without saying that if you hear from your husband, please call me," Vaill said, passing over his card.

"I can't promise that."

"As you wish."

The two agents had driven more than a mile before McCall spoke.

"That was masterful, man," he said. "Truly masterful. I know that picture was a tough thing for you to show, but you did it. And just at the right moment, too. This DVD could be the break we need."

McCall had his phone out, dialing the field office while he was driving and talking.

Vaill was facing away from him, face turned toward the passenger window, eyes closed tightly. The blinding pain behind his eyes had come on with unrelenting force.

CHAPTER 19

Secrecy is tantamount to success and therefore to know a Neighbor's true identity is to strip them of a fundamental power.

—LANCASTER R. HILL, *100 Neighbors*, SAWYER RIVER BOOKS, 1939, P. 100

"I created a spreadsheet and I think the Bake-a-Thon could raise a thousand dollars," Emily said.

Lou was back at work at the PWO when his fourteen-year-old called with the latest development in her campaign to raise money for Cap and the Stick and Move gym. Much to her mother Renee's chagrin, and Lou's delight, she had been training with Cap for more than eight months and was actually showing serious potential in the ring. Not surprisingly, she absolutely adored the man, and was desperate to do what she could to help pay his mounting bills and save the gym.

"That's great, sweetie," Lou said, cupping the phone's receiver and speaking softly. With well less than nine hundred square feet of office space, no matter how quietly people spoke, conversations in the PWO were rarely private. With the other associate director Wayne Oliver in the next cube over, and secretary Babs Peterbee almost directly across from them, it was hard not to know one another's business.

Meanwhile, Lou was eyeing the mountainous stack

of paperwork Babs had just deposited on his cluttered desk. She appeared unfazed that the carpeted floor inside his cramped cubicle was already serving as an auxiliary work space. In the span of less than a week, the usual pile of documents and paperwork had multiplied like rabbits. Lou stopped multitasking so he could give Emily his undivided attention, not that she needed it. He had seen his daughter take up the banner of a cause before, and knew what an unstoppable force she could be.

He thought back to the time her computer crashed, and with it the term paper she had finished less than a day before. There were no tears. No throwing things. No rants. She did not talk about asking for an extension. What she did instead was to berate herself for not making a backup, then vowed never to repeat the mistake again. Finally, after a bowl of her favorite mint chocolate-chip ice cream, she gathered her reference books and rewrote the entire eleven-page paper in one marathon session.

A+.

In the game of life, divorce or no divorce, Lou's money was on his kid.

She was just four when Renee decided that Lou's amphetamine addiction was bigger and stronger than their marriage and, quite understandably, bailed. For a couple of years, it was hard going for all of them. But gradually, understanding, flexibility, and communication took the place of anger, and Emily became a tribute to what was possible when a husband and wife refused to allow the failure of their marriage to mar their commitment to their child and the strengthening of her self-esteem. Now, a by-product of that commitment had been the reestablishment of the friendship and mutual respect with Renee that years of Lou's self-serving drug use had destroyed.

Mental . . . Physical . . . Spiritual—like water from a pipe leaking in the attic, Lou's alcoholism and other addictions had seeped down and destroyed the fabric of all three aspects of his being. Now, recovery and hard work had restored them, and in doing so, had stabilized the life of a kid who was already making a difference in the world.

"I think what you're doing is great, Em," Lou said. "You've got my full support."

"I don't need support. What I need is a hundred and fifty boxes of brownie mix."

"Hey, I thought we were trying to raise money, not spend it."

"We are," Emily said. "I'm looking for donations."

"Donations? Who are you soliciting? Betty Crocker?"

Emily got quiet.

"Well, actually . . ."

"Hey, wait, I was kidding," Lou said. "You really did solicit Betty Crocker?"

"It's General Mills," Emily replied, "and yes, I've been in touch with the public relations department. I put together a PDF of all of Cap's good deeds and got testimonials from some of the kids he's helped get off the streets."

"A PD-what?"

Emily sighed. "PDF, dad. Portable Document Format. It's . . . it's like a brochure for the Web."

"Oh, I was thinking of the other PDF. Listen, I really want to help, so just let me know what I can do."

"Check out the pages I made on GiveForward, Fund-bunch, and GoFundMe," Emily said, "and let me know what you think. I'm trying to put together a street team through my Facebook friends."

"What do you need to get the ball rolling?" Lou asked.

"Just money from you and Mom, and Grandpa Dennis, and Nana, and Uncle Graham, to add to the five hundred the people at General Mills will be sending."

"Consider it done," Lou said.

He left out the part where he was scheduled to meet with his tax guy later that afternoon to help him figure out which of his raggedy collection of mutual funds he could sell. Based on hours of phone calls with Cap's doctors in Atlanta, and his own research, Lou estimated the total cost of his sponsor's care would exceed 150,000 dollars.

Still, brownies were a great start.

"I'll e-mail you the links," Emily said. "Can you get back to me in, say, an hour with your ideas?"

Once again, Lou eyed the stack of work surrounding him—the forms and follow-up reports dealing with the docs he was monitoring—each in serious, potentially career-ending trouble. Somehow, someway, he would find the time to do it all, including his weekend plans to fly back to Atlanta. The only person who might get squeezed out of seeing him was high-powered attorney Sarah Cooper, but their on-again, off-again relationship had been steadily drifting toward off-again, anyhow.

"Of course, sweetie," he said. "Send the links my way and I'll give them a look. Together, and with Mom's help, we can pull this off."

"You bet we can, Pops."

"I love you, princess."

"Love you, too."

As Lou was hanging up, Walter Filstrup marched past his cubicle without a word or even a glance, then left the office. The usually bombastic director, as difficult to read as time on Big Ben, had been icy and distant since Lou's return from Atlanta. With the man's wife out of the ICU and improving from her cardiac problem, it was clearly the lost election that was continuing to vex him—the lost election and the man he believed was responsible for it.

CHAPTER 20

That which is attained without conflict or strife
is rarely worth attainment at all.

—LANCASTER R. HILL, PERSONAL
  COMMUNICATION TO ROBIN BROADY, 1942

Three days later, Filstrup's gloomy state of mind was unimproved. The man had not once mentioned the election results and had shown no curiosity at all regarding Cap's condition.

Pleasantville.

Several times, Lou ticked through what he had explained to Filstrup in the call from Arbor General. He and his best friend went for a run. Cap fell, sustained a compound fracture of his femur, and nearly bled out. Lou administered first aid and possibly saved Cap's life. They took a helicopter to the hospital, and Lou missed giving the speech. A reasonable sequence and explanation if ever there was one.

Now, Lou was debating rolling out plan B—earnestly sharing with Filstrup his gut instinct about the unlikelihood of the man's ever squeaking out a victory in the election, even if Lou *had* given his speech. For the moment, he chose to shelve the idea. He expected his boss would evolve back to his baseline, self-absorbed, testy state in a matter of no time. He always did.

This time, Lou was wrong.

He had opened the top folder on his bottomless stack of dictations while awaiting a return call from Emily regarding the bake sale, when his desk phone rang.

"Hey, sweetie," Lou said. "What took you so long?"

"Excuse me," answered an unfamiliar male voice, "I'm looking for Dr. Louis Welcome."

Lou cleared his throat, heat from the embarrassment crawling up the back of his neck.

"I'm sorry. I thought you were my daughter calling back," Lou said. "This is Dr. Welcome. How can I help you?"

"Dr. Welcome, this is Dr. Win Carter, I'm the president of Arbor General Hospital in Atlanta. Do you have a minute to talk with me about Mr. Hank Duncan?"

Lou went cold. He clutched the lip of his desk, steeling himself against a rush of panic. Barely able to catch his breath, he tried, willing his racing heart to slow down.

"I'm fine," he managed. "I mean, this is a good time. Is he all right?"

Everyone at Arbor, it seemed, had heard about Lou and Cap's exploits in the woods, so he was not that surprised his name had reached the hospital president's desk. Maybe while Cap was still in the hospital, they wanted Lou to give a grand rounds talk to the medical staff about the treatment—bring Cap down for his version. Maybe the call was about Cap's ballooning hospital bill. The thoughts were quickly replaced by a far more frightening one. He was Cap's medical proxy. Something bad—real bad—had happened. But the two of them had just spoken yesterday, and aside from some new aching in the leg, everything seemed okay.

Hey, easy does it! he shouted at himself. *Easy frigging does it.*

"Actually, that's why I'm calling," Carter was saying. "I'm sorry to disturb you at work, but I wanted you to know that we've begun work to contain an infection in your friend's leg."

Lou strained to pick up any clue in Carter's voice regarding the severity of the infection, trying to block out the reality that Carter simply making such a call was all the indication that was needed.

"He told me yesterday he was experiencing some new discomfort," Lou managed.

Why is the president of a huge hospital calling to tell me this?

"Well, his surgeon has done an aspiration of pus from an area beneath the incision. A drain was placed there during the surgery as a precaution, but apparently it wasn't enough. They've called in the infectious disease consultant on the case, and have changed antibiotics. But what we have learned has made us all a bit nervous here, and Mr. Duncan's team is considering taking him back to the operating room."

"Nervous?"

The word was unusual in this context, and Lou had picked up on it immediately.

"It's complicated," Carter said.

Anxiety was now swarming in Lou's throat like army ants on the march. He had little doubt Carter was holding something back—something big.

"Complicated?" Lou asked, feeling like an idiot for repeating the man's word again.

"It looks like Mr. Duncan is the second case we've had at Arbor General of a very unusual bacterial infection. Something we're not entirely sure how to contain."

Very unusual?

Lou stopped himself at the last possible instant from another echo. He sucked in a breath and gritted his teeth as though expecting to take a punch to the gut.

"Please, tell me what you know," he said.

"Truthfully, it's best not discussed over the phone," Carter said. "Obviously, I am calling you instead of having Dr. Standish do it because this germ is of concern to the whole hospital."

"How is Cap at the moment? Can I call him? I was planning on flying down this weekend."

"To be frank, Dr. Welcome, you may want to consider coming down sooner. I just came from visiting him. Your friend isn't very toxic yet, but he is febrile, and there clearly has been a turn. When you get here, you can stop by my office if you wish, or better still, go to the seventh floor of the Baron Building, and have them page Dr. Ivan Puchalsky, the ID consultant handling this case."

"I'll do that. I'll do it as soon as I can. Thank you, Dr. Carter. Thank you for calling."

Lou ended the call and popped up from his chair as though it had become electrified. He raced out of the cube and was passing Babs Peterbee's desk, headed to Filstrup's office, when she held up her hand.

"Dr. Welcome, I wouldn't go in there. He's asked me to hold all his calls."

Lou leaned over and saw that the secretary's desk-top switchboard had no "in use" lights on. The maneuver was one of Filstrup's favorites.

"Sorry, but that call was from Cap's hospital. It's an emergency, Babs."

Lou knocked twice and opened the door an instant before Filstrup gruffly invited him in.

"Sorry to butt in, boss, but I just got a call from Arbor General in Atlanta. Cap's getting toxic from a wound infection. His condition has started to deteriorate."

Seated behind his immaculate desk, Filstrup, wearing his typically wrinkle-free white dress shirt and power-red tie, lowered his glasses and eyed Lou with a chilly look.

"Oh," he said. "I'm sorry to hear that."

"Yes . . . Well, they've asked me to come down to Atlanta. I'm quite worried."

"To dash away from your job, you must be *very* worried," Filstrup said, sounding not at all worried or even that interested.

"I'm certainly concerned," Lou said. "As you know, he's the best friend I have. I give him credit for turning my life around. I'll take some work with me. Nothing that will violate any confidentiality, of course, but I'll get stuff done."

"No need," Filstrup said.

"There's a lot to catch up on," Lou said. "I realize I'm behind, but I'll make up the time. From what his surgeon said, Cap needs me there."

"That's fine," Filstrup said. "But there's no need for you to take any work."

"Excuse me?"

"I think you understand. There's no need for you to take your work with you because you no longer have a job here."

"Walter, what are you saying?"

"I'm saying you're fired, Dr. Welcome. Now, go pack up your desk. I wouldn't want you to miss your flight back to Atlanta."

CHAPTER 21

It is not our nature to suffer, and most of those who are offered government handouts in place of effort will take them.

—LANCASTER R. HILL, *Climb the Mountain*, SAWYER RIVER BOOKS, 1941, P. 11

Kazimi had never seen anything like the Great Room.

While growing up in Kohat City, in the Khyber Pakhtunkhwa province of Pakistan, he believed all homes were made from dusty brown clay bricks. The densely clustered buildings of his youth were still etched in his heart and mind. As he grew older, he escaped his daily travails through books, and began to excel in school. Finally, he was accepted as an exchange student in Los Angeles, and from there, off to Stanford.

Kazimi loved America . . . much of it, at any rate.

The over-the-top opulence of Red Cliff and its whiskey-gulping master were well more than he could take. Doug Bacon, and his dedication to eliminating programs assisting the poor, was an anathema to Kazimi as was One Hundred Neighbors, the extremist organization he embodied. And despite his captor's self-important attempt to use Kazimi's religion to enlist his help, the overriding consideration for him was still escape.

For the better part of two days, he had kept to himself, waiting. He ate well, exercised, used the sunlamp in the bathroom for vitamin D, and slept as much as he could manage. He was determined to build his strength. The opportunity to escape might at any minute present itself. When he was not meditating, he prayed to Allah using the prayer rug and beautiful copy of the Koran Bacon had supplied, while at the same time forcing thoughts of escape from his mind.

After his afternoon prayer, and after seeking Allah's guidance, Kazimi had summoned Harris to his room.

"I want to meet with Bacon," he said.

Red Cliff was vast, and the butler was slow. It had taken ten minutes to reach the Great Room. Most of the trip was down—both straight and spiral staircases. At the head of the first flight, Bacon's two buffalos met them and took over as Kazimi's guides. There were no windows along the way, and even had the guards not been there, he had no sense that escape was possible. The stone passageways, lit by gas lanterns, were dank, smelling increasingly of mold and, surprisingly, of the sea.

The sea . . . Where was this place?

He had been unconscious from the moment Alexander Burke injected him until he awoke in his bedroom prison. Where in Allah's name was he? How long had it taken to get there? Fortunately, there was some comfort in his resignation to whatever fate was determined for him. Still, he had decided, any action he could take that would return him to his laboratory, he would take. Many times each day he had recited the hadith attributed to Imam Tirmidhi:

If you put your whole trust in Allah, as you ought,
He most certainly will satisfy your needs, as He
satisfies those of the birds. They come out hun-
gry in the morning, but return full to their nests.

After a long walk, the guards guided him past a pair
of French doors through which, for the first time,
Kazimi got a glimpse of where he was. Beyond the
doors was a narrow gravel path, bordered by a fringe of
lawn, and just beyond that, and far below, was the ocean,
stretching to the horizon. Before he could ask any questions, the huge men motioned him through an arched
opening, and into a cavernous stone room. The scientist's mouth fell open. To his right was an enormous
bank of windows, at least twenty feet high and, in
total, perhaps fifty feet across.

Incredible as the windows were in both size and
scope, it was the view outside that held Kazimi spellbound. He was gazing out from the edge of a cliff,
easily a hundred feet high, at a steel-gray ocean capped
this day by frothy waves. No land. His sense told him
East Coast and north. The cliff was daunting. The
gravel path and strip of grass were all that separated
the spectacular windows from the sea. Any attempt
to escape from here could well end in a plunge to his
death.

"After we talk I'll take you outside so you can see
the waves crashing against the shoreline. It's truly a
marvelous sight."

Bacon, speaking from behind a huge leather easy
chair, was dressed in crisply pressed gray slacks, a
double-breasted blue suit, and a white oxford shirt

accented by a silk paisley ascot. His right hand was clasped around his lion's head cane, and his left cradled his ubiquitous half-filled crystal tumbler.

"North Atlantic?" Kazimi offered.

"Maine, actually. I'm glad you've requested this meeting. As I have said, time is of the essence, and people are dying."

"I refuse to succumb to your guilt ploy. Any deaths are your fault, not mine."

The overcast skies and stone walls kept the room cool, although the blaze in a fieldstone fireplace big enough to park a car took away much of the chill. There were leather armchairs, couches, and marble-topped tables spaced throughout, and a mélange of wondrous oriental rugs.

A castle in Maine.

Bacon led Kazimi to a sitting area for two in front of the windows. The breathtaking view, like the opulence of the place, only strengthened Kazimi's discomfort. There was either an elevator or a kitchen, because after just a few minutes, Harris appeared, wheeling a cart carrying covered platters of food. The aroma, even with covers in place, was exquisite.

"Goat cooked in desi pickle curry, or perhaps you'd prefer to try the chicken nihari?"

Kazimi glared at Bacon.

"My appetite for company may return with my freedom," he said. "Until then, I prefer to dine alone."

Bacon took a contemplative sip of his drink.

"Your choice."

He nodded toward his butler, and Harris bowed, swung the cart around, and wheeled the food away. Kazimi shifted his gaze back to the mesmerizing vista.

"What is this place?" he asked, making no attempt at eye contact.

"My home," Bacon said.

"I assumed that."

"Red Cliff is on a hundred and fifty secluded acres on the coast of Maine. It was built in 1890 by an eccentric engineer named Gerhardt, who held more than three hundred patents, many of them quite lucrative. Gerhardt indulged his passion for castles by bringing one over here from Germany, stone by stone. The rebuilding took three years. Gerhardt lived to be more than a hundred. During his waning years, when he became aware of the Society of One Hundred Neighbors, he willed it to us, along with enough money to maintain it in this wonderful condition. As the current head of our society, I have the option of living here—an option I was only too pleased to exercise. Have you ever been to Maine before, Ahmed? Or would you prefer I use your birth name, Nazar."

Kazimi swung around. Generally, Pakistani males were given the first name of Muhammad. The practice of referring to people by their most used name, a second or even third name given at birth, served as a unique identifier. Bacon's use of Nazar suggested extensive research and comprehensive knowledge. He was both showing off and announcing that One Hundred Neighbors were well armed.

"Yes, we know very well who you are, doctor," he said. "We also know where you're from. We know who and where many of your relatives are, as well as the names of your former graduate assistants back at Stanford. We know virtually everything there is to know about you, except for one very important item."

Kazimi, now seething, glared at Bacon. "I presume this one item is the reason you've taken me hostage. What is it you want? What do you intend to do with me?"

Bacon leaned back in his chair, appraising his captive with his sharp eyes.

The man was a psychological predator, Kazimi thought—a stalker, always on the hunt for any angle to exploit, be it a word, an inflection, or even some subtle bit of body language. In spite of himself, Kazimi felt naked and exposed in his presence.

"To be perfectly forthcoming," Bacon said, "we need you to complete your work on the antibacterial treatment for the Janus strain. That's the name we have given to the bacteria we have developed."

Bacon's accent, a countrified twang really, registered stronger to Kazimi's ears than it previously had. Perhaps it was the drink, exposing the Southern gentleman for who he really was—a man not born into great wealth, but someone who had acquired it without ever forgoing his roots.

Kazimi's jaws clenched. The situation, as presented, was dire. Bacon wins, and countless people living in poverty become disenfranchised and ignored while countless others are refused hospital care for conditions that might be easily treatable. Bacon loses, and countless people die from an infection as horrible as the worst of the plague.

"Janus," Kazimi mused aloud, "the two-faced god of contradictions. Gram positive . . . Gram negative. Very appropriate choice."

"I'm not surprised you made the connection so quickly. There are few who would have. As our research has disclosed, you are certainly a highly intelligent man."

"Maybe not that intelligent, Mr. Bacon. I cannot figure out why you would kidnap me to *continue* my work and not *kill* me to stop it. . . ." Realization of the answer to the conundrum took just a few seconds. Kazimi laughed sardonically. "Your germ has bested you, hasn't it? Like Frankenstein, you have created a monster, and now you have no way of stopping it. Your scientists should have known, sir. They should have known that sooner or later this would happen. Now you are in danger of losing your leverage."

Bacon calmly took another sip from his tumbler, but there was no slyness in his expression. No playfulness.

"We created our hammer for a singular purpose," he said finally, "and that purpose is working. However, for our plan to be a total success, the government has to believe without a doubt that we can contain the Janus strain—turn it on and off at our will. But as you suspect, the geometry of the spread of infection has deviated from our precise statistical modeling. An anomaly if you will. It appears the bacteria has mutated into something even more potent then what we had designed. It is beginning to spread and is appearing in people we did not infect. The treatment our scientists developed, which has worked perfectly for several years, and which we are prepared to make available to you, is no longer effective."

"Your scientists are mad to have thought they could contain it for any length of time. The lessons of antibiotic history have always been available to them."

"We have means at our disposal you cannot begin

to imagine. We will resolve this bump in the road one way or another, with your help, or without. We are here to orchestrate change. Massive change. It is in our charter as it has been since our inception."

"Yes, the twisted charter of One Hundred Neighbors," Kazimi said.

"I'm sure your employers have given you a distorted view of our mission and our methods," Bacon responded acidly.

"Your man Burke has given me all the view that I will ever need. I believe the government's portrayal of you is accurate, Mr. Bacon, just as is their portrayal of the Oklahoma City bomber, and the Unabomber, and the master of Waco, and all the other deranged killers who follow your tenets, whether they are members of your precious society or not."

"Tell me, Dr. Kazimi, have you ever read *100 Neighbors*?"

"I am more than a little familiar with Lancaster Hill's manifesto," Kazimi replied, startled by the vehemence in his own tone. *Control your emotions,* he warned himself. *Your freedom depends on clear thinking.* He took a moment to compose himself and then added, "Published by Sawyer River Books in 1939, and immediately decried as subversive. Hill, a congressman from Virginia, resigned from office soon after its publication. He made it his mission to undermine the national rebirth brought about by President Franklin Roosevelt. But soon, the impact of *100 Neighbors* faded from the public eye, forgotten like the madman, himself."

"Not forgotten," Bacon corrected. "Hidden in plain sight. And as you now well know, Hill was more than a little successful in his endeavors. He assembled his society of patriots in secret. As he divined, the organization consisted of people from every walk of life, people who look perfectly unremarkable on the outside, and often hold positions of influence in one of the six essential disciplines."

"Military, scientific, policy, finance, communications, and intelligence," Kazimi recited, his tone mocking. Now it was his turn to show off.

Bacon ignored him.

"Our vision of America is the purest reflection of the Constitution by which we must all abide, even immigrants, such as yourself."

The way Bacon spit out the word "immigrants" lifted a cloak on his deep-seated racism. Kazimi heard in his tone a xenophobic fear, bordering on paranoia. And for that, his dislike for the man and his cause approached hatred.

"I really don't need to hear any more of this," Kazimi said.

Bacon continued without pausing.

"Our accomplishments are more impressive than those of almost any organization dedicated to social change. We have blocked congressional appointments and forced politicians to resign. The list of legislation passed into law through our influence would be a lobbyist's dream, as would those bills we have blocked. We began as one hundred, and we have kept the society to that exact number because, as Lancaster Hill predicted, it works."

"One man can dream, a handful can plan, thousands can strike, but a hundred can reshape the world," Kazimi said in a singsong voice.

"So you *are* intimately familiar with Lancaster Hill's work. I'm impressed."

"I'm not. My parents brought me up to have only loathing for extremists, madmen, and murderers."

Bacon's expression darkened, in concert it seemed with a bank of storm clouds gathering in the east.

"You will help us, Ahmed, Nazar, or whatever you wish to be called. You will see to it that we reestablish an antibacterial treatment for the Janus strain."

"So you can continue to use it for leverage?"

"What we do with the treatment is of no concern of yours. What should be of concern is that you will be saving countless lives." Another sip of Scotch. "The deal is this, dear doctor. We are immediately prepared to provide you with the lab space and all the equipment you require to complete your work. In addition, we will bring in the developer of the Janus strain and treatment so that you two can collaborate. In exchange, we wish to know the names of all the microbiologists you have been working with, and what their contributions have been to your research. I think you'll agree it is a simple trade, and one that gives us the best chance of quick success."

"What do I get in return?" Kazimi asked.

Bacon's smile reminded him of a shark.

"You will get your life," Bacon said. "In addition to the lives of those already infected with the bacteria that the press is calling the Doomsday Germ. Oh, yes, in addition, you will be saving the lives of every single person you hold dear. I promise you that. They will die and you will be spared until last so you can watch it happen."

CHAPTER 22

In the years to come, citizens will wonder with
dismay why a fertile America has turned fallow,
when they themselves have sucked all the
nutrients from the soil.

—LANCASTER R. HILL, MEMOIRS
   (UNPUBLISHED), 1937–41

For Lou, the final hour of the flight to Atlanta was an
emotional one—not unlike returning to the scene of
the crime. The glide path to Hartsfield-Jackson International Airport might have passed directly over the
Chattahoochee forest—directly over the lodge . . . and
the trail . . . and the cliff; directly over Floyd and Rebecca Weems's cabin, and their field. The images were
as indelible as they were painful.

Lou rested his head against the window and allowed
his eyes to close. His thoughts wrapped around another
indelible, painful image—Walter Filstrup's disgust-
ingly smug expression as he fired Lou from the PWO.
Stunned, Lou had asked on what grounds Filstrup would
tell the board of directors he was being dismissed.
The answer was vintage Filstrup—dereliction of duty.

"My best friend could have died," Lou protested.

"You shouldn't have been out on a run in the first
place," Filstrup countered. "That demonstrated extremely poor judgment."

"Walter, this is ridiculous. We run all the time together. It was just a freak accident."

"You had no contingency plan, Welcome. Nothing
in place in the event you were unable to perform your
assigned task, which in addition to office-financed at-
tendance at the meeting, included the presentation of a
very important speech. Your failure to appear was an
embarrassment to us on a national stage."

You mean an embarrassment to you.

"I'm very sorry about that, but I wasn't expecting to
be on a med flight to Atlanta. And as far as our reputation goes, everyone I spoke to when I stopped back
at the conference, and I do mean everyone, was absolutely understanding of the circumstance. Nobody felt
that hearing your speech would have altered the result
of the election. One of them said they were sure that
next year you would win. The only concern anyone expressed was for Cap's well-being."

"He shouldn't have been there in the first place. My
primary obligation is to this organization, and, in my
professional opinion you demonstrated a considerable
lack of foresight with your actions. Now you're hurting us again by demanding time off that you simply
don't have coming to you. Lack of foresight, lack of
perspective, lack of loyalty, lack of solid judgment. Tell
me when to stop."

"Walter, the only measure by which I should be
judged is my ability to reinstate licenses suspended by
the board of medicine and if you measure me by that
benchmark I'm the best we ever had here."

"We'll, since I'm the boss, I guess I get to decide
which benchmarks matter most."

"Jesus, Walter."

Filstrup busied himself with his computer, while Lou, still dumbfounded and flushed, stood by with nothing to do but watch. When the psychiatrist finally looked up, his expression was one of utter triumph.

"I just informed Mrs. Peterbee of your termination," he said. "She'll take care of all of your exit paperwork. Thank you for your service, Dr. Welcome, but as of this moment, those services are no longer required. If you need a reference, I'll be happy to provide one."

"Well, that makes me feel so much better, thanks."

"I hope you don't take this personally."

"When you come up with another way for me to take it, just let me know."

"Please understand I have to do what's best for the PWO."

There was an intense buzzing in Lou's ears. His fists clenched and loosened rhythmically. If only they were in the ring. Or perhaps he could just pretend they were, and flatten the pompous ass's nose across his face. He loved his job and had always taken pride in doing it well. Plus he certainly needed the income. Now he'd been terminated. The entire situation felt surreal.

And worst of all, the one person he most needed to turn to was lying in a hospital bed more than six hundred miles away, sick enough so that the president of the hospital had sent for Lou.

Use your imagination to play through the situations where you might drug or drink. It was an AA tool that had helped Lou get through the hard times accompanying the early days of his recovery. Now, breathing slowly and deeply, he sank into his desk chair and let his mind wander down the alley where, nearly eleven years ago, he frequently went to meet his supplier. The man was absolute slime, but his product, which Lou bought in pill form or as nose candy, was the best. There was no fatigue, no disappointment, no stress that the drugs—heroin or amphetamine—would not make him feel better . . . at least temporarily. His mouth went dry. He was inhaling through his nose now, actually tasting the crystals.

I'm not doing it anymore, he heard himself say. *I'm finished*.

He stopped inhaling and then opened his eyes. The image faded quickly. Despite the resentment boiling inside him, the years of dedication he'd given to this job, the cases he'd be deserting, the people who might not understand, and might think the worst, Lou decided to go out with class, refusing to sink to Filstrup's level. The people who really mattered, Emily, Renee, and Cap—they would understand. But only if he stayed clean.

"Dr. Welcome, are you okay?"

Babs Peterbee stood by the opening to his cube, concern clouding her face. Tears were welling in her eyes.

Lou's thoughts snapped back to the moment.

"I'm not happy, if that's what you mean," he said. "But I'm going to be okay if *that's* what you mean. I'm going to be fine."

"And your friend?"

"We'll have to wait and see, but the people in Atlanta sound like they are on top of things—at least for the moment."

"Dr. Welcome, I'm so sorry. I knew Dr. Filstrup was upset about not having his speech read, but I had no idea he would do something like this."

Lou felt the last of his fear and anxiety blow away

like mist. No projections. One of Cap's favorite lessons crossed his mind.

In any situation, there are only two possibilities: What you want to have happen . . . and something else.

It was time to adjust to the something else. And then, there would be two new possibilities.

"Not to worry," he said. "I'm going out like John Wayne, riding off into the sunset. I'm not going to throw a fit, no tears will be shed, no long good-byes said. Off into the sunset."

Peterbee sniffed and used a tissue.

"It's just so unfair," she said. "I'm going to fight to get you your job back."

Lou brushed aside the idea with a wave of his hand.

"You'll do no such thing, my friend. I'll be fine. Remember, I do have another job."

"But you're so good at this—"

"You and I will have lunch at O'Rourke's when I get back from Atlanta. I'll pay the tab, and you'll tell me all about how you're not making any waves on my account. Deal?"

"I—"

"Deal?" Lou asked again.

"Deal," Peterbee relented as she reluctantly plunked down a set of exit papers.

Lou accepted them and took the photo of Emily from his desk. He could do without the cheesy stapler and tin of paper clips. Smiling now, he walked past the secretary and out the office door.

"I really like John Wayne," he heard her say.

CHAPTER 23

Entitlements are like a house of mirrors: the more mirrors there are the harder it becomes to find a way out.

—LANCASTER R. HILL, *100 Neighbors*, SAWYER RIVER BOOKS, 1939, P. 200

Still dealing with the inner conflict of getting out from under Walter Filstrup on the one hand and being shut out from a job he loved on the other, Lou took a cab directly from the airport to the hospital. He would stop later at the hotel and remain in Atlanta for as long as Cap needed him. The department head at Eisenhower Memorial, the anti-Filstrup, had juggled the ER schedule, and had readily handed over the five days remaining in Lou's vacation account. Lou was prepared to put his ER job on the line if he had to, but this was another of those first-things-first situations.

There was a text waiting when they touched down at Hartsfield-Jackson Airport. Hospital president Win Carter had been called out of the office, and Lou should meet Dr. Ivan Puchalsky of infectious disease at the isolation suite on Baron 7. During the ride into town, Lou read up on the man. Russian-born and educated at top U.S. hospitals, his résumé was impressive, and his area of expertise was nosocomial disease.

Nosocomial.

Infection acquired in a hospital. The word, itself, sounded nasty. It had always bothered Lou that such a term even had to exist. As they weaved through the busy streets toward Arbor General, he absently tried the dictionary connected to his iPhone, and was surprised that *nosocomial* wasn't in there. A nonexistent, ugly word referring to a condition that had only come into being because there were hospitals.

Nice.

After paying off the cabbie, Lou followed the signage to the Baron Building, and took one of four gleaming elevators to the seventh floor. The isolation suite was located behind a set of closed double glass doors at the end of an ominously long corridor. What he noticed immediately on exiting the elevator was the quiet. If Arbor General was a subway, this section of the hospital was the last stop on a line that headed into a very scary part of town. Not many people wanted to be around patients deemed too contagious to be cared for within the general hospital population. Lou could not believe this was where the magnificent man, who had done so much for him and for others, had been relegated.

He flashed back on the misty morning, a lifetime ago, when the two of them were stretching beside each other on the perfect emerald lawn of the lodge, getting ready to begin their second run into the mountains. As a doc in the ER, he had been forced to confront the ultimate truth countless times—life was all so fragile . . . so precious . . . so unpredictable. He had never managed to disengage himself from that reality, nor did he ever want to. But this was Cap.

Battling the fullness in his throat, Lou pressed the

button on the intercom, announced himself, and was buzzed into the unit.

Waiting for him by the central nurses' station was a lanky, high-jumper-tall man, dressed in a knee-length white lab coat with scrubs underneath. He was clean-shaven and youthful, although Lou put him at fifty. Above his Slavic cheekbones, his pale blue eyes were darting from left to right as though he were agitated by something—perhaps Lou's presence. Above the eyes, his thin, straight hair was prematurely white.

"Dr. Ivan Puchalsky," he introduced himself with a pronounced accent, probably Russian.

His handshake was like a mackerel on ice.

"Welcome. Dr. Lou Welcome," Lou responded, imitating James Bond without meaning to.

"I was told you'd be here ten minutes ago," Puchalsky said.

No *How was the trip?* No pleasantries whatsoever, for that matter. The irritation in the man's voice made Lou wish he had tried even harder for the Bond.

"Thank you for being here to meet me," he said.

"Coming from the chief of the hospital, it was a request I could not easily refuse, although I am not certain why he chose me. As I understand from Dr. Carter, you are an emergency room physician, and a friend of Mr. Duncan's. Is that correct?"

I'm a clinical instructor in medicine at George Washington Medical School, with boards in internal medicine as well as in ER and addiction medicine, Lou wanted to counter, but didn't. Puchalsky sounded determined to talk down to him regardless of his résumé.

"Correct," he said instead.

"My work on nosocomial infections is very complex

and deeply involved, even more so now that I have entered into an arrangement with the genetics department, and have opened a lab where we are sequencing the genome of dangerous bacterial pathogens to trace their origins within and outside of the hospital. So rather than explain what we do in my labs, and what we are working on with Mr. Duncan, suppose we go down the hall and you can ask me questions."

During his years as a doc, Lou had dealt with many brilliant, caring, memorable men and women. But being in medicine, especially academic medicine, also meant dealing with overinflated egos. Clearly, Ivan Puchalsky fit in that latter category.

Suppressing the fleeting image of the Hindenburg exploding, he followed the ID specialist to the doorway of a small conference room. He wanted desperately to go in and see Cap first, but he sensed Puchalsky wasn't ready to be left standing.

"Please tell me about Hank Duncan and the germ you're concerned about," Lou asked.

"Generalists such as yourself," Puchalsky responded, "don't often understand the nuances and contradictions involved in a case like this one. This is a complex situation, Dr.—"

Bond. James Bond.

"Welcome. Lou Welcome. Dr. Puchalsky, why don't we pretend, just for a moment, that this isn't a big waste of your time, and for the sake of my friend in there, clue me in about what's going on with his infection. If it helps you to think I wouldn't understand, feel free to use simple terms or to speak slowly."

Lou was not sure how sarcasm translated in the Russian culture, but judging by Puchalsky's slightly raised eyebrows, he figured the intent had registered. If anything, the man seemed resigned to extending Lou the requisite professional courtesy, albeit the minimum he could get away with.

Puchalsky sighed.

"We're not entirely certain of the nature of this particular germ," he relented. "The truth is, until the last six months or so, I've not encountered anything quite like it in all my years in medicine."

Lou's pulse accelerated. This was not a man to share such a thing easily. For someone with Puchalsky's experience never to have encountered a germ of this type before had Cap sailing in stormy, uncharted waters. Lou had come to Atlanta expecting to find his friend in trouble, but the threat level here could be the medical equivalent of DEFCON-2—one step removed from nuclear war.

"What's so unique about the germ?" he asked, barely controlling the quaver in his voice.

"Did you by any chance read in *Time* magazine six or eight weeks ago about a cheerleader who had surgery on her fractured elbow after a nasty fall during a cheerleading competition?"

"As a matter of fact, my daughter, Emily, showed me a video of the fall on YouTube. It was just awful, and at the time I saw it, there had already been something like two or three million views."

"Well, the girl was cared for at White Memorial Hospital in Boston, which as you know is as good as any hospital in the country. A week or so after her open repair, she developed an infection with an unusual bacteria. As you may know, with very rare exceptions, all bacteria are classified as either Gram positive, or Gram negative, depending on whether they become purple or pink when stained."

Inwardly, Lou groaned. This was introduction to undergraduate microbiology stuff. He nodded, keeping his expression blank. Puchalsky had to be allowed to do it his way.

"Please go on," he said.

"What is unusual about this germ is that it appears to fluctuate between the two states. There is no pattern that we can discern to this fluctuation. Nothing we can find that is cause and effect. But the result is an organism that isn't consistently sensitive to any antibiotics."

Lou went cold. The Doomsday Germ. He had read a newspaper article about it, but had seen nothing in the medical literature, and had categorized it in his mind as a variant of MRSA—methicillin-resistant staph aureus.

"What happened to the girl?" he asked.

"She lost her arm, and then one leg. She was extremely ill at the time of that operation, and she died on the table."

Jesus. Cap was in isolation because of a nosocomial infection—a germ he had caught from simply being in the hospital.

"Have there been many other reported cases?"

"Some. We had one at this hospital about six months ago—an elderly diabetic woman who came in for treatment of a foot ulcer and got a secondary infection with the bacteria. She died quite rapidly and unpleasantly."

"What do the sensitivities of Hank Duncan's cultures tell you?" Lou asked.

Apparently Puchalsky liked the way the question

was phrased. His impatient demeanor lightened just a bit.

"The antibiotic sensitivities are inconsistent and not encouraging. We've tried methicillin and two different carbapenems, individually and in combination. Next will be vancomycin. But so far nothing seems to be working. At the present moment, I am not entirely sure how to battle this particular germ. I have no idea of its origin, how it managed to infect your friend, or how many people may be at risk for exposure now. We've contacted the CDC of course, and are working at it in my lab over in the Smith Pavilion."

"What's the current situation?" Lou asked, his voice breaking in spite of himself.

"The infection is getting worse. Mr. Duncan's surgeons have put in drains, but we're contemplating opening the incision."

"And your investigation?"

"The germ is actually easy to grow in culture, but with the resistance it is showing to our drugs, it's seeming clearer and clearer that we will have to go in another direction."

"Such as?"

Puchalsky sighed again.

"Dr. Welcome, this just is not the time to go over my work with you or anyone for that matter. I mean you no disrespect, sir, but I am just too busy for this. And I will get even busier the moment a third case crops up in our hospital. And believe me, doctor, it is only a matter of time before that happens. Feel free to visit with your friend. Stay in his room as long as you like, but if you have any questions specific to his condition, I ask that you direct them to his attending physicians, or his nurses. I plan on delivering a similar message to Dr. Carter. Are we in agreement here?"

Puchalsky clearly wanted Lou just to dry up and blow away. That didn't matter. Lou had plenty of experience with people who, for one reason or another, wanted the same thing. Besides, the man had reminded him that just down the road was a resource that could prove far more helpful than he was—bacteria-worshiping Sam Scupman of the CDC's Antibiotic Resistance Unit. But before he let the incorrigible infectious disease specialist walk away, Lou had one more question.

"At the rate Hank Duncan's infection is progressing, what's the next logical course of treatment if a new antibiotic remains elusive, and combinations of existing antibiotics continue to be ineffective?"

Puchalsky's expression and isn't-it-obvious gesture suggested he was in no mood for a long-winded reply.

"His leg would be amputated and we would continue to remove infected parts of his body, until either the germ vanishes, or he dies."

CHAPTER 24

To follow our government blindly is to walk
blind with no cane just waiting to hit something.

—LANCASTER R. HILL, LECTURE AT PRINCETON
UNIVERSITY, NOVEMBER 12, 1938

"Let me guess, you heard all that."

Lou pointed at the discrete microphone attached to the tray of Humphrey Miller's wheelchair. Humphrey, who had been making a delivery in the med room, motored over as soon as Puchalsky had left the isolation suite, and flashed what seemed to be a consoling look. His arms were somewhat more spastic than Lou remembered, as though Humphrey were reacting to Lou's angst.

"Ivan sounded more cordial than expected," Humphrey said. "Must like you."

Lou chuckled.

"Happy to see you again, Humphrey. You don't have to shorten your sentences for me unless you want to."

"Saying everything more tiring. At least you bother listen what I say. It's refreshing."

"So long as you do it for you and not for me."

"Believe me, much easier talk to you. Been follow situation with your friend."

"And?"

"And everyone's nervous."

"Puchalsky said this was the second case Arbor has had of this germ."

"That's right. Older woman."

"So he told me."

"Rapidly flesh-eating. Pretty grim."

Lou's mouth became dry.

"From our experience with flesh-eating bacteria at my hospital in D.C.," he managed, "the treatments aren't great, but they eventually work."

"Not with that lady."

For a time, neither man spoke. Humphrey appeared to be mulling something over.

"Lou, I really do like you," he said finally. "You're not like others."

"What others?"

"Other people. They don't take me seriously. You're different. Can tell. That's why I want to show you something."

"Sure," Lou said. "But it's going to have to wait until after I see Cap."

"Understand. How about meet me in main lobby in hour."

Lou checked his watch, a gift from Emily, and wondered how she was doing with her fund-raising effort. He would not have been surprised if a truckload of brownie mix was already en route to the house in Virginia where she lived with her mother and stepfather when she wasn't in D.C. with him and Diversity, their cat.

"An hour," he said, tapping Mickey for emphasis.

Humphrey's smile was oddly enigmatic. He seemed extraordinarily pleased and excited about the prospect of showing Lou whatever it was.

"You're going thank me, Dr. Welcome," he said. "Guarantee it."

The antechamber to Cap's isolation room was not much bigger than a modest walk-in closet. A wall-mounted placard instructed Lou to don a surgical mask, hair cover, gloves, shoe covers, and a gown. He had followed a number of highly infectious patients at Eisenhower, so he knew the drill well. Arbor General had assigned Cap the strictest of isolation categories, requiring the most stringent precautions. Brightly colored warning signs on the doors and walls made certain Lou understood his visit could be dangerous and would be made at his own risk.

After checking himself one final time, he pulled on the door to Cap's iso unit and felt the tug of resistance caused by the negative pressure environment. Powerful purifiers were drawing contaminated air through an elaborate filtration system. The room was hi-tech and short on warmth, with no furniture beyond a built-in nurse's computer station with a tall stool, a pair of Danish-modern chairs, a TV, and the ubiquitous hospital tray table. Waste and used linens were stuffed inside specially labeled sacks and would be disposed of or laundered in a secure environment.

Separate. Isolated. Alone . . . Frightening.

Cap's bed filled the center of the Spartan room—an island in a gray linoleum sea. Lou took in a sharp breath. He'd mentally prepared himself for this moment, but seeing his friend looking so beaten and tired hit him like a sucker punch. In spite of himself, he flashed back to the moment right before they started on the trail, when Cap had suggested they give running a rest for that day, and get their workout in the gym. Had Lou not persisted, the man would be back at Stick and Move, and Lou would probably still have his job with PWO. Cap could tell him not to blame himself all he wanted, but unless he could also change Lou's twin live-in monsters, responsibility and guilt, it was going to be a wasted effort.

The head of the bed was slightly elevated. Eyes closed, body unmoving, Cap lay there, a magazine splayed open on his belly. Lou approached, pausing to watch the ragged rise and fall of his chest, each breath strained. One IV line in each arm was infusing fluid and piggybacked smaller bags of medication. So far, it seemed clear that all the fluids and meds were no contest against the deadly germ savaging his leg. The leg itself, still suspended above the bed and braced inside a metal frame, was cocooned within layers of gauze, stained in the front with bloody drainage. Lou resisted the urge to unwrap the bandage and inspect the infected area, but what lay beneath the wrap wasn't hard to imagine.

Placing a gloved hand on Cap's muscled shoulder, Lou nudged him awake.

"Hey, sponsor-guy, it's me."

Cap's eyes blinked open. He took a moment to get his bearings. Then his parched lips bowed in a thin smile.

"Can you come back in a bit?" he asked, his voice hoarse and dreamy. "I'm supposed to have a dance lesson in five minutes. Tango."

Lou poured a cup of water from the plastic pitcher, stuck in a straw, bent the end, and helped Cap take a much-appreciated sip. He seemed to have lost ten pounds since the beginning of their ordeal.

"I spoke to your dance instructor and told her you'd reschedule," Lou said. "She said you're hot, so she'll be back."

"Good. You making meetings?"

"Don't you even give me a chance to ask how you are?"

"The leg hurts and they can't keep my temp down. There. Now, you getting to meetings? Don't bother answering. I can see it in your face. Don't trust your disease, Buck-o. Even though you think you're an old-timer now. Don't trust it a bit. While you've been growing, it's been growing, too. I assume if you're not going that there are problems. Work? Emily?"

Sponsors.

Like most of the other good ones, Cap had a sixth sense.

At that moment, his face scrunched up.

"Pain?" Lou ventured.

"A little spasm. Nothing I can't handle. So, is it your job?"

"Let's just say me and Filstrup have had a parting of the ways."

"He is such a jerk. It'll work out. You're the best thing that ever happened to that place and those docs. I promise you that what goes around, comes around. Say a prayer for him to be absolved of being an asshole."

"If I can pull it together, I will."

"Do that, brother. You ain't no good to me or anyone else all messed up again. So, Filstrup notwithstanding, thanks for coming back down."

"Nonsense. We're gonna get you through this."

"Duly noted. So, have you met my new friend Dr. Ivan, the friendly undertaker?"

"I just talked to him. Knock knock."

"Who's there?"

"Ivan."

"Ivan who?"

"Ivant to suck your blood."

An appreciative snort was all Cap could manage.

"Nothing like a corny Welcome knock-knock joke to cheer me up. Especially compared to the stuff that Russian beanpole has been doing to me. Talk about humorless. He makes you look like Chris Rock."

"Hey, watch whose humor you're disparaging. So, here's a good one I just heard. This guy's wife goes into labor big-time, and she's a screamer. 'Get me to the hospital! Get me to the hospital!' So he bundles her into the backseat and races across town only to find there's not one parking place in the hospital lot."

"And his wife keeps screaming."

"Exactly. Like a jet engine. So the guy is desperate. He looks to the heavens and calls out, 'God, get me a spot and you have my word—no more drinking, no more gambling, no more smoking, no more flirting.' At that moment, right ahead of him, a car pulls out and in he goes. 'Never mind,' he calls up. 'I found one.'"

"Better. How much do you want me to pay you to stop cheering me up? Name your price. Speaking of not cheering me up, what did Ivan-the-terrible tell you?"

"He said he's wicked smart and he's going to cure you."

"Don't BS me. I trust you, doc. You're family."

"I'll never lie to you," Lou said. "Puchalsky says you have a very serious infection in your leg and they're trying to figure out how best to treat it. This is a terrific hospital and these are very competent people. They're going to do everything that needs to be done to get you back on your feet again."

"Yeah, or foot. Think there's much of a market for one-legged boxers?"

I'll never lie to you. . . .

"Don't say that. You're not going to lose your leg."

"You tell me that with truth in your eyes and I'll buy it."

"I'm telling you that."

"Buddy, just remember two things," Cap said, lifting the hand with the thin IV tube attached so he could hold up fingers for emphasis. "First, you promised never to lie to me."

Cap maintained his hard stare, boring through the layers of Lou's uncertainty and fear.

"What's the second thing?" Lou managed, feeling his conviction dropping as if a sinkhole were opening up beneath him.

"The second thing," Cap said, this time flashing him a forgiving grin, "is to remember that despite my performance on that trail in the mountains, I'm not stupid."

CHAPTER 25

The Director shall oversee the Hundred, but
shall not supersede any one of them.

—LANCASTER R. HILL, *100 Neighbors*, SAWYER
RIVER BOOKS, 1930, P. 102

By the time Cap's nurse, a full-figured woman named
Elisha, bustled into the room and shooed Lou out,
he was already five minutes late for his meeting with
Humphrey. Cap dozed through some of their hour together, but in general, he forced himself to stay awake,
asking about the kids he had been training at the
gym, including Emily, his prize pupil, and also about
some of their other mutual friends.

For the moment, Stick and Move was being covered
gratis, but no one connected with the gritty inner-city
joint had any money to spare. Thanks to Walter Filstrup, Lou's calendar had lightened some, but he was
determined to spend his newfound free time right there
at Arbor General.

Mostly, though, the two of them skirted the money
issues, both surrounding the business and also Cap's
mounting hospital bills. The overriding problem—the
elephant in the tub—was Cap's leg infection. Once that
behemoth was sent back to the jungle, they could focus on redecorating the bathroom.

"He needs his rest," Elisha said.

Given the sheen of perspiration coating Cap's fore-head and the clammy feel of his hand, Lou was not about to disagree.

"I'll be back, pal," he said.

The nurse placed a firm hand on his shoulder and turned him toward the door.

"He'll be fine," she insisted as if addressing a grade-schooler.

Lou wished he felt buoyed by her reassurance.

It took him a bit of time to discard his paper cloth-ing, ride downstairs, and wend his way through the bustling corridors of the hospital. Humphrey was wait-ing to one side of the modestly busy lobby, but from what Lou could discern, he looked less cheerful than usual.

"I'm sorry for being late," Lou said. "Cap isn't in good shape."

"That's want discuss with you," Humphrey replied, wheeling past the bank of elevators and the massive in-formation desk to an unoccupied nook. As usual, Lou saw people stare at the man as they passed, then un-comfortably turn away.

"I'm not sure I understand what you mean," Lou said. "What is there to discuss?"

Humphrey held Lou's gaze as best he could. When he finally spoke, he abandoned his shorthand speech and did his best to carefully enunciate every word.

"I believe your friend is dying, Lou, and there is nothing anyone can do about it. . . . Except me."

With those few words, it felt as if Humphrey had completely altered the dynamics of their connection. He was suddenly not the affable, upbeat, indomitable cripple, struggling along despite his limitations and the disregard of so many. He was no longer desperately grateful for Lou's understanding and respect. He was, instead, a stern, deadly serious man.

"Go on," Lou said, sensing he was as much annoyed as engaged by the change in his unusual new friend.

"Before we talk. Before I show you what I mean, there's something you need to watch."

Humphrey didn't give Lou the chance to question the order. He depressed a large button on the right side of his tray, and a modest-sized computer screen rose smoothly in front of him, already booted up.

"Game versus Henri Delacourt," he said.

Many might have had trouble discerning Humphrey's thick speech, but the computer had none at all. In seconds a chessboard appeared on the screen. Lou could play a half-decent game, but over the last six months or so, Emily, a fierce game player at everything from jacks to Monopoly, had begun to win their encounters more often than not. He knew enough to see that the game on the screen was already in progress, but it wasn't clear whether white or black was winning.

Henri, it's Humphrey. Are you there?

The words he spoke printed out in a dialogue window below the board.

Right here, my friend.
How are things in Paris?
Rainy as usual. And there in Atlanta?
Hot. I believe you are in some trouble, good sir.
I believe you are right, Monsieur Miller. One

more move, and if it is the right one, I am afraid you will have beaten me once again.

In that case, it is time for us to plan our next encounter. Ng1-f3 discovered check.

On the screen, the black knight moved from the first space in the *G* row to the third space in the *F* row.

There was a prolonged pause, and then the word RESIGN appeared on the screen, followed by a few words of gentlemanly congratulations, and the promise to schedule another match as soon as time allowed.

The chessboard was replaced by a screen saver showing an eagle in constant flight.

"Nice going," Lou said, not bothering to ask the obvious question regarding the connection between Cap's situation and Humphrey's victorious online encounter. He did not have to wait long for at least a part of the answer.

"Henri Delacourt's bio," Humphrey said to the console.

In seconds, a handsome, aging face appeared, topped by a thicket of silver hair. Lou was only a few lines into the man's résumé, when he understood at least some of the demonstration. Delacourt, a professor of physics, was an international chess grandmaster, and the champion of his country seven times.

"Quite a pedigree," Lou said.

"Seldom lose to him, or any of ten grandmasters I play."

"You must be very good."

"Correction," Humphrey said. "I must be very smart. Need you believe just how smart before we can move to purpose of this little trip."

"Well, that was quite a demonstration. I am genuinely interested in what this is all about if that's what you mean."

A genius . . . Not just smart, a frigging genius.

Lou had no trouble seeing how difficult it must have been throughout Humphrey's life, being thought of first and foremost as broken and unappealing, especially with an intellect as remarkable as his obviously was. How difficult and frustrating over the years for the pharmacy tech to be unable, for whatever reasons, even to approach his potential.

"Okay, then," Humphrey said. "Let's travel."

"Where are we going?"

"Down," was the terse reply.

He spun his chair around and motored to the elevators, with Lou hurrying to keep up. The car at the far end was labeled as FREIGHT ONLY. With practiced skill, Humphrey took a custom-made rod created out of metal and plastic, and hanging off his tray table. A key card was fixed to one end. Then, with difficulty, he drew the card along a slot on the wall, and the elevator door glided open.

The padded car had only two buttons: SB 1 and SB 2. Humphrey, clumsily turning the extension wand around, used a rubber tip to press the bottom button. Lou found himself wondering if the repeatedly vanquished chess masters had any idea of the nature of the man who was drubbing them again and again.

The elevator came to a stop, the doors slid open, and in moments Lou was following Humphrey along the poorly lit corridor of Subbasement Two. On either side were closed metal doors, labeled in black-painted block letters with the equipment and supplies stored within.

In the dense quiet, the soft hum of Humphrey's wheelchair was the only sound. Lou's eyes had adjusted to the dim light when they turned a corner and came to a stop facing a metal door labeled simply STOCK OVERFLOW.

"What is this place?" Lou asked.

"Where we're going to save Cap's life."

There was a note of excited pride in his voice as he inserted the key card straight into a slot above the handle of the door. Instantly, a lock clicked, the door swung open, and they entered an extremely chilly room—in the fifties Fahrenheit, Lou guessed.

"Impressive," Lou said.

"Choose friends carefully," Humphrey responded. "One is hospital engineer. I ask, he makes."

"Why so cold?"

"Muscles less spastic."

Grinning, Humphrey lifted an arm, and Lou saw somewhat of an improvement, although not a great one.

The faint spill of light from the corridor partially illuminated a high-ceilinged room approximately the size of a two-car garage. Lou could see the outlines of boxes, stacked in towers and arranged in neatly ordered rows. When Humphrey used his extender to flip on the lights, Lou saw two ten-foot-long Corion-topped tables with storage units built underneath. A side-wall table with a built-in sink occupied one corner of the room, and opposite that was an antivibration table—a workstation specifically designed for vibration-sensitive imaging applications. There were some other items not boxed, including a small refrigerator, a freezer, and even an ice machine, but most of the supplies were still sealed inside their cartons.

In addition, there was a pair of large incubators against the far wall. And from what Lou could tell, both of them were functioning, and contained labeled petri dishes of microorganisms.

Humphrey wheeled around to face Lou.

"You like?" he asked.

"Humphrey," Lou said, struggling to find his voice. "What's going on?"

"Less exhausting if I write this."

Humphrey set his hand around his joystick. His screen featured an alphabet and a large number of word combinations. His text was produced slowly, but accurately, and faster than even his verbal shorthand would have produced. Lou read patiently.

I told you I had many interests besides chess—mathematics, the Japanese game of go, physics, anthropology, classical music. When a person of great intelligence is chained to a computer and the Internet, there is no limit to the world available to him. Chief among my areas of expertise, the one I am much more adept at than any of the others or any board game, is microbiology. That bacteria eating away at your friend's leg is known by those working on it as the Doomsday Germ. With your help, we are going to cure it.

CHAPTER 26

The French revolution's *régime de la terreur* was a means to establish order during a period of turmoil, and was embraced equally by the populace and political establishment. If these so-called terrorist acts can create order, it is logical to conclude they should be employed to prevent the turmoil in the first place.

—LANCASTER R. HILL, LECTURE AT LEHIGH UNIVERSITY, FEBRUARY 18, 1940

Lou was stunned—absolutely incredulous.

Even though Humphrey's chess demonstration and subbasement secret lair made some sense, Lou could not put them into context. His efforts to understand the man's speech and to learn more of his strength and how he managed to get it together to come to work each day, had all at once been dwarfed by these new revelations.

Humphrey glided over to him.

I know what's infecting Cap. It's a bacteria developed by some sort of terrorist organization. I don't know the name of this organization, or what their goal is. They could be Al-Qaeda or an off-shoot. They could be U.S. radicals. But what I do know is that the germ is real.

Lou could only stare at the screen.

"Please explain, Humphrey."

"From beginning?"

"The temperature's a little below my comfort zone, but I'll tell you if I want you to cut corners."

Two out of every one thousand births end up to a greater or lesser extent like me. The numbers haven't changed in forty years or more, even with advances in obstetric care. It used to be that poor obstetric care was considered the leading cause of cerebral palsy, but epidemiological studies have largely refuted that assertion. Some studies have suggested maternal bacterial infection as a causal factor. This interested me. Was it bad luck, bad genetics, or some environmental factor? I wanted to know the history of me. How I'd come to inhabit this crippled body. As I explored this question I fell in love with microbiology as a scientific discipline.

"You're doing great, Humphrey. Go on."

My parents were embarrassed by me. They pretty much left me to my own devices so long as I stayed in my room with my computer, or went to special classes at special schools. Their expectations of me were zero or less than zero.

"They couldn't have missed by much more," Lou said, aching for the man's early years.

It probably comes as no surprise that growing up I lacked confidence. I knew what my brain was capable of doing, but my body always held me back.

To maintain his composure, Lou looked away from the screen briefly and glanced around at the cartons. There were towers of boxes, some stacked like matryoshka dolls, the largest on the bottom perhaps containing pipettes and glassware, the next size labeled shakers, and at the top, a vacuum pump.

"The Internet rescued you," Lou said finally.

It was wonderful. There were forums and blogs and bulletin boards where researchers exchanged all sorts of information. In that virtual world, without my body to hold me back, I could keep up with the most advanced minds out there. When I was sixteen, I was answering questions some top research scientists and mathematicians didn't even know to ask. My reputation spread online and I became a bit of a celebrity within this very small cluster of intellects. That's how I came to the attention of Dr. Nazar Farooq from Stanford. Very brilliant.

Lou checked the time. An hour and a half had passed.

"I'm going to nudge you ahead a little," he said. "Connect the dots to Cap, and then we need to go back upstairs."

Dr. Farooq and I became more or less colleagues. We spoke online as many as several times a week. Then one day, Farooq disappeared. Just like that. Gone. I couldn't find a word about him except that he had vanished one night, and the police were involved. Several months passed before I heard from him again, but not as Dr. Farooq. He called himself Ahmed Kazimi. It took me months to figure out who he was, and he did his best to keep his identity from me.

"How did he say he learned about you?"

He said he got my name from notes found in Farooq's files. He swore me to secrecy and claimed to be the head of a government project tasked with creating workable defenses for fictitious biological terrorist attacks. I didn't say anything after I realized Kazimi and Farooq were one and the same. He never told me why he disappeared or needed an alias. For my part, I was happy to be a member of this cutting-edge virtual team.

Fascinated, Lou barely breathed during the account. The deep chill in the room stopped affecting him.

"And you never told him about yourself?" he asked.

I used my real name at the very beginning of our online connection, so I kept that. But then I changed all the other details of my life. There were times when I couldn't remember the story I had told. I made myself a hermit, who had shunned academia after my Ph.D. thesis was rudely and crudely rejected.

"It's incredible you were that ashamed when you were so accomplished. What about Stephen Hawking?"

Humphrey sneered as though he'd played that argument out countless times and always to the same conclusion.

"Hawking known at school as Einstein," he said. "ALS not begin until twenty-one. Already premier intellect then."

"Point taken," Lou said, raising his hands to defuse what he perceived as escalating tension.

Humphrey required a moment to regain his composure.

"Kazimi not entirely honest with me, or rest of team."

"In what way?"

He told us our work on an antibacterial treatment for a germ that fluctuates between a Gram positive and Gram negative state was a fictitious scenario. There was no way for him to know that I worked in a hospital that had actually encountered a real case.

"The older lady with the foot ulcer."

"Exactly."

Thoughts of the woman's horrible demise segued to Cap's situation. Lou had to look away.

I said nothing to Kazimi about this. I didn't want to jeopardize my role on the project. But I knew we weren't part of any theoretical think tank. We were under attack by a real terrorist organization that had developed this potent biological

*agent capable of resisting any antibacterial treat-
ment we could throw at it.*

"So you and Puchalsky are both working on a treatment?" Lou asked.

Humphrey scoffed and visibly exhausted himself
with the vehemence in his verbal response.

"Puchal arrogant joke. Kaz's team already working
on germ when he started research. Heard him talk
once. Totally misdirected. Don't think Kazimi ever
made him part of think tank."

"And your role in the project?" Lou asked.

"Removed," Humphrey replied simply.

"By Kazimi?"

"Yes. My mentor . . . my friend. Just like that."

"Why would he remove you from the project?"

"I suggested alternate approach—new theory I'd
developed."

"And the theory goes?"

Lou, completely transfixed by the man, crouched
low to get at his level, and focused on every syllable.
Was this Floyd Weems, stepping from the dense under-
growth of the Chattahoochee forest at the moment he
was most sorely needed?

"My work uses bacteriophage," Humphrey said.
"Three strains, actually. You know about phage?"

"Some. I know they are viruses that infect a specific
bacteria, and as often as not, kill it. There are many
different kinds."

"Not bad. Think we need get away from chemical
antibiotics. Kill the Doomsday Germ with phage before it can adapt."

"Your approach was rejected?"

Humphrey had to rest several minutes before he resumed typing.

Kazimi and I had a heated online exchange. As I said, I had always given him the utmost amount of respect, but on this point I firmly believed he was headed down the wrong road. He was like Puchalsky, locked into familiar notions and traveling well-worn paths, fixated on established approaches, blind to the fact that this germ plays by a different set of rules.

"So, why haven't I heard much about this germ? It's sensationalist stuff. You'd think it would be in all the papers."

Humphrey's expression darkened.

Do you think the government wants this sort of news widely known? Think of the panic it would cause. There are outbreaks of SARS or infections like SARS all the time, all over the world, but we rarely hear about them because of the damage it would do to tourism and consumer confidence.

We count on the vigilance of our scientific community to sound the warning bells, but in this case the most brilliant minds don't even believe the germ is real, while the hospitals are under a gag order to keep it out of the public domain. I know this for a fact.

"How do you know?"

"Very good with computers," Humphrey under-

stated. "Have ways. Exchanges between our hospital
and FBI following initial case."

"You hacked the hospital."

"Not so hard."

Humphrey laughed merrily.

"What makes you think Kazimi won't come around
to seeing it your way?"

"He's cut me off—gone silent. No word since argument."

"Are you sure he's all right? Could something have
happened to him?"

Humphrey returned to his joystick.

*He's working for the government. I'm certain
they are keeping him closely guarded. Unless I
miss my guess, at the moment, Kazimi is hard at
work in some secret lab. And he's failing, just as
our friend Puchalsky is failing. But you and I,
Lou, we're going to succeed. I can develop the
treatment that will save Cap Duncan's life and
the lives of anybody infected with this Doomsday
Germ. But I can't do it without your help.*

"My help?"

Humphrey gestured to himself.

"Look at me, Lou," he said, eschewing his shorthand
speech for emphasis. "I have aides to help me get
dressed, eat my meals, and go to the bathroom. I can't
even unpack these boxes let alone set up a lab or get any
significant work done in it."

He sank back, gasping for breath, utterly spent.

"But you do your job here at Arbor General, and do
it well from all I can tell."

"Thank God for Bat-chair, and Americans with Disabilities Act, and all who load and unload my med cart."

Lou was unable to get a total read on Humphrey's emotions, but the bitterness was clear.

"Where did you get all this equipment, anyway?" he said, angling to lessen the tension.

"Stockpiling for a while. Inefficient purchase order system here."

"Humphrey, that's like grand theft."

Again, a laugh.

It's not theft when everything purchased is still here in the hospital. Besides, the end will justify the means. I'm sure of it. If you don't help me, Lou, you'll be leaving the fate of your friend to Puchalsky or Kazimi or maybe others. All will fail. I promise you that. I also promise you that there is a terrorist attack happening right now, right under our noses, and I am the only person who can stop it. Will you help me?

Lou was pacing now among the cartons. He wasn't concerned about the criminality of what Humphrey had done—he had crossed that line in the past and if he had to, he would cross it again. No, his concern was more about Humphrey Miller, himself—whether, in fact, he was something of a misguided megalomaniac, driven by the anguish and frustration over his profound disability, layered on what was undeniable, but vastly underappreciated, genius.

"Why not do this aboveboard?" Lou asked. "Tell someone what you know."

I tried telling Kazimi, and look what it got me.
Lou, nobody will find out about this lab, if that's
what you're worried about. Hardly anyone ever
comes down to this floor, and when they do, they
never have any reason to look in here. In fact,
their keys won't even work. My engineer friend
and I have seen to that. Maintenance will give up
long before they go running around looking for
an explanation or a solution.

"I need some time," Lou said, turning his back.

"You saw how quickly Cap's deteriorating."

The man was pushing—the surest way to get Lou, or most other docs for that matter, to dig in and resist. He gazed up at the drop ceiling and ran his hands through his hair. He had connections at the D.C. hospitals.

Becoming Humphrey's arms and legs would be time-consuming and possibly counterproductive, to say nothing of what might happen should they get caught and arrested. Humphrey's chess demonstration was certainly compelling. Now, Lou was wondering if it was possible to get any further information about the man and his offbeat theories on using various bacteriophage to destroy an indestructible germ. The ones who kept crossing his mind were Dr. Sam Scupman and his associate Vicki Banks.

"Tell me, Humphrey, what were you doing for this Kazimi if you couldn't work any lab equipment?"

"Computer modeling. Heady stuff that you wouldn't really understand."

"Make me."

"What?"

"I was near the top of my class in med school. If you want me to be your assistant, make me understand your work."

Humphrey thought for a time, then wheeled to a far corner of the room where a small, built-in desk was set up. On it was a cup of pens, pencils, and markers, as well as a laptop. He used his extender to open the drawer.

"Take out the notebook," he said.

Lou removed a thick, green three-ring binder, filled with what looked like articles and printouts. Humphrey took most of ten minutes to type out an explanation.

This notebook contains the basis of my theories and an instruction manual on the bacteriophage I believe will do the job. Read it over carefully. Take notes. Be ready to ask questions. I've used advanced computer models to predict the response to the phages, and bacterial growth based on various levels and combinations of treatment. The mathematics will not be easy for you despite your intelligence, but take it from me, it is irrefutable. I ask that you take care of this. It is the only hard copy in existence, although I can duplicate it from my computer.

Lou thumbed through the pages, impressed by the depth of the research.

"I want to look it over," he said.

"Trust you be discreet and careful who share this with. But I need you."

"How much time do I have?"

"Have another look at your friend, Dr. Welcome. Then you tell me."

CHAPTER 27

To extinguish the fires of American prosperity, we need only to suffocate them under a blanket of government programs.

—LANCASTER R. HILL, *A Secret Worth Keeping*, SAWYER RIVER BOOKS, 1937, P. 1

Lou spent the night holed up in his hotel room, examining Humphrey's research notebook a page at a time. The task would have been near impossible had Humphrey not included a five-page summary of the most significant papers and professional exchanges.

By 3:00 A.M., not even the discipline acquired through medical school and residency could keep him focused, or keep a deep melancholy from taking hold. Despite his commitment to Cap, he missed his life in D.C.—his place above Dimitri's Pizza, the ER, and most of all, Emily. He also worried about his docs at the PWO. Walter Filstrup's precipitous action was forcing him to acknowledge how much of his identity revolved around that now defunct job.

A man doesn't know what he has until he loses it. . . .

The tune took up residence in his head and began a loop. Where did it come from? A musical, maybe. Whatever. If the identical situation had come up again, even knowing that his job at PWO was on the line, he would have done nothing any different.

This was where he was supposed to be, and helping Cap in any way he could was what he was supposed to be doing. Arbor General was a world-class institution, but it and other hospitals were being outwitted, outmatched, and outgunned by an organism just a couple of microns in diameter. And at the core of the struggle, almost six feet tall, and as powerful for his age as any man had the right to be, was Cap Duncan. Seeing his mentor so depleted continued to fuel Lou's resolve to do everything in his power to save him, even if that everything included helping Humphrey Miller run an unsanctioned, illegal laboratory, dedicated to turning theory into reality—abstract beliefs into lives saved.

From what Lou could glean from the notebook, Humphrey had done meticulous and incredibly well-documented research. What he did not know, and could not know without some expert guidance, was if the brilliant pharmacy tech's approach really did have as much or more chance of succeeding than the traditional ones.

One thing seemed certain—Dr. Ivan To-Drink-Your-Blood was not up to the task, nor would he take Humphrey's work seriously, even if he had done research on bacteriophage. Puchalsky would never be able to see the genius imprisoned within Humphrey's tangled body. Still, some sort of expert evaluation of Humphrey's proposals seemed like the only way to go at this point.

With that in mind, Lou had contacted Vicki Banks and arranged a time when she and her boss, Sam Scupman, could meet with him. Seven more hours, and he might have some answers.

Now, if only he could sleep.

* * *

It seemed like a year since Lou last sat in the library conference room of the CDC's newly constructed Antibiotic Resistance Unit. Certainly, in terms of eventfulness, it had been. As before, he had been escorted to the room by an armed security guard and informed of a delay in Dr. Scupman's and Dr. Banks's schedules. While he waited for them to arrive, he once again skimmed the five-page abstract of Humphrey Miller's thesis, the only part of the thick notebook he had chosen to bring. After hours of study, he sensed he was getting a handle on things. And what he was understanding, he liked.

Humphrey's bacteriophages—*bacterio* for the target germ, and *phage* meaning to devour—were three of thousands of types of viruses, readily available in soil, shallow ocean water, and other ecosystems, capable of invading specific bacteria and interfering with their reproduction. The irony of a flesh-eating bacteria being eaten from within by another microorganism was not at all lost on Lou. Prior to their discovery in 1917, phages had been linked to miracle waters—rivers in India and other places with the power to cure diseases from leprosy to cholera. Only later did scientists, examining a naturally occurring treatment for dysentery, discover these "cures" were phages, feasting on and eradicating the disease-causing bacteria. Use of cultured phages to fight bacterial infections had not been without controversy, and had not at all enjoyed universal acceptance. Humphrey's proposal would push the boundaries of what the virus could do beyond all known limits.

But Lou sensed the theory was solid, and very well

might work. With time running out for Cap, it simply *had* to.

While Lou worried Scupman might balk at offering his professional assessment based on the five-page summary, he was equally concerned with revealing Humphrey's identity. Humphrey had left it up to him, but they both knew that the wrong word to the wrong person might mean the end of his lab before it was even up and running.

Ten minutes later, Sam Scupman entered the conference room, followed two minutes later by Vicki Banks. Scupman was even more frazzled and unkempt than Lou remembered, and had probably not changed his knee-length lab coat since then. Lou took extra notice of the dark circles encasing the man's green eyes. Nothing like a flesh-eating, untreatable infection to induce insomnia in a microbiologist. For her part, Banks looked as interesting and unflappable as before, with her heavy, black-framed glasses and her raven hair knotted in a bun. If there was any change in her since their last meeting, it was that she seemed less reserved than Lou remembered, and quicker with a smile.

"Dr. Welcome," Scupman said. "Nice to see you again. You're the one who asked that excellent *Pseudomallei* question."

"Thank you for remembering."

Lou shook hands with the two scientists before they took their seats at the conference table. Banks's hand was smooth, and despite the air-conditioning, quite warm.

Scupman spoke first. "In your phone conversation

with Dr. Banks, you mentioned wanting to speak with us about a special type of bacteria. I admit your caginess pertaining to the specifics intrigued me. Unfortunately, my time today is short so we'll have to get right to the point."

"Not a bacteria, Dr. Scupman. A bacterio*phage*."

"Oh?"

The scientist seemed to perk up.

"A patient at Arbor General named Hank Duncan is in trouble. He had a compound fracture of his femur a little over two weeks ago, and is now toxic from a flesh-eating bacteria for which it appears there is no treatment. Hank runs a gym in D.C. and is known around the city as Cap. He is my closest friend."

"The splint!" Banks exclaimed.

"Pardon?"

"You're the ER doctor who splinted the fracture in the wilderness north of here, aren't you?"

Lou couldn't completely pin down the expression in her eyes, but it was one he liked.

"It appears the Arbor General grapevine moves information as fast as ours does in D.C," he replied. "I splinted the leg, but couldn't have done it without my friend's help."

"So I heard," Banks said. "Quite a story. Sorry there have been complications."

"Thanks. That's why I'm here. The ID specialist consulting on the case, Dr. Ivan Puchalsky, used the term *Doomsday Germ* when he spoke with me."

Lou passed across two copies he had made of Humphrey's abstract.

"Is this from Puchalsky?" Scupman asked with a

disdain that immediately lifted his standing in Lou's mind. "Arrogant son of a bitch," he then muttered, earning a few more points.

"No," Lou said. "Puchalsky has nothing to do with this. I made calls when I learned what was going on with Cap. One of my friends faxed me this."

Scupman scanned more than read the pages. His eyes narrowed and Lou sensed an immediate souring in his demeanor. His body language, arms crossed, leaning back in his chair, seemed more guarded.

"You sure this wasn't put together by Puchalsky? Actually, never mind. It doesn't read as if it were something he would have come up with. Excuse me for saying so, but as a microbiologist, primarily interested in nosocomial infection, he really is quite limited in his scope and in his respect for the power of bacteria. Would you agree with that, Dr. Banks?"

"Actually, Sam, I think you're being a little hard on the man."

Lou suspected the same could be said for Scupman's reaction to most of his colleagues. He wondered if Ahmed Kazimi had included the man in his cyber think tank. It wouldn't surprise him in the least if he hadn't.

"I'm looking for any information that will help my friend," he said.

"I'm sorry to have to tell you this," Scupman responded, "but most of our work with this bug is classified. That's the way it is with a government lab. But I can assure you that if we had a treatment breakthrough of any kind, it would already be inside your friend."

"That's why I wanted you to see this document," Lou said.

"Who wrote it?"

"I promised to pass on your reaction to what's written there before disclosing who wrote it."

"The truth is," Scupman said, "it really doesn't matter who wrote it. From what little material you brought me, I can say with some certainty that it's not going to work. What do you think, Dr. Banks?"

Lou had watched as Banks went through the pages a second time. At least one of the scientists had shown Humphrey's work that much regard.

"Dr. Welcome," she said, "the truth is, Dr. Scupman and I have done some phage work, without much in the way of encouraging results. We haven't done anything with the combination of phages that is discussed on pages three and four, but the information presented here is scant."

"Scant?" Scupman broke in. "It's thin as a wafer. And what's this with these footnotes? They don't refer to anything. There's no bibliography and nothing at the bottom of the pages. Whoever wrote this obviously has more information than he chose to include here. Why is that?"

"I can't say why," Lou answered, "but I can tell you that there is more. A lot more."

"Well, bring it in if your mystery scientist wants, but at the moment there's not enough here for me to promise I'll get to it in the next couple of months. Dr. Banks, anything to add?"

"It's clear how much your friend means to you. The truth is, I agree with Dr. Scupman that the theories presented here are interesting, but nothing that new. However, if it's really that important to you, I will try and go through the total material over the next week."

"I'm afraid I'm going to have to insist that you don't," Scupman said, his expression pinched, and his irritation apparent.

Banks's cheeks reddened.

"But I would be doing it on my own time."

"Dr. Banks, as long as I am your superior at this lab, your time is my time. We are locked in a death struggle here against one of the most cunning, baffling, powerful bacteria man has ever encountered. Think Attila and Genghis Khan and Hitler all rolled into one. If you have free time on your hands, I strongly suggest it be used to further your work on the antibiotic you and your staff are developing."

Lou felt a rush of heat across the back of his neck.

"But—" he began to protest.

Banks, her eyes riveted on his, stopped him with a minute shake of her head, and Lou pulled back.

Was Scupman protecting something . . . or someone? he wondered. He had expected the bacteria sycophant to behave eccentrically, but by shutting the door on a concerned physician, as well as on his own second-in-command, he had taken a step over the line between eccentric and rude. Lou had already decided that because of Scupman's behavior, he was going to help Humphrey set up his lab no matter what. Still, one final try at getting some encouraging information from the division chief seemed called for.

"Dr. Scupman, Dr. Banks, I know you've taken a look at the effect of bacteriophage on the Doomsday Germ, but what do you think about the proposal of using three different types of phage administered simultaneously—one directed at the Gram positive, and two directed at the Gram negative?"

Scupman pushed himself away from the table and stood.

"Scientists have invented a dozen different antibiotics in just the past few years, and we are on the doorstep of creating a dozen more. One of them, or a combination, will eventually be enough to bring the so-called Doomsday Germ to its knees, at least until the tyrant figures out what's going on and mutates. We have known about bacteriophages for close to a century. There is a reason why they haven't caught on as an antibacterial agent."

Lou was disappointed when Banks also stood. He had no choice but to join them.

"Three different forms of phage is an interesting approach," she said. "It would be like forest rangers setting a fire to fight a fire. It seems a long shot, but maybe the proposal does have some merit. Sam?"

"The only thing I'm willing to concede," Scupman said, "and I'm sorry to have to say this so bluntly, is that I think it's best if you light a candle for your friend. We only have the time and manpower to follow very promising lines of research. Bacteriophage therapy is most certainly not one of those. Now, as I said, I have another appointment, and Dr. Banks has some promising work I want to take a look at before that. Thank you for your effort, Dr. Welcome. I appreciate your sad situation. Now, if you'll excuse us."

Lou felt stunned. Either Scupman did not like his opinions being questioned, or he hated the notion of this super-germ being vulnerable in any way. It was as though he were rooting against a cure—hoping that super-germ never stumbles onto any kryptonite.

Scupman pointedly moved to the desk at the far end

of the conference room, made a phone call, and began talking more loudly than he probably had to.

Banks gave Lou a sympathetic look and said softly enough so only he could hear, "I'm sorry for Sam's behavior. He isn't a bad guy, he just has very strong opinions, and as you seem to suspect, he's under a huge amount of pressure."

"But you don't agree with his opinions?" Lou asked, gathering his papers.

Banks pursed her lips, giving her next words careful consideration.

"I think there is something to what you're proposing," she replied. "But Sam isn't wrong. It would probably take a long time to perfect, and more manpower than we have."

Or, Lou thought, *the most brilliant microbiologist nobody has ever heard of.*

"I don't have many options left," Lou said. "Thanks, Dr. Banks. You gave me something important."

"And what is that?"

"You gave me a bit of hope."

Banks returned a weak smile. *Hope,* her expression said, *would not be enough.*

"Please call me Vicki. Listen, Lou, I'm really very sorry about your friend. I deeply hope he makes it."

"You and a lot of other people," he said. "Thanks again for caring."

Scupman was still on the phone, and Lou wondered in passing if there was anyone on the other end of the line. He had taken a step toward the door when Vicki blurted out, "Would you like to go out and get a drink sometime? I hate to think you're by yourself in a city that's not your own, dealing with what's on your plate."

"Thanks. I'm going to spend some more time reading about bacteriophage," he said, thinking about the work that awaited him in Subbasement Two of Arbor General. Then, quickly, before she could acknowledge that turning her down was okay, he added, "Oh, hell, I'd love to. What works for you?"

"How about the day after tomorrow?" she said. "We have budget meetings this week. You can meet me outside this building at five. It's a few blocks' walk to a little place I like. The Blue Ox—long on atmosphere, a little short on delicacies."

"How'd you know?" Lou asked.

"Know what?"

"How'd you know I needed a friend?"

Vicki's smile was radiant. "I've always had an overabundance of woman's intuition," she said.

CHAPTER 28

Mark my words: August 14, 1935, is a date
Americans will come to rue.

—LANCASTER R. HILL, PERSONAL
  COMMUNICATION TO JAMES KINCHLEY, ESQ.,
  MARCH 1936

All the mice were dead.

Twenty cages, each occupied by one mouse of a genetically pure strain, were lined up along a bench in
Kazimi's laboratory. The Janus germ was not an airborne contaminant, but as a precaution, powerful HEPA
filters droned on, continuously purifying the air. To
prevent accidental spread, the lab contained a rack of
level-B hazmat suits and a chemical shower for the de-
contamination process.

A few hours before, the mice had been bustling—
scurrying about, squeaking, sniffing, and standing on
their hind legs as they tried to scale the plastic enclo-
sures. Two hours after Kazimi injected their peritoneal
cavities with the Janus bacteria, they grew listless. An
hour after that, they were all dead.

Kazimi took one mouse from its cage and carried
it respectfully to the table where he performed his
autopsies.

Using a scalpel, he made a careful incision from
belly to neck, and pried apart the skin and sternum with

stainless-steel spreaders. The results were the same as those from his earlier trials. The mouse's insides were gone, simply liquefied. Kazimi sliced open five more mice. Their organs had melted away in a similar fashion. In a few of the dead animals, he could actually see the liquefied rot through a portal the bacteria had eaten in the peritoneum.

He had expected a fast reaction time as he had inoculated the mice with an unusually heavy dose of the germ, but the speed of morbidity, then mortality, was truly chilling.

The lab, as promised, was perfectly equipped for Kazimi's work. He might still want to collaborate with the developer of the Janus strain, as Bacon had offered, but for now his preference was to work alone. It had taken three days to grow this latest preparation of bacteria, which was designed to protect the mice against Janus. The approach was a form of competitive interference, using a genetically "neutered," nontoxic bacteria derived from the Doomsday Germ.

The idea was to flood the mice's bodies with the harmless, modified bacteria, which would compete with the virulent form for binding sites. At the same time, the competing bacteria would stimulate the immune system to make antibodies against both itself and Janus.

Only all the mice were dead.

Kazimi packed the tiny liquefied carcasses in airtight cartons, and shuffled off to the chemical shower. He was feeling more and more like a man trying to type with no hands. Once in street clothes, he went to the vast lounge and slumped onto a leather easy chair, cognizant that he was almost certainly on camera—probably more than one. He'd been working with little sleep, and exhaustion was taking a toll. The damp chill of Red Cliff was seeping into his bones and causing him to shiver. Someone had built a blaze in the massive fieldstone fireplace, but the warmth did not reach across to where he sat. He considered moving closer, but his legs were rubber, and his back ached. Instead, he grabbed a throw from a nearby sofa, wrapped it around himself, and closed his eyes, searching for sleep that just would not come.

From the reports he was receiving, the Janus strain was becoming even more deadly. The bacteria, which before required a deep wound to take root, could now enter the bodies of its victims through even a tiny cut. Epidemiologically, the Doomsday Germ was spreading with increasing speed, and in some hospitals had already breached containment protocols. Before long, Kazimi feared, the devastation could become unparalleled.

Chilled as much by the terrifying prospects of a pandemic as he was by the stone walls, Kazimi knew that the persistent failure of his research made it even more critical that he escape. If One Hundred Neighbors did not carry out their threat to kill every person he held dear, Janus might eventually do the job for them. He had to be fearless. He had to warn the people in Washington of the looming crisis. The time for his secret lab was over. He had given it his best shot, and he was failing.

It was nearing Asr—midafternoon prayers. As he was doing more and more, Kazimi was staying in the lab to pray. He forced himself to his feet, crossed to the massive windows, gazed down the nearly sheer cliff at the craggy shoreline, and reviewed what he had learned about Red Cliff. The wing housing the lab and the great room was attached to the massive main structure by the winding corridor that was constantly guarded. As far as Kazimi could tell, there was no other way in or out.

Jutting into the sea below, arising from the rocky base of the cliff, was a wooden dock, next to which was a well-maintained boathouse. Several times, he had seen a cigar-shaped motorboat with powerful twin engines bringing in supplies. What he could not figure out was how those supplies were transported up and into the castle. Some of them, at least, had to be destined for his lab. There were no stairs or pathways from the ocean—none that he could see, anyway. There had to be some way to the boathouse that didn't require scaling a one-hundred-foot cliff.

But where?

Kazimi became aware of a shift in the atmosphere of the lounge. He turned to see that Doug Bacon had entered from the corridor and was approaching him. The mogul's cane snapped against the stone floor like the popper of a bullwhip. Kazimi thought Bacon's limp seemed more pronounced. Perhaps it was the chill. His face appeared pale and drawn. Stress. Janus was getting to its creator as well as to its pursuer.

With a subtle nod, Bacon dismissed the huge African American guard he called Drake, who had followed him in. Kazimi's stomach soured at the thought of being alone with the man. For a moment he contemplated taking Bacon hostage, and using him to barter his way out. Bad idea. He needed the space that trust was giving him. Escape seemed nearly impossible as it was.

"I came to see how you were doing," Bacon said.

"You have the cameras and the screens. How do you *think* I'm doing?"

"The latest pass?"

"The mice are dead. All dead."

"Sorry to hear that. You look exhausted. Why don't you get some rest?"

"Scientists always believe that the next experiment is going to do it."

"I understand," Bacon said with a tense smile. "That which is attained without conflict or strife is rarely worth attainment at all."

"True enough."

Kazimi recognized the quote from Lancaster Hill's manifesto, but kept that fact to himself. He had no desire to share his views on Hill's misguided thinking with a zealot like Bacon. "Tell me about the situation," Bacon said.

"Despite this failure, I believe my theories of competitive inhibition have merit," he said.

"I admire your commitment. More mice have arrived. You're certain you don't need our scientist?"

Kazimi had balanced the loss of what little privacy and mobility he had against the possibility that the microbiologists working for Bacon could help him succeed where they had continued to fail.

"Not yet," he replied.

As he continued gazing out at the slate-gray ocean, Kazimi found himself thinking about the mystery man of his task force, Humphrey Miller.

Of all those on the team he had created, Miller seemed to be the most inventive, and the most outside the box. The irony was that they had never met face-to-face or even spoken to each other. Miller had connected with him some years ago via an Internet forum. After a stream of e-mails and exchanges of information, Kazimi still hardly knew the man at all. Miller had written a number of amazing papers, but had not published any of them as far as he could tell. His name, if indeed it was his name at all, was not associated with any university faculty. Still, his brilliance and creativity were unquestioned.

The mystery man.

Over the month or two before he was kidnapped, Kazimi had lost patience with Humphrey Miller persistently blaring the trumpet of his bacteriophage theory. In fact, although his deal with Bacon included the disclosure of his entire online team, he had omitted Miller as not being relevant. Now, as he endured one failure after another, he considered sharing Miller's offbeat approach to the Janus conundrum with Bacon. The last thing Kazimi wanted was to put Miller, or anyone else, in harm's way. But the situation was growing desperate. The answer as always would be to pray to Allah for clarity and vision.

"Okay, then," Bacon was saying. "Continue as you are. And if there is anything you require, do not hesitate to ask. But I remind you, time is growing short."

He turned to leave.

"Bacon, listen to me," Kazimi blurted out. "You've got to let me and your scientists work with the government. You miscalculated the power of Janus. Now, you rightly say that we're running out of time. We need more resources."

"Then take the scientist I've offered you," Bacon said.

Kazimi shook his head. "We need a vast, coordinated, combined effort here. The mutation has changed the rules of this game. Even my group of experts wouldn't be enough."

Bacon turned to him, his eyes glowing like the embers buried deep within the fireplace.

"I'm afraid that's not possible," he said. "So long as we have the leverage of possessing the means of stopping the Doomsday Germ, we can move even this ponderous government to accede to our demands. We have come too far not to make this happen."

"But you don't possess the means to control what you created. Sooner or later, even if Congress passes the laws you are demanding, even if they agree to change the way our government does business, it will become clear that you cannot deliver on your promise."

Bacon slammed the tip of his cane on the stone.

"And that is precisely why you must succeed, Dr. Kazimi," he cried out, his voice shrill and unsettling. "You must succeed at all costs."

"Tens of thousands, even millions could die."

Bacon went apoplectic.

"Without the sort of change we are demanding, there are hundreds of millions in this country who are at risk! At risk for poverty! At risk for global irrelevance! Hundreds of millions who will be left destitute as this country goes broke. We are not here to save a life, Dr. Kazimi, or even a few hundred lives. We are here to save a country!"

"You are insane! All of you."

The fire in Bacon's eyes receded, replaced by a disturbing look of vision, determination, and peace.

"Many people are depending on your success, doctor," he said evenly. "Don't disappoint them."

Turning his back, Bacon ambled over to the bar where he poured himself a drink. Kazimi stood by the towering windows, his arms dangling at his sides, his head bowed. There was to be no reasoning with the Society of One Hundred Neighbors. Not now, not ever.

"Come, sit by the fire," Bacon said. "I'll get us something to eat."

He raised a finger to his behemoth guard, and the man silently vanished into the darkness of the corridor.

Fifteen minutes later, Harris arrived wheeling in their splendid meal on the usual silver cart. Famished, Kazimi ate. A hunger strike would not do him nor the rest of the world any good. As they dined, he came close several times to bringing up Miller's name. Each time, though, he resisted. If his next trials failed, if this new batch of mice died, and if he found no escape from Red Cliff, he would have little recourse but to share Miller's name with Bacon. Then, having witnessed Alexander Burke's guile, he had little doubt the society would find him.

After lunch, Kazimi decided to remain in the lab for Asr prayers. In the short corridor connecting the Great Room with his lab, he passed the other of Bacon's bodyguards—the white, acne-pocked, bullnecked thug named Costello, who was carrying a large carton that had probably contained lab supplies, but now appeared to be empty. Kazimi intentionally averted his gaze. He saw no reason to look the man in the eye.

"I left the mice and some other stuff in the animal room, doctor," Costello said, his voice rough as new sandpaper. "I'll be back after dinner to clean out the cages."

"Good enough. Thank you."

Kazimi paused to watch as the giant lumbered past him, down the connecting corridor, and into the Great Room.

But instead of turning back and heading into his lab, he remained transfixed, staring at the Great Room door. Something did not make sense.

Had Costello gone into the lab while he was having lunch with Bacon? Not possible. The giant would have had to pass right by them. Could Kazimi have fallen asleep by the fire and missed the man entering with large cartons and boxes of mice? Again, no way.

But if Costello had not come through the Great Room to get from the boathouse to the lab, how had he gotten there? Bacon had been clear that there was only one way to get to the lab, and that was via the Great Room.

It surely wasn't the first time, and most definitely would not be the last, but the master of Red Cliff had lied.

CHAPTER 29

Social insurance puts at risk America's economic
stability and therefore should be viewed not as a
path forward, but rather as an assault on our
very liberty.

—LANCASTER R. HILL, ADDRESS TO JOHN
BIRCH SOCIETY CONVENTION, MEMPHIS,
TENNESSEE, SEPTEMBER 21, 1962

Lou kept to the shade of a maple tree near the entrance
to the Antibiotic Resistance Unit and waited for Vicki
Banks. Two days had passed since they had agreed to
meet, and Lou was surprised at how much of that time
she had been on his mind. She was certainly attractive
enough in a bookish sort of way, but it was more her
calmness and intellect, as well as her perceptiveness in
sensing how much he needed someone to talk with. His
mood, rooted in the loss of his job, the time away from
Emily, and the situation with Cap, was boring in like a
deer tick.

The days had been a stressful amalgam of hours at
Cap's bedside, and even more hours under Humphrey's
excited, watchful eye, slicing open boxes and setting
up his lab. One thing the man was right about—so long
as they looked as if they knew what they were doing,
going up and down in the freight elevator, moving

through the bowels of the hospital, no one seemed in the least interested in them.

The clinical situation with Cap was deteriorating, albeit slower than Lou had anticipated—credit to the boxer's spirit and incredible conditioning, and perhaps to the antibiotic combinations being put in play by Ivan Puchalsky. Still, as Sam Scupman had so tactfully put it, time was not a commodity Cap possessed in any great abundance. The leg was hour-to-hour. His physicians met frequently to decide whether or not the infection needed to be opened up, drained, and irrigated. It was still too early to make the larger, more frightening decisions, but if the infection spread to another limb that process would have to be sped up considerably.

Vicki emerged from the building, glanced around, and waved cheerfully when she spotted Lou. Her vibrant smile, appealing shoulder-length hair, white jeans, and turquoise blouse instantly dashed his vision of a constrained academic. Her figure, trim and sensual, had hardly been well presented beneath her knee-length lab coat. To complete the transformation, her thick-lensed, black-framed glasses were gone, replaced either by contacts or near-blindness. They shook hands, but her expression suggested they could have just as easily exchanged a quick embrace. Immediately, Lou's battered spirits felt somewhat buoyed.

"Hey, there. How are you holding up?" she asked.

"I'm okay," he replied with less conviction than he had hoped. "However, I'm not sure I'll be such a great conversationalist."

Vicki gave him an understanding look.

"Don't worry. Sometimes it's good just to have company. Are you up for a little walk? The place I was thinking we could go is a couple of blocks from the main entrance."

Lou had parked his rental in the lot by the museum, but the late-afternoon sun was still warm and the lush air, sweetened with the scents of spring, begged for a walk. Initially, they made their way in a comfortable silence along the walkway that snaked through the vast research complex.

"So how was your day?" Vicki asked finally.

"It was hardly one of my best. I spent it mostly with my friend Cap."

"The reports we've gotten from Arbor General aren't so good."

Lou grimaced.

"The reports are right, I'm afraid. He talks when he has the strength to carry on a conversation, but mostly he sleeps. He's a rock-hard, vibrant man, and it's terrible to see him like this."

"He's lucky to have a friend like you."

She took his arm in a totally natural, empathetic way.

Lou decided not to tell her about Cap's nurse finally caving in and allowing him to help change his dressing. The two of them had begun by unwrapping several layers of putrid, drainage-soaked gauze, and tossing them into a red biocontainment bag. The stench was nothing Lou hadn't encountered before, but the fact that it was a man he knew so well made it hard to take. At one point, he actually felt his blood pressure dip and had to block his nose off with the base of his tongue.

"The hardest part for me has been dealing with all the what-ifs," he said. "What if we had turned left instead of right where the trail forked? What if I had been just a foot farther over?"

"You know it wasn't your fault."

Lou felt the heaviness in his chest recur.

"I know. And it's not like me to snivel. But this has been one of the worst stretches of my life. I've lost my job at Physician Wellness for insisting on coming back down here. Even before this all happened, my significant other decided that she had enough problems in her own life without trying to deal with anyone else's. Then, last night, I had the first drunk dream I'd had in months."

"You're in recovery?"

"You know about that stuff?"

"I have my own issues," she said, "but alcohol and drugs aren't among them. You go to meetings?"

"Not many since all this happened."

"Well, you can't put this infection on yourself, Lou. Sadly, nosocomial infections are a common occurrence—close to three hundred thousand reported annually in the United States alone."

"Not a reassuring statistic."

"Sorry. That wasn't very sensitive of me. Sam and I discussed this some more after our meeting with you. He is impressed that this is a very unusual microbe. But when I told him you and I were getting together, he apologized for talking about how powerful it was and asked me to tell you not to give up hope. Saying anything derogatory against his precious bacteria is not like Sam."

"I've never met anyone quite like him. At certain times he seems seriously in love with the little beasties."

"Sam is definitely unique," Vicki said. "I've been working with him for four years and that's the way he's always been."

"Well, I wish he had as much faith in the power of science as he does in the power of microbes. His enthusiasm for the germ that's eating my closest friend is certainly testing my sobriety like few things ever have."

"How long since you've had a drink?" she asked.

Ironically, at that moment, they turned a corner and were standing in front of the Blue Ox Tavern.

"Ten years give or take," Lou answered, holding the door for her.

The tavern was beamed and dimly lit, with dark paneling throughout. The bar was impressively stocked, and there were no empty stools. His kind of place. The whole scene was too familiar, and immediately started tapes running in his head.

"It's always crowded here this time of day," Vicki said, speaking loudly enough to be heard above the din. "Between the CDC and area hospitals, the owner is probably a millionaire many times over."

"Judging by all those steins, I might say that what Sam Scupman is to bacteria, this guy is to beer. Only a beer obsession pays better."

Vicki returned a serious look.

"You don't do my job for the money," she said. "Sam and I at least have that much in common."

At Lou's request, a hostess led them to a booth in the dining area away from the noisy bar. They slid in across from each other and scanned the laminated menus. Bob Seger's mildly depressing "Turn the Page" was playing on the jukebox.

Here I am on the road again. . . .

"I've told you a lot about me," Lou said, setting his menu aside, "but I hardly know anything about you."

Vicki appraised him thoughtfully.

"I usually don't talk much about myself," she explained.

"Up to you, but I could sure use the distraction."

Before she could respond, the waitress, young and perky and in her early twenties, came over.

"Something to drink?" she asked.

Vicki looked across at Lou for permission, and he shrugged and nodded that it was okay.

He also subconsciously ran his tongue across his lips.

"Jim Beam and water," she said. "A little bit of extra ice."

"A bourbon girl. A lady after my own heart."

"I'm not a fan of fruity cocktails, and beer makes me feel like a tub."

"I'll have the same," Lou heard his detached voice say. "Neat."

Vicki's eyes narrowed. Even though he'd been engaged by her, thoughts of Cap and the grotesque infection ravaging his leg hung in his mind like a Cape Cod fog. Partial amputation . . . reamputation . . . sepsis . . . weakness . . . death. For years he had fought to stay in the moment—to vigorously avoid projecting outcomes into the future. Now, he was solidly planted in possibilities. No matter what Vicki or anybody else said, he felt responsible for what happened to his sponsor. It was his fault. And dammit, this was the moment—he wanted a drink.

"You sure?" Vicki asked.

The waitress stood by patiently.

"Yeah," Lou said finally. "I'm sure."

The girl smiled, nodded, and promised to be right back.

"I'm not your babysitter, Lou," she said. "You're a big boy and you can make your own decisions."

"Okay, then. I'm deciding I want to know more about you."

Her expression darkened.

"It's not the happiest of stories," she said.

"In that case, clearly you've come a long way."

"Well, let's see. I became damaged goods very early in life. I was an only child and my parents were both very abusive to me."

Lou cringed. "Physically?"

"And mentally, but mostly physically. They were religious fundamentalists, who believed in the importance of discipline. I'm not talking a spanking now and again. I have the scars to prove it was a whole lot more than that. After my father put out his cigarette on my backside when I had just turned fourteen, I decided it was time to leave home for good."

Lou was sickened by the thought. He could not imagine ever laying a hand on Emily, let alone burning her.

"Where'd you go? Did you move in with a relative?"

Vicki shook her head. "No, I didn't trust anybody. Not even the police. I worried they wouldn't believe me and I'd be sent back to live with my parents, so I just ran. For a long time I lived on the streets."

Vicki's story was interrupted when the waitress returned, set their drinks down in front of them, and asked if they wanted to order food. When there was no response from either of them, she pledged to be back and scooted off. Lou had been too occupied with Vicki's story, and now his drink, to respond. His drunk dream last night was like a Ouija board message, telling him that ten years was quite long enough and that he had earned what he was about to get. He imagined the taste—the wondrous velvety burn of a good bourbon.

Jim Beam.

Lou hefted his glass, swirling the amber liquid onto the sides with a movement that came back as easily as starting over on a bicycle. He knew that Vicki was riveted on him. It didn't matter.

Get it over, the voice in his head insisted. *You've earned this. Just get it over. Afterward you can just stop.*

He brought the drink closer to his lips. The aroma drifted up his nostrils like smoke from a French cigarette. His mouth was desert dry.

Then, with the rim of the glass just an inch from his lips, he hesitated. He could feel the pull—a gravitational force beyond his control.

Just get it over. . . . Ten years is enough. . . . This one drink, then start over. . . . You've earned it, man. . . . Dammit, you've paid your dues. . . .

He tilted the glass until the distance between the bourbon and his lips could be measured in millimeters. The white noise of the tavern gave way to a deep silence. This was it. He just had to get it over with. Then, in the moment before he drank, a vivid image of Emily filled his mind. She had been a child the last time he had lied to her—too young to understand his dishonesty or to be ashamed of him. She was not too young now.

The spell shattered like dropped crystal. Lou pulled the heavy glass away from his mouth and set it down.

"Not today," he said, wondering if Vicki could tell he was shaking. "I'll get to a meeting later tonight."

"Good idea. We should go ahead and order something to eat. Then maybe you can go right from here."

"The list is online. I'll check it after you finish your story. I'm okay now, I really am."

They ordered burgers, Lou went online as promised, and Vicki exchanged their untouched drinks for Diet Cokes.

"I'll give you the short, waiting-for-cheeseburgers version," she said. "So I was living on the streets of Cincinnati, occasionally sleeping at homeless shelters, but sometimes I just found a bush in the park and slept under it. Cincinnati has beautiful parks."

"How long did you do that for?"

"About a year. Then I was semi-adopted by a couple I'd met at one of the revivals. They didn't have children of their own, so they took me in. Really nice people. They got me enrolled at an alternative high school and I took my GED exam. Next thing I knew, I was getting a scholarship to Ohio State, and after that my masters in micro. Then I got a part-time job at the CDC and finished my doctorate at Emory, and here I am."

"From a GED to a Ph.D. Slightly impressive."

"Not your average, everyday fairy tale, I'll give you that."

"And your parents?"

"My real parents, you mean? I haven't spoken to them since I ran away from home. Sadly, the couple who took me in died years ago, heart attack for one and cancer for the other."

Lou was grimly silent. Cap had no children of his own, but had taken any number of street kids in over the years. Nearly every one of them was the better for the connection.

"Every day needs to be lived to the fullest," he said.

"Every day," Vicki echoed.

They talked through dinner about their lives and work. Then Vicki announced that she and a girlfriend were headed to an art lecture, and slid out from the booth.

"Meeting for you?" she asked.

"All set. I've got the address and there's a GPS in my rental."

Lou would do the meeting, then visit Cap, then meet Humphrey in Subbasement Two for what would probably be their first actual experiments. Easy night, thanks to Emily.

"You're a good man, Lou Welcome," Vicki said. "A very good man. If there's anything I can do for you, just give me a call." She drew a business card from her wallet, wrote a number on the back, and handed it to him. "That's my cell. No one gets this except you and the president. At least he will as soon as he asks for it. Call whenever." This time they did hug. "I'm glad you liked the Diet Coke," she whispered.

She kissed him lightly on the ear. Then she was gone.

He sat down again, breathing in what remained of her. A few seconds later, two men slid in where she had been—directly across from him in the booth. Both wore suits. One of them was a light-skinned African American, young, and athletic looking. The other had a hard face, strong jaw, and close-cropped hair.

"I'm not leaving just yet," Lou said, an alarm starting up in his head.

"Actually, we were counting on that," the tough-looking man said. He flipped his billfold open. There was an ID on one side and a badge on the other.

"Special Agent Tim Vaill with the FBI. My partner, Special Agent Charles McCall. Are you Dr. Louis Welcome of Washington, D.C.?"

Lou gripped the edge of the table and did a prolonged examination of the ID, buying time to will the bass drum throbbing in his chest to slow down.

"Yeah, that's me. Why?" he managed.

Vaill looked pleased. "Well then, doctor," he said, "if that's who you are, we'd like to ask you a few questions."

CHAPTER 30

Our country is under attack by forces far more powerful than those in Central Europe or the Far East.

—LANCASTER R. HILL, LECTURE TO THE
PENNINGTON SCHOOL, JUNE 6, 1939

Only one way in . . . and one way out.

Kazimi was giddy with the significance of Bacon's huge bodyguard casually emerging from the lab and lumbering past them and across the Great Room. Until that moment, Doug Bacon, the master of Red Cliff, had led him to believe there was only a single passage into that wing of the castle. Leaving the lab as the bodyguard did had to have been a mistake.

Now he stood in the lab, just inside the closed door through which Costello had come. He was wary that the giant, or Drake, the other huge guard, would open the door at any moment, and even the smallest sound from the other side caused his pulse to skip. Another concern was the security camera mounted close to the ceiling in one corner of the lab. An identical electronic sentry kept watch from a similar spot in the annex. Perhaps the guards would realize the significance of what he was about to try, and would be on their way to stop him as soon as he got started. Kazimi gritted his teeth, then cursed his inability to stay cool. This was a time for action, not apprehension.

Almost certainly, there was a hidden passage—a secret way out of the wing, and most likely down to the boathouse at the base of the cliff. It was time to find it and to escape.

Where to start?

As a scientist, Kazimi prided himself in his ability to work out problems. The X-factor here, of course, was not only figuring out the solution to the puzzle, but doing it without getting caught. Step one, always, observation. From large to small, broad to compact. Stay casual, look busy, and examine every bit of the lab and the annex—the stark animal containment room the guards had taken to calling the "mouse house."

Mindful he was probably being watched, Kazimi moved around the perimeter of the spacious lab, doing menial tasks as he scanned the gray mortar and fieldstone walls, as well as the concrete floor, looking for cracks, ill-fitting rocks, or any part of the construction that appeared to have been patched. It took most of an hour to make several passes, all the while continuing to prepare culture agar and growth medium.

Nothing.

His enthusiasm dampened. Sooner or later, someone would be in to check on him. Sooner or later someone would realize the repetition of his actions and speak to Bacon if, in fact, Bacon wasn't the one currently watching the monitor screens.

Don't give up became Kazimi's mantra. If he got caught, he would deal with it. But he had to keep trying.

Don't give up. . . .

On his initial tour of the wing that included the Great Room and laboratory, he wondered about the prior use of the lab space and annex. The two rooms, hastily renovated, had almost certainly served as storage areas. There were no windows in either of them, and the mouse house, perhaps fifty feet long by twenty-five wide, included a huge built-in freezer/refrigeration unit, which had certainly been around for a while. The lab, identical in length and larger in width by at least a third, had shelves fixed to the stone wall, nearly all the way around.

It was easy for him to imagine the rooms filled with pallets of canned food, cleaning supplies, paper goods, and other items needed to operate the fortress. But it made little sense to him that things were carried or wheeled along the winding access tunnel and through the Great Room only to be stored and then brought back into the main building by the same route. But it was certainly possible. If there was a trapdoor, it would have been kept clear of any major obstruction, and would have to be fairly large. That ruled out the heavy benches in the lab, the incubators, the delicate electron microscope, and the refrigeration unit in the mouse house. On his next pass, Kazimi focused on the floor, squinting to spot any section of stone that was different from the rest.

Again, nothing. No sign of a secret passage. The space was a prison . . . a tomb . . . a mausoleum.

Only one way in . . . and one way out.

A sudden scraping caused Kazimi to freeze—footsteps echoing from the Great Room. A janitor? One of the guards? He strained to pick up the tapping of

Bacon's cane on stone. Drake or Costello. It was most likely one of them. He wondered what their directive was should they catch him trying to flee. A quick snap of his neck, perhaps. It didn't matter. Ahmed Kazimi was not afraid to die.

But he did fear Janus.

The germ's startling transformation was unlike anything he had ever encountered, and was fraught with terrifying possibilities. He studied his hands and saw at least a half-dozen small cuts, a torn hangnail, and a slight scrape by the knuckle on the index finger of his left hand. They were barely slivers to his eyes, but represented a gaping portal through which Janus could march into his bloodstream and kill him horribly. Doubtless, hospitals were trying to contain the spread. It would be, he felt certain, a futile effort. In time, not much time at that, a handshake would become the equivalent of a gunshot. Although there might be no visible entry wound, the victim's organs would dissolve from the inside out.

The government had to be warned. Without a treatment, a pandemic was on the way that would make SARS and bird flu look like a summer cold. The time of an individual hospital using its isolation procedures to deal with Janus was passing quickly. The world was far too interconnected now. Every minute Kazimi stayed locked up inside Red Cliff was a minute too long.

Don't give up.

Kazimi turned his attention to making a more detailed inspection of the mouse house. If he believed in what he saw when Costello crossed the Great Room, and he believed there was nothing to be found in the lab, then the passage had to be in the annex. He passed through the doorway into the secondary structure. The plastic cages were lined up on shelves across one of the end walls and extended along half of one adjacent long wall. About half of the cages were occupied, and as they always did, the mice reacted to his arrival with a prescient step-up in activity. The large, stainless-steel refrigeration units were at the other end of the room.

Kazimi noted the areas that were almost certainly blind spots to the security camera. He stood in one of them, directly beneath the camera lens, and once again carefully surveyed the room. At first glance he saw nothing unusual. Then, after a minute or so of quiet observation, he did. It wasn't a defect in the fieldstone or shelving or floor. It was the distance from where he stood to the opposite wall. It looked shorter than the length of the lab next door. Not a lot shorter, but . . .

Keeping as far to the left of the camera as possible, Kazimi nonchalantly paced off the distance. Twenty-three strides. At approximately three feet per stride, the room was sixty-nine feet long.

Swallowing against the dryness of excitement that had materialized in his throat, Kazimi moved back into the lab and, mixing a bowl of liquid agar, casually measured the length of that room. Twenty-six strides, once, then a second time. Seventy-eight feet. The annex, which he initially had thought was identical in length to the lab, was three strides less.

Nine feet were missing.

Why would the contractor of the place cut nine feet off a room that, at first glance, looked to be exactly the same dimensions as the room adjacent to it? Perhaps rock on the other side of the wall prohibited going any farther. But that made little sense considering the whole wing—Great Room and storage areas—was hewn out of solid rock.

He peered across at the door to the Great Room. The footsteps, whoever they belonged to, had vanished. Perhaps a janitor, who had moved to the far side of the vast room.

Kazimi prayed to Allah for protection and guidance. Then he took a flashlight and, easing along a line that he hoped was beyond the angle of the camera, made his way across to the shelves of cages filling the far wall. Everything appeared normal until he dropped to his knees and shined the light under the bottom shelf, which was three inches above the floor. At the very base of the wall, there was a gap—a dark space no more than half an inch wide, but it was there, running the full length of the wall.

It took only seconds for him to reason out the most likely significance of the narrow gap. He stood and, reaching between two cages, pushed with all his strength. Grudgingly, the wall pivoted inward two inches. His heart pounding like a bucking stallion, he inched along the wall and turned off the fluorescent overheads. Then, shielding the flashlight beam, he returned to the spot between the cages and pushed once more. The pivot was precisely at the midpoint of the wall. The small opening expanded to more than a foot. He turned sideways and in an instant, he was behind the wall.

His mind visualized a single bacteria of the Janus strain, entering a body through a small cut. Like that Doomsday Germ, he was inside his target.

Now to cause some serious trouble.

The wall glided closed more smoothly than it had opened. The darkness was impenetrable. Kazimi took in a breath of musty sea air, and switched on his flashlight. A wall switch was just a few feet away. A moment later, the secret space was bathed in dim incandescent light.

Kazimi's grin was triumphant. "Don't give up," he said out loud as he illuminated a grated metal staircase, descending from the center of the narrow room. "Don't ever give up."

At the base of the first five stairs was a rectangular platform, lit from a sconce. If Red Cliff was an exact, modernized replica of a medieval German castle, then this was the escape route should the master's soldiers fail to hold the keep.

Kazimi climbed aboard the sturdy platform, flicked on his light, and peered down through the grate into what appeared to be a crudely cut vertical shaft. Then he noticed the cables . . . and the pulleys . . . and finally, the bands of corroding metal that formed a largely open cage.

He was standing in an ingeniously constructed elevator.

Sea air filled his lungs. From below, he could hear waves crashing on rock. He pictured the boathouse he had seen jutting out from the base of the cliff. That had to be what lay beneath him now. He was standing in the artery that pumped life-giving supplies up into Red Cliff from the sea.

Protruding from a strut to his right was a switch box with two unlabeled buttons. With a final glance upward, Kazimi pressed the lower of them, and instantly, the elevator rattled to life.

CHAPTER 31

Where blood has been shed for liberty and the
freedom to improve one's lot, the wound from
which it spilled will heal in time.

—LANCASTER R. HILL, *Climbing the Mountain*,
SAWYER RIVER BOOKS, 1941, P. 97

There was nothing at all friendly or engaging about the
way FBI Special Agent Tim Vaill looked across at Lou,
or made small talk as they settled in. The muscles in
his chiseled face had not once relaxed. Compared to
him, his partner McCall was mellow.

At times, the two men actually seemed to have completely separate agendas—one of them to put Lou at
ease, and the other to tighten the screws that kept his
internal organs in place.

"We were surprised to learn that you had a record,
doctor. Wanna tell us what that's all about?"

Lou asked more than once if he should be contact-
ing a lawyer, and was assured each time, by both agents,
that would not be necessary. Not once did either of
them suggest that he could feel free to do so if he
wanted, and he found himself wondering what they
would say if he insisted.

Finally breaking his stranglehold eye contact with
Lou, Vaill gave McCall a sidelong glance.

"It's a bit noisy in here, don't you think?" he said.

He returned to Lou. "What do you say we go outside and walk and talk?"

Another query from Lou about whether he should contact a lawyer. Another negative response. More of the uneasy feeling that there would be no lawyer until the agents got what they wanted.

"Before we go anywhere, what do you say you two tell me what this is all about?" Lou risked.

There was nothing about the encounter that encouraged the smart-ass side of him to leap to the fore, rapier wit at the ready. He worried about aggravating the situation, whatever the situation was, but he was equally concerned with getting back to Humphrey and the lab. It seemed pretty clear that this walk and talk with Vaill and McCall was not an offer he could easily refuse. Vaill leaned across the table, obviously not concerned with invading Lou's personal space.

"How about you ask for a check and we go outside?"

Clearly the man intended to keep his responses cryptic. While Vaill seemed ready to pounce, McCall stayed relaxed.

"I'd do what he asks," McCall suggested.

Lou studied both men. He wasn't a big TV guy, but he'd watched enough dramas with Emily to know the good cop/bad cop routine when he saw it—even when the players were as good at it as these two.

"No harm in taking a walk," Lou said with a shrug.

He signaled for a check and to speed matters up, reluctantly eschewed a credit card for most of the cash in his wallet. He headed for the door with McCall and Vaill behind him like highway tailgaters. The agents waited until they were outside to put on dark sunglasses. Lou took a moment to appraise them, and was unable to keep his mouth in check.

"Now you guys look like real FBI agents," he said, gesturing at their blue suits and shades.

There was no response. Bad sign.

"So, where are we walking to?" he asked, still more curious than frightened.

"We parked just down the road," McCall said, nodding.

"You didn't use customer parking?"

Lou wondered if they had steered clear of the lot to avoid any kind of public scene with him in case he went ballistic. He glanced at his watch. Any chance to make a meeting had just about passed.

"We needed the exercise," Vaill said.

The three started in the direction McCall had indicated. The sidewalk was wide enough for Lou to be kept sandwiched between the men. His apprehension was beginning to mushroom. Even though he had no intention of running from two almost-certainly armed FBI agents, they apparently were taking no chances.

"So what's this about?" Lou asked again, this time with a mix of anxiety and impatience.

Although he could not see their eyes behind their shades, he got the impression neither of them could care less if he were upset.

"It's about you making inquiries into a very dangerous germ," Vaill said finally, his gaze straight ahead.

Lou stopped walking.

"How'd you know about that?" he asked.

"We're with FBI," McCall said, presenting Lou a mocking grin. "It's our job to know these things."

A brief stare down ensued and Lou realized he was more at ease moving than he was standing still. He started to walk and again the agents kept pace.

"Is it a crime to ask about a bacteria?" Lou questioned, ticking through the people to whom he had even mentioned the Doomsday Germ—check-in calls to Puchalsky, hospital chief Win Carter, and surgeon Leonard Standish, as well as some nurses in the iso unit, and two people he knew in ID at Eisenhower Memorial. Then, of course, there were Samuel Scupman and Vicki Banks. "It's savaging my friend's leg. If it can't be stopped they're going to have to amputate. And his doctors will keep amputating parts of his body until the infection is either contained or my friend is dead. So that's why I was asking around."

"I'm sorry about your friend," McCall offered in a sincere tone. Lou was not surprised he'd be the one to show some sympathy. For whatever reason, Vaill kept up his menacing act, as if Lou somehow repulsed him. He felt judged guilty of some crime without even knowing the charges. Again he sensed there was something off with Vaill, as if one wrong word or a misinterpreted hand gesture would be enough to set him off. Lou reminded himself to remain calm and proceed with extreme caution. Until he knew their agenda, these agents were not to be trusted.

"So, Dr. Welcome, how is it you've come to know so much about this germ?" Vaill asked.

"I got a briefing from Cap's doctor," Lou said. "Ivan Puchalsky. He's the head of infectious disease at Arbor General."

"We know Puchalsky," Vaill said. "We spoke to him already."

"So then you know. Why are you asking me?"

McCall took out a small notebook and referenced it as they walked. "What about this thing called a . . . a bacteriophage?" he asked. "You ever talk to anybody about that?"

Lou felt his face get hot. He eliminated Puchalsky, Carter, and the nurses from his list.

"Who contacted you? Was it Sam Scupman?"

"Never mind that," Vaill said. "My partner asked you a question. You ever talk to anybody about a bacteriophage?"

Lou nodded. "I did, yes," he said. "I brought it up a few days ago as a potential idea for a treatment to Dr. Sam Scupman of the CDC's Antibiotic Resistance Unit." Both McCall and Vaill nodded as if they knew that tidbit already. "So is that why you're here? Is it a crime to try and save your friend's life these days? Don't you guys have better things to do, like fight terrorism or something?"

Vaill gripped Lou's arm tight. "I think we know best where and how to spend our time."

Lou wanted to break his arm. Instead he just pulled away.

"Sorry about that," Vaill said in a tone that was not even a little apologetic.

"What's this about, guys?" Lou asked.

McCall stopped in front of a silver Chevy Impala parked on the side of the road.

"How'd you come up with the bacteriophage theory?"

Lou's pulse quickened. He knew he had to tread carefully. One wrong slip risked exposing Humphrey. It would mean the end of the lab and quite possibly Cap's life. Somehow without Lou realizing, Vaill and

McCall positioned themselves so that his back was up against the car. They both kept their eyes locked on him.

"I'm a doctor," Lou said. "I simply suggested a potential medical treatment for my friend's condition."

Vaill said nothing. He seemed to be giving Lou a chance to change his answer.

"Yeah," Vaill said. "Well, I don't think you want to go down that road."

"What are you talking about?" Lou snapped.

"I'm talking about what we know," Vaill said. "I'm talking about information we have that you don't that says you couldn't have possibly come up with that approach on your own, unless you're a trained microbiologist. Are you a trained microbiologist, Dr. Welcome?"

"Before you answer him," McCall said, "we already know your résumé."

"We also know you just got fired from the Physician Wellness Program in D.C.," Vaill added. "You worked for Walter Filstrup."

No reference to any notes. Vaill knew this from memory.

"Why are you guys checking up on me like this?"

The agent ignored the question. "And we know about your problems with drugs and alcohol," he went on. "So we know a lot about you. But funny thing, nothing we've learned suggests that you're a trained microbiologist. So what do you say, doc? How'd you come up with this theory of yours?"

They could goad him all they liked, but Lou was not going to give up Humphrey's name.

"Agent Vaill, Agent McCall, if you guys know

so much about me, you must also know I'm a really smart guy."

McCall lowered his shades so they rested on his nostrils. "If you're really that smart, you'll tell us the truth. Where'd you get your information?"

"I did research."

"With what source?" Vaill asked.

"The Internet, at the hospital library, my friends at Eisenhower Memorial. I can be quite resourceful when I'm motivated."

Lou regretted the words the moment they tumbled out. He had smart-assed himself into a corner with claims he couldn't prove. Vaill jumped on the opportunity.

"So there are people at the hospital library who will corroborate your story?" he asked. "You have to know we can search your computer and see records of what you were looking at. In fact, I wouldn't be the least surprised if we did that anyway."

Lou did not answer, which in FBI parlance was probably tantamount to an admission of guilt.

"I'm going to ask you one more time," Vaill said. "Where did you get your information about the bacteriophage?"

"I told you. What more do you want me to say?"

Vaill grabbed Lou's shoulders, flipped him around, and jerked his arms up behind his back.

"Hey!" Lou shouted. "What in the hell are you doing? You can't do this. I have rights!"

He felt the pinch of handcuffs being snapped into place.

"Dr. Welcome," Vaill said, "you're under arrest."

"What's the charge?"

Lou's demand came out rife with indignation but his voice was also more than a little shaky. The cuffs were incredibly uncomfortable, and in moments his arms began to throb. He tried to reposition his wrists, but the slightest movement caused the manacles to tighten even more.

"I have rights!" he protested. "I want to speak to a lawyer. I'm not telling you anything more until I do. You can't just take me in like this. Jerks! I haven't committed any crime."

Vaill turned Lou around to face him. His smile was scornful and smug, as if this was the best part of his job.

McCall opened the Impala's rear door, and with some difficulty, the two men stuffed Lou into the backseat.

"When it comes to terrorism," Vaill said, "the law has a lot of latitude regarding who we take into custody and how we do it. And as for rights, thanks to your unwillingness to cooperate, and Miranda's public safety exception, I'm sorry to inform you that you don't have any at all."

CHAPTER 32

Social/Political philosopher Lancaster Hill's
growing popularity should be a source of
concern to us all.

—DAVID CARP, *New York Times* Op-Ed,
MAY 8, 1940

The elevator ride to the bottom of the granite shaft took
Kazimi no more than thirty seconds. The platform
shuddered and shimmied. Machinery, corroded from
the salt air and water, groaned. With each passing foot,
the sound of waves grew louder. Faint natural light
filtered up through the elevator's grated platform, and
the complex smells of the ocean grew more pronounced.
The eerie descent ended with the locking of gears and a
jolting stop.

Kazimi peered upward. He saw the lights embedded
in the walls and nothing more. There was no trace of
the stairway on which he had entered the shaft. Still,
he had to hurry. It was only a matter of time before
Bacon's thugs came looking for him. Kazimi exited the
platform and followed a wooden walkway out an opening carved through the cliff face. Twenty feet down
the narrow dock he entered the boathouse. There he
paused, savoring the wind on his face, and breathing
in the heavy salt air.

Freedom!

A few feet more and the dock widened to form the floor of a storage area—marine supplies, engine parts, oil and gas cans, life jackets, ropes, bumpers. Not unexpectedly, the construction was first-rate—hardwood walls, beamed ceiling, four good-sized windows. The dock continued as two extensions, one along each wall. At the center of the construction, bobbing on its moorings like a glistening mahogany torpedo, was the boat.

It was a stunning inboard—a Chris-Craft, long and sleek, with foldaway seats that increased its transport area.

Please, let there be a key. Please . . .

The boat looked as if it were ready to speed off just by willing it so, but that simply wasn't going to happen. Nothing in the ignition.

Please . . .

Kazimi hurried back to the shelves, and quickly scanned them and the walls for any kind of a key hook or holder.

Nothing.

He returned to the cockpit, pausing to listen for any sounds from back beyond the storage area. Then he loosened the dashboard cover and searched for a way to cross wire the ignition. The computer that controlled the speedboat's functions looked as complicated as the ones he worked with in the lab.

Rarely an impatient or easily frustrated man, Kazimi cursed his situation and his limitations. There was a single paddle on the floor. Untying the boat and trying to row it out to sea was a possibility. But the afternoon was giving way to dusk, and the gray, choppy, uninviting ocean was frigid. To make matters worse, the brisk wind was onshore. In all likelihood, if he could even get the heavy inboard boat past its boathouse, it would end up wrecked at the base of the mammoth cliff.

His odds of making it away from Red Cliff, he decided, were considerably better on land. He scrambled off the magnificent craft, carefully stepped around the edge of the boathouse, and jumped to the rocky shoreline. To his left, the cliff face rose almost straight up, like a massive arcade climbing wall. Between its base and the lapping waves were five feet of sand, pebbles, and stones.

The wind and salt air stung Kazimi's lips as he made his way along the treacherous shoreline, slipping on seaweed-covered rocks. When he fell, he pushed himself up and plunged ahead. When he got hurt, he ignored it. His plan was simply to keep going. Sooner or later he would have to come to a trail that would cut up away from the water. For a few moments he considered trying to scale the cliff wall itself, but for years his exercise had consisted solely of half-hour walks around the streets of D.C. once or twice a day. A climb like this one, challenging for an expert, just wasn't going to happen.

One foot . . . the other. Again . . . Again.

The going was painfully slow, and now he had another concern—another enemy. The width of his treacherous and narrow escape trail was shrinking. The tide was coming in. He estimated he had traveled maybe two hundred yards, perhaps a little more. The trail was now half the width it had been when he started. To his left, the cliff was just as sheer. The wind was noticeably picking up, and the thin outfit he had worn to the lab was not fending off the chill. With every step, the taste of his newfound freedom was becoming more bitter.

It was at that moment, with the late-afternoon shadows moving across the water, that Kazimi thought he saw movement on the rocks well ahead. He tensed, uncertain if the vision was a seabird, a person, or his imagination. If it was one of Bacon's massive bodyguards, there was nothing he could do except try to escape the way he had come—this time sloshing through deepening water all the way.

A few more tentative steps, and he could make out a figure, standing on top of a large boulder. The figure, really a silhouette in the deepening shadows, was waving to him with both hands. Thankfully, it became quickly apparent that the man—for it almost certainly was a man—was tall and lean, not at all like either Drake or Costello.

Slipping on rocks and wading in the cold seawater, Kazimi waved back and quickened his pace. Allah had heard his prayers and answered them. Whoever this man was, he would know of a passageway along the rocks that could bring him to the top of the cliff. The Janus strain was going to be the next great plague unless Kazimi could warn the government to abandon all pretense of secrecy and to put as concerted an effort into stopping Janus as it had the AIDS virus. Hopefully, there was still time to stop it from happening.

"Hello!" Kazimi cried out. "I need help! Help me, please!"

His words were swallowed by the wind and the building sea.

Racing ahead, he stumbled, lost his footing, and fell heavily onto a wet, barnacle-covered rock, slicing his palms and knees like a nest of razors. He cried out at the pain, but it was of no matter. Whatever the price of escape, he would pay it. In seconds he was up and shambling ahead as best he could, peering through the gloom at his savior, mussel shells crunching beneath his feet. The man ahead remained motionless except for his arms, which continued to wave rhythmically back and forth.

As the distance between Kazimi and the man narrowed, he slowed his pace. The fellow's features were coming into focus. There was something familiar about him—something about his narrow face and corn-colored hair.

Burke!

It was far too late for Kazimi to turn and run now. The killer, dressed in a navy blue sweat suit with white stripes running down the sleeves, casually slid a pistol from a shoulder holster, and trained the weapon on him.

"From this distance I can shoot you in plenty of places that would be terribly painful, but won't keep you from working," he called out.

Kazimi kept his distance, so Burke, wearing high-cuts, jumped nimbly from his boulder and closed the gap between them until just a few feet remained.

"Did you really think we'd just let you walk away?" he asked.

"How long have you been watching me?"

"The whole time," Burke said. Kazimi could hear the breezy pride in his voice and it disgusted him. "We had cameras on you, but Bacon wanted to see if you'd figure it out. Maybe he was starting to think you weren't as smart as you were advertised to be. You passed that

test. Now you get to pass another one. If you don't follow me back to Red Cliff, the tide is going to come in,
and soon you'll be swimming in sixty-degree ocean
water."

"Then it would be Allah's wish," Kazimi said.

Burke dismissed that notion with a wave of his
pistol.

"No, it would be *your* wish—your death wish. But
my wish, no, make that my orders, are to bring you
back to your lab. You've got work to do."

"I will do no such thing. I'm finished."

Burke did not look surprised. "Bacon told me you'd
say something like that." From a pocket in his sweat-
pants, he retrieved a cell phone and held it up for
Kazimi to see.

"I've got a number here on speed dial," he said. "It
will call an associate of ours in California. He's been
stalking a former graduate assistant of yours, Dr. Amy
Gaspar. Do you remember Amy? She's a pretty girl
with brown hair and a really sweet smile."

"Please," Kazimi said, holding up his hands, im-
ploring Burke to be merciful. "There is no need to
hurt her."

"One call," Burke said, shaking the phone, "and it's
bye-bye, Amy. Nothing as quick as a bullet, though. We
decided on hanging."

"What do you want?"

"I told you. I want you to go back to Red Cliff and
stop trying to escape. We have no patience for this
nonsense."

"Listen to me," Kazimi said. "Bacon does not understand what is at risk here. The Janus germ has mutated. He has lost control of it. The result will be a new

plague, worse than polio, worse than smallpox, worse than AIDS. Millions of people will be eaten alive from the inside out."

Kazimi turned toward the sea. In the distance a large tanker was churning north through the gray water.

"Thinking of trying to swim to that boat?" Burke asked. "You'll freeze before you get fifty yards." As if to emphasize that point, a sudden gust of wind kicked up, whipping their hair about. "You'd be far better off returning to Red Cliff with me."

Kazimi sank to his knees, ignoring the rush of pain caused by barnacles digging into his skin.

"Please," he said, his hands clasped together. "Please just let me go. You don't understand what is at stake."

"Go back and do your work," Burke said, holding up the cell phone and speaking as if he were dealing with a schoolchild. "It'll be easier for everyone involved."

Kazimi looked up at the man fiercely.

"I can't succeed," he rasped.

"Repeat that?"

"You heard me. My theories were misguided. I was wrong. The Janus strain has beaten me. If I am indeed smart, then it is smarter—far smarter. As things stand, my efforts will continue not to succeed, and Janus will do what it will do."

"I've heard enough, doctor." Again he brandished the phone. "And believe me, Amy Gaspar is not the only one you care about who will die."

"Burke, you can talk about death all you want. This is all about death. Do you wish to see my mice? Do you want to see for yourself what will happen to your wife if she were to become infected with Janus? You must let me go. You must help me get away from here so I can warn the president."

"I said enough! In another minute I will make the call, and Dr. Gaspar will hang and it will have been your fault. We want you to succeed at what you're do-ing here, Dr. Kazimi. What is it you need to make that happen? More equipment? More money? We will get it for you, whatever it is."

"I need a miracle," Kazimi said.

"I've got news for you, pal. *You* are the miracle. Now, tell me what you need."

Kazimi again looked toward the sea. The ship was just vanishing in the distance, leaving a blanket of dark clouds in its wake.

I've got news for you, pal. *You* are the miracle.

"I need someone's help," Kazimi suddenly heard himself saying.

"Bacon has already offered you our best scientists," Burke replied. "We'll get them here ASAP."

"No," Kazimi said, shaking his head vehemently. "I don't need your scientists. I need one of mine."

"A name. Just give me a name."

"His name is Humphrey Miller."

CHAPTER 33

Benefits for those deemed less fortunate are organic. They spawn a feast of greed and corruption. Civil War pensions, for example, seemed a moral right, until they sprung a cottage industry of unscrupulous lawyers whose sole purpose was defrauding the federal government by securing pensions for those who had not earned them.

——LANCASTER R. HILL, *Climbing the Mountain*,
SAWYER RIVER BOOKS, 1941, P. 33

The FBI field office in Atlanta was a featureless, twelve-story office building nestled within a corporate industrial complex and approached via a series of wide, tree-lined streets. Vaill drove them around back to a controlled-access parking area, protected with chain-link fence, topped by barbed wire, and guarded by two armed men. Lou had multiple run-ins with the law during his drug-using days. None was pleasant, and every one made him feel as he did at that moment—like a hardened criminal. Vaill flashed the guards his credentials and the chain-link gate glided opened.

"What's up with the barbed wire?" Lou asked. "I'm not going anywhere."

"Nice to know," McCall said. "But just in case you decide otherwise, there's no place you *can* go."

The pit in Lou's gut widened.

Vaill drove to a single-story redbrick outbuilding at

the rear of the enclosure, and parked the sedan next to a large van with multiple antennae and satellite dishes on the roof. There were signs for an electronics repair shop, and the bay doors of an automotive repair facility. The two agents escorted him into the building by way of a side door and down a hallway to a small room with a drop ceiling and bile-yellow walls. Recessed fluorescent lighting reflected harshly off the white linoleum floor.

"Welcome to wonderland," Vaill said with no humor. "This is the booking room."

The space was no more than twelve feet to the back wall, where an electronic kiosk and a camera were set up for photographs and fingerprinting. Vaill and McCall bypassed the area and led Lou to a small alcove where they deposited their weapons into a metal lockbox.

"From booking to detention," McCall said.

"So does this mean you're going to uncuff me?"

"Just follow the white rabbit. You're expected in the interview room."

"Expected by whom?"

"Well, by us, of course."

"In that case, you mean interrogation room, don't you?"

Vaill returned a pleased-with-himself grin that gave Lou the shivers.

"Whatever works for you," he said.

The interview room was even smaller than the booking room, with a table, three chairs, a box of Kleenex, three small plastic bottles of water, and not much else. There was a wall-mounted camera in one corner that provided a feed to a monitor on the other side of the door.

"You're never alone in wonderland," Vaill said, gesturing up to it.

The tight quarters, intense lighting, spartan furnishings, lingering body odors, and incompetent air circulation enhanced Lou's sense of powerlessness. No doubt the setup was by design. *Nice job.*

"This is all useless," he said. "I don't know anything."

Vaill, his face brooding and eyes unkind, forced him into a seat at the table, and roughly undid his handcuffs. Lou tried to get the blood flowing again by rubbing at the deep creases persisting on his aching wrists. His chair was slat-backed wood with a flat seat and no cushioning. *Uncomfortable* wouldn't have done it credit.

Intimidate . . . terrify . . . control . . .

"Are you doing all right, doctor?" McCall asked.

Only then did Lou realize he was hyperventilating.

"No, I'm not doing all right. You guys are messing with me and I don't like it, and I want to know what I'm doing here."

The men sat down opposite him, their expressions disinterested.

"Look," Vaill began. "We don't want to do this dance. We're on your side here. We want to help you out. But for us to help you, you've first got to help us."

"How's your buddy Duncan doing?" McCall asked. "You call him Cap, right?"

The statement was a warning. They knew things and could catch him in a lie.

"I wouldn't know," Lou said. "I'm here and not with him like I should be."

"You two were running in the mountains when he fell. You do a lot of that trail running?"

They had to have seen Cap's medical record. So much for HIPAA and patient confidentiality.

On absolute red alert, Lou merely nodded.

"I've been thinking about trying trail running myself," McCall went on. "It's a good workout, huh?"

"Go ask Cap," Lou said. "Look, is this part where you guys act nice to me? We develop a rapport and I cave in? I've seen enough cop shows to know this act. Well, it's not going to work. First of all, I don't know anything that would be of interest to you. Second of all, I haven't done anything wrong, and I don't belong here. Give me a phone and let me call a lawyer."

"Where are you staying in Atlanta?" McCall asked.

Lou gave them the name of a hotel, but said he did not know the address.

"When did you get here?"

"You mean this time? Five days ago."

These two were clearly empowered to trample on civil rights if it suited their purpose.

"You right-handed or left?" Vaill asked.

"What has that got to do with anything? Okay, okay. I'm right. Now, what in the hell is this all about?"

Vaill and McCall were looking intently at his eyes. Suddenly Lou recalled a book he had read on neurophysiology that included a section on using eye movements to separate truth from lies. According to the authors, if a subject were stating a fact, his eyes tended to drift or flick to the right. If he were making up a story, it was more likely for them to move left, unless they were left-handed, in which case the telltale movements were reversed. The question about his hand preference strongly suggested Vaill and McCall were aware of that tidbit—probably from interrogation 101 in agent school. Now, by asking simple, easy-to-answer questions, they were establishing a baseline by which they could judge Lou's physical response to telling the truth.

He sensed, correctly, that the softball questions were about to end.

"Did someone give you the bacteriophage theory?" Vaill asked.

Jesus!

For a few seconds Lou couldn't breathe. Who in the hell were these guys? He half expected them to begin asking about Arlene Silver, his fourth-grade girlfriend.

"I came up with it myself," he said as quickly and evenly as he could.

Humphrey! They have to be after him.

He tried to control his eye movements, but suspected he hadn't succeeded.

Meanwhile, McCall's expression gave Lou the feeling that this was his favorite part of the job.

"You're going to stop lying to us, doctor," the agent said. "Believe me, it's not the right way to go."

"We know you didn't come up with this phage theory on your own," Vaill added. "Where did you get your information?"

He spoke in an even, unflappable voice—the kind Lou used whenever he needed to calm an especially nervous patient. Lou had the sense that, like an ultra marathoner who could run hours on end without tiring,

Vaill could do the same when it came to interrogating a suspect.

The older agent got up from his chair and came around to Lou's side of the table. The stuffy, staged discomfort of the little room was becoming increasingly effective. Sweat was running down Lou's spine. He knew what they were after now.

"Do you want to know what we think?" McCall said.

"Not really," Lou answered.

"We think you guys are in a pickle. You've created a monster with this germ, but for whatever reason, you've lost control of it. So, now you've got all your smart medical guys tasked with developing a treatment before this nasty bug really breaks out."

"What do you mean 'you guys'?" Lou asked, all at once genuinely curious.

"Hey, we're doing the talking!" Vaill snapped. "You'll get your chance soon enough."

"We don't know how you got recruited into One Hundred Neighbors," McCall went on, "but I promise sooner or later you're going to tell us."

"How long have you and your terrorist pals been working nonstop on this?" Vaill asked. "Turning over every rock, vetting every possible theory, looking for a cure because, without it, you've got no leverage. You're just a bunch of murderers. Mass murderers at that."

One Hundred Neighbors . . . Terrorists . . . Murderers . . .

Lou searched the men's faces for any sign he was being toyed with and found none. He felt as if he had stumbled into quicksand, and his legs were no longer

capable of pushing himself out. Where in the hell had
they gotten their information? Dead-on with their information one minute, coming from Mars the next.

"I'm not part of any terrorist organization," he insisted.

"Of course you are," Vaill said. "We have proof."

"What proof?" Lou was outraged now. "You're
making up stuff just to rattle me."

"Are we?" McCall asked.

At that instant the realization hit. *They're going to
hold me indefinitely.*

Everyone had heard of suspected terrorists being
kept without ever being charged—kept and eventually
waterboarded. From his conversations with Humphrey,
Lou knew there was some sort of terrorist connection
to the germ, but even Humphrey did not know exactly
what it was. To give these guys even that much information would eventually lead them to Humphrey—
probably at Lou's bodily expense. For now at least, he
vowed to maintain ignorance . . . at least as long as he
could.

"Do you know a group called One Hundred Neighbors?" McCall asked.

"Never heard of them."

"You're lying," Vaill said. "You're part of them."

"What about a scientist named Ahmed Kazimi, do
you know him?"

"No," Lou said again, wincing because he was sure
his eyes had darted left. Vaill definitely noticed.

"You and your crazy group are bent on destroying
America, aren't you?" McCall said.

"No! No!" Lou shouted. "I would never do that. I
love this country."

Vaill stood again and came around the table.

"Now we're getting somewhere," he said, his voice turning softer. "That's good, that's real good, Lou. You love this country. You didn't mean to create this plague. It just got out of control. You're trying to set things right by coming up with a workable treatment."

Lou was feeling flustered and a little unsure of himself. He had no trouble imagining this line of questioning going on for hours, circling back to his prior statements as he became more exhausted by the second. He had no doubt that given enough time, coupled with hunger and lack of sleep, it was possible they would extract some sort of a confession.

"I know about your group's motives," McCall said. "I've read up on them. You did this for the love of your country. You think you're doing us Americans a huge favor."

"Nah," Vaill said. "I think this guy is doing it for the power. Do you get off on what you're doing?"

"I'm an American citizen just like you," Lou countered. "I have rights."

"We discussed that already," McCall said. "We've slapped you with the public safety exception to the Miranda Act. You know what that is?"

"Miranda? I think so."

"Being a smart-ass doesn't suit you, doctor. The public safety exception is for terrorists like you. It means you got very few rights in this situation because we say so. Got that?"

"Then think of me like a journalist. They have the right to protect their sources."

"So you're admitting there *is* a source."

Lou cringed.

"I'm admitting nothing. I'm just saying that if I had a source I would have the right to protect it."

Vaill shook his head. "A shield law? Really? That's the best you can come up with? Sorry, pal, but last I checked, the federal government hasn't enacted any shield laws, so how about you try again. Who's your source?"

"Whoever put you on this track missed," Lou said.

The small room felt like a sauna.

"It's evident to me," Vaill said, "that you don't understand how serious this situation is. Our country—the country you purport to love—is under attack, and you have information critical to our national security. Okay? Is that being clear enough for you?"

Lou decided not to answer.

"It's sure clear to me," McCall said.

"Do you know what sort of charges you're facing?" Vaill asked.

"I haven't committed any crime! I'm doing research to help my dying friend."

Vaill ignored him. "We're talking major conspiracy charges here," he said. "Conspiracy to commit offense against the United States will get you five years and some hefty fines, but, material support to a known terrorist group, that's another charge you're facing and that could get you fifteen plus."

"Not if someone dies," McCall interjected.

Vaill nodded appreciatively. "Oh yeah, thanks. You're right. If someone dies then you could be locked up for the rest of your life. But don't worry. I'm sure you can get posted in the prison infirmary—at least until the guys realize they won't let you handle any drugs. Then there'll be no one to protect you."

"This is crazy. I'm not a terrorist."

"You *are* in your government's eyes. Now, who's your source?" Again, Lou said nothing. "You don't have the right to remain silent," Vaill went on. "You have the right to be charged for a very serious set of crimes. So I'll ask again. Who is your source?"

"Think about your daughter," McCall said.

Lou's eyes sparked. Vaill was locked on him.

"Emily. That's her name, right?" he said as if congratulating himself for remembering. "Look, Lou, do you think she wants her daddy put on trial as a terrorist? Doctor by day, mass murderer by night. What press." He dramatized the headline in the stale air. "That's a terrible thing for a kid to go through."

"She'd be bullied something awful," McCall chimed in. "I mean the worst."

"Probably have to drop out of school." Vaill's turn.

"It would most likely ruin her life. You guys are close, right?"

"Keep my daughter out of this!" The back of Lou's neck was on fire. This whole tact was a ploy, a charade, but it still stung like a swarm of hornets.

"You see, that's the problem, Lou." Vaill again. "She would be like collateral damage. There's no keeping her out of it unless you start talking. Everybody you love, everybody you care about. They're all going to be questioned. This business is at the head of the government's to-do list—our list of priorities. We're going to bring on more manpower to turn over every single stone in the life of every one of them. We'll dig into their pasts as hard as we're digging into yours."

The agents continued with skill and teamwork.

McCall took over. "Your pal, Cap," he said. "How

is he on his taxes? If he survives this germ, you think he'll still have a gym to work out of when we're through? And what about your ex, Renee? And her husband, Steve? Do they have any little skeletons in their closet they wouldn't want the FBI to know about? That law firm of his doesn't seem like the kind that would tolerate the agency nosing around. You really want to bring all this down on the people you love the most, Lou?"

"People have died, Welcome," Vaill said, his voice up half an octave and louder by several decibels, "and until we get something good from you, as far as we're concerned, you pulled the fucking trigger."

Lou noticed a legitimate, pained look cross the man's face, and recalled how Vaill's agenda seemed to differ from McCall's when they first accosted him at the Blue Ox Tavern.

"Did someone you love get killed around this?" he asked. "Is that why you're being so hard on me?"

"Shut up," Vaill snapped.

Lou continued to press. "Was it your daughter? A son? A wife, perhaps?"

In an explosive burst of movement, Vaill seized Lou by the shirt. Lou was ten or fifteen pounds heavier, but adrenaline took care of that. With a powerful jerk, Vaill yanked him out of his chair. McCall rushed around to pry his partner's fingers open. Vaill slumped back and dropped into his chair, breathing heavily, his eyes daggers.

"Okay," McCall said. "We're going to start this dance all over again. Where did you get your information?"

CHAPTER 34

When the cause is right and just, victory is
inevitable.

—LANCASTER R. HILL, *100 Neighbors*, SAWYER
RIVER BOOKS, 1939, P. 161

Jennifer Lowe knew that she was going to die.

Not die someday, but die soon.

It was her fifth day in the isolation unit, only this
time it was as the patient, not the nurse. She remembered one of her favorite instructors in nursing school
saying that the best shortcut to being a better nurse was
to be a patient. This hospitalization was definitely one
of those shortcuts, except that the chance she would
ever get to becoming a better nurse was remote. The
sheets had become sandpaper, the meals contained
nothing she wanted to eat, the time-consuming isolation procedures made it almost impossible to have her
bodily needs met in any timely fashion even though her
caregivers were all her friends and terrific at their jobs.
And her left arm—swollen and throbbing—felt as if it
were to fall off, which, one way or another, it almost certainly was going to do.

Even the wonderful view of Boston's skyline was becoming tiresome.

From as far back as she could remember, Jennifer

had always been a positive person. When she first encountered a hospital nurse during her admission for a ruptured appendix, she knew in her heart that she was going to become one, herself—not just a nurse, she decided as she learned more about the profession, but a nurse in a physiologically demanding part of the hospital like the operating room or the ICU.

As it turned out, she fell in love with respiratory physiology and had ended up first working in White Memorial's medical ICU, and then in the hospital's new isolation unit. Now, irony of ironies, she was going to die in that very unit—there, or in the operating room like Becca Seabury.

It was crazy. Absolutely crazy. She was young and healthy. She had done absolutely nothing wrong. She was a spiritual person with a deep belief in God, and a commitment to helping those less fortunate than she was. And yet, as things were unfolding, hope was vanishing by the hour.

She tried to shift the position of her arm, which was now the size of a torpedo, but burning, neuritic pain, and swelling from fingers to shoulder prevented her from doing so. Instead, she pressed the button signaling her intravenous infusion pump to send down some more morphine through her peripherally inserted central IV catheter—her PICC line. It was always a surprise to find out she hadn't yet called for the maximum narcotic the machine would allow. Well, dammit, she deserved the relief.

Jennifer knew she was in trouble just a day after the tragic death of her patient and friend Becca. The cheerleader had gone from a fairly straightforward elbow fracture to a wound infection with a virtually untreatable bacteria, labeled the Doomsday Germ by the press, to the amputation of her arm, to the spread of infection to her other limbs and her heart, and finally, to a fatal cardiac arrest on the operating room table.

That was precisely what Jennifer believed was in store for her.

Looking back now, she knew the Doomsday Germ had already entered her body by the time she stood on a riser in the operating room and witnessed the final chaotic, violent minutes of beautiful Becca's life. The bacteria—possibly even a single germ, the ID people had told her—had gotten in through an odd little patch of eczema, or a small scrape on her hand, or maybe— irony of ironies—through a scratch caused by taking her engagement diamond on and off for work.

The ring represented Andy Gulli, her fiancé, and Andy represented the answer to her prayers. Handsome, athletic, bright, funny, and caring, he would have been the answer for most girls.

The IV beeped the new infusion of pain medicine and in seconds a reassuring warm pressure settled in her chest. The terrible aching began to abate—not vanish, it never fully did, but at least lessen. She smiled to herself as Andy's reassuring voice made its way through the haze in her mind. It wasn't really him, but it was certainly the best part of the morphine.

"Jenn? . . . Baby?"

I'm dying, Andy. Come and hold me and keep me from dying.

"Jenn? . . . Can you hear me?"

He was there—really there, gowned and gloved, hair covered and masked and shoes covered. She opened her eyes and blearily saw him standing there, looking like an alien. Had she kissed him for the last time?

"I thought you were in a dream," she said.

"It's the morphine. I had some when I had my knee rebuilt. There were times when I considered purposely tearing up the other knee so I could get more. I went into PT instead, and swore off basketball. How's the arm?"

"On a scale of three, proportional to the number of antibiotics I'm on currently, that would be three. I love you, Andy."

"I love you, too, baby."

"Still want to marry me?"

"Of course I want to marry you. More than ever."

"Even if I only have one arm or no arms, or no arms and no legs?"

"That's not funny."

"I'm sorry. I'm just scared. These people are the best doctors in the world and they don't seem to have any idea what to do. And this arm keeps getting more swollen and more painful. Tomorrow they're going to have to slit open the skin all the way from my armpit to my fingertips just to keep the pressure of the swelling from killing the muscles and nerves."

"I'll check with the nurses and find out what time, and I'll be with you when they do the procedure. Be strong."

"It's Becca. I can't get her out of my mind."

"That's understandable."

"Sometimes I can actually hear her calling me to come and be with her."

"That's just the meds and the pain, honey. You're going to be all right."

He didn't believe it. She could hear it in his voice. He didn't believe it for a second.

"Andy?"

"Yes, honey?"

"Want to know the worst thing?"

"What's that?"

"As fast as I'm losing my arm, I'm losing my faith faster."

CHAPTER 35

The Social Security Act disembodies us from our pioneering spirit, the very foundation of America, and it shall lead, in no uncertain terms, to new social insurance programs, which ultimately will bankrupt the country sure as the sun shall rise.

—LANCASTER R. HILL, PERSONAL
CORRESPONDENCE TO NICOLE SMITH,
JUNE 1936

Seven hours.

Lou remained firm, but he was fading. Each of those four-hundred-and-twenty minutes was taking a toll on his muscles and joints, as well as on his spirit. The only redeeming feature of the grueling interrogation was that the two agents—especially Tim Vaill—also seemed to be wearing down.

Lou's primary advantage, he decided, was years on the graveyard shift, immersed in the sort of pressure that only an inner-city ER could bring. Throughout the grilling, he kept to his story, more or less improvised on the fly. He was doing research on his best friend's situation, for which he felt partially responsible. He wanted to validate something he had read, and so reconnected with Drs. Scupman and Banks, whom he had met several weeks before on a tour of their facility at the CDC. Vicki Banks had suggested meeting for a drink a couple of days later at the Blue Ox Tavern, and that was when the men in shades had shown up.

Because of the dire situation with his best friend, Lou had considered an alcoholic drink, but ultimately had ended up with a Diet Coke.

Keep it consistent. Keep it simple.

More than once during the interrogation, Lou had asked to make a phone call. Each time his request was denied. Fortunately, he had been granted a couple of bathroom breaks.

His rights, simply put, were that he had the right to be kept in this room for as long as his captors were not satisfied with his responses.

Whose law was that again?

Once, when Lou's eyes closed and his head began lolling to one side, Chuck McCall got him a protein bar, a plastic bottle of Gatorade, and a cup of coffee from a vending machine. Other than those brief men's room breaks, he remained imprisoned in a space not much bigger than the examining rooms at Eisenhower Memorial.

No rights . . . no freedom . . . no letup . . . no way out . . .

As they were entering the eighth hour, Vaill whispered something to McCall. Moments later, in the first real letup in their grueling routine, the younger agent rose and left the room.

"Let me guess," Lou said. "You guys are union, and he's going back to the hotel, right?"

"Not funny. You think we like doing this?"

"You don't really want me to answer that."

Lou's voice was weaker than he had expected. A gulp of his Gatorade made no difference.

"He's getting something to show you."

"Do you mind if I stand? My legs are going numb again."

"Just back away from the chair and keep your hands where I can see them."

"Illegally held prisoner makes daring escape using child's desk chair as weapon. I like it."

"A smart aleck to the end."

Not *smart-ass,* Lou noted. *Significant?* He also sensed that Vaill's demeanor and expression might have softened a bit.

Lou rose unsteadily and backed away from the chair, hands raised. Vaill remained seated. Lou was now in something of a power position, standing tall, facing his antagonist. The agent leaned back, a distant look in his eyes. Lou had the impression that for the first time since the questioning began, the man wasn't locked on him.

"When we first started our conversation," Vaill said, "you asked about my wife."

"As I recall, when I did that you tried to strangle me."

"Believe me, doc, when I want to strangle someone, they get strangled."

More softening . . . Was it just fatigue?

Vaill leaned forward, elbows on the table, and for an uncomfortable minute gazed off at nothing. When his attention returned, Lou sensed that whatever was to follow would be from the heart.

"My wife's name was Maria," Vaill began. "She was with the agency like me, and she was and will be the only woman I have ever loved. Alexander Burke, a mole working for One Hundred Neighbors—actually, he was probably one of them—shot her between the eyes from seven feet while he was kidnapping Ahmed Kazimi. She was dead before her knees even started to buckle. She and I were on duty together at the time, so I watched her die. After he took out Maria, Burke shot me twice. I was falling backward down a flight of stairs and had my vest on, or he would have hit what he was aiming for—heart and head. The head shot missed being lethal by like an inch. The bullet ended up between my skull and brain and was removed. His mistake."

Vaill gestured to a thick, recent scar arcing above his right ear.

As much as Lou despised the man, he could not dismiss his genuine heartache for what he had been through. All along, Lou had sensed that Vaill's agenda had differed from McCall's. This was not just about investigating a terrorist threat for him—it was personal. Highly personal.

"I'm really sorry," Lou said. "But I honestly had nothing to do with your wife's murder."

"Look, I'm not saying you're one of them."

"So you do believe me?"

"I'm just trying to get at the truth," Vaill said, rubbing his eyes.

"And *I'm* just trying to save my friend's life."

It was apparently the right thing to have said. Vaill's expression reminded Lou of men he had sparred against to a draw, including Cap on those rare days when the difference in their ages caught up with him. There was an exhausted, grudging admiration. Lou sat back down when he realized he was bouncing on the balls of his feet, getting revved up for another round.

"Let me ask you another way, Vaill," he said. "You don't honestly think I'm a terrorist, do you?"

"Believe it or not, I'm trying to keep you out of jail. But I do think you're holding out on me. This isn't your war, Lou. It's ours. You've got to give us the ammunition you're holding back so we can fight it."

McCall returned at that moment with a thin manila folder, which he set down on the center of the table. Lou reached for it, but Vaill set his hand there first.

"Before I let you open this," he said, "let me tell you what happens from here. We're going to transfer you to the U.S. Marshal's holding facility. You'll still be the responsibility of the FBI until we get you in front of a U.S. magistrate at the district courthouse. When that happens will depend on when we decide we've had enough of you. At court, you'll be officially charged with conspiracy and material support to a known terrorist group. At that point our job is done. You'll be assigned a lawyer and the U.S. government will sic their most vicious doggies on investigating every moment of your life, and on getting you convicted."

"Why are you telling me this?"

Vaill glanced down at the folder. But in that instant, Lou saw a strange, bewildered look in his eyes. He was squinting as if the lights in the ceiling were painful for him. McCall, standing behind his partner, seemed unaware anything unusual was happening. Vaill tentatively drew his hand away. He looked dazed.

What in the hell is going on with him? Lou wondered.

The man, self-assured and confident throughout the entire night, was in serious pain. Lou felt the physician part of him kicking in. Something bad was going on.

Vaill's eyes closed tightly, and he began to squeeze his temples.

A stroke? Lou wondered. Some sort of hemorrhage? An expanding aneurysm?

"Vaill," he asked. "Are you okay? Hey, McCall, something's going on with your partner. Maybe a migraine. Maybe something worse."

"I'm okay," Vaill said in a near mumble, squinting against what seemed like unbearable pain. "I'll be right back. Chuck, keep an eye on him."

McCall was still not in a position to see how un-okay the man was at that moment. His eyes tearing, Vaill stood, knocking his chair over backward, and more or less staggered from the room.

"He gets migraines," McCall said.

"They usually come on slower than what I saw, and give some sort of warning."

"He'll be fine."

"This wasn't a typical migraine. Let me check him out. I promise I won't try to take off. You can come."

McCall looked bewildered.

"Just stay right there," he said. "Vaill gets these."

After five minutes, McCall dialed his cell, leaving it on speaker.

Vaill picked up after six rings.

"I'm okay," he snapped. Then he hung up.

Five more minutes passed, then another five.

"All right," McCall said. "Let's go and—"

The door slammed open and Vaill entered, still somewhat unsteady. His eyes were bloodshot, and the odor surrounding him said he had gotten sick.

"Sorry," he muttered. "I'm fine. Let's get on with this."

"You sure?" McCall asked.

For a moment, Lou sensed the older agent was about to explode. Instead Vaill breathed in deeply through his nose, apologized again, and took a swig of Gatorade.

"Let's get on with this."

Lou looked for any signs suggesting a stroke, but clearly the man was improving. Vaill slid the folder over to him, and Lou, shrugging, opened it.

It contained a picture of Emily, extracted from her Facebook page, showing her with her two best girl-friends, both of whom Lou knew well. It was taken outside of Carlton Academy, with the girls' arms draped around one another.

"What is this all about?" he exclaimed, pushing the sheet away as if it were on fire. The odd, distant look on Vaill's face had now vanished, and it was as if the strange episode had never happened.

"It's what you have at stake here, Lou," he said.

"Why are you showing this to me? How dare you bring my daughter into this cesspool?"

"You don't get it, do you?" Vaill said, on his feet once more. "Your daughter is a very big part of this. Listen to me, Lou. You're facing some serious charges here. Chances are you'll go away for a long time. Don't do this to your kid. Think about it. We're not your enemy. I told you about my wife. I was honest with you because I care. But we've got a job to do, and dammit, we're gonna do it. So study that picture. My wife is dead, this girl is very much alive. You don't want to ruin her life or humiliate her. You want to be around to take her to a ball game, go visit colleges, or whatever else lies ahead. And you'll be able to do those things, too—but only if you cooperate. Give me a name.

Where did you get the information about the bacterio-phage?"

Lou stared at Emily's image and touched it with his fingertip. He imagined only seeing her through the Plexiglas of some federal prison visitor's room. Every-one knew of injustices done to innocent men and women by the vagaries or intentions of the government. He also knew that Humphrey would be useless with-out his help, and Cap would suffer as a result. Could he simply make up a name?

No chance.

How long would he be in prison? Could they actu-ally do it to him? He was caught in a scenario that would do Kafka proud. Theater of the most absurd, only this drama was for real. And as Vaill had said about his wife, the real victim here would be the per-son he loved more than anyone in the world.

Emily . . .

"Humphrey Miller," he heard his voice say in a strained whisper.

Vaill leaned forward.

"Again?"

"Miller. Humphrey Miller," Lou repeated, more forcefully this time. He felt a weight lift from his chest, but there was no sense of relief. "He's a pharmacy tech at Arbor General, but he is also a brilliant microbiolo-gist. He was part of a team that was helping Kazimi develop a treatment for the germ."

"So, what happened?"

"They had a fight—a falling-out because Kazimi didn't believe Humphrey's phage theory would work. Humphrey was either kicked off the team or he dropped out."

"I think you're messing with us."

"Think what you want. I don't believe Kazimi ever even met him. Humphrey isn't a scientist. He's a plain old hospital employee, who has debilitating cerebral palsy. He and Kazimi have communicated for years online, but they've never met."

"This is ridiculous!"

"Well, it's the truth. Humphrey never spoke to anyone at the hospital about his talents because people often ridicule him, and have trouble understanding his speech, and because the blowhard in charge of infectious diseases would never have taken him seriously. But Humphrey grew to trust me, and I understand his speech and respect his theories. I believe Humphrey can cure this infection using killer bacteriophage. If you've been researching it, you know it's possible. They use the method in Russia and other countries."

"Jesus," Vaill murmured. "Why didn't you tell us this?"

"Because Humphrey is wheelchair-bound. He has poor use of his hands and not much of his legs. He wanted my help setting up a lab in a storage space in Arbor General, so we could conduct experiments to prove his theories, and I needed him to do it quickly."

"You mean an unsanctioned lab?"

"Yes, in the subbasement. He hacked into the hospital's computer system and ordered all the supplies and animals he needed. Thanks to me, it's all ready to go. Now please, Cap's life is at stake. You can't stop Miller now."

"Jesus," Vaill uttered again, shaking his head.

He turned to McCall.

"Chuck, call Beth and give her the name Humphrey

Miller, a pharmacy tech at Arbor General. See what she wants to do."

"You got it. Meet you at the car." He hesitated at the door and gestured toward Lou. "Tim, you believe this guy?"

"I don't think he's a whack job if that's what you mean. But I'm not the least bit sure I can say the same thing about this Miller."

Vaill helped Lou to his feet and put handcuffs on him once more.

"What now?" Lou asked.

"Now, you get to take a nap in a bedroom with bars at the U.S. Marshal's place, and we get to do what we do."

"I told you what you wanted to know. Aren't you letting me go?"

"Um, let me see. . . . No."

The word echoed like a judge's gavel.

Vaill escorted Lou out the door and past McCall, who was already on his phone, presumably talking to their supervisor.

Lou knew that he had made a mistake caving in. The government was famous for messing up situations like this one. There was no chance they would ever step back and let Humphrey do his work. No chance for Cap.

Vaill guided him out of the building and into the cool, early morning air. Overhead, the sky was drenched with stars.

"What time is it?" Lou asked.

"Two thirty in the morning," Vaill said, checking his watch.

Lou took a deep breath, no longer sure if he'd ever breathe fresh air as a free man again.

CHAPTER 36

A Neighbor often needs a community to reach his goal. Therefore, if deemed reliable, others may be hired or enlisted into the order for specific purposes, but they shall not be offered a number unless there is an opening and they are acceptable to the director.

—LANCASTER R. HILL, *100 Neighbors*, SAWYER RIVER BOOKS, 1939, P. 57–8

Vaill rarely felt sorry for criminals, but he made an exception for Lou Welcome. From his read, Welcome seemed like a decent guy, a caring father, and a devoted physician who got caught up at the wrong time in a deadly set of circumstances. But the laws were the laws, and more than a few men and women were trudging around in orange jumpsuits with numbers on their backs because they made bad choices.

Putting his feelings aside, Vaill had done what had to be done. As an agent for the FBI, it was his duty to conduct sensitive national security investigations and to enforce hundreds of federal statutes. Regardless of what Lou Welcome was holding back, he was involved in a case the government considered priority one, and Vaill had done his job and done it well. Next it was up to the federal prosecutors to build a case and officially charge him with a crime. Meanwhile, Vaill would do his best to support those efforts, while in this case secretly rooting against them.

It was four o'clock in the morning when he finally emerged through a side door of the Atlanta City Jail. McCall had elected to stay at FBI headquarters for the rest of the night and write what was sure to be a lengthy report on the events leading up to and following their encounter with Lou Welcome at the Blue Ox Tavern. After that, he would get a ride back to their hotel from one of the guys, and they would meet later in the morning.

There had been virtually nothing said between them about the episode in the interview room. As before, he had lied to his new partner about having migraines, and as before, as far as he could tell, McCall had bought it.

Sometime around nine, Vaill would retrieve Welcome from his cell and ferry him to a magistrate's hearing in the courthouse. After that, it would be up to Lady Justice to decide the man's fate, and Vaill could, and most certainly would, join his partner in continuing to track down Alexander Burke.

During the short walk to the jail parking lot, Vaill tried with no success to immerse himself in the serenity of the early morning. Something wasn't right with his brain, and the headaches seemed to be getting worse and more distracting. Once he had nailed Burke, he would consider going back for a consultation with Dr. Gunter, his neurosurgeon. Maybe another MRI. But not until Maria's killer was behind bars . . . or dead.

Vaill's cell phone had rung several times before the sound intruded on his thoughts. He checked the caller ID and was not surprised to see his boss's name.

"McCall gave me the lowdown," Beth Snyder said, "and we've started running things down. Good job on the interrogation, Tim."

"My pleasure, ma'am."

"You think this Humphrey Miller is really a player here?"

"Could be. Lou Welcome, the doctor, is safely tucked away until he goes to court in a few hours. By then, I hope we'll have something on Miller."

Vaill's knees and back creaked as he climbed into the motor pool sedan, and the rumbling in his stomach had him considering a frozen burrito from the first all-night convenience store he could find. But there was another stop he wanted to make first.

"Have you gotten Miller's address yet?" he asked. "I'll drive over there right now."

"No," Snyder said, perhaps a little too quickly. "Take a rest until you're due to pick up Welcome. I want to get a search warrant to check out this secret lab of Miller's. If it's there, getting a probable cause warrant to search his apartment will be a no-brainer. Better to get all our *I*'s dotted and *T*'s crossed when we make the move on him. Last thing we want is for Miller to get off on some technicality, especially if this handicap of his is as severe as McCall tells me it is. Chuck didn't think we had to rush on this one, and I agree. Besides, it sounds like you could use some rest. In case you've forgotten, you've been through a lot."

I'm not resting until I find Burke.

Vaill kept the thought private. Having worked under Snyder for many years, he knew how she'd respond: *The FBI is not the place for personal vendettas. Agents go on vendettas, agents die.* Something in the way Beth

ordered him to get some rest had him wondering if
McCall had said anything to her about the headaches.
He didn't want to give away the intensity of the problem by making a big deal about it, but perhaps it would
be best if he and Chuck had a talk.

"Actually, I'm feeling surprisingly perky," he tried.
"It's no problem to do a quick drive-by and at least
check out Miller's place from the outside. Knowing the
setup there might make it easier serving the warrant
when you get it."

"That's a negative, Tim. What you're feeling is the
adrenaline left over from a very long, grueling interrogation. You promised me you'd take care of yourself if
I let you get in on this case. Well, getting some rest is
taking care of yourself. I've got to protect my soldiers,
especially ones who had their head operated on not so
long ago. So the answer is no. Now, you've got a few
hours. Go back to your hotel and get some shut-eye.
Whether you believe it or not, you need it."

"You ask, I do," Vaill said, knowing this was a battle he couldn't win.

"That's the old agency spirit. I'll have the gift shop
send you out a pennant and a mug. So listen, Tim, while
you're on your way to your hotel, tell me what your take
is on this Dr. Welcome. Who's he playing for? How
hard should we put his feet to the fire?"

"Believe it or not, Beth," Vaill said, turning onto the
near-empty highway, "after working on him for most
of the night, I think he's playing for his friend."

CHAPTER 37

Any piece of legislation passed by Congress,
approved by the Senate, signed by the president,
that in turn erodes liberty must not be viewed
by the American people as the law of the land,
for it is in truth the beginning of the end of our
world.

——LANCASTER R. HILL, MEMOIR
     (UNPUBLISHED), 1940

Humphrey Miller had four different in-home aides who
assisted him throughout the week—three women and
one man. There were others who tended to his needs
on weekends. The aides generally worked for two
hours then left or accompanied him to the van for
transport to his job at Arbor General. The nighttime
help took care of preparing his dinner and the subsequent cleanup, addressed his bathing and grooming
needs, changed him into his bedclothes, and physically
moved him from his wheelchair into his adjustable bed.

While he slept, many of Humphrey's CP symptoms
went dormant along with the rest of him, offering a
brief but welcomed respite from his daily physical
travails.

On weekday mornings, Humphrey's favorite aide,
Cassie Bayard, would let herself into the apartment to
help get him ready for his workday. He always wished

her time with him could last longer. Cassie was a strikingly beautiful Jamaican woman, tall and long limbed, with ebony skin and caring eyes, and was the focus of most of Humphrey's fantasies. He often lightly referred to her as Mama Teresa, but it really was a fitting moniker. Dependable as sunrise, Cassie, a single mother of three, always brought a lift to the start of Humphrey's day. Like many with CP, most of life's many mundane tasks were mini-mountains he was forced to climb time and time again. Cassie's enthusiasm made his daily trudges up Mount Life all the more manageable.

Humphrey had a mixed form of CP resulting in symptoms of both the spastic and athetoid types. Not easy. He endured involuntary movements of his face, arms, legs, and body, difficulty swallowing, drooling, and slurred speech, in addition to having tight muscles, which limited his movement altogether. He credited Cassie with keeping him from wallowing in self-pity.

Cassie knew he was bright and respected him for that. But he had never bothered to try to demonstrate to her just *how* bright. He was embarrassed to show off in that way, and feared he would intimidate her and drive her away. Now, with the newfound help of Lou Welcome, he wouldn't have to demonstrate his brilliance to anyone. Universal recognition of that was certain to follow when word got out of his achievement and his role in defeating the Doomsday Germ.

Following their morning routine, Humphrey was dressed and at his desk, a specially constructed workstation. While Cassie busied herself with the breakfast dishes, Humphrey used the joystick controls for his computer, which allowed him to search, type, and code with almost the same ease as an able-bodied person. Prior to Lou, Humphrey had used this time each morning to enlarge on his bacteriophage theories and computer models. Now that his lab was about to be functioning, he was instead preparing for the first round of serious, confirmatory experiments—studies that would rapidly lead to the cure for the deadly germ, and the sort of fame that would transcend his disabilities.

Cassie emerged from the kitchen with her denim jacket over her arm, a signal that their time together this morning had come to an end. She was rushing because if Humphrey did not make it to the curb on time, the van would simply leave without him.

"You've been extra happy these past few mornings, Humphrey," she said, her lilting Jamaican accent like a birdsong. She paused at the door, contemplating. Then, with the trace of a smile, she asked, "Mr. Miller, have you got a girlfriend you're keeping secret from me?"

Humphrey's smile was ebullient.

"Never compared to you," he said.

Cassie's hands went to her hips. She gave him an appraising look, but not because she had any difficulty understanding his speech.

"She better not, mister, or I might get jealous."

She opened the door and Humphrey, who had glanced away for one last, longing look at the other love of his life, his computer, heard two strange popping sounds. He turned to see Cassie fly backward, feet off the ground, arms beating the air. She landed on her back with crimson welling through two holes punched through her white blouse and into her chest.

With blood beginning to flow onto the floor beside

her, a man entered the apartment and softly closed the door behind him. It was only then that Humphrey cried out—a weak, strangled scream. The man was tall and thin, with blond hair and pale eyes as cold as ice. Humphrey, staring down in utter disbelief at the inert body of the woman who loved him more than any other he knew, began to hyperventilate. The tall man gingerly stepped over Cassie, careful to avoid the expanding pool.

"Hello, Miller," he said. "Sorry if I seem surprised. Nobody told me anything about you being a fucking cripple. My name is Burke, Alexander Burke, and I'm going to take you out of this shithole . . . now."

Humphrey's fear spiked, triggering a chain reaction in his body. His CP symptoms were often affected by his emotions and he had already lost most of what control he maintained over his limbs. His arms and legs jerked chaotically. His facial muscles tensed, distorting his features. His thoughts became a blur.

"Oh, my God," he finally managed. "Why did you do that?"

Burke looked at him curiously.

"I don't understand you," he said, reaching for Humphrey's motorized wheelchair. Instinctively, Humphrey pulled on the control stick and backed up, but in the small apartment, there was really no place for him to go. Burke, at once bemused and repulsed, watched his efforts. After creating a couple of feet between them, Humphrey pawed at the medical emergency alert device linked around his wrist. The killer moved to stop him, then paused and grinned. His prey, at least for the moment, was helpless. Beside Humphrey,

Cassie's blood glistened on the hardwood floor, and filled the room with a nauseating, coppery smell.

"This must be horrible for you," Burke said. "Help is just a button push away and yet you can't even do it. Why in the hell do the Neighbors want you so much anyway?"

He ambled across the room, grasped the emergency bracelet, and ripped it off Humphrey's wrist with one hard yank.

"Who pays for all this?" he asked, holding up the bracelet, and using it to gesture around the room and down at the lifeless woman on the floor. "Who pays for this whore to come to your apartment and tend to you? Wait, don't answer that. I already know."

"What . . . what . . . do you want?"

Humphrey continued to quake.

Burke ignored the question, quite possibly because he could not understand it.

"Where is your family?" he demanded. "How come they don't take care of you? Wait, don't answer that. It's because it's easier for Uncle Sam to foot the bill, that's why. Fucking leeches. Entitlement. That's what's made such a mess of this country. Your mother boozed or smoked or drugged or all three when she was pregnant with you, and we all end up paying for it for as long as you live. Trillions of dollars. That's what your entitlement programs cost the rest of us. Trillions!"

"What do you want?"

"What do I want? Is that what you said? Hey, I understood what you said. Okay. I'll tell you what I want. I want you to get your materials related to the Janus bacteria together so you can make us an antibiotic that works. Our scientists and our laboratory are waiting for you."

"No . . . I don't know . . ."

Burke slapped him violently across the face. Bright blood began coursing from one nostril over his lip and into his mouth. Grabbing one handle and the control stick of his wheelchair, Burke drove him over to his computer. There was a large gym bag nearby. The killer, virtually out of patience and composure, emptied the clothing from the bag, swept up the mass of papers and articles covering the cluttered desk surface, and jammed everything into it. Then he pulled open the drawers and a file cabinet, and did the same. The bag was bulging by the time he finished.

"Okay, what do you want to print out from that computer? I have the address of our scientist in case you just want to send it. You had better get everything you need, because if you screw this up and don't make the antibiotic we need, you're going to die, one tiny piece at a time. And I tell you, I'm going to love doing it. Understand? I said, *do . . . you . . . understand?*"

Burke raised his hand menacingly and seemed about to swing when he spotted a joystick near the computer and slid it over. Normally, Humphrey could maneuver the device with ease and some speed. This time however, he fumbled with it. The smell of Cassie's clotting blood made it difficult to concentrate, and in addition he was having no luck at all processing who could possibly have sent for him this way. At that moment, he felt Burke's hand on the back of his neck. A burning, electric pain shot across his shoulders and down his spine. His vision went white.

"I can press on this nerve even harder if you'd like," Burke said. "You won't ever pass out. Never ever. Trust me on that."

Humphrey had been verbally abused for much of his life, but this was the first time anyone had purposely inflicted physical pain on him. He feared this man more than he had ever feared anything or anyone.

In truth, there was little in his electronic files that he did not know virtually by heart, but what little control he might have over whatever was in store for him depended on no one seeing what was in those files. He had a backup system, but the only hard copy at the moment he had given away to his new lab assistant.

Carefully, he wrapped his hand around the joystick and launched a special program he had designed to protect his work from being pirated—a program he called Kill Switch. His program would delete not only all the files from his computer, but from the backups for those files as well. If he ever had to use Kill Switch, he would rely on his memory.

It took just three seconds.

With Burke watching, Humphrey pressed a sequence of keys and the computer monitor flashed and flickered as though it had been powered off and quickly turned back on. Sensing trouble, Burke bent over and stared at the screen. Items he had noted on the electronic desktop had suddenly vanished.

"What did you just do?" he demanded.

Humphrey's speech, rapid and legitimately frightened, was muddled beyond the killer's ability to understand. Barely able to control his movements, Humphrey used his joystick to bring up a blank text document into which he typed:

> *kill application all data deleted forever gone from backup servers too GO FUCK YOURSELF!*

"You stupid, crippled jerk!"

Violently, Burke tipped over the surprisingly heavy wheelchair, groaning at the effort and sending Humphrey sprawling through the half-clotted pool of blood and into Cassie's body. For a minute, he let him lie there, a hermit crab ripped from its shell.

"Now," he said after regaining a modicum of composure, "you're going to learn a little of what happens to people who fuck with me."

Burke set the toe of his boot across the fingers of Humphrey's left hand, stood on it with all his weight, and held it there.

"From what I've been told, you're a very brilliant scientist. But you're also very stupid. I have orders to bring you back to the lab at Red Cliff, but I wasn't instructed to bring back all of your fingers."

He finally stepped back and crossed to the tiny kitchen, returning with a large carving knife. Careful to avoid the blood, he got down on one knee and pressed the tip of the knife into the knuckle of one of Humphrey's injured fingers.

"One little push, and you'll never use this finger to pick your nose again."

"P-please stop!"

"Now listen and listen good. I know scientists. Scientists don't ever leave themselves without a copy of their data somewhere. You have to have a backup.

You have one, don't you." It was a statement, not a question.

The knife point pierced the skin and entered the knuckle.

Humphrey, screaming without sound, managed a nod.

"Good," Burke said, twisting the blade. "Okay, this is it. Tell me where you keep the backup or you are minus one finger. And I'll still have nine to play with. Understand?" A nod. "Ready to cooperate and not do anything else stupid?"

"Y-yes."

Burke pulled the wheelchair upright, lifted his prey off the ground, and dropped him like a rag doll into the seat. Humphrey's teeth snapped closed on the side of his tongue. Blood frothed out of the corner of his mouth. Burke pushed the bloody apparition to his computer and again shoved the joystick at him.

"Okay, where is the backup copy?" Burke asked.

Humphrey, spitting blood onto his shirtsleeve, fumbled with the joystick, but finally, the letters appeared on the screen.

There is no data backup.

Burke put the knife to Humphrey's wounded knuckle once more.

"I told you not to mess with me! There is a backup somewhere. Now, where is it? This is your last chance before pieces of you begin to fly. And do it fast. I'm running out of time."

Humphrey's hands were shaking too much to type.

"Please, take knife away," he said.

Burke did not oblige.

"Jesus. I can barely understand a word you're saying. Just nod. Is this guy in Atlanta? . . . Good. Can you tell me where? . . . You don't know? Okay, type what you do know. Remember. One lie and that finger goes, and I'm gonna love doing it. . . . Hospital. He's at the hospital? The one you work at? . . . Excellent. If he's there, I can find him. If he's not, this knife and I are going to pay you another visit. Now, once more, type out his name. . . . Good. Now, grab anything you need because you won't be coming back here for a long time. And don't think for an instant that this Dr. Lou Welcome won't turn your work over to me. Unless he's as badly deformed as you are, he'll have plenty of fingers for me to work on."

CHAPTER 38

When it comes to commitment, you are either
fully engaged or not, for there is no gray area.
Half measures will avail us nothing.

—LANCASTER R. HILL, *100 Neighbors*, SAWYER
RIVER BOOKS, 1939

His ringing cell phone roused Vaill from a dreamless
sleep. Even before answering it, he began testing himself. Stiff sheets, unfamiliar mattress, LG TV propped
up on the dresser at the foot of the bed. He was in a
hotel—a Marriott in downtown Atlanta. The room curtains were like lead shields, and if the sun had already
come up, it was impossible to tell. The ringing continued. Vaill fumbled for the phone, knocking over his
bottle of Tylenol. His voice was sleep-drenched.

"Yeah, Vaill here."

"Tim, it's Chuck."

Vaill brightened.

"Hey, buddy, what's going on? What time is it?"

"Sorry to wake you, sleeping beauty. I actually
thought you'd already be gone. It's eight-thirty."

"Shit."

Vaill sat up and felt a twinge behind his eyes, but
nothing materialized. He had planned to get Welcome
to the Richard B. Russell Federal Building and the district court magistrate judge before nine. Now he'd be

hard-pressed to make it there by ten. No big deal, he supposed.

"Don't worry about it," McCall said. "It's probably just as well if Welcome's not moved around too much."

"Yeah? Why's that?"

"I just got a call from the team Snyder sent over with a warrant to Miller's apartment. They found the place trashed, and a dead body in a pool of clotted blood in the middle of the floor. Humphrey's gone. The guys are knocking on doors now, but so far no one saw or heard anything. The victim's name is Cassie Bayard. She works for a company that provides home health services. Took two in the chest from close range."

Burke!

"Shit," Vaill muttered again. "What's the T.O.D.?"

"The police forensic guys checked body temperature and stiffness of the corpse and put the T.O.D. between five-thirty and seven-thirty this morning, but the pathologist should be able to narrow that down even more."

"What did Snyder say?"

"She's freaked and so am I. It was her call on my advice to get the search warrant for the lab first and use that as probable cause to get a warrant to search Miller's apartment and question him. That may have cost us a couple of hours. Now she's feeling the heat from above."

Vaill never questioned Snyder's decision to move cautiously on Miller. She never acted impulsively, which is why there were jokes about her sleeping with the FBI's procedures manual under her pillow. Snyder's commitment to protocol was probably the reason she'd risen in the ranks while Vaill was still in the field.

Now, in spite of himself, Vaill began considering a rushing stream of other explanations for this latest disaster—especially the possibility that Burke wasn't the only one in the agency who was working for the Society of One Hundred Neighbors.

The first mention of Humphrey Miller and his connection to Ahmed Kazimi had come from Lou Welcome at two-thirty that morning, and had almost immediately been relayed to Beth by McCall. Who she talked to after that was anyone's guess. Now Miller was gone and a woman was dead in his apartment, with the stench of Alexander Burke's close-range M.O. hanging heavy in the air. Even after exhaustive backtracking, to this day, nobody knew how the killer had infiltrated the organization. Did he have help from the inside? If so, someone else in the agency was on One Hundred Neighbors' payroll.

"Chuck," Vaill asked, "did you put Humphrey Miller's name into the I.D.W. after you phoned it in to Beth?"

I.D.W. stood for Investigation Data Warehouse, and it was where all leads associated with active cases got logged in by the investigating agents. Vaill knew that he was being intentionally cagey with his partner. Their pairing was fairly new. How much did he really know about the man? What if McCall had worked his way onto the investigation team the same way Burke had infiltrated Kazimi's security detail?

Vaill's mind was spinning.

This was the second major security breach. Who in the hell could he trust?

"Right after I called Snyder I keyed the new leads into the I.D.W. from my phone," McCall replied.

More possible sources of leaks. The I.D.W hadn't been in place long, and already had a reputation as a sieve.

Vaill pried the curtains apart. Bright sunlight hit him like a straight-on jab. He squinted against the glare and the renewed throbbing, and sucked down three extra-strength Tylenols without any water. In passing, he considered reporting his suspicions to Internal Affairs. But if the leaker turned out to be someone high up the food chain, they'd probably get Vaill kicked off the investigation within hours, if not out of the agency altogether. For the moment at least, he decided that his best chance to avenge Maria would be to operate in the shadows while keeping his mistrust for the FBI a secret.

"So," McCall was saying, "how about letting Welcome fester a bit longer in jail and come check out Miller's apartment with me?"

There were rules for how long Welcome could be detained without due process, but like anything pertaining to terrorism, those rules could be bent or even broken. Still, McCall had unknowingly brought up yet another consideration. If One Hundred Neighbors wanted Humphrey dead or captured, it was reasonable to assume they could be targeting Lou Welcome as well. Those two men were more than passing acquaintances. Since he no longer trusted the FBI, Vaill knew he alone had to protect Welcome, at least until he got more facts.

"I'm getting another call, Chuck," Vaill lied. "Hang on the line a second."

Vaill cupped the phone and counted slowly to twenty. Maria often complimented his ability to think creatively. Exhausted as he was, he at least had not lost a step in that regard.

"Chuck, are you still there?" he asked finally.

"I'm here."

"That was Welcome. Apparently he's got more information to share about the Neighbors, and he wants to cut a deal. But for whatever reason he says he'll only talk to me, and he won't do it there. I'm going to go and get him."

"Then what are you going to do?" McCall asked. "You need help?"

"Not as long as there are handcuffs in the world. I'll take him into protective custody and just learn what he has to say."

It was a good lie because McCall would have no reason to bring it to Snyder's attention . . . unless the two of them were connected in other ways.

"Okay," McCall said. "I'll be at Miller's. Call or meet me there after."

He gave Vaill the address.

"Sounds good. I'll be there as soon as I can."

Vaill showered quickly and got dressed, thinking that if McCall turned out to be the mole, he'd have no problem shooting to kill.

CHAPTER 39

Where there is no entitlement, there is no
iniquity.

—LANCASTER R. HILL, *100 Neighbors*, SAWYER
RIVER BOOKS, 1939, P. 12

The electronic release buzzed open a heavy steel door,
and the two burly U.S. Marshals who had handcuffed
Lou's wrists behind him escorted him into the small
foyer of a rear entrance in the Atlanta jail. Having been
briefed on the punch list of procedures he could expect,
Lou was a bit surprised his ankles and wrists hadn't
been chained for this trip to the courthouse. He was
also surprised that there was no other security ready
to transport him. The only one waiting in the dim light
was FBI Special Agent Timothy Vaill.

"The face is familiar," Lou said, pointing at him.
"Haven't I seen you some place before?"

"These guys take decent care of you?"

"They wouldn't look like they're both on steroids if
they had to eat the food here, but yes, they've all been
okay. Thanks for caring. Now, about the lawyer I never
got a chance to call."

"Oh, yeah. Well, the court would have appointed one
for you, and he or she would have scheduled an arraignment date. No big deal, and no matter. You're

still my prisoner, and I have some things I need to speak with you about."

Even in the subdued light Lou could see the strain enveloping the man's eyes. Something had gone wrong.

"You don't look so good," he said.

"Neither do you."

"Got me there," Lou said, grinning.

He had caught a glimpse of himself in a mirror in the guards' room as they passed by. His five o'clock shadow had grown to about quarter after eleven, and the date clothes he had worn to meet Vicki—dark jeans and a nice oxford shirt—looked like they had been rescued from a gas station's collection bin. The orange jumpsuit, he had been told, would come after he was returned to his cell to await arraignment. In truth, even the nasty times on the street had not prepared him for this experience.

But now it didn't seem like court was in his immediate future. Instead, it appeared that something had gone wrong. Maybe very wrong. His first thought was Cap.

A nod from Vaill, and the burlier marshal with the nameplate Gomes pinned to his tan shirt undid Lou's handcuffs long enough to have them replaced by the ones brought in by Vaill.

"You're still my prisoner until you've been formally charged," he said, "so no screwing around or I'll hurt you."

"Nicely put," Lou said. "Very nice."

"He's all yours, my friend," the marshal pronounced. "If he doesn't work or should he break, just bring him back for a full refund."

"Thanks, boys. I'm hoping the good doctor is going to be more cooperative this time around."

Vaill signed some papers then took hold of Lou's arm and led him out. The familiar, nondescript gray sedan was parked nearby. Lou settled into the backseat, turned away from the mesh screen, and watched the jailhouse shrink from view as they drove away. There had been times when the American justice system had actually been kind to him. The last eighteen or so hours had not been one of them.

"You're not going back there again, doc," Vaill said, eyeing Lou in the rearview mirror.

Lou swung around to face him.

"No judge?" he asked.

"No judge. Things have changed."

Vaill pulled the car to an abrupt stop, opened a rear door, and unlocked Lou's handcuffs.

"You were right when you said I was entering wonderland," Lou said.

"You want to sit up front?"

"Okay, I get it. This is some new form of torture to replace waterboarding, right? Confession by confusion. I'll come up front, but only after you tell me what this is all about."

Vaill sighed.

"Your pal Humphrey Miller has gone missing," he said. "A woman was found shot dead in his apartment and Miller is nowhere to be found. I have a strong feeling that the person who shot her was the son of a bitch who killed my Maria. If so, that means the Neighbors have both Kazimi and Miller. I think I mentioned the bastard's name last night. Burke—Alexander Burke. Listen, you're not a prisoner anymore, doc, so join me up front if you want."

"Tell me everything," Lou said, numbly sinking onto the seat Vaill's partner had occupied.

"We sent agents to Miller's place and to your basement lab at Arbor General. The lab was right where you said it was. Miller didn't show up for work this morning. Now we got a dead body and another missing microbiologist. I'm guessing he's been kidnapped, not killed—at least not yet. The Neighbors are getting desperate, but damn, they are good. That's where we stand."

Lou buried his face in his hands as Vaill eased back into traffic.

"Cap," he whispered.

Vaill shook his head, making no attempt to mask his empathy.

"No miracle cures waiting to happen," he said. "I'm sorry."

For a minute, two, there was only silence.

"So, what do you think?" Lou was finally able to ask.

"I think there's a significant security breach at the FBI. That's what I think. If there is, that's how Burke got onto the detail that was guarding Kazimi. Until now, I thought he did it on his own—learned enough about the Neighbors and their beliefs to locate them and offer himself up or else just sell Kazimi to them. But now that the information we got from you somehow already made it back to the Neighbors, I have to believe there's someone inside the agency who turned Burke. I just don't know who."

Vaill appeared genuinely distraught. If this was subterfuge and gamesmanship on the part of the FBI, designed to squeeze more information from Lou, it was a masterful performance.

"Tell me you didn't know there was a leak when I gave up Humphrey's name," Lou demanded.

"I didn't know. I swear it."

"What does McCall think?"

Vaill looked over at him.

"Do you see him riding with us?" he asked.

"You think McCall could be part of this?"

"I don't know what to think or who to trust. Right now, I'm navigating by instinct. I may have already cost two people their lives and I'm not about to do it to a third."

"You mean me," Lou said.

Vaill said nothing, which was answer enough.

Lou knew when he gave up Humphrey that he'd made a mistake. But the government had far surpassed his expectations for screwing up, and now Humphrey was either a prisoner of the Neighbors or dead. Lou had one card left in his hand—the notebook Humphrey gave him. And until he had reason to do otherwise, he vowed to hold that card close to his vest.

But time was running out for Cap.

"I shouldn't have told you his name," Lou said, as much to himself as to Vaill.

Vaill looked over at him.

"Hey, we're just as good at what we do as you are at what you do, doctor. You didn't stand a chance against us."

The remark took some of the guilt away.

"So what now?" Lou asked.

"Too bad you gave us your hotel. McCall probably

included it in his report, and whoever the mole is, if there is a mole, would have access to it."

"Except that I lied."

"What?"

"I made up a hotel. At the time you asked, I had decided not to make anything easier for you."

Vaill pumped his fist and clenched his teeth.

"Yes!" he said. "Then no one can possibly know. First I've got to be certain we're not being followed. Then we get you to your hotel and you double-lock yourself in and turn on a marathon James Bond retrospective or whatever."

"You really think I'm in danger?"

"Listen, I get what you were doing with Humphrey," Vaill said. "You wanted to save your friend's life, no matter what you had to do, even if it meant being an accessory to grand larceny and setting up an illegal lab. Hell, I'd probably have done the same thing. But the truth is, like it or not, you've gotten yourself connected to the Neighbors. We can take a chance on putting you back in jail, but those people are heavily financed and very resourceful. If they want you, you're not even safe behind bars."

And I have something they may really want, Lou thought, picturing Humphrey's book.

"Let's see," he said, "my hotel room or a return to jail . . . Tough choice. What are you going to do in the meantime?"

Vaill peered through the rearview and side mirrors and began a series of turns clearly designed to pick up a tail.

"Wish I knew this place better," he muttered, swerving

onto a freeway entrance at the last possible instant. "God bless GPS, that's all I can say. After I drop you off, I'm going to pick up some stuff from my hotel and meet up with McCall at Miller's place or headquarters—wherever he is. For the moment, he and my boss, Beth Snyder, think you're with me. I'm going to tell them I dropped the charges against you and stashed you at a hotel until we can figure out how big a risk Burke is to you."

"What about McCall?"

"I'm just going to tell him the truth—that I believe there might be a mole embedded in the agency, and that he's on my list of possibilities. I've never been much at sparing people's feelings if I thought it would help me get the job done."

"Let me help you," Lou said. "I need Humphrey to save Cap. Even with him, I'm afraid he may not make it. Without him . . ."

Lou's voice trailed away.

"Give me two days to find the mole," Vaill said. "At least I'll feel you're somewhat safe while I'm tracking him—or her—down."

"I've got to get to the hospital. I've already missed time. Then I'll tell you how long I'm willing to stay holed up in my hotel."

Vaill made some more evasive turns and glanced over at him.

"I told you these bastards are resourceful. I don't suppose I could talk you out of going to the hospital for like a day."

"You don't-suppose right."

"They might be watching for you there."

"If they're that good, they deserve to have me."

"Okay, okay," Vaill relented. "I've got an extra FBI Windbreaker and hat in the trunk. We'll both wear them and shades when we go inside Arbor."

Lou regarded Vaill with gratitude and appreciation.

"So, does that mean we're partners now?"

Vaill kept a stony expression as he watched the rearview and punched the gas to be the last car through a yellow.

"No," he said making a U-turn in what Lou hoped was the direction of Arbor General. "It means I'm putting my paranoid mistrust of you on the back burner until you give me reason not to."

CHAPTER 40

Government needs people to govern and so creates a subservient class upon which it can thrive and rule.

—LANCASTER R. HILL, *A Secret Worth Keeping*, SAWYER RIVER BOOKS, 1939, P. 64

From the earliest days of their friendship, Lou had kept no secrets from his sponsor. That included the news about the secret life of eccentric Humphrey Miller, and Lou's decision to help him open his subbasement lab. Now he wished he hadn't said anything. Cap had enough to deal with without having that rug of hope pulled out from underneath him.

It had been less than twenty-four hours since Lou was last in Cap's isolation room, but there had been a noticeable change in the man. A change for the worse.

Lou and Vaill were together in the tiny antechamber. Both men had replaced their FBI caps and Windbreakers with the required safety garb. In spite of himself, Lou felt different swaggering around wearing the dark shades and displaying the iconic letters on his back. Special. Tough. Then he thought about the people Vaill and the other real agents had to deal with every day—people whose life or way of life often depended on killing them.

No thanks.

He checked Vaill over to make sure he was properly gowned before giving a strong pull against the negative pressure door. Vaill had wanted to wait outside, but Lou requested he come in. Like in the ER, it was always more motivating to put a face on the people one was dealing with, and he expressed that feeling to himself, then out loud.

This is the man you've heard so much about. This is the life we're trying to save.

For an agent accustomed to clashing with dangerous criminals, Vaill seemed affected from the moment they opened the door to Cap's room. Perhaps it was the purulent, blood-soaked bandages, perhaps the scent of pus that was hanging heavier than ever in the air.

"Are you all right?" Lou whispered to Vaill, soft enough not to rouse Cap, who was sleeping sonorously on his back, with a sudoku puzzle book splayed across his chest.

Vaill nodded. "Yeah, I just have a little thing about hospitals. Understandable considering I got out of one myself not too long ago. Believe it or not, it was my first time."

Lou pointed to the rainbow scar.

"I imagine you're in the minority of your profession to have made it that long."

"Quick reflexes or incredible good luck. Probably both, combined with Kevlar vests."

Since Cap's ordeal began, the proprietor of the Stick and Move Gym had gone from a cruiserweight, just below the unlimited heavyweight rank, down close to a light heavyweight, and his wonderfully handsome face showed it. But as his eyes fluttered open, there was no mistaking the spirit in them.

No surprise.

"Hey, buddy," Cap said, grunting as he reached for the adjustable bed controls.

As always since the infection began, Lou cringed. Watching his boxing coach and best friend struggle with even small movements was heartbreaking. Cap pushed a button and a motor whined as it elevated the bed to an angle more comfortable for him, although comfort, with his leg in a frame and up on pulleys, was certainly a relative term.

Cap gestured toward Vaill but was too weak to shake hands. Lou noted the flush in the agent's cheeks and sensed he hadn't given the man vivid enough preparation—probably by not accounting enough for the changes they were seeing in Cap's condition.

"Looking pretty good," Lou managed.

"Don't bullshit me, Welcome," Cap replied before being cut short by a brief coughing spasm. "Why don't you just sell me some swampland in Florida. There's a mirror in my tray table, remember. I look like crap and we both know it. They've even decided I'm too dangerous to take me for any more hyperbaric treatments."

"You always did have a lousy self-image, my man. More meetings. That's what you need. Cap, meet Tim Vaill from the FBI. He arrested me yesterday afternoon for obstructing justice, threw me in jail, and then changed his mind this morning about exactly what justice was."

The two men greeted each other with their eyes and a nod.

"You don't want to shake hands with me, even with those rubber gloves on," Cap said. "According to Dr.

Puchalsky, my charming mortician-turned-infectious-disease-specialist, this bug inside me has mutated again. He's a specialist in infections you get from just being in a hospital. Believe it or not, there's actually a name for that. I'm not a big fan of people who are full of themselves, even when they're smart."

"I have exactly the same take on him. Holier than thou doesn't even cover it."

"He thinks I might have to be moved to some kind of special facility in Wyoming or Nebraska or one of those other states that are all corners, in order to get me even more isolated than I already am. He said it to me like he was announcing what dietary was going to give me for dessert."

"Great image of the man. I got it."

"Believe it or not, when all this started, he actually asked me what kind of insurance I had, so he could find out if I was covered for certain experimental anti-biotics."

"What a strange thing to ask you. What did he say when you told him you didn't have any?"

"The truth is, I was so upset by the question and his tone, I didn't tell him anything except that he should check with you."

"Well, he must have worked things out, because he never mentioned it."

"He's worried about the germ spreading to more patients, and for that I don't blame him. But that's going to be after."

"After what?" Lou asked.

"After something not so good. So, what are you doing with the FBI anyway? Are you in trouble with the law again? Good gravy, I can't trust you anyplace. Now, don't you go bringing any heat down on me, buddy, I've got enough problems to deal with as it is."

"No heat," Vaill said. "I'm here because this germ of yours was initially discovered by some very bad people, and now the government is interested in putting them out of business."

"It involves our friend, Humphrey," Lou said.

"Is he bogus? He seemed like such a sweet little dude."

"No, not bogus. Not bogus at all. He's missing. A guy killed the aide who was getting him ready for work, and kidnapped him."

"Ouch."

"I know about the lab in the basement, Cap," Vaill interjected. "The doc, here, told me about it and said he had told you as well. We think the work Miller was starting down there is why they took him."

"Damn," Cap muttered, clearly grasping the significance.

No miracles.

"We think we know who did this, and we're going to find him," Vaill said.

"Better make it quick, brother."

The way Cap said the words was ominous.

Lou put his gloved hand on the fighter's forehead, feeling the burn even through the latex.

"Cap, what's going on?" he asked. "What's the not-good thing you mentioned?"

Vaill backed up a step, giving the two friends a little more space to connect.

"It's ugly, Lou," Cap said, his voice coming out like the hiss of air from a punctured tire. As he did during every visit, Lou poured a cup of water from the plastic pitcher and angled the straw so Cap could take a sip.

"What do you mean 'ugly'?"

"I mean I got some news yesterday from Puchalsky and my surgeon, and it ain't good."

"Talk to me, big guy, what did they say?"

"I got a few days, Lou. A week at the most."

Cap's voice cracked mid-sentence.

"What do you mean a week? A week for what?"

"The germ is spreading to the rest of my body. If they can't get the infection under control, they're going to take my leg. Dr. Standish, my surgeon, says that if they do it, they're going to cut it off way up here. He was going to let matters drop there for the time being, but fucking Puchalsky—excuse my language, officer—felt the need to add that the operations may not stop with the leg."

CHAPTER 41

To remove responsibility from the individual is
no different than to laden them in shackles.

—LANCASTER R. HILL, LECTURE AT MARIETTA
COLLEGE, OHIO, MAY 1, 1938

Lou leaned up against Vaill's sedan and gazed sky-
ward, stealing a moment's rest along with the chance
to contemplate the gut-wrenching new developments.
The man lying in the isolation suite was hardly the warrior who could once go fifteen rounds opposing ranked
professionals. The visit with Cap had lasted fifteen
minutes before he started to fade. Lou left with a promise to return soon, but kept the timetable vague. They
had returned the FBI-issued Windbreakers to the trunk
and Vaill had his suit jacket back on.

"Tim, this changes everything," Lou said. "I can't
be locked up anywhere, my hotel room included—not
if they could operate on Cap at any time. More important, I've got to keep looking for Humphrey or someone like the people at the CDC who can put his theories
into practice."

Vaill looked at him disapprovingly.

"You can't do that, Lou. Anything you do right now
risks compromising my work. I've got to manage this

investigation, and unfortunately, because I can't trust anyone connected with the agency, I have to do the important parts alone."

"Look, I know how—"

Lou stopped speaking. Tim Vaill wasn't listening. Instead, he was staring up at the glass and steel façade of the main building, his eyes squinting rhythmically. It was the same distant look Lou had seen in the interview room.

"Oh, God," Vaill murmured.

Hyperventilating, he dropped to one knee, pressing his hands across his eyes.

Lou dropped down beside him.

"Another headache?"

Vaill managed a nod.

"I'm going to get you into the ER."

"No!"

Lou checked his pulses, paying closest attention to his carotids.

"Is this the same as you've been having—the same as the one last night in the interview room?

Another nod.

Lou opened the passenger's-side door, and helped him in. The hyperventilating was becoming even more marked.

"Jesus," Vaill muttered, now holding his head on both sides as if to squeeze the pain into submission.

Standing outside the open door, Lou gently lifted his lids apart and checked his pupils. Abnormally dilated, but equal in size, and symmetrically constricting a bit to the light.

Almost certainly not a stroke, hemorrhage, or clot.

"If you need to get sick, just do it out here, Tim. You sure you don't want me to get some help and get you into the ER?"

"I'll . . . be . . . fine."

In his years as an ER doc, Lou had seen every kind and degree of pain. Kidney stones and acute gout were high on his list of those he did not ever want to have, along with aortic artery leaks and, of course, from all he could ever tell, childbirth. But also on the list were big-league headaches—migraines or even worse, cerebral aneurysms. Vaill's pain seemed right up there with any of those, although, as the previous night, it seemed to have come on faster than a typical migraine. Had he not had that prior experience, Lou would have called for help. Instead, he kept his fingers alternating from Vaill's carotid to radial pulse, and waited.

There was a large manila envelope on the driver's-side floor. Lou emptied its contents on the floor and fitted it as best he could over Vaill's mouth and nose to allow him to rebreathe some of the carbon dioxide he was blowing off.

"Easy, pal. Easy."

Gradually, the rapid breathing began to slow. Lou checked the time. Twenty minutes.

An elderly couple, who had apparently been watching from nearby, came over to ask if they could help. Vaill, his eyes now open, waved them off.

"Let me stand up," he said.

Lou helped him to his feet and for another few minutes, Vaill braced himself against the car roof.

"I'm not certain what is causing those headaches," Lou said, "but I don't think I want one."

"Believe me, you don't. I'm okay now. Thanks."

"Tim, listen, you are really in no condition to be going after Humphrey or Burke on your own—especially if you're getting an attack every day. You need a partner, and since you can't trust anyone you work with, I want to come with you. I have as much at stake here as you do."

"No. Absolutely—"

"Dammit, Tim, you've got to trust me and let me help."

"Exactly what do you think you could do?"

Time was becoming as big an enemy as One Hundred Neighbors and the Doomsday Germ. It no longer seemed important to keep Humphrey's research notebook a big secret, and Lou told him about it.

"There's a lot of Humphrey's work that isn't over my head," Lou said. "I can help in that regard. Is there any way you could share with me what you've found so far?"

"Everything? We have reams and reams of reports and interviews."

"Where is all that?"

"I can't believe I'm caving in on this," Vaill said. "Okay, listen, we've got a new system, the I.D.W., for Information Data Warehouse, where we log in all the evidence and leads we collect on a case. It's supposed to help improve efficiency with our task forces. Physical evidence stored in evidence rooms gets logged in so we know where it is. We even take pictures of it, so we can look at it remotely. Any electronic evidence—photographs, videos, that sort of thing, is uploaded to the I.D.W. as well."

"And you have the codes and passwords to access that warehouse?"

"Of course, doc. That's the idea."

"Sorry. Between Cap and you, I'm a little rattled."

"Okay, I'll check what McCall and I have entered into the warehouse."

"Burn as much as you can onto a CD and we can go over it together."

"What are you going to do in the meantime?"

"I'll take your advice and go back to my hotel room and reread Humphrey's notes. Then I can start making calls to my ID contacts in Washington. If we can't find Humphrey, maybe I can locate another microbiologist who could help put his theories into action."

"We need to just stay away from any government scientists for a couple of days until I figure out where the leak could be coming from. If I don't find it in two days, you're the boss. This is all on us, doc."

"And you're feeling all right?"

"A few patches of fog still hanging around, but I'm okay. You just protect that book."

"Check."

"We're going to bust this thing, Lou."

Where there had been confusion and pain in Vaill's eyes, now there was only fury—a hunger for vengeance.

"You got it," Lou said. "I'll stay in the hotel long enough to change out of these clothes, shower, call Emily, pack, and try to understand as much of Humphrey's research as possible. You go check out that warehouse, make a CD, and maybe find us a place that's safe away from McCall and anyone like my former clients and family who might know where I'm staying."

"Sounds like a plan," Vaill said. "Two hours?"

"Make it three and be extra careful picking a place for us."

The new allies shook hands, climbed into the sedan, and drove off.

If, when they first arrived at the parking lot, they had glanced toward the hillside three hundred yards behind them, one of them well might have seen sunlight glinting off the lenses of a powerful pair of 30-160x70 Sunagor mega-zoom field glasses.

Now, had they looked, they would find the hillside empty.

CHAPTER 42

A civilization is viable so long as there is trust
between the people and the government.

—LANCASTER R. HILL, *A Secret Worth Keeping*,
SAWYER RIVER BOOKS, 1941, P. 11

Alexander Burke loved stalking his prey even more
than he loved killing them.

When on a job, he frequently envisioned himself as
a tiger, padding through the brush on huge, soundless
paws, getting closer by the second to administering
violent death . . . and closer.

He had come to Arbor General Hospital prepared for
a long surveillance, having brought a knapsack of energy bars and water in addition to night glasses and binoculars. As it turned out, he didn't even need the night
glasses. Now, lowering his binoculars, he wished he
had bought a laser microphone so he could have listened in on the conversation between his former co-
hort Tim Vaill and the man that photos told him was
Dr. Lou Welcome—the prey he was actually stalking.

He'd been watching the parking lot and main entrance to Arbor General from a perfect vantage point
on a hill overlooking the main lot. The full resources
of One Hundred Neighbors were working nonstop to
locate Welcome's hotel room in Atlanta. But Burke was

certain the hospital was the most likely bet, so he had taken that watch himself.

It had required more work on Humphrey Miller's fingers, but eventually the pathetic cripple had given up additional and useful details, including the existence of a secret lab in the hospital subbasement, and the name of Welcome's hospitalized friend, Hank Duncan. Duncan was in bad shape and was being cared for in some kind of unit. If Welcome and Duncan were as close as Miller had said, odds favored Welcome would be visiting soon—and those odds had been on the money.

The tiger had no trouble spotting the two FBI agents as they headed for the lobby entrance. He identified Vaill right away. He'd never forget the face of the only man he had ever failed to kill. But it took a moment to realize the agent with him, also wearing shades, an FBI Windbreaker, and hat, was Dr. Lou Welcome. Clearly, they were wary.

The doctor wasn't the only one to have altered his appearance. Because he was now one of the FBI's ten most wanted—number one, actually—Burke had applied a fake beard to minimize the shape of his jawline, and heightened the contours of his face with makeup that added years to his age. He also traveled with a number of different disguises, and his current choice—a brown wig, brown contacts, and a latex covering that altered the shape of his nose—fooled the FBI agents who had swarmed Arbor General several hours before. He had even followed two of them down the stairs to the subbasement, although he refrained from getting any closer to the lab that Welcome must have told them about.

Seeing Vaill and Welcome together put a new wrinkle

into Burke's plans. He wanted to learn more about Welcome's relationship with the FBI. Did they know each other from before? Why did they seem so close? Had Vaill gone rogue? Was that why he snuck Lou into Arbor dressed as an agent? If so, to what end? For now, their unusual association would be information to report back to Bacon and nothing more. He doubted this unexpected development would compromise his mission, but if Bacon gave the kill order, the tiger would gladly eliminate them both. Even though he actually liked Tim Vaill, there was no real emotion involved, one way or the other.

It was different for the woman, Cassie, whom he had taken out on the way to Miller. She was an anathema, a representation of the wasted entitlement spending the Neighbors had vowed to eliminate. He would have killed the freeloading Miller, too, as retribution for all money stolen by the government from those who had earned it to fund the broken man's so-called entitlements. But his mission called for a different course of action.

When Vaill and Welcome finally drove away, Burke was just a few car lengths behind, countering every one of Vaill's evasive maneuvers with one of his own. The streets here were fairly wide and traffic lights lasted longer than most, making it easy to maintain his tail. Burke had sped up anticipating and avoiding a yellow light, when his phone buzzed. Bacon.

"I've got a visual on Lou Welcome right now," Burke said.

"And hello to you, too," Bacon replied in a cool tone.

Burke often forgot Bacon was a Southern gentleman

who, even at the oddest times, demanded civility and proper etiquette.

"Hello, Thirty-eight," Burke said, correcting himself. "I'm on to Welcome."

"Well, I was calling to tell you that we've found his hotel room. He's staying at the Miralux Towers on Grand Street, room six-seventy-five."

Burke keyed the address into his GPS, careful not to lose visual contact with Vaill.

"My GPS says they're headed in that direction right now."

"Good. I trust you'll be able to resolve this matter fully."

In Bacon-speak that was his way of ordering termination.

"First I'll get the book Miller said he gave Welcome. One interesting thing—he showed up at the hospital with Tim Vaill."

There was a pause.

"Why have those two come together?"

"I don't know. Vaill gave Welcome an FBI Windbreaker to wear into the hospital. There's got to be a reason."

"Your call there," Bacon said.

Burke knew it was Thirty-eight's way of saying it was up to Burke's discretion to let Vaill live or die.

"Understood. Is Miller safely there?"

"Yes. Nice job. The Gulfstream touched down a few hours ago and we transported Humphrey to Red Cliff by van. Of course, he'd be more useful to us with his data, but you're about to make that happen. This is a vital part of our mission now, Forty-five. You have a substantial role to play, and I trust when we are victorious, and Western society is changed forever, history will shower you with the accolades you deserve."

"I'm proud to do my part."

Burke pulled to within three car lengths of Vaill's sedan. Vaill was good at evasion, but the tiger, driving a burgundy Buick LaCrosse, was able to predict his moves. Even if he lost them, the turns Vaill was taking had him headed directly toward Grand Street. Miller's book and Welcome's life—one-stop shopping. The decision regarding Vaill could wait.

As expected, fifteen minutes later, Vaill stopped in the drive of the Miralux and remained in the car, engine running, as Welcome hurried past the uniformed doorman and into the modest, family-type hotel. Five minutes later, Vaill took a call on his cell, spoke for a couple of minutes, then drove away. Obviously, Welcome was safely inside his room.

Time to make the doughnuts.

Keeping the weapon in his lap, Burke mounted his Gemtech suppressor to the barrel of the SIG Sauer 9mm MK25—the preferred weapon of the Navy SEALs. Then he slipped the exquisite gun inside his gym bag. Finally, he worked his trusty Strider SJ75 folding knife into his back pocket and exited the Buick. The knife was lightweight and the thin profile made it easy to forget it was even there.

If possible, he would kill Welcome with the Strider. It was a powerful weapon, great for the quick draw. However, if it was more practical, the suppressor would take care of matters well enough.

Either way, Dr. Lou Welcome had just minutes to live.

CHAPTER 43

Poverty is not an addiction, and as such is remediable. But the treatment for the condition is most certainly not a paid vacation from life.

—LANCASTER R. HILL, *100 Neighbors*, SAWYER RIVER BOOKS, 1939, P. 7

From the small balcony off his sixth-floor hotel room, Lou had a view almost straight down at the kidney-shaped pool below. By the time Vaill and he arrived at the Miralux, the sky had transformed from bright blue to battleship gray. Now ominous clouds forming in the west warned of an approaching storm. As instructed, Lou had passed slowly through the small lobby to the elevators, keeping an eye out for anyone sitting down, reading, or otherwise appearing to be simply hanging out.

Nothing.

Once inside his room, he checked the closet and the bathroom, which had a glass shower stall, but no tub, and confirmed that the king-sized bed was on a frame that left little room underneath. Humphrey's notebook was where he had left it, locked inside the surprisingly ample room safe.

Before Lou exited Vaill's sedan, the agent gave him his business card with a mobile phone number written on the back, adding that at least they could count on him remembering that Lou had put the card in his wallet. Lou's smile in reply held little mirth. Not being able to predict when Vaill might suddenly go blank was a bit like playing Russian roulette.

Last, Vaill tried to give Lou his pistol, promising to pick up another one at the field office. Over his life as a doc, Lou had treated many more gunshot wounds than the number of times he had actually held a gun.

"They give me the creeps," he explained, refusing. "Chances are I would end up shooting myself or some innocent bystander before I hit anyone I was actually aiming at."

"Suit yourself," Vaill replied. "I don't have time to talk you into it, or to give you an in-service lesson."

"Believe me, Tim, the world will be a better, safer place."

After the careful search of his room, Lou called to confirm all was well.

"Okay," Vaill said. "Now flip on a James Bond marathon and watch how he handles a gun."

"I thought Bond films were all Hollywood bogus."

"They are, but he never misses."

Finally able to stretch and relax, Lou plugged in his cell, stripped down, and fell onto his back on the bed, tired, hot, and sweaty from what was probably the worst twenty-four hours in a life that gave them stiff competition. The thought of a quick dip in the pool began to wriggle its way into his mind, but that simply wasn't going to happen.

Survey says: shower.

As if placing an exclamation point on the result of his one-man audience poll, there was a volley of lightning nearby, followed by resounding thunder. Lou peeked out between the balcony drapes. Sixty feet down, the pool was emptying out, as it should have been.

The shower won high marks in the hotel category by only twice shifting without warning to icy cold. He dried off, changed into jeans and a knit polo, and by habit shifted his wallet to his left front pocket. Moments later, another flash and a booming clap of thunder announced the rain.

The sound of the kids racing into the lobby or back to their rooms made Lou realize that he had not spoken with Emily in two days. One or two was their average when he was in D.C., closer to one those rare times when he was away.

"Keep a close watch on her," his father, Dennis, had warned when Emily was a newborn. "You blink, and they're driving. And sometimes, like the day your brother Graham drove my Plymouth through the garage door, they're only twelve."

Ensconced in the storm-darkened, womblike comfort of his room, Lou reflected on the many times he had urgently raced to get Emily out of the water before a thunderstorm. The memory brought a tired smile, and he picked up his cell phone. She would do most of the talking, which was good, but he really needed to hear her voice, to know she was at home in Virginia, and most important of all that she, like the children from the pool, was safe.

The balcony door was open, allowing a fresh breeze stirred up by the impending storm to cool down his stuffy room. He checked to be sure there was no rain blowing in on the carpet, then sat on the edge of his bed and dialed her cell.

One minute they're crawling and the next they're on your data plan.

That would be his quote to his daughter after her firstborn.

"Daddy!" Emily squealed.

"Hey, baby girl." Her voice was a symphony. "How's my favorite chiquita in the universe? I miss you."

"I miss you too, Daddy. How's it going? How's Cap?"

"He's okay, sweetheart. He's hanging in there."

"That means he's not doing so good."

"It's a bad infection, but you know how much strength and courage he has. He's going to do all right."

Lou fought back a sudden swell of emotion. His heart filled with uncontainable love for his daughter. It was right for him to have caved into Vaill and McCall's grilling and threats. He could not imagine being locked up in a cell somewhere, kept away from her and shielded from the fullness of what her life would become.

"Dad, are you okay?" Emily asked.

He'd gone quiet for too long.

"Yeah, sweetie. Tell me about you. What have you been up to?"

Just talk to me . . . I need to hear your voice.

"I'm doing everything I can think of to raise more money for Cap," she said. "It's going great. I mean, we've still got a long way to go, but people are really rallying behind me."

"Is General Mills still contributing?"

"They are!" she announced with pride. "In addition to the five hundred they're donating, they're also sending all sorts of mixes so we can have a big bake sale. The street team has been picking up steam, and my fund-raising sites have raised over two thousand dollars so far."

"Two thousand," Lou repeated. "That's wonderful! Congratulations, honey. Well done. Very well done!"

"Thanks, Dad. You sure you're okay?"

"I'm fine, kitten. I'm just a little—"

A sharp knock on the door interrupted him.

"Lou, it's Vaill," he heard the urgent, somewhat muffled voice say. "We gotta talk."

"Sweetheart, let me call you right back."

Lou got up from the bed.

"Okay, Daddy, I love you."

"Love you, too," he said on his way to the door. "Talk to you soon."

Such a kid.

Lou wondered what news Vaill had returned to share, thinking it was something too serious to discuss over the phone. He turned the knob and had pulled the door open barely an inch when it sprung inward on him, rammed from the other side. Knocked off balance, Lou staggered backward. He was confused by Vaill's sudden aggression until he realized it was not Vaill. This man had a beard, dark brown eyes, brown hair, and carried a pistol with a silencer pointed at the center of Lou's chest.

"Don't make a sound, not a single noise or you die," the intruder said. One look at his flat, lifeless eyes, and Lou had no doubt the threat was real. The man stepped farther into the room, closing the door behind him with his foot and reaching back to dead-bolt it, which Lou knew would automatically engage the Do Not Disturb notice on the outside. "Keep your hands chest-high where I can see them," he demanded.

"Who are you? What do you want?"

Lou's stomach cartwheeled. His heart slammed again and again against the inside of his ribs. This was not a man to be tested.

"Doesn't matter," the gunman replied, "you have something I need."

Missing pieces quickly dropped into place.

"You kidnapped Humphrey, didn't you? You're Burke. You killed Tim Vaill's wife."

Outside, the wind and the downpour had intensified, but Lou, desperately sizing up his situation, was barely aware.

Alexander Burke returned an indifferent shrug. "So I am," he said. "But to repeat—you, sir, have something I need. A notebook your friend Miller gave you."

The killer moved closer, one cautious step . . . then another. His gun hand was as steady as a steel rod. Lou was on one side of the king-sized bed, Burke on the other, but the bullets in his gun shortened the distance between them immeasurably.

More lightning . . . more thunder . . . more wind . . . more rain.

Neither man moved to close the flapping drapes, but Burke flipped on one bedside light.

Lou searched for an advantage—any advantage. They were about the same height, and Lou had the sense that in an even-up fight he had a chance—except for the gun.

"I don't know what notebook you're talking about," he said.

Burke sneered.

"We're not really going to play that game, are we?"

"I don't know what—"

"Cool it, Welcome. Just stop right there. You have one chance to save your life. Right now. Only one. I'm going to shoot you if you scream . . . or stall. Ever been shot? Well, you have my word that I'm going to do it— more than once, and in places that won't kill you. I'm going to shoot you if you try to escape, if you cough, or sneeze, or argue, or do anything other than give me what I came here to get, which is a notebook that Humphrey Miller gave to you. Is that clear?"

"Please . . . let's—"

"—I'm counting to five, then it starts."

"I have it, I have it."

"Four. I don't care if you have it. I want you to give it to me. Three . . ."

"It's here, it's right here!" Lou shouted. Any vestige of coolness or composure was gone from his voice. This was a man with no soul. He had killed Vaill's wife without a blink, and he had undoubtedly gotten pleasure out of gunning down Humphrey's caretaker at close range. There was no way even to try to reason with him. "Don't shoot me! I'll get it. I'll get it."

Lou continued desperately to search his mind for a move or a word that might forestall the inevitable and turn even one thimbleful of the tide that was threatening to sweep him away forever.

"It's locked in the safe," he said, pointing.

Another round of wind and thunder. Rain was now being blown through the open sliders and onto the carpeted floor. The curtains billowed inward like spinnakers.

Burke came around to Lou's side of the bed. Five feet separated them—an easy kill shot, but too far for Lou to make any reasonable attempt to attack him.

Another look into Burke's empty eyes told Lou everything he needed to know about how this was going to go down.

He's going to kill me. Once he has the book, I'm dead.

"Open the safe," Burke said.

Time was almost up. Lou decided he wasn't going without a fight. He wasn't going to wait to be shot. Crouching rather than dropping onto his knees, he opened the cabinet door and took in a deep, steadying breath. There was no way Burke would accept the combination to the safe. He wanted the notebook, not any of the distractions that could result from dialing numbers.

Distractions . . .

Lou glanced out the sliders, and the germ of an idea formed . . . and began to grow. He worked quickly but carefully to press the correct number sequence—03051009, a mashup of his birthday and Emily's and the only combination he was guaranteed not to forget. The safe clicked open and he retrieved the thick, bound document. As he stood, Lou turned back around to face Burke.

Could the notebook stop a slug? he was wondering.

He needed time. Just a second or two.

Another bright flash of lightning drew Lou's attention to the balcony where raindrops continued pelting the stone floor.

"Slide the book over to me," Burke said, motioning with his gun hand. Clearly, he did not want Lou even within arm's reach.

Lou swallowed hard.

One chance . . . I have one chance. . . . What does it feel like to be shot?

He bent down and slid the book on the carpeted floor, but angled it in such a way that it slid underneath the bed.

Burke's expression remained pure ice, but his eyes were daggers.

"That's going to cost you," he said.

Keeping his gaze locked on Lou, he used his foot to feel under the bed. The Neighbors had Humphrey Miller, and Burke had been able to make him hand over Lou. The notebook was insurance in case Miller suddenly refused to cooperate anymore . . . or died.

Lou tensed. He was a sprinter on the blocks, and the starter's pistol was about to go off.

The Neighbors had probably given up on Kazimi's antibiotic approach, and their scientists had not been able to keep up with the mutations of the Doomsday Germ. They were getting desperate. The good news was it now appeared Humphrey well might have been correct in his bacteriophage theory. The bad news was that Lou was essentially finished. His only hope—an incredibly thin one—would involve leaving the notebook behind.

Come on and look away. Look . . . away.

Lou's eyes were fixed on the man set to kill him.

Look down. Now, dammit! . . . Now!

Burke extended his foot another inch under the bed frame. Then a wisp of a smile bowed on his cruel mouth. He had located the notebook.

Bending at the knees, Burke kept his eyes on Lou, and the gun fixed on his chest.

Get ready . . .

Burke looked away for just two seconds, long enough to dip his shoulder and reach underneath the bed with his hand. When he glanced up again, Lou was already in motion. In the instant before he moved, Lou flashed on the parents rushing their kids out of the swimming pool. He took two giant steps, pushing past the curtain and onto the balcony. From behind him came two silenced shots—like champagne corks popping. He sensed bullets whizzing past his head. One might have shattered the sliders.

This was it.

There was no time for hesitation, no time to calculate . . . or to direct his leap. Barefooted, Lou swung one foot up onto the railing, and in a fluid motion, pushed off with all his strength.

Live or die.

He was six stories above the pool and falling fast. The scene rushing up from below was crystal clear. Indelible. No kids. Air being forced from his lungs. Unable to breathe in.

Lou peddled frantically as though astride an invisible bicycle. His arms pinwheeled to gain balance and shift himself into a seated position. He had heard someplace that going in butt first would do the least damage. Or maybe it was feet first. He also remembered to try to stay loose. Tight muscles would limit the cushion around the spine and contribute to compression fractures.

Of course, no maneuver would help a whit if he landed short.

The pool was coming up with dizzying speed. He could see now that he was going to hit water. His last thought before impact was whether he was about to land at the deep end, or whether, in fact, there even *was* a deep end. The force compressed his chest and stomach. Banshee wind and stinging rain lashed at his face.

It was time. He would survive this, or he would shatter and die.

He was upright now, about to hit legs and butt first—a cannonball from six stories with absolutely no idea what it was going to feel like when he hit, or if he was about to blow apart on the bottom. The impact was intense, and the simultaneous explosion was worthy of any cannon. Every bit of remaining air burst from his lungs. He pinched his nostrils just in time to keep water from shooting up them and through the top of his head.

A moment later, he hit bottom. The jolt was stunning, but not lethal. Disoriented, he flailed with his arms and foolishly tried to take a breath, filling his lungs with chlorinated water. With panic taking hold, he hit the bottom of the pool again, but this time he pushed off with his legs and shot upward, gagging mercilessly as his head broke the surface. Adrenaline and the realization that he was probably not dead carried him to the side of the pool.

Hanging on to the tile and coughing nonstop, he peered up at the balcony of his hotel room. Burke was there, silenced pistol in hand, taking aim. Then he lowered the weapon as a group of concerned parents with children in tow came rushing out of the lobby to Lou's aid. Burke pointed two fingers at his own eyes, and then at Lou, before he vanished into the room. Groaning with the effort, Lou pulled himself out of the pool, and pushed himself to his feet. Burke was on his way down. Shivering from the shock of the ordeal, Lou eyed the crowd gathered around him.

"Kids," he said, "don't ever try this at home."

CHAPTER 44

Senator Huey Long's Share Our Wealth program is emblematic of America's failed entitlement policy. Choosing to forgo our agrarian roots, to turn our collective backs from extended family in exchange for urban living, to become dependent on handouts at the cost of self-reliance should have consequences not rewards.

—LANCASTER R. HILL, *Climbing the Mountain*, SAWYER RIVER BOOKS, 1941, P. 99—100

Like the Red Sea, would-be rescuers and good Samaritans parted to let the sodden, barefoot specter hurry past. On his way into the lobby, Lou grabbed a towel from an oversized bin and coughed what seemed like a gallon of chlorinated pool water into it. There was still time, he was thinking, to catch Burke inside the hotel before he could get away with Humphrey's notebook. Then he flashed on Vaill's description of the ruthless murder of Humphrey's caretaker, and of Vaill's wife.

It was possible, likely even, that with his prize in hand, Burke would not come after him. But it also seemed certain that given half a chance, it would be a pleasure for the professional to finish what he had been about to do. The best chance Lou had with the least amount of risk to people was to call security and the police. He wondered if hotel security officers were like mall cops, or if they carried guns. Even if they did, he would be sending them to their death against Burke.

Still coughing into his towel, Lou braced himself against the front desk. Water dripped down his face and pooled on the granite surface. The attendant, a quick young man with black-rimmed glasses, a dark suit, and a name tag that read REYNALDO used a hand towel to blot the mess before it reached his keyboard.

"May I help you?" he asked, cool as a Popsicle.

Lou was speechless,

Don't you notice anything unusual about me? he wanted to say. *I just did a six-story cannonball into your pool because a man broke into my room with a gun and was about to kill me. Would you please call security and the police?*

Then it occurred to him that Vaill was keeping him hidden because the agent no longer trusted the FBI. The worst thing he could do now was to get the authorities—any authorities—involved. What he really needed was to get away from Burke, and to reconnect with Vaill. . . . Oh, yes, and to pick up some clothes and a pair of shoes.

Reynaldo stood by, waiting patiently.

"Um, the shower in my room is broken," Lou said, using the coughing towel on his hair. "I was looking to see if the shampoo was in the stall, and the shower just went . . . on. Full blast, no warning."

Improvised lying. He had been a master at it during the drinking and drugging years. It seemed that like his alcoholism, the ability to improvise a lie was never really far from the surface.

"I'm very sorry about that," Reynaldo said. "I thought you might have been caught in the rain. Sir, what's your room number?" he asked as if Lou had simply requested another pillow. "I'll send maintenance up right away."

The young desk clerk was clearly destined for bigger things.

Again, Lou found himself speculating on how Burke might escape the hotel, and wondering if it would be wise to go after him. Again, the internal debate ended quickly. Alexander Burke was a man to stay away from unless Cap's life or Humphrey's depended on bringing him down.

"No worries," Lou said to the desk clerk. "It only did it once. Just wanted you to know."

From the corner of his eye, Lou saw some would-be rescuers making their way in from the pool, and hurried off. In spite of himself, he ignored the mismatch of a soaking wet doc versus a heavily armed killer, and skidded to a stop at the elevators. There were four of them, two on each side of the bay. All were in use, but none of them was on the sixth floor. At that moment, his common sense took over. It was doubtful Burke was anywhere near the sixth floor. He could have taken the stairs or gone out a service entrance. Either way, he had the notebook. The Neighbors would want it ASAP, and Lou would most likely be put on his to-do list.

Lou avoided the front desk and Reynaldo, and hurried out the revolving doors. The rain had largely abated, but the wind remained, along with a thick band of humid air that gave his sodden clothes the heft of a suit of armor. Ignoring the uniformed doorman, Lou climbed into a cab that was idling on the hotel's circular driveway.

The cab lurched forward, and the driver, an African

American man with a congenial smile, glanced over his shoulder.

"Going to the aquarium?" he asked.

"That was pretty funny."

"I have my moments."

The cabbie slowed, waiting for instructions.

Stubborn to the last, Lou was still scanning for Burke.

"Just drive," he said.

"Your dime."

There was reason to be hopeful, Lou was thinking. Horrible as it was, it was telling that Burke killed the home health aide, but not Humphrey. One Hundred Neighbors were frantic. According to Cap's doctors, the germ had mutated. It could be the Neighbors had lost their leverage to negotiate with Washington, but were keeping that fact secret for as long as possible. Assuming their treatment was no longer effective, it made no sense that Humphrey was dead.

Lou removed his sodden wallet from his pants pocket and gave the driver the address to the FBI's Atlanta field office.

"Do you have a cell phone I could borrow?" he asked.

The driver looked at Lou through his rearview mirror.

"You're not going to call a girlfriend in Canada, are you?" His laugh was genuine.

"No, I'm going to call my brother at the FBI," Lou said, deadpan.

The man's expression turned serious.

"Oh, well, in that case . . ."

He passed his phone back. The numbers Vaill had

scrawled on his card were still legible, although the ink was running. Reluctant even to consider going into the field office, Lou didn't have a plan B. As things shook down, he didn't have to. A second after he hit the last number, Vaill answered.

"Yeah, Vaill here."

"It's Lou."

"What number is this?"

No pleasantries, no small talk. The man was all business, and totally suspicious of everything.

"I borrowed it from my cabdriver. I'm on my way to you now."

"Just stay away from the front of the building," Vaill said. "Park across the street and a block down. Believe it or not, I was just going to call. I've put together a DVD like you suggested. There's one thing I think we should go over together—it's a DVD recording Burke sent to his wife. It's been checked by the evidence analysts, but it may be worth looking at again."

"Well, I've learned a little bit about Burke, too," Lou said. "He just showed up in my hotel room. He used your name to get me to open the door. Then he tried to do his thing."

"How'd you get away from him?"

"Let's just say I got a seven from the Polish judge."

Lou heard Vaill suck in a breath.

"You dove?"

"Cannonball. I did a six-story cannonball. I'm sore but okay. Tim, he's got Humphrey's notebook."

"As long as he doesn't have your scalp on his lodge-pole. Do you need anything?"

"A change of clothes and size nine New Balances."

"We'll find a place to do that. Have the cab park near

the Starbucks across the street. I'm going to pack up and meet you. Where are you now?" Lou got the address from the driver and relayed it back to Vaill. "Okay, I think you're about fifteen minutes away. And, doc?"

"Yeah?"

"That puts you and me together in a unique group."

"What group is that?"

"As far as I know, we're the only two Alexander Burke has ever tried to kill and didn't."

CHAPTER 45

Secrecy and discretion are more important to a tactical revolutionary movement than numbers.

—LANCASTER R. HILL, *100 Neighbors*, SAWYER RIVER BOOKS, 1939, P. 156

Burke showing up at Lou's hotel had only heightened Vaill's paranoia and his conviction that they were dealing with a mole in the agency. Moments after Lou hung up, he had called back to move their meeting place down two blocks.

As the cab cruised past the field office and neared the spot, Lou dropped two limp wrinkled twenties onto the front seat and bolted before they had come to a complete stop. As best as his still-saturated jeans would allow, he got into a crouch and weaved to Vaill's passenger's-side door like a man afraid of getting shot by a sniper, which, essentially, he was.

Alexander Burke had proved his skill as an agent as well as his viciousness and absolute remorselessness. Now it was time for Vaill to take charge and lead them in some sort of counterstrike. Two problems: even in top form, it was unlikely he was a match for the killer, and at the moment, post-op with a rainbow scar and unpredictable, disabling headaches, he most certainly was not in top form.

"Buckle up, buddy," he said. "If I pick up a tail, we're going to have to do some fancy driving to lose him, or even better, to come up behind him. Just like the fighter pilots."

"I don't think he's out there, Tim. At least not right now."

"Explain."

"He's got what the Neighbors want, Humphrey's notebook, and now he's got to deliver it to wherever they are, probably as quickly as possible."

"I suppose."

"That doesn't mean forget about him, but I am willing to take the chance he's postponing coming after either of us until his mission is complete. Then maybe he'll come after us instead of taking a well-earned vacation to the Caribbean or something. All that is by way of saying I need to get out of these damn clothes and into something dry."

"How about we find a place to stay first?"

"How about we stop by a store for some sweats and a pair of sneakers? My inner thighs can only take so much of this."

For the first time, Vaill cracked a smile.

"You got it," he said.

To the credit of the staff at Richie's Sporting Goods, no one reacted to the disheveled, sodden, shoeless customer with an "M.D." following the name on his MasterCard, which, not surprisingly, failed to work after its soaking. Vaill quickly pulled out a wad of cash before the clerk even started keying in the account number by hand. Fifteen minutes of rapid shopping, and Lou left the store with a set of sweats, a sharp pair of New Balance running shoes, shorts, socks, underwear, T-shirts, an Atlanta Falcons jacket, an Atlanta Braves cap, an Atlanta Hawks sweatshirt, and $270 owed to his new partner.

"My delicate inner thighs thank you," Lou said as they drove away.

"In nearly a month working together, Chuck McCall never cost me a dime," Vaill replied. "And he never mentioned his delicate inner thighs, neither. Now, let's first make certain Burke isn't even better than we fear, and then find somewhere to settle in and look at this evidence I brought."

The place they settled on, after nearly half an hour of evasive driving, was a no-frills Great Southern Inn and Suites. In truth, the Great Southern was the exact sort of place Lou would have picked had he not accumulated an abundance of credit card points. The irony was not lost on him that those points had most likely saved his life. There was only a micro-sized pool at the two-story motel, and no balcony from which he could have jumped.

Vaill registered as Gregg Campbell from Houston, and had a license and credit cards to back that up.

"I have half a dozen of these sets," he said to Lou in a more than passable Texas drawl. "Passports, letters of credit, the works. Gregg Campbell is one of my favorites, although the truth is he would probably never stay here. Oil, dontcha know."

"Our tax dollars at work," Lou said.

He liked it when Vaill shed his grim mantle, but he well understood why he didn't do it often.

The Great Southern was up a long drive, about a quarter mile off a sparsely traveled highway. They found it because of a large sign on a very tall pole. Lou wondered what a six-story-tall pole would look like. After they registered for a second-floor suite, Vaill waited in the shadows near the entrance for a good while, fixed on the driveway and the parking lot. Finally, satisfied enough, he led Lou up to their room.

"I wouldn't put it past the monster to leave his car someplace and walk a mile or so to come up behind this place," he said.

He pulled the small desk over in front of the closed pullout, set up his laptop, and inserted one of two DVDs.

"I thought we could start with the one Burke's wife gave to me and McCall. I showed her graphic photos of what he did to Maria, and she cracked and gave this to us. There's nothing really of use on it, but I thought it would be a good place to start. Want me to go out for some popcorn for the matinee?"

"Let me see if I can recall what happened the last time you left me alone in a hotel room," Lou replied.

"Okay, no popcorn, no Raisinets."

"So there's not much to this recording?"

"It's a tearjerker featuring a murderer. Doesn't even get a PG rating."

"Sounds like at least you guys are making use of the warehousing technology."

"This is a video of Burke, sent to his wife. It's been analyzed by one of our very best intelligence people. No, make that our absolutely best intelligence people. Like I said, he didn't come up with much. But if nothing else, it presents some interesting insights into the man."

Vaill hit play and Lou felt his insides go cold. The screen lit up with the image of Alexander Burke, although not the Alexander Burke who had attacked him at the hotel.

"Amazing disguise he wore," Lou said.

"Believe me, this one's the real deal."

This man, clean-shaven, had gray eyes, a different-shaped nose, and straw-colored hair. He was totally at ease, and dashingly good-looking, perched on a high, bar-type stool, set on a swath of brownish green lawn. Behind him, an endless expanse of steel ocean churned before an arcing horizon, and on either side, small groves of trees set off his carefully staged tableau. A small plastic device—a remote, Lou assumed—dangled in his hand. The camera, rock steady, was probably set on a tripod, and it did not look as if the killer had help in making the recording.

"Hi, Lola, hey, sweet baby." His voice was nothing like the one Lou had heard in the hotel room. His inflection was warm and full of love, incongruous with the cold eyes and the harsh memories Lou held of him. "You're not going to hear anything from me in the coming months. But sooner or later you will, and none of it is going to be very flattering. I wish I could be there with you when it all comes out, in order to comfort you in what is going to be a difficult time. But I can't. I have to be where I am, doing what I will be doing."

Vaill paused the recording.

"Like I said, this has been analyzed by our best. But it's good that we're starting at the beginning. Pay attention to voice, his manner, the way he holds himself. I guess the best thing we could hope for is some clue as to where this film was made, but I believe that's asking too much."

"Got it," Lou said. "Keep rolling."

Burke's image again became animated.

"You understand our cause," he was saying, his tone far calmer than the white-capped ocean behind him. "You know what's at stake. It's not just about our future, but the future of this country. Somebody has to take a stand. The politicians have had their chances and it's time for my organization to step up and make a real difference.

"I told you when we first met that I didn't want children, because I didn't want them raised in this corrupt and weak society. But every day I wished we had a bunch. You would have made an amazing mother, and I would have been the luckiest man in the world. As it is, *I am* lucky. I'm blessed to have the opportunity to make it possible for other people to have children and raise them in a country that is as strong and as financially stable as the original foundation upon which our forefathers built it.

"I miss you, Lola, and I love you with all my heart and soul. I want to tell you that I will come for you when it's safe. If there is a way, I will come get you. But that might not happen. More likely is that I will be a wanted man—wanted for doing what I believe in my soul is right. But know this: my heart is pure, my conscience is clean, and my conviction in the cause is as unwavering as my love for you."

Burke raised the remote control and the image on the screen went to black.

Lou sat quietly, stunned by what he had just watched. Nothing leaped out at him, except that the emotion expressed in the recording was as true as a bullet—as bright as the torch Lou still carried for Emily's mother, Renee. Also, it was clear that Burke was not simply a hired gun. He was invested in the principles espoused by the Neighbors. Their cause was his, and he was willing to kill to support it.

Lou shared those thoughts with Vaill.

"Anything else?" Vaill asked. "Anything that would give us other insights into the man, or maybe something that would give us a clue as to where this was made?"

Lou shook his head. "The only things I saw were ocean, trees, grass, the stool, and a few large rocks, mostly embedded in the earth."

"Come on, doc. More. You're doing fine."

"Well, I feel stupid even saying it, but he was up high."

"On a cliff," Vaill said. "It's like he chose the most scenic, romantic spot around wherever he was. And his face was well lit—no shadows."

"Good. His shadow sitting on the stool wasn't very long, and it went out behind him, toward the water, so he's probably facing west."

"Past noon, facing west. That's it, partner. That's the idea."

"I can't make out the few trees to his right, but there are leaves with some color on them, and just a few on the ground. Doesn't look like winter."

"Or summer," Vaill said, "judging from his clothes. There are a few wispy clouds and the water is a little choppy, so that's a half point against summer and winter, too."

"I agree. My money's on autumn, maybe six months ago. Sorry, Tim, but at the moment, I can't come up with anything else."

"Then we're going to do what any decent FBI agent would do in this situation."

Lou shot him a curious look. "And that would be?"

"First we'll go over the other material I recorded in order to bring you up to speed. Then we watch this recording again, and we keep watching it until we're fried—until our eyes bleed or we find something else of value. At the moment, it's really all we have."

"In that case," Lou said, "before we settle in for a quintuple feature or whatever it turns out to be, maybe they have a vending machine here with some Raisinets."

CHAPTER 46

Liberty cannot exist without sacrifice, nor can sacrifice exist without suffering. Blood may be shed, but should the suffering of the part in the end save the whole, it is a pain we are obligated to endure.

—LANCASTER R. HILL, *A Secret Worth Keeping*, SAWYER RIVER BOOKS, 1939, P. 199

Tim Vaill's exhaustion was a concern.

Med school and a grueling residency had trained Lou for endurance studying and long shifts, so it wasn't surprising that he felt solid after five straight hours of reviewing the evidence from the Information Data Warehouse, and then plunging back into the Burke video.

Lou had supposed that Vaill, who was about his age, was put together similarly, having survived the punishing tests of Quantico and hours spent cooped up inside various vans conducting surveillance. But at the moment that seemed not to be the case.

Lou eyed the scar arcing along Vaill's right temple, speculating on how much the injury and subsequent surgery might have affected his stamina. This was the second time in the past hour the agent had drifted off in his chair during a playback. Lou would have let him rest, except this time he had begun to snore, making it hard to study the nuances in Burke's speech, even though Lou had already committed every word and vocal inflection to memory.

Making matters even more difficult, the air conditioner was on high, even though the room at the Great Southern Inn and Suites still felt humid and stuffy. For a time, Lou busied himself folding empty Domino's pizza boxes and forcing them, the Diet Coke cans he flattened, and the wrappers of each item in the motel vending machines into the wastebasket. Finally, after some stretching and a hundred double-crunch sit-ups, Lou tapped Vaill on the shoulder. The agent came awake with a start.

"I'm fine, I'm fine," he said, pawing at his eyes. "What'd I miss?"

Lou appraised him thoughtfully.

"Only our one hundredth viewing of Alexander Burke. You want to take a real break? A lie-down nap?"

Vaill again massaged his eyes and then wet his lips with his tongue. He still looked glazed, so Lou passed him a half-empty can of warm Diet Coke, which Vaill drained in one gulp.

"No," he said emphatically. "I want to keep watching."

It was intense work, but Lou believed they were making some progress, even though a *Eureka!* moment continued to elude them. Having focused on everything Burke was saying—every word, every nuanced change in his vocal inflection—Lou had compiled a complete transcript of the killer's impassioned speech for Lola, and was now dissecting it for hidden clues—a message within the message.

"If there's really anything encoded in this," Lou

asked, "why wouldn't Lola have told you what it was when she gave it to you?"

"Inner conflict, I suspect. Maybe guilt kept her from making it too easy for us."

With Lou perched on the pull-out and Vaill on the desk chair, they watched the killer again—viewing number 101. Afterward, Lou crumpled a ball of the white copy paper he had gotten at the front desk, and tossed it with frustration at the wastebasket, which blocked his shot with the top edge of a folded Domino's box.

Despite this latest disappointment, he continued to pursue the latest possibility—that the letters of each word Burke spoke could be used to form new and more revealing sentences. So far, only gibberish. At Vaill's suggestion, they had diligently recorded each time Burke had blinked, thinking perhaps he was using Morse or another code to send Lola his location. If there was a subliminal message hidden within the recording, it was proving to be as elusive as an *A* was in Lou's college organic chemistry class.

"You okay?" Vaill asked.

"Maybe a little pizza-ed out, but I'm fine."

"Then let's play it again," Vaill said. "We'll shoot for Chinese delivery in another couple of hours."

By run-through 105, Vaill's chin and eyelids were heading south again.

"Honestly, Tim, I think it's time we take a break," Lou said.

Vaill lifted his head and Lou saw the fire he recognized from the interrogation room.

"I'm not going to give up because Burke is out there," Vaill said, tapping the killer's image with the butt end of a pen. "That piece of garbage murdered my wife, is stealing your best friend's life, and is laughing at us for coming after him because he doesn't believe we'll ever catch him until he wants us to catch him so he can kill us."

Lou's own resolve felt strengthened by Vaill's intensity, and he was about to hit play, when they were interrupted by a series of sharp knocks on the door.

"Hey, Tim," came a voice Lou recognized with virtual certainty, "it's McCall. Open up."

Lou froze. Usually unflappable, his pulse kicked off like a jackrabbit's. Vaill, by contrast, appeared unfazed.

Whatever exhaustion Lou had seen in the man was gone, and he was instantly on the move, his actions rapid and purposeful. *Situations like this are his ER,* Lou thought—the equivalent of a doc being confronted by the multiple victims of a car crash. Calm as a summer breeze, Vaill put a finger to his lips, moved the stuffed wastebasket to a remote corner with his foot, pointed to the laptop then to Lou, and lastly to the bathroom. The unspoken message was clear: this was quite possibly a threat.

As Lou headed into the smallish bathroom, he saw Vaill smoothly check his gun and stuff it into the rear waistband of his jeans, concealing it underneath his T-shirt.

"What do you want, Chuck?" Vaill called out without rancor. "It isn't a great time to talk."

"What are you doing in there?" McCall implored. "Come on, Tim. Let me in!"

Lou closed the bathroom door behind him and threw his still drying clothes into the tub. Then he climbed in himself, forcing the damp clothes beneath his knees, clutching the laptop, and pulling the plastic curtain closed. The tight fit reminded him why he never chose a tub over a shower unless it was a good-sized Jacuzzi.

Willing himself to control his breathing, he listened, using his imagination and ears to create details he could not see. It was clear Vaill was going to allow his partner in. Lou imagined him crossing the room, then checking through the security peephole. Next came a click and a faint creak of unoiled door hinges opening then closing. Chuck McCall, in Vaill's mind the chief possibility to be an agency mole working with Burke, was in the room.

"Are you doing drugs?" McCall asked.

"What are you doing here, Chuck? How'd you find me?"

"When I couldn't get a hold of you, I checked to see if anybody was using your credit card or one of our fake ones, and saw activity on the Gregg Campbell VISA. Wasn't hard to track you down from there."

"Next time I'll be more careful."

Lou decided to mute Vaill's laptop in case an e-mail or other warning tone sounded. Gingerly, he lifted the cover and killed the volume. Burke's face stared out at him.

Where are you? Lou asked the face. *Where have you taken the notebook? Did you kill Humphrey? Torture him?*

"What in the hell is going on with you?" he heard McCall ask. "Where's Welcome?"

"I let him go. I called Beth and told her."

"You did what?"

"I let him go. We were off base on him. He's not involved in any way we don't already know about."

Lou had no trouble picturing McCall's disbelief.

"You can't just do that," he said.

"Why not? I work for the FBI. We make those decisions all the time."

"But I'm your partner! You're supposed to make them *with me*."

"Speaking of that, I'm thinking of putting in for a few weeks off. Medical leave. My headaches are getting worse."

"Yeah, well, I'm thinking about putting out an APB for Lou Welcome. I can't believe you let him go."

"Don't do that, Chuck. As your partner, I'm asking you to back away from this. Miller and Welcome aren't terrorists. A doctor and a scientist. That's all they are. They're victims of One Hundred Neighbors, not their allies. I think the murder in Miller's apartment is proof enough of that."

A long pause ensued. Lou's eyes traveled back to Burke's frozen image. Without sound or movement, he could better focus on other details—the dusky blue of the sky cut off by the gray of the sea, the angle of the sun on Burke's face and straw-colored hair, and the carpet of grass running from the killer to the cliff's edge.

But for the first time in more than a hundred viewings, something else in the frame caught Lou's eye. Like the audience of a magician using misdirection to perform a trick, Lou realized he had missed seeing the object because he'd been so focused on other details— the timbre of Burke's speech, his words, his eye blinks. But this new discovery, frozen in the field just beneath the horizon, might be real, provided it was not just a figment of the filming or something the endless plays had done to the disc.

"Look, Tim," McCall was saying, "I know I can never replace Maria, but that doesn't mean I can't care about you as a partner and a friend."

"Good to know. If you care, you'll head out."

"Just like that?"

"Just like that."

"What about the job?"

"I'm going to take some time off. I've already given Snyder the heads-up. I need to rest."

McCall went silent.

"It's that bad?"

"I'm taking a leave, aren't I?"

"Promise me you'll check in with your doctor."

"If you promise me you'll back off Welcome."

Lou's lower back was starting to ache. He wanted desperately to shift positions, but worried that even the slightest movement might cause a sound. Instead, he focused on the image to distract himself. As before, the object was there, nearly lost in the whitecaps and the horizon and the scattered clouds.

Maybe, just maybe . . .

"I need you to go, Chuck," Vaill said. "Please. I need my time and space to heal. Can you do that for me?"

The younger agent exhaled loudly.

Lou pictured his discouragement, but now his own pulse was beginning to quicken. McCall was just seconds from leaving.

"Mind if I use your bathroom before I go?" he said suddenly.

Lou's breath caught and he braced himself against the sides of the tub. There was nothing he could think of to do except to remain motionless and keep his breathing slow and soundless.

"Sure," Vaill replied. "But then I need you to go."

The door opened. McCall stepped in and closed it behind him. Lou could think of nothing around the sink that would give his presence away. He clutched the laptop to his chest like a life preserver and stared up at the showerhead as the agent did his business two feet away.

McCall flushed the toilet and washed his hands, standing not much farther away than the thickness of the vinyl shower curtain. Lou held his breath. The porcelain tub was feeling like it was made of shirt pins, and the damp clothes were becoming bothersome as well.

Then the bathroom door opened and clicked shut.

"I'm really worried about you, Tim," McCall said.

"I appreciate that."

"If you change your mind about staying on the team, call me."

"Roger that. I'll see you again soon, Chuck. Don't worry about me, okay? I'll be fine."

The door to the outside corridor opened and closed with the rusty squeal and a soft click. Two endless minutes passed before Vaill called out.

"He just drove away. I don't think he suspected anything, but we've got to think about getting out of here to another place. That was really stupid of me with the damn credit card, especially when I have one with a fake name that I don't think the agency knows about."

Lou unfolded to his feet, stepped into the room, and glared at Vaill.

"I can't believe you let him use the damn bathroom. Why couldn't you have told him the toilet was plugged or something?"

"I didn't think of it. Next time," Vaill said. "Nice going in there. You have the makings of a decent agent."

"Actually, thanks to your partner's visit, we might have caught a break."

"Explain," Vaill said.

Lou brought the laptop back to the desk.

"Take a look at this. Because I turned the sound off and paused the DVD, I just lay there and stared at this one image. I can't believe we missed this every time. Top center."

Vaill looked at the screen for just a few seconds.

"Jesus," he murmured. "There's a ship out there."

"A tanker, I think. And at that distance, I would guess it's a large one."

"I'll be damned. Our analyst must have missed it, too. He never mentioned a word about it."

Lou ran the disc back and forth a few times. Now the tanker was obvious, cruising from their right to their left, just below the horizon.

"Okay," Vaill said, "we've found something. Now, how is it going to help us?"

"That depends."

"On?"

"On how good your analyst is at enhancing images. If he's really good, and I mean *really* good, maybe he can get us a look at the markings on that ship."

CHAPTER 47

Roosevelt's New Deal needs an adversary worthy of its bloated aspirations, to force a retreat from its initial advance. In this regard, *100 Neighbors* will be mightier than any military for our means to an end will not be subject to any of the rules governing war.

——LANCASTER R. HILL, PERSONAL
  COMMUNICATION TO CARL LAGRECA,
  SEPTEMBER 1936

Vaill and Lou packed what little they had and headed off for the Wendover Suites, five miles east of the Grand Southern. Halfway there, Vaill, who had been pensively quiet, looked over at his passenger. There was reverence in his eyes.

"Do you realize what you just did back there?" he asked.

"Well, I know I noticed something we had missed seeing after hours of studying that video. Was there something else?"

"The amazing thing is, *mi amigo,* we're not the only ones who had missed it."

"The bureau analyst?"

"Not just any analyst," he said. "You just beat the Slugger."

Lou knitted his brows.

"The who?"

"Remember how I told you this video was logged as evidence and thoroughly analyzed by one of our best intelligence agents? No, make that our *top* intelligence agent."

"I sort of remember you commenting about an analyst, but I don't remember anything about a slugger."

"Itsuki Sakura," Vaill said, "not *a* slugger, *the* Slugger."

"Confusion reigns."

"It's an internal nickname we have for the guy," Vaill said. "Sakura played minor league pro ball in Japan for a short while before he moved to the States and became a legend at the agency. He's a baseball fanatic, and I don't mean your garden variety either. This guy is a living encyclopedia of American *and* Japanese baseball trivia, facts, and statistics. He's an amazing intelligence analyst, but sometimes people use him as a last resort because he can be a bit, how should I say, *tiring* when it comes to getting him to focus. That aside, when the Slugger is locked in, man, he never misses."

"Slugger. I love it," Lou said.

"Tell me that after you've met him. Anyway, the Slugger looked at the video, too, but he saw nothing of real value."

"Guess I got lucky."

Vaill dismissed that notion with a flick of his hand.

"No. In the agency you learn that you make your own luck. This time, the FBI fell short and when the Slugger reviews this video again, he'll be the first to agree."

"He wasn't prepared for the ship, that's all. We watched that video more than a hundred times."

As a rabid Washington Nationals fan, who took Emily to two or three games a year, Lou felt he needed to defend the Slugger's honor.

"Whatever you say," Vaill replied, "but I do understand what you mean. We once took a class at Quantico about observation and selective attention. They played a video of six people whipping a basketball around randomly in a circle. We were told to count the number of times the ball changed hands. Afterward, some had the right answer, some didn't. Then the instructor asked who saw the gorilla. Nobody raised a hand, but sure enough, when he played the video back, a guy in a gorilla suit had wandered into the middle of the circle while the ball was being passed, did a little dance, and then wandered off. The class was so focused on counting the tosses, that the ape never registered."

"Terrific example. That's exactly what happened with us, and probably to the Slugger as well. We were so focused on what Burke was doing and talking about, we never noticed the gorilla steaming along in the background. In medicine, when we read an x-ray, say, a chest x-ray in a patient with a big patch of pneumonia, we are taught to examine everything *except* the lungs first, because otherwise you lose yourself in the object of your interest. That's how things get missed in, like, the ribs or the heart."

After twenty minutes of relatively uninspired evasive driving, they picked up forty dollars' worth of Chinese takeout and checked into the Wendover Suites, which was a notch or so below the Grand Southern.

As soon as they were in their room, they called Itsuki Sakura in his San Diego office, to give him instructions. For the next several hours, Lou and Vaill ate, rested, talked about their lives, and waited for the

Slugger to get back to them, this time on Skype. Lou had picked up only snippets of Vaill's conversation with the man, but it was enough to know the analyst was not at all pleased with his own performance.

The Chinese food was actually decent, but to Lou, his exchanges with Vaill were better. Not unexpectedly, much of what he had to say led back to Maria. Every time, Vaill's eyes would grow distant and his heartache became a presence in the room. Lou found himself wondering if, after Renee, he'd ever feel like that toward another woman again. He talked about his enduring love for his now-remarried ex, his brief relationship with high-powered attorney Sarah Cooper, and even his growing attraction for Vicki Banks. Could he ever love a woman besides Renee the way Vaill treasured Maria? The jury, they concluded, was still very much out on that one.

Skype's ringtone electrified the moment. Vaill raced over to his computer and in a few seconds, Lou was introduced to Itsuki Sakura, a.k.a. the Slugger. Lou's first impression was surprise at how young the analyst looked, having imagined a thin, wizened man with wise eyes. The Slugger, by contrast, had a mop of dark unruly hair, gold-rimmed glasses, and a delicate nose and mouth. Dressed in a white shirt and black tie, he reminded Lou of a graduate student more than a seasoned FBI intelligence analyst.

Seated on the pullout, Lou crowded in close to Vaill so that they could both be seen in the camera's limited field. When they were properly positioned, the Slugger gave them a thumbs-up.

"You are very bright man to see what you saw," the Slugger said.

According to Vaill, Sakura had become a natural-ized citizen only ten years before.

"I just got a little lucky," Lou replied.

"You know who considered self to be luckiest man on face of earth?"

Vaill leaned over, briefly blocking Lou's view entirely.

"Slugger, we've got to focus here."

"Lou Gehrig, that who," Slugger answered. "He said so in farewell address to baseball. But he never really left game. He still one of most loved players of all time. So maybe he was lucky, like you, but that does not lessen your accomplishment any, or his."

Lou liked the man immediately. Having worked with plenty of rhino-sized egos over his years in academic medicine, he took notice whenever somebody was not threatened by teamwork.

"That's great, Slugger," Vail said. "Now, what have you got for us?"

"You Lou Welcome, eh? That your name? Welcome?"

"That's right," Lou said.

"Good. Good. No relation to Welcome Gaston? Great-grandson, maybe?"

"Who?" Lou asked.

"Pitched for Brooklyn Bridegrooms from 1889 to 1899. They ancestor of Brooklyn Dodgers. Betcha not know that!"

"I do now. What a pearl," Lou said.

"Slugger, the video!"

"Yeah. Well, video very good quality. Sorry I read it so poorly first time. Now that we know freighter is there, easy to enhance and see IMO number."

"IMO?" Lou asked.

"IMO, International Maritime Organization. Each ship has unique identifier. Can track back to registered shipowner and management company. Ship in video belong to Exceed Maritime. Headquarters in New Haven, Connecticut. Name of ship is EM *Sustinet.*"

"That's great work!" Vaill exclaimed, with Lou nodding his assent.

"Still feel like Bobby Richardson for missing ship altogether."

"Feel like who?" Vaill asked.

"Bobby Richardson," Lou said. "Second baseman for the Yankees. The only player ever to win the World Series MVP while playing for the losing team."

"Very good, Lou Welcome! Remember Bill Mazeroski? He hit home run to win that 1960 series for Pirates. Major, major upset. But Richardson, he hit .367. Drive in twelve runs. Hit grand slam, too."

"Slugger, can we get back to the video?" Vaill pleaded. "Could you pick up the location?"

Slugger smiled.

"At first evaluation, video was only a double. No home run."

"Why only a two-bagger?" Lou asked, already comfortable with the analyst's colorful patois.

"I know time of day because of position of sun and shadows," Slugger said. "Video taken close to one o'clock in afternoon."

Important stuff. By knowing the time of day they could contact the shipping company and examine the ship's logs to determine where the vessel was located at that particular hour. Then, using maps, they might possibly be able to pinpoint Burke's location.

"But there still problem. You went two for three with data, but you still missing key piece."

"What piece of data do we need?" Vaill asked.

"What day is it?" Slugger replied. "I know hour, approximately one P.M., but I don't know day. True position of sun depends on location and month. Also, ship has many logs. Need the day or close to it to make equation work."

Lou's enthusiasm lessened.

"Lou Welcome!" Slugger cried. "You look like you strike out with bases loaded. No worry. We come back like Cleveland beating Seattle down twelve runs in seventh inning. Okay?"

Lou, whose father, Dennis, could still give the Slugger at least a run for his money, immediately picked up on the reference to one of the greatest comebacks in Major League Baseball history. In 2001, the Indians were losing to the Mariners 14–2 and came back to win the game 15–14 in eleven innings.

"Sorry, Slugger, but I threw my last strike with the ship. Not sure how I can be John Rocker here."

Slugger beamed. "Rocker! Yeah, good! Crazy man but damn good pitcher. John Rocker won game. Lot of luck there! But Rocker was no forester, and he was no intelligence analyst, either."

Vaill now. "What do you mean 'forester'?"

"Foliage in background," Slugger said. "It is what forest people call peak. Best autumn colors. I check with forestry expert and he confirm."

"But that won't tell us *where* it was peak," Lou said.

"We know based on sun and trees this East Coast," Slugger replied. "But I call forestry expert and give him screen grab. Nothing revealing. He sees mix of deciduous trees and firs—blue spruce, white pine, maple, cedar, and balsam, which tell him Downeast Maine, maybe Washington County, which include city of Calais, first place in United States to see sunrise. You know that, Lou Welcome?"

"No. No, I didn't. This is amazing work, Slugger."

"Like Teddy Ballgame Williams, last man to hit four hundred for season. Four-oh-six for Red Sox in 1941. But it get better, Lou Welcome. Peak foliage in Downeast Maine depend on previous summer weather, but because climate warmer around coast, and no killing frost, peak for Washington County anywhere from fourteen October to twenty-five."

"Which means you can check with Exceed Maritime and see where the EM *Sustinet* was on those dates," Vaill said.

Slugger nodded his appreciation of Vaill's insight. "More specifically, I made call and ask if ship was within thousand yards of coast in Washington County at one o'clock any days between fourteen and twenty-five October."

Lou's mouth had gone dry. "And?"

"And it was," Slugger said, as matter-of-factly as if he had just shared the top item on his grocery list. "On twenty October. I make printout of exact location of land from shipping coordinates. So I know where video was recorded, but could not have figured it out without Lou Welcome's help."

"Itsuki, you can't tell anybody about this," Vaill said urgently. "Please. It's highly confidential."

"Understood."

"Where?" Lou asked. "Where was this filmed?"

"According to my map and other sources, video recorded on property of private residence. Big, big place called Red Cliff. Here nice photos from Google Earth and also one of our satellites."

Lou and Vaill peered first at one, then the other remarkable pictures of what appeared to be a sprawling medieval castle, complete with moat, perched on a cliff over the ocean.

"Home run," they said nearly in unison.

CHAPTER 48

At some point, and this is a guarantee, the trustees overseeing the finances of Social Security will issue a report informing the American people that the fund is bankrupt.

—LANCASTER R. HILL, LECTURE AT DUKE UNIVERSITY, NORTH CAROLINA, MAY 21, 1947

Electronically distorted images of the seven Neighbors flickered and glowed on the screens filling one wall of Bacon's magnificent study. The financier, N-38, was flushed with excitement—a condition that had little to do with the tumbler of twenty-one-year-old Glenlivet he was clutching. Victory was again within reach. He inhaled the aroma of his Scotch and savored the smoky taste of a more lusty swallow than typical for him. There were still mountains left to climb, obstacles to overcome, but with each hour, each piece of news, he was feeling more confident. As director of the Society of One Hundred Neighbors, it was time to share the latest regarding AP-Janus with the members of the project board.

Good news indeed.

"We are all here, Eighty," Bacon said. "Please begin with an update on the medical."

Academic surgeon Dr. Carlton Reeves, known by

name to Bacon but only as Eighty to the others, was the coordinator of Action Project Janus. It was he who initially investigated the bacteria discovered by N-71, saw the possibilities, and formed an advisory committee consisting of several of the society's members—each with an expertise that would help make the possibilities a reality. The advisors were selected by summaries of their backgrounds, accomplishments, and abilities, and submitted to Eighty by Bacon.

From his control panel, Bacon sent the physician's distorted image to the rest of the board. Except for him, none of them would know Reeves by anything other than his number, unless their paths had crossed by coincidence. It had been that way since the organization's inception.

Secrecy and discretion, Lancaster Hill had written in 1939, *are more important to a tactical revolutionary movement than numbers.*

"Welcome all," Eighty said. "Due to the unpredicted mutation of the Janus strain, the government's efforts to develop an effective antibacterial treatment are languishing. We are seeing an acceleration of infections in hospitals caused by the bacteria, which has been labeled by the media as the Doomsday Germ. However, the microbe that our scientist, Seventy-one, initially discovered is no longer the same as the current incarnation of Janus. Correct me if I'm wrong, Nine, but it is clear that as things stand, earlier estimates of the potential for spread are low—actually quite low."

Bacon made a mental note to cycle back to Nine, the analyst/strategist, who, by protocol, had been given her late predecessor's number when she was first inducted some years before. Even without her verification, everyone on the board knew that Eighty's assessment was correct. First though, Bacon wanted a report on how the government was responding to the increasing rate of spread, and whether they had concluded that the treatment guaranteed by the society was no longer effective.

"Forty-four," he asked, "can you offer information on the government's efforts to combat Janus?"

The center of the display flickered and filled with Forty-four's distorted feed. In addition to secretly brokering the backroom deals to end the Janus attacks, Forty-four, a senior senator from Rhode Island, was the point man in dealing with the president and the secretary of Health and Human Services.

"As you know, Washington has formed a global consortium," Forty-four said, "employing scientists from various disciplines, but nobody is pleased with the progress thus far. The good news is since Dr. Kazimi was brought in to work with us, the government's efforts are being coordinated through the CDC, making it possible for Seventy-one to intentionally mislead the consortium wherever necessary. We believe we can continue this internal sabotage without risk of exposing Seventy-one's affiliation with us."

"I doubt these efforts will be necessary once the entitlements are revoked." Speaking was Twenty-six, a specialist in mass psychology.

"Explain yourself," Bacon said, switching the man to the center of the board members' screens.

"Once Social Security, Medicare, and Medicaid are revoked, along with all the other related programs, a sea change will take place among the population. My research, in conjunction with supporting evidence from several top economists, has confirmed this theory. There will, of course, be unrest, but the American people will see immediate tax relief, followed soon after by a massive reduction in the deficit. Our economy will be greatly unburdened, resulting in higher levels of employment and a fast-growing GNP. Our country can be made great again, and once the entitlements are gone, it will not take long for all to become convinced of that fact. In other words, we won't need Janus. People will begin to demand less and less government involvement in the daily lives of its citizens. They will come to see and understand the parasitic nature of Washington taxing us all to care for those who refuse to care for themselves."

"Yes, it's true," Bacon said. "Fear has been keeping us in chains for far too long. We know what is necessary, but like an opiate addict, we cannot rid ourselves of the very thing making us sick. It is, and always has been, the goal of our society to cut off the shackles binding us to this failed system, and to remove the blinders from the eyes of all so that they might finally see the truth."

"If what Twenty-six says is true," Eighty interjected, "then we need only delay the government's efforts for a short while—long enough to put a set of new laws in place. But without an antibacterial treatment of our own, this is all moot. We have no leverage. We have only the specter of a pandemic."

Bacon was smiling now.

"Our Neighbor at the CDC is one of the brightest minds in all of microbiology," he said. "I've been assured the bacteriophage theory proposed by Humphrey Miller not only will work, but members of this newly formed government consortium are not close to considering the three types of phages needed for his treatment. Thanks to the work of our number Forty-five, nobody else has this information. None of you have actually met the latest arrival in our lab, so I would like to give you all a glimpse of Mr. Humphrey Miller at work. Please do not be distracted by his appearance or lack of academic credentials. I have it on the authority of number Seventy-one as well as our own Dr. Kazimi that this is a brilliant scientist who has been thinking outside the box on this challenge for some time."

Bacon threw a switch, and the center of each board member's screen filled with rotating camera views of Ahmed Kazimi and Humphrey Miller, communicating with each other in the impressive incubator room and laboratory, mixing plates of agar growth medium, and tissue culture bottles, and generally seeming congenial toward each other and in good spirits.

"As you can see," Bacon went on, "these men are well on their way to giving us back the control of the Janus strain that will give us all the leverage we need for complete and total victory. I have been and remain supremely confident in our efforts and I know you share my sentiments. We do not have the antibiotic treatment as of yet, but rest assured the pieces are in place for us."

"What is the current status of Seventy-one?" Eighty asked.

"A few hours ago, Seventy-one arrived here at Red Cliff, bearing tissue cultures growing the three types of bacteriophage that will be used to reestablish our control over the Janus strain. The viruses have just been delivered to Kazimi and Miller, and as you see, they are working together to get the phages ready for an all-out assault on Janus. It could be as little as a day or two before we have a viable new antibacterial."

"But until we do, how many deaths will Janus cause?" asked Ninety-seven, a mechanical engineer and mathematical wizard from MIT. Even with the verbal distortion, her concern was apparent.

Nine, as usual, had the data ready.

"We project less than a six-month lag from the time we have a perfected therapy to the date when the entitlement laws are revoked. Given the mutation and rapidity of bacterial spread, we estimate five thousand casualities during that time. But I would caution you all that might be a conservative figure."

"Five thousand?" Ninety-seven repeated. "That seems quite high. Is there anything we could do to lower that figure?"

Bacon responded vehemently.

"We *should* do nothing and we *will* do nothing until these entitlement programs are revoked." He snapped the tip of his cane down against the stone floor like exclamation points. "Lancaster Hill expressed it best," he said. " 'Liberty cannot exist without sacrifice, nor can sacrifice exist without suffering. Blood may be shed, but should the suffering of the part in the end save the whole, it is a pain we are obligated to endure.' "

Silence followed. Most, like Bacon, could recite the words from Hill's hallmark treatise by heart. But hearing them from a man of Bacon's stature was powerful and compelling. They served as a call to action, and a reaffirmation of the oath each Neighbor once took.

"I understand your discomfort, Ninety-seven, really I do," Bacon said. "The situation is regrettable, but by no means should it deter our efforts. I never expected this action program to go without a glitch. AP-Janus is a massive undertaking that is going to change the landscape of this country and fulfill the dreams of our founders."

"May I remind you," Nine said, "that thirty percent of Medicare payments are spent in the last year of life, and forty percent of *those* dollars cover care for people in the last *month*. The last month! Our country is deficit rich and cash poor, and as sure as metastatic cancer, our entitlement programs will kill us."

At that moment, the door to Bacon's study opened softly, and the butler, Harris, shuffled in. He was one of several employees who worked at Red Cliff but were not members of the Society of One Hundred Neighbors. One of the reasons why the faces on the video system were blurred was to conceal them from those who were not part of the order.

Harris whispered in Bacon's ear. The director nodded, then stood awkwardly, wincing from the stiffness in his deformed foot.

"My friends," he said, "I need to excuse myself for a moment. Nine, if you could provide the group with the update you gave me earlier, we won't have to waste any time."

Bacon followed his butler out of his study and into a nearby room, which had been soldiers' quarters in the original castle, but was used now as a library annex. A rugged man with a thick goatee and shaved head stood in front of one of the floor-to-ceiling bookshelves. His name was Ron Jessup, and he was responsible for security and surveillance at Red Cliff. Bacon had hired the mercenary for his technical abilities, but he was also an experienced sniper and an expert with most weapons.

"Our radar has picked up a boat moving up the coast from the south," Jessup said in a calm, authoritative voice. "Collins and I looked at it together. Something small, maybe a fishing boat. About a quarter mile from here. You asked to be notified of any possible security threats, so I wanted to inform you right away."

"You did the right thing, Ronnie," Bacon said. "Send Collins out to have a look and keep me informed of any developments."

Jessup left with Harris while Bacon gazed out the window at the darkening skies. Gray clouds were moving in from the west, pushed by a steady wind, strong enough to bend the tops of trees. Bacon guessed the seas would be six to seven feet high, with whitecaps. It was not the sort of ocean for pleasure cruising, and professional fishermen seldom hugged the coastline around here. Still, it could be a crabber or a lobster boat.

Chances were it was nothing else.

But Bacon was not a man who left anything to chance.

CHAPTER 49

Where's the money coming from?

—LANCASTER HILL, PERSONAL
CORRESPONDENCE TO AYN RAND, 1939

Swirling fog shrouded most of the imposing cliff face.

From the rocky shoals, Lou could see about five feet in any direction, including up. Ankle-deep in frigid seawater, sneakers in his hand, Lou reached out to feel the rocks. They were slick with ocean spray and were going to be a bear to climb, but he found a boulder near the base of the cliff to sit on and put his sneakers back on. Moments later, Vaill settled in next to him, and did the same with his boots.

Following frantic preparation, Lou had caught only a few hours of sleep during the fifteen-hour journey from Atlanta to this remote stretch of Maine coastline, and he worried fatigue might hinder his ascent. Vaill, on the other hand, seemed energized. There was no doubt why. Almost certainly, Alexander Burke was close. The two of them had taken a plane from Atlanta to Portland and from there, caught a flight on a small jet to a regional airport near the Canadian border, some fifty miles from the coast.

A cab brought them to the quaint port village of

Mount William, once a bustling community featuring granite quarries, tide mills, and canning businesses. As those companies vanished with the times, fishing became one of the few ways to earn a living. With dwindling catches and mounting government regulations, Vaill and Lou had an easy time renting a lobster boat and seasoned captain to ferry them to this remote section of beach, a quarter mile from the castle. For most of the hour-and-a-half trip, the seas were blanketed in fog and extremely rough. The spray was ice-cube cold, but the tide was receding, and the fisherman managed to get just a few feet from the rocky shoreline.

"It appeared a lot easier on Google Earth," Vaill said as they peered up, searching for an ascent that looked possible.

"Should we have gotten off the boat closer to Red Cliff?"

"The cliffs along this stretch of shoreline are at a more forgiving slope than the ones closer to the castle. We'd need real climbing gear to make that ascent. Besides, there are woods south of the castle we can use to our advantage."

On the plane ride from Atlanta, they not only studied maps of the coastal terrain, they also, thanks to the Slugger, had found building plans to go along with a complete history of Red Cliff. They had learned about the eccentric inventor, who had painstakingly overseen the stone-by-stone reconstruction of the castle he had shipped over from Germany.

Following a careful study of the plans, Vaill suggested they would be best climbing from the south and circling to the north end, where there appeared to be no windows. If the plans were right—what the

Slugger had found were faded and not that easy to read—the package of C-4 Vaill had taken from the FBI's weapons stock was capable of creating a door where none existed. Also in Vaill's tactical backpack was a rope, a Swiss Army knife, an extra pistol, some power bars, a flashlight, a bottle of Gatorade, and a couple of radios in case they needed to separate.

"Make sure your gun is snapped into the holster and the holster is on tight."

After some debate with Vaill, Lou had agreed to carry a weapon. He removed his backpack and Windbreaker to double-check the nylon straps of his harness, which allowed for a horizontal carry of the Glock G27 pistol Vaill had supplied.

"If I get in trouble, I'm going to count on you to get me out," Vaill had said. "Just point and shoot."

As Lou tightened the straps, he flashed on Cap, as he often did, running alongside him in the Chattahoochee forest. Then, out of his control as usual, his mind began reliving the fall, and in particular, Cap's eyes.

Please hold on . . . please!

I've got your back, Tim Vaill, Lou was thinking as he double-checked the snaps locking the Glock into its holster. *I've got your back.*

They stood shoulder-to-shoulder at the foot of the cliff, trying to see through the fog. If the skies opened up, the climb would become next to impossible. Lou's suggestion on the flight that they get backup had been brusquely dismissed. Not only was a mole in the agency still a possibility, but anyone who could own a place like Red Cliff could own the town nearby as well. There was only one thing left to do.

Climb.

"Maria and I actually used to climb together from time to time," Vaill said. "God, but she was good at it. Just follow my line and keep your body as close to the wall as possible. If you get tired, reach up and tap me on the leg if you can, and rest. Otherwise, just rest. Got it?"

At that moment, a wicked gust of wind kicked up, followed by a spray of seawater that soaked the rock face and stung Lou's eyes.

"Got it," he said with little enthusiasm.

With his hands stretched high above his head, Vaill felt around the loose stones and jagged rocks until he found a suitable purchase. A moment later he hoisted himself two feet off the ground, and soon after his feet were well above Lou's head. Moments later, he vanished inside the fog.

Now it was Lou's turn. Keeping his body tight to the cliff, he found a crevice with his fingers, lodged his foot into a V-shaped formation in the slick rock, and lifted himself as Vaill had done.

One push at a time . . . one pull . . .

As he hauled himself up another few inches, a final spray spattered up from below, soaking the rocks and his clothing. His hands almost immediately became wet and raw, and he began to shiver.

One more push . . . one more pull . . .

Above him, he could just make out Vaill's shoes. Ignoring the salt sting in his eyes, Lou made several pulls in succession and then risked a glance down. The ocean was gone. Above him was only heavy mist. It was like being in an airliner, taking off through dense clouds. Fortunately, as Vaill had predicted from the photos, the angle of the rock face was not as bad as it might have been. More and more as they spent time together, Lou was coming to admire the man and his abilities. He forced himself to maintain at least some eye contact with his boots, and pushed on, following his line.

Soon though, the tips of Lou's fingers began to throb and burning needles shot up into his arms. From above, stones were kicked free and pelted against his face. Even well above the ocean, every hold was slick and potentially disastrous. There was no reliable footing here, and no trustworthy holds. But there was also no way to stop.

Keep climbing . . . just keep climbing.

Ten feet more were negotiated—maybe twenty. There was no way to tell where he was or how far he had traveled, nor was there any way to know if Vaill was looking back for him.

One hand . . . then the other . . . steady . . . steady . . . It had to end. . . . All bleeding eventually stops. The infallible ER maxim. *All bleeding eventually stops. . . .*

Another surprise gust of wind nearly loosened Lou's handhold, but he clawed at the rock until his fingers sunk into a micro-thin crevice. He was about to make what seemed like it might be his final push when he saw the bottom of Vaill's boot emerge from the fog just a few inches from him.

Why had he stopped climbing?

Vaill bent at the waist so Lou could see his face through the murk. He held his finger to his lips and then pointed upward. From somewhere above them, Lou heard a sudden burst of radio static. Next came a gravelly voice.

"Collins, here. I'm around the spot now."

"You see the boat?" The voice on the other end of the radio came through quite clear.

"Forget seeing a boat, I can't even see the ocean. The fog is really thick up here."

"Well, climb down and go check it out. I've lost it on the screen here."

"What am I, a fucking mountain goat? There's no way I'm getting down there."

Lou held his breath, ignoring the ripping pain in his fingers. His arms began to tremble as he struggled to maintain his hold.

Don't speak . . . don't breathe . . .

Another minute and the throbbing in his arms became unbearable. As he adjusted his hold, his footing slipped. A stone came free and clattered down the cliff face.

"Hang on a second," the man above him said. "I just heard something. I'm going to take a closer look."

The radio crackled again. "If you see anyone," the voice on the other end said, "find out what he's doing there, and then if his answer makes sense, kill the fucker. If it doesn't, put a bullet in his leg and I'll come out and help you bring him back here. Understood?"

"Yeah, understood."

Lou looked above him for guidance, but it was nearly impossible to see the agent's face through the thick haze. Then it registered that Vaill was motioning for him to go around him and continue the climb. At first, Lou hesitated, but his arms were killing him and he needed to move, so he elected to trust his partner and work his way to the right so he could pass. He was

within a foot of the top when the barrel of a gun materialized, pointed at the center of his forehead.

*What in the hell was going on? Vaill had to have
forgotten the man was up there.*

"Come up nice and slow," Collins ordered.

Lou hauled himself over the top of the cliff, grunting with every movement. Once on the edge, he stole a
glance behind him. He could see for just a short ways.
Beyond that was only white. No sign of Vaill.

"I . . . I'm hurt," Lou pleaded, improvising.

"Get up. Who the fuck are you? What are you doing here?"

With painful slowness, Lou rose from his crouch.
The killer, a hard-looking, acne-scarred man with the
long, blond hair of a Greek god, and a build to match,
continued holding his gun at Lou. Searching as in-
conspicuously as he could for any sign of Vaill, Lou
stumbled, at the same time inching back toward the
edge of the precipice.

"I asked what you are doing here," Collins demanded. "Are you here with anybody?"

Lou laid his performance on thicker, his voice
quavering.

"I'm here alone. I'm just a hiker. Please put that gun
away. Don't hurt me."

Collins cocked a half smile.

"I'm not going to hurt you, buddy, but I am going to
kill you unless I get some answers. One last time: Who
are you and what the fuck are you doing here?"

Collins raised his gun, but before he could pull the
trigger, a hand shot up through the fog and caught him
hard behind the knee. A powerful yank and the knee
buckled, sending the man down. In almost the same

movement, the hand grabbed his jacket, and pulled him over the edge. Two seconds—that's all it took. Maybe less. His arms and legs slicing through the mist, the killer bellowed as he fell. The screams ceased abruptly with the sound of shattering bones. Lou had no trouble picturing the man exploding on the rocks below—blood and brain splashed everywhere. It was then he heard Vaill cry out.

"Lou, help, I'm losing my grip!"

Panicked, Lou scrambled forward, leaning as far over the cliff's edge as he dared. His arm became an oar, sent out searching for a drowning man.

"Lou, Jesus, I'm falling!"

"Vaill, grab my hand, dammit! Grab my hand."

Lou could see enough now through the fog to know that he was inches short of Vaill's outstretched hand.

"Lou!"

Lou pushed himself ahead another half foot, no longer aware if he was at or over his balancing point. It didn't matter. At what seemed the last possible moment before they both followed Collins down, Vaill grabbed hold of Lou's right wrist. Clawing into the damp, stony earth with the fingers of his left hand, Lou twisted his right arm around until he was able to grab hold of Vaill's wrist.

"Hang on, brother!" he shouted, certain that any moment, he was going over.

Don't let go . . . for God's sake, just don't let him fall. . . .

Not this one, he vowed. *Not this one.*

With all his strength, forcing his stiff, chilled fingers even deeper into the pebbles and dirt, Lou pulled, driving his knees into the muddy earth, searching for leverage. Through the mist, Vaill's eyes were Cap's, pleading with him for strength.

Driven by that image, Lou clenched his jaws and drove back even harder, the muscles in his back and arm burning.

One inch . . . another . . .

Not this time . . . Lou pulled to the rhythm of his words. *Not . . . this . . . time.*

Below him, Vaill's grip remained fast, but Lou's own was weakening.

Not this time . . .

Then, with a ferocious, warrior's cry, Lou gave one last yank as he rolled backward. Vaill came shooting up out of the fog like a missile and landed in a heap beside him, both men gasping for air. Vaill regained his breath first.

"Come on, you lightweight," he said, rolling to his knees. "Someone's sure to be calling splatterboy back and wondering why he doesn't answer."

He was upright by the time Lou could even turn over.

"Lightweight, huh," he said. "Well, take it from me, no one could ever accuse you of being that."

He made it to his feet. The two of them exchanged fist bumps.

"I owe you big-time for that one," Vaill said. "Thanks, my friend."

"Nonsense. I just felt we had fed the seagulls enough for one day."

CHAPTER 50

It is illogical to believe that bloated spending on parasitic entitlement programs exists within a vacuum, for these will put a drain on other worthy causes, such as our defense force, which our Constitution obligates us to maintain.

—LANCASTER R. HILL, *100 Neighbors*, SAWYER RIVER BOOKS, 1939, P. 88

Lou led the charge through the fog-shrouded woods toward the south side of the castle. Cliff-climbing might have been Vaill's forte, but trail running was squarely in his domain. He was in his element, moving by instinct and feel. The mist made it difficult to anticipate problems, but Lou could still spot precarious roots and rocks faster than most. Vaill ran just far enough behind him to make adjustments. Here, the forest floor was uneven, but the trees were dense, and were clearly helping to conceal their approach.

There was no debating whether to walk or run. Lost time could be the difference between Humphrey living and Cap losing his leg or quite possibly his life. The mist transformed the woods into the setting for a fairy tale. Knowing what awaited them beyond the forest's edge made the scene even eerier. Lou's eyes darted from his feet to what little he could see ahead and Vaill labored some, but still had little trouble keeping pace.

Soon, Lou saw diffused light in the distance. The trees began to thin. Slowing to a trot, he hid behind a tall pine. Vaill came up alongside him. He was breathing heavily and rubbing at the rainbow scar.

"Does running hurt that?" Lou whispered.

"Nothing I can't handle."

End of discussion.

Continuing to move from tree to tree, Lou led the way toward the light. To his right, he could hear the pounding of surf mixed with the cries of seagulls. He imagined the birds swooping through the fog, perhaps diving for morsels of the man who had just tried to kill him. The guard's disappearance had to have been alerted inside the castle, and whatever men were still about, possibly Burke included, would come looking for him. Jogging now, Lou continued to use the trees for concealment. His exhaustion was gone. From behind, he could hear Vaill breathing heavily, but keeping up.

Tough guy.

Another few minutes, and the woods gave way to closely trimmed spring grass. Thirty yards or so ahead of them, looming up as though being borne by the mist, was the brooding, imposing south façade of Red Cliff. Having studied the castle's layout, Lou knew it was surrounded on three sides—south, west, and north— by a moat that featured two drawbridges, and on the east by the ocean. But no map could do the imposing structure justice. Set behind a stone outer wall were tall turrets with crenelated roofs. It wasn't hard to imagine defenders of the huge keep pouring boiling oil down on the heads of an attacking army.

Well, he warned silently, *better get ready. Here comes a marauding hoard of two.*

"Jesus," Vaill whispered, "will you look at that place? Wonder what their real estate taxes are."

The drawbridge on this side was up, and the moat—twelve or so feet across—shone like black opal. Beyond the drawbridge, an imposing portcullis made of heavy timber and iron fortified the southern entrance. Glimmering in the stone somberness of the place were dozens of tall windows, every one of which seemed to be lit.

According to the plans they had reviewed, there were far more windows on the south side than on the north. Lou could actually see movement inside the first-floor room closest to where they were standing. The space, a study or library, was at the base of a mammoth turret, and was semicircular, with a row of elongated, mullioned windows curving around it like sentinels. Spectacular.

Keeping low, Lou pointed to the room, and then to his eyes. Vaill nodded. Counting down from three on his fingers, Lou broke from the trees and raced toward the castle with his partner right behind. When they reached the moat's edge, they dropped to their knees. There was absolutely no cover, only carefully manicured lawn. But from what they could see, the area was deserted.

They peered into the elegant room, albeit at an upward angle. What they observed ran quite contrary to the ancient stone construction. Just to the right of the entrance a highly sophisticated videoconference was set up. The huge screen was divided into multiple sections—at least seven of them, several of which appeared to have active images. A man was walking toward them, but judging by his portly build, it wasn't

Burke. In addition, he looked to be walking with a limp, and probably was using a cane.

Lou was engrossed in searching for a means to cross the moat, and was considering ways they might get in through one of the many windows, when Vaill nudged him and pointed to their left. A figure had appeared on the lawn, no more than fifty or seventy-five feet away—a dark silhouette, at least as large as Collins. Even through the heavy air they could hear the man's radio crackle to life, followed by the sound of his voice.

"Yeah, Drake here. I'm not seeing any sign of trouble. Still no word from Collins? . . . Let me finish checking this side, then I'll go take a look for him. . . . Yeah, I know it's getting dark. I'm not a fucking ninny, Ronnie. I can see. I got a flashlight right here."

Out in the open, with no place to run to or to hide, Lou and Vaill were just seconds away from being discovered. They remained flattened on the damp grass, asking questions of each other with their eyes. To Lou, their only option, a poor one, was somehow to disappear over the bank and slide down into the moat. But even if they tried, it was doubtful they could complete the maneuver without being detected.

After pausing to use his radio, the huge guard was on the move again. And as if locked onto their position, he was lumbering directly toward them. The behemoth was perhaps twenty feet away when his gaze hit on what must have looked like a boulder.

The seconds it took him to work out what the odd shape was proved lethal.

Vaill sprung to his knees and fired a single shot that seemed muffled by the heavy air. The bullet struck Drake square in the throat, and the big man instantly crumpled to the ground, spewing crimson from the hole in his neck and from his mouth. Inside the study, Lou saw stirring. The portly man approached a window and peered out. Drake lay on his back in dense shadow, sputtering as he drowned in his own blood.

With the odor of gunpowder wafting around them, Lou and Vaill remained motionless, staring across the moat at the majestic windows. Fifteen seconds . . . twenty. They could see the portly man searching from side to side. Finally he turned and headed back to wherever he had been sitting. The dreadful gurgling from Drake was dying away. A few spasms of his arms and legs, and he went still.

Lou stared spellbound at the corpse. Vaill had been right. It was just point and shoot. Just like a camera. He was wondering if he would ever have the cool to do the same if he had to, when he became aware of Vaill tugging at his Windbreaker sleeve.

"There can't be too many of these monsters about, or one of them would be here by now," he said. "But just the same, I think we should get around to the north side."

At that moment, following a burst of static, the dead man's radio went on again.

"Drake, you big baboon, where in the hell are you? Drake, it's Ronnie. Did you find Collins?"

"As a matter of fact," Vaill said as he and Lou raced across the expansive lawn, giving the melancholy castle a wide berth, "he did."

The west side of Red Cliff was also the main entrance. There was a circular gravel driveway abutting islands of lawn adorned with stone fountains, concrete planters shaped like Grecian urns, flower gardens, and even a topiary. Several high-end luxury cars were parked along the drive. Wealth was clearly consistent with the Society of One Hundred Neighbors' philosophy. Graduated income taxes, on the other hand, almost certainly were not.

Linking the driveway to the castle was another raised drawbridge, with a narrow footbridge crossing the moat next to where the main bridge would lie. The oversized rusting portcullis looked capable of withstanding the sort of battering ram featured in Hollywood films. Vaill examined the massive door with a small pair of field glasses and verbally confirmed that impression.

"We're too exposed out here to cross the footbridge and set up a detonation," he said. "Even if we manage to blow that monster without killing ourselves, we might as well announce our arrival with a bullhorn. I say we move north."

The moat essentially turned Red Cliff into an island, with the east face resting atop the imposing cliff for which the place was probably named. Though he took pride in his ability to solve complex problems, Lou was as yet unable to connect with an idea for getting the two of them inside. Meanwhile, the darkening evening sky was becoming their ally.

At the edge of the north woods, their luck continued. Lou discovered a small building with a single window on the west side nestled ten feet or so inside the tree line.

"A guardhouse," he said, leading Vaill around the fieldstone structure. "The matted brush and these broken branches suggest it gets used. No idea what for.

And look, right here, headed back toward the castle, tire tracks."

He shined a flashlight through the window and Vaill came over to look with him. The place was dusty and a little cobwebby, but there were sconces on the wall, a coffeemaker and cups on a low shelf, a small wooden table with two chairs, some cookie tins, a hot plate, and a boom box.

"What in the hell do you think this place is for?" Vaill asked.

"It doesn't really make sense just standing here like this, disconnected from the castle."

"Maybe it was there in the sixteenth century or whenever it was built, and the inventor just brought it over."

"Maybe," Lou said, "but that explanation sounds a little thin and . . . Bingo! Tim, look there in the floor behind that chair."

Vaill took the flash and trained it on the outline of a two-by-two square cut into the wood of the floor. There were two hinges on one side and a rusting metal ring in the center of the other.

"Bingo is right, brother," he said. "Any doubt as to where that trapdoor leads?"

Lou pumped his fist.

"None," he said. "Absolutely none. All we got to do now is get in there."

The unadorned door to the stone house, probably steel, was facing south. Without being told, Lou unholstered his Glock, stepped back two paces, and discharged three well-aimed rounds into the keyhole, each sending out a small burst of sparks. The rippling echo of gunfire rolled away like a cresting wave. Vaill inspected the keyhole, tested the thick metal handle, and shook his head. Then he removed his backpack and opened it up.

"Time to sic the Doberman on it," he said. "His Christian name is C-4, but he'll answer to almost anything. Stand by, my friend."

Lou knew very little about plastic explosives. Obviously, it was a moldable material, but he had little knowledge of the chemistry that made it work. Vaill took a wedge of the whitish putty from a tinfoil wrapper, and shaped it in and around the keyhole and along the hinges.

"As with most decent explosives," Vaill said, "serious energy is needed to initiate the chemical reaction. That's what these blasting caps are all about." He inserted one into each lump of putty, and rolled out enough detonator wire for them to get a safe distance away. "You can shoot bullets into C-4 all day and it won't go off," he went on. "Put a match to it and it'll just burn slowly. What we need is a smaller explosion to trigger a bigger one."

Vaill held up a black metal box about the size of a deck of cards—the detonator. He flicked a switch and a green light came on. Then he attached the three wires to a spool. His thumb hovered over the red button on top of the box.

"Ready?" he asked.

"Are we far enough away?"

"We're about to find out. Move behind that tree and hold your ears, pal."

Lou shrugged and did as asked, and his partner depressed the button. The three simultaneous blasts were more intense than Lou would have ever anticipated given the size of the explosives. Even behind the tree, the shock drove him back a foot and seemed as if it momentarily stopped his heart. Debris shot out in all directions. Lou peered out as the wall of smoke quickly dissipated. Astonishingly, the door was still standing.

"What happened?" Lou asked, stunned.

Vail looked nonplussed as well. Then he strode to the door, inspected it for a moment, grabbed the handle with just two fingers and tugged lightly. The steel rectangle fell toward him as if it had fainted, landing with a muted thud facedown on the forest floor.

Vail turned to Lou, his expression a mix of pride and absolute amazement.

"To Red Cliff," he said.

"You don't have to ask twice," Lou replied.

CHAPTER 51

If financial solvency is of concern to any of us,
then Mr. Roosevelt's entitlement programs
should be of grave concern.

—LANCASTER R. HILL, LECTURE TO THE
COLLEGE OF WILLIAM AND MARY, VIRGINIA,
FEBRUARY 22, 1937

Lou was standing on a rough-hewn, centuries-old plank
floor, staring down through a trapdoor that might have
been the gate to hell. And in that instant, in what seemed
like a heartbeat, realization caught up with him.

Their presence had to be known.

The element of surprise was gone.

Soon, he was likely going to die—painfully and
violently.

Maybe it was the horrible deaths of the two guards.
Maybe it was the realization of how much was at
stake—how many lives. Maybe it was the notion of
never seeing Emily again . . . or Cap . . .

It had been twenty-five years since he last felt as panicked as he did at that instant, and as he stared down
into the abyss, memories of that night so long ago filled
his thoughts.

It was the second of July. He was in his final year of
internal medicine residency and had made the decision
to switch to emergency medicine the following year.

First, though, he had to rotate as chief resident in a large V.A. hospital. The day, his first as chief, had gone easily. He loved the vets and the challenges of caring for them, and was gaining confidence by the hour in what he knew.

Then night came.

The hospital, with hundreds of patients, many of them quite ill, quieted down. Much of the support staff went home. And soon, responsibility for medical care fell to a pair of interns, a junior resident, and him. Always in the past, when he looked over his shoulder in a tense situation, someone senior to him was there with a calming word and useful advice. That night, there was no one. Weighed down, it seemed, by various beepers, he stood in the doorway of the ICU, staring at the monitors and watching the intern in her first harried day as a doc, going about her mountain of work.

It was then that legitimate, gut-wrenching, throat-tightening panic took hold.

His stomach knotted. A wave of nausea swept over him, and he knew he was going to get sick. Just one day earlier, he had been a junior resident. Now, whatever happened in the hours ahead to hundreds of patients putting their trust in their caregivers, he was the ultimate authority. There was no one looking over his shoulder. No one with reassurance that he was doing the right thing—making the right decision. His panic lasted for more than an hour, and he twice got physically ill. But when the first code blue was called, the fear ended abruptly, and his life as a doc moved up a notch.

Now, as then, he was paralyzed.

"Hey, pal, what gives?"

Vaill's voice, ironically, from over his shoulder, brought him back to their reality.

Lou turned slowly, wondering if, as in the V.A., he was going to get sick. "I'm okay."

"That isn't the look of someone who's okay," Vaill said, pulling his flashlight from Lou's face and directing it through the trapdoor, where a flight of corrugated metal stairs disappeared into darkness. "I'm surprised this didn't all hit you awhile ago." He set his hand on Lou's shoulder. "You're doing amazing, doc. Better than I could have ever expected. Look, we have no idea what's waiting down those stairs. I'd be worried if you *weren't* scared. You didn't bargain for any of this, but you never backed away. And you could have. There have been plenty of chances. Hell, this is a chance right now. I promise I wouldn't think any less of you if you decided to just head into town and take your chances with the locals there."

"Don't worry, I'm in," Lou said. "Thanks for the props."

He turned, about to go down the stairs, but Vaill brought him back by the elbow. The agent's eyes were flint.

"If you're in, you're in all the way," he said. "Somebody could be down there right now waiting to ambush us. If they are, I don't want any hesitations. None."

Lou unholstered his Glock and straightened his Kevlar vest. God, but he wished he could hold Emily one more time.

"I'm ready," he said.

"Just keep doing the next right thing, doc. You do that and don't hesitate, and we'll be all right."

The stairs, maybe ten of them, led down to a surprisingly wide, dank, coal-black tunnel, hewn into the rock, and permeated with the distinct odor of the ocean. The rugged ceiling was low enough to make for an uncomfortable, stoop-shouldered passage. Footprints in the dirt-covered floor, like the tire tracks outside, suggested the setup was still in use.

"We've got to be passing under the moat," Lou said.

Vaill panned his flashlight over the ceiling, where a row of inlaid light fixtures ran the length of the tunnel. High-tech. At the far end of the passage was a metal door. Where the other one was latched, this one, rusted in places from persistent exposure to salt air, had a knob.

"I'm surprised nobody's come for us already," Vaill whispered. "Either they didn't hear that explosion, or with two guards dead, there aren't that many more left in there, and they're gonna wait for us to come to them. That's what I'd do."

Lou was first to reach the door.

"I got this," he whispered back.

Vaill took up position to the right, with his back against the wall, gun drawn.

"If it opens, it's gonna swing toward us," he said. "Use it for cover. If it's locked, we may have to unleash the Doberman again and fight it out right here. No hesitation, though, right?"

"No hesitation."

Lou's pulse was hammering as he turned the knob. The door pulled open easily and he slipped behind it, creating, for a moment, a makeshift shield. Vaill dropped to a crouch and sprang forward, his weapon leveled at the darkness ahead.

"We're in," Lou said with some excitement.

There was nobody waiting on the other side, no targets for him to shoot. Vaill had to be right. What remained of the fortress guards were waiting for them inside.

Lou's nerves were crackling now. They banished the blackness with their lights. To his left, Lou could quite clearly discern waves churning.

"You hear that surf?"

Vaill nodded.

"How could we be close to the ocean here? The tunnel went straight and level. The ocean would be down and to the left."

Again, Vaill panned his beam through darkness. He settled it on a rectangular corrugated metal platform, no more than ten feet away. On the other side of the platform was a set of five metal stairs that ascended to a narrow elevated area, lined by a metal pipe railing. Vaill crossed the platform and climbed up to the new space. Lou followed. Below them was a man-made shaft—a long passageway that extended down through the rock, almost certainly to the ocean below.

Lou used his light to indicate a series of partially corroded cables and pulleys, and all at once the layout made sense. From the satellite photos they knew there was a boathouse at the base of the imposing cliff. This platform was part of an elevator, and this shaft a way to move supplies in and out of the castle by sea. They huddled together at the railing, and focused on that section of the castle on their map.

"We're behind this room right here," Vaill whispered. "It could be some sort of storage area for things brought up by the elevator. There are two other spaces adjacent to where we are. From that larger room, a doorway leads to what's labeled "Great Room," with windows opening onto the cliff. Then there's a corridor off of the Great Room that connects with the rest of the castle. I think this bottleneck is where they'll be waiting."

Lou agreed.

"Two ways inside," he said. "One from the stone house, maybe for a truck making large deliveries to the storage areas, and the other from the boathouse down below."

"So how do we get into the supply rooms?" Vaill asked. "No doors."

Lou stood in the center of the space and listened. Then he put his hands against the cold concrete of the one wall.

"I hear machinery," he whispered.

"A humming. I hear it, too. Coming from behind here."

"So there's almost certainly got to be a way inside. Otherwise this space makes no sense. Maybe from farther down the elevator shaft?"

Vaill withdrew another small black box from his pack, about the size of the detonator, and connected to a pair of cushioned headphones to it. Coming off the other side of the case was a small microphone.

"The future is now," he said. "You can hear through five feet of concrete with this baby. I almost didn't bring it." He placed the small, disc-like receiver against the wall and then motioned for Lou to come take the earphones. "I hear voices," Vaill said, "and I'm almost certain one of them is Dr. Kazimi. I think there's only one other, another male, but it's hard to make out what he's saying. Here, have a listen."

Lou donned the headphones. The humming noise he heard was louder now, but did not drown out the voices. It took some time for Lou to attune his ears to the sounds behind the wall.

"What do you need now?" he heard an accented voice say.

"Bring over agar and pour into petri dishes five millimeters deep."

There was no mistaking the dense, shorthand speech of the man giving orders.

Humphrey!

Vaill took the device and listened some more.

"It sounds like they're alone, working," he said, "but I can't be sure."

"We've got to find the way in."

"It's a risk."

"You going chicken on me, Agent Vaill?"

Vaill was about to protest when the listening device slipped from his hand and slid underneath the railing, clattering noisily down the stairs to the elevator platform. The seconds that the echo persisted seemed like an hour.

Lou pulled his gun and tensed. If Kazimi and Humphrey were not alone, this could be it. A moment later, they heard a slight scraping sound. Before they could pinpoint the source, the wall began to move, pivoting precisely at its midpoint to reveal an opening several feet wide. They watched, guns raised, as the figure of a man emerged. Focused on Vaill's repeated warning not to hesitate, Lou trained his weapon on the shadowy target, and tightened his finger on the trigger.

CHAPTER 52

If only allowed to flex its muscle, the bond of
family would prove stronger than allegiance to
any government.

—LANCASTER R. HILL, *Climb the Mountain*,
 SAWYER RIVER BOOKS, 1941, P. 33

"Don't shoot! Don't shoot!"

Committed to avoiding hesitation at all costs, Lou's
finger was tightening on the trigger when Vaill reached
over and grabbed his wrist.

"Jesus, you almost killed him, Lou. Next time you
decide you're not going to hesitate, stop and check with
me. Dr. Lou Welcome, Dr. Ahmed Kazimi."

The men, would-be killer and would-be victim,
shook hands.

"Please speak softly," Kazimi said. "There is a surveillance camera in the room behind us. We will meet
you by the elevator shaft where we cannot be heard or
seen by them."

The scientist vanished back into the castle, while
Lou risked a quick peek into the space beyond the wall.
Instead of the storage area he had expected, the room
was a microbiology laboratory, with a stainless-steel
autopsy table, a sink, and several large refrigeration
units, along with a rack of hazmat suits and a portable
chemical shower. Craning his neck sideways, Lou

could see clear plastic cages lining the pivoting wall. White mice scurried about, disturbed by the sudden movement of their habitats.

Lou stepped back to make room for Kazimi in the space overlooking the elevator shaft. Humphrey, whose motorized wheelchair barely fit through the opening, followed. Kazimi applied pressure to a spot, and the wall glided shut, enclosing them. A nearly concealed switch turned on a trio of corroded sconces.

"You were the last person I expected to be knocking on the wall, Agent Vaill," Kazimi said as the two men shook hands. "I saw what happened that night to Agent Rodriguez. I am terribly, terribly sorry."

"I'm here to rescue you and to avenge her," Vaill said without emotion.

"Well, I am glad you are alive to do so," Kazimi replied. "Dr. Welcome, Mr. Miller has had many fine things to say about you."

"I'm glad we've found you both. Humphrey, I confess I feared the worse for you. It's *very* good to see you again."

"Good to be found," Humphrey said.

"I'm saddened about your aide. These are very bad people we are dealing with."

"Especially that Burke."

"No time for happy reunions," Vaill said. "How long do we have before whoever is monitoring those cameras notices you're gone?"

"No idea," Kazimi said, "but I would think not long."

"How many guards?"

"Again, I do not know. But Burke is here. I know that much."

Lou expected Vaill to react to the news, but his face looked blank. It was the expression Lou had seen in the Arbor General parking lot and before that, in the interrogation room. Hopefully, if a headache was developing, it would either be minimal or short-lived. Lou feared otherwise.

"That's important information," he said. "Anything else you can tell us?"

"You should know that it is my fault that Mr. Miller is here. Burke forced me into giving up his name by showing me proof they were ready to harm or murder my friends and family."

Vaill suddenly brightened, and seemed to connect with what was being said.

"Do you mean *you* told Burke about Humphrey? I thought there was an informant in the FBI."

"Burke is the only informant I know of," Kazimi said, "but he is enough—a violent, violent man."

Lou and Vaill exchanged understanding looks. There was no additional mole in the FBI. Under great duress, Lou had disclosed Humphrey's identity to Vaill and his partner, while Kazimi, imprisoned fifteen hundred miles away, had given up the same information to Alexander Burke.

"You did what you had to do, Dr. Kazimi," Lou said. He glanced at Vaill. "We both did."

"It appears summoning Mr. Miller may well be the key to solving this crisis. Mr. Miller and I connected online many years ago. I had never met him in person, so I was unaware of his disability while he was part of my team. But I did appreciate his brilliance. My decision to ignore his good council was predicated on my arrogance alone and nothing more."

"You've made up for that now," Humphrey said.

"Thank you for saying that. I believed in my approach to eradicating this germ. I was wrong. Thankfully, I have since seen the light, as it were. I now believe Mr. Miller's theory about a combination of bacteriophage may well be the correct one. If his well-thought-out approach is proven in our trials, it will destroy the Janus germ, as it is referred to here, without harming the host."

Instead of looking terrorized or weakened by his ordeal, Humphrey seemed aglow with pride.

"Very sad about Cassie," he said, "but getting recognition I deserve means a lot."

"What did he say?" Vaill asked, clearly impatient.

"He said he's glad things are working out."

"Tell him that if his theory works, he'll be a national hero."

"Tim, he can hear and understand you," Lou said, suppressing most of a grin. "It's just his speech that's off."

"Very confident will work," Humphrey said. "Don't need lab at Arbor, Lou. We're about to get cure!"

His eyes were sparkling.

"He says—"

"I got it. I got it," Vaill said, cutting Lou off. "Now, we need to get going. Let me ask you both one last time: Do you know of anyone else here besides Burke?"

"And that man, Ron, handling the radio from the security office," Lou reminded him.

"I know of two other guards besides Burke," Kazimi said. "One is a big, blond man named Collins and the other is an even bigger fellow named Drake. They seem very dangerous."

Again, Vaill and Lou exchanged looks.

Not anymore . . .

"Anybody else?"

"Doug Bacon is here. Another bad man. I think he runs the entire organization. He limps and walks with a cane, and I think he has a drinking problem. But he is very smart and not to be underestimated."

"Okay, last chance. Anyone else?"

"There's a butler—an older man named Harris. Nobody else I know of. We have been told the microbiologist who first identified the Janus strain has arrived at the castle with tissue cultures growing the three strains of bacteriophage Mr. Miller believes will be the key, but we haven't been introduced yet. That's all."

Vaill's eyes were smoldering.

"Where is Burke?" he asked.

Good, Lou thought. *False alarm. He's back.*

"I don't know where he is right now," Kazimi said again. "He comes back here a lot."

Vaill removed the Red Cliff plans from his backpack and laid them out on the cement floor.

"Show me the way to Bacon," he said. "If Burke is here, he'll be guarding the head of the dragon."

Kazimi used his finger to trace the best route from the laboratory to Bacon's videoconference study on the north side of the castle.

"The details of the map are small and blurry, but I believe this route will get you to Bacon's study."

"You two stay in the lab. We'll be back to get you."

Vaill retrieved the extra pistol he had brought—a Glock like the one he'd given Lou from his backpack—and tried to hand the weapon to Kazimi.

"Ever fire one of these?" Vaill asked.

Kazimi held up his hands in refusal.

"I study microbes and the Koran, Agent Vaill. You know that."

"As you wish."

"Keep low and to the wall as you go through the mouse room and the main lab. There are two cameras in the Great Room, but I don't know how you might avoid them."

Vaill nodded, replaced the gun, and Lou retrieved the listening device that had fallen onto the elevator platform. Kazimi reopened the secret door. Moving forward on their knees, careful to hug the wall, Vaill and Lou followed Kazimi into the adjacent main lab—an impressive facility that spoke volumes of the resourcefulness and resources of the Neighbors.

Leaving the two scientists behind, Vaill and Lou crossed into the opulent Great Room. Each pointed to the mounted security cameras, and together, they elected to stand up. The message was clear: the time for stealth is over. Come and get us!

Vaill took the lead. Lou's stomach felt knotted and raw but the Glock in his hand was actually somewhat reassuring. With Kazimi and Humphrey back in the lab, anyone else they encountered would be the enemy.

This time, there *would* be no hesitation.

Lou was mindful of his breathing—slow in, slow out—as he fought to quell his rumbling anxiety. He and Vaill entered the Great Room side by side. Lou paused momentarily to observe the spectacular bank of floor-to-ceiling windows lining the east-facing wall. Like the trappings of the Great Room, without a doubt the daytime view through those windows was spectacular.

They were halfway across the room when they heard

a radio transmission echoing from the passageway to their right—the central passageway through the castle.

Burke.

"I just left Jessup. He called me down because he just discovered he has them on camera," he was saying. "Two of them, using what looks like C-4 to take the guardhouse door off. Can't make them out in the dark. Looks like professional work. Probably FBI. Any word from Drake or Collins? If the intruders who did the guardhouse are FBI, they're both dead."

Vaill did not react.

"He's right over there, in the passageway," Lou whispered urgently. He gave a hard tug on Vaill's sleeve, asking him to pull back and find a hiding place for an ambush. As if under a spell, Vaill remained rooted where he stood, out in the open. He was squinting. Tears of pain had formed at the corners of his eyes.

This was no false alarm.

"Tim, take cover," Lou said more urgently now.

The agent stood rigidly upright, his pistol dangling at his side. His eyes were nearly closed.

". . . The situation certainly looks dangerous," Burke went on, his voice getting louder as he approached. "I think we should keep Miller and Kazimi in the lab. I'm going there to check on them now. I'll bring them to your study to meet the new arrival once I clean up this mess."

Burke, radio to his ear, strode into the Great Room and immediately spotted first Vaill, then Lou, both out in the open. Vaill was a step in front, partially blocking Lou's line of sight. Burke wasted no time reaching for his weapon. Vaill, holding his at his side, was clearly too distracted by the pain in his head to move.

Lou leveled his Glock, but with Vaill out in front, could not get off a clean shot.

"That's Burke!" he shouted. "Dammit, Tim, shoot!"

The delay was an eternity. Not even bothering to seek cover, Burke calmly raised his gun and fired, hitting Vaill squarely in the chest once, then again. It was as if he assumed Vaill was wearing Kevlar, and was purposely firing to stun, not to kill. The impact knocked Vaill off of his feet and onto his butt. Lou dove to his right, ducking behind an oversized armchair, wondering how much protection the cushions might afford. Twenty feet toward the massive windows, Burke stood erect, scanning the scene in front of him. It was then Lou realized the man was smiling.

Lou poked up from behind the chair just long enough to fire off several shots, all misses.

The bright flashes made his eyes tear; the acrid stench of gunpowder assaulted his nostrils; and the shots were temporarily deafening. He was a neophyte in a gun battle with a highly trained killer. Not good. Keeping his head down, he shot almost blindly toward where he thought the man was standing. He hit a window, shattering one of the panes, and at least forcing Burke to take some cover beside a leather sofa.

To Lou's left, he saw that Vaill had clumsily retrieved his gun and stumbled to his feet. The vagueness in his eyes persisted. Lou could see the holes where at least two bullets had torn through his shirt and slammed into his bulletproof vest.

Thank God for Kevlar, Lou was thinking. But he knew it was just a matter of time—and not much time at that. In his condition, Vaill was even more of a mismatch for Burke than *he* was.

"Tim, get down!" he cried.

He fired another burst, this time, it seemed, with more patience and control. In fact, his third shot struck Burke somewhere in the upper leg. The killer swore and immediately fired back an angry volley, striking the sturdy easy chair inches from Lou's ear. The way Burke lurched backward but did not fall, Lou felt certain that the wound was muscle or merely flesh, not bone.

Ignoring his leg, which was already bleeding through his khakis, Burke inserted a new ammo clip, hobbled to his right, and stopped in front of the massive windows, not fifteen feet from Vaill, who was still raising his weapon. Burke, his expression nearly serene, leveled his gun at the man he had not long ago failed to kill.

Lou, twenty-five feet away, and almost directly behind Vaill, watched the terrible scene unfold as if it were in slow motion.

"Maria," he heard Vaill whisper, once and then again. "Maria."

Lou stood and quickly moved to his left to open up a line of fire. He was Vaill's backup. They were partners now. He trained his Glock in Burke's direction and fired.

The click from his empty chamber was as loud as any gunshot.

An instant later, the Great Room erupted. More noise, more flashes, and more stench of gunpowder. One of the bullets from Burke's gun struck Vaill in the neck. Another slammed into his shoulder, where the Kevlar offered no protection. A geyser of blood erupted from the neck wound spraying in all directions, bathing his face and clothes, and turning the floor at his feet crimson.

Lou stood helplessly as Vaill dropped his gun and stumbled back a step. But somehow, he refused to go down.

"Maria," he said, louder than before. "I . . . love . . . you."

Then, to Lou's astonishment, the wounded agent, more dead than alive, charged forward, blood spraying from the grotesque holes in his neck and shoulder. The killer fired once more from no more than ten feet. Then again. The first shot shattered Vaill's forearm. The second went through his mouth and out his cheek. Legs still pumping furiously, Vaill cleared the last five feet.

Burke was wide-eyed, raising his gun for a center forehead killshot, when the bloody apparition lowered his shoulder and hit him with intense force. In that same motion, Vaill locked his arms around Burke's midsection, and drove him backward like a linebacker tackling in the open field.

The two enemies, one essentially dead, one about to be, slammed against one of the massive windows, and then continued through it into the ebony night.

Amid the sound of glass raining down onto the stone floor, Lou swore he heard Vaill cry out his wife's name one final time.

CHAPTER 53

It is folly to consider that spending on bloated,
parasitic entitlement programs occurs within a
vacuum, for each expenditure will put a drain
on other worthy causes, such as our defense
force, which our Constitution obligates us to
maintain.

—LANCASTER R. HILL, *A Secret Worth Keeping*,
SAWYER RIVER BOOKS; 1937, P. 18

A strong wind blew through the shattered glass, scattering loose papers from an end table into the air, and briefly turning the elegant Great Room into a snow globe. Lou rushed to the gaping window. His powerful flashlight beam could not penetrate the lingering mist, and probably would never have reached the base of the cliff even if it had. He listened for confirmation of what he knew was true, but heard only wind and waves. Dazed, he surveyed the gruesome trail of blood—all that remained here of Tim Vaill. Given the man's neurologic damage, it was doubtful he would have ever been able to function as an agent again. And given the depth of his anguish and hatred, he had accomplished what he had come to do.

You got what you came for, my friend, Lou thought, gazing out into the night. *Now you can rest.*

He heard the hum of Humphrey's motorized wheel-chair approaching from behind, and turned to see the two scientists.

"Agent Vaill?" Kazimi asked.

"Gone. He died for us and took Burke with him."

"May Allah speed him to join his beloved wife in Heaven."

"I promise to finish my work for him," Humphrey added.

"This isn't finished," Lou said. "Let's go over the guards again."

Kazimi repeated what he knew. Burke . . . Drake . . . Collins . . . Bacon . . . an old butler named Harris . . . Again, Lou added the man Ron.

"Then there's the scientist who discovered the Janus strain," Kazimi said. "I don't know his name, and we haven't met him yet, so I cannot tell you how much of a threat he is."

"How disabled is this Bacon? I saw him through his study window, and it looked like he could still put up a fight."

"Especially if he has a gun," Humphrey said.

Was that all? Lou guessed there could not be many more left, or the cameras overseeing the horrible gun-fight would have brought them in by now.

"There is someone else," Humphrey said. "I saw him in a room filled with monitors."

"That's probably the one I heard on the guard's radio—the one named Ron."

"Big man," Humphrey said. "Broad shoulders. Bald with thick eyebrows and a goatee."

"Where did you see him? Where's that room with the screens?"

"I think it's at the other end of that passageway. Near the main castle."

"I know that door," Kazimi said. "I've never seen it open and I assumed it was just for storage."

"That's got to be Ron."

Lou understood this was a significant crossroads. He had to decide whether to go deeper into the castle and neutralize all threats, or try to escape and get help. Vaill had been wrong about there being a second mole in the agency, but chances were he was right about the control Bacon's money had over the people in Mount William—especially the police. The choice seemed clear.

"What are we going to do?" Kazimi asked.

"We're going down that corridor," Lou said. "If the door is open, whoever is in there, I'll take them out."

"That may not be the best plan," Humphrey said. "If there is a guard, he will be armed and better trained than you. He also would be ready."

Lou thought about the number of shots he took at Burke before he ran out of ammunition, and the number he missed.

"You have a better idea?" Lou asked.

"In fact," Humphrey said with a spark in his eyes, "I do."

Kazimi hurried back into the lab, and emerged with the needed things. When he caught up with Lou and Humphrey, they were already moving slowly down the stone corridor. Lou had put a new ammo clip inside the Glock.

After handing over the supplies, Kazimi returned to the lab to gather up Humphrey's notes. Lou had given him orders to escape from Red Cliff through the guardhouse tunnel in the event anything happened to him. If for any reason Lou failed to take down Bacon, someone had to get the Janus research to the authorities.

Humphrey seemed more concerned with getting his research completed, and he urged Kazimi to stay and work with him and the other scientist.

They entered the passageway and paused for Lou to don a pair of rubber gloves and to review their plan. He had misgivings, but the thought of once again testing his mettle as a gunfighter held no appeal, either.

Not surprisingly, the door to the security room was closed.

Humphrey maneuvered his wheelchair to face it, while Lou, pistol in his waistband, pressed his back against the wall to Humphrey's right. In one hand, he held Vaill's listening device. In the other, he gingerly cradled a beaker half full of the concentrated sulfuric acid that Kazimi had retrieved from the lab.

The headphones fit snugly. He put the microphone up to the wall and listened.

"Bacon, it's Jessup here," Lou heard a man say. "Burke is dead. One of the intruders I reported about carried him through one of the big windows in the Great Room. They're both gone. I'm back in my office now. No sign of the other guy or the two scientists. They were all there a few minutes ago, but now they've all vanished. Remember, the cameras have blind spots, and there are only a few of them down at that end. . . . So, what do you want me to do? . . . Yes, boss, I'll stay right here and keep my eye on the screens. But if you want me to go after them, just say the word. Yes, sir.

Yes. I understand. Protect the scientists at all costs—especially the one in the wheelchair."

Lou put the listening device away and tightened his hold on the beaker.

He was surprised at how calm he was feeling compared to his state of utter panic staring down through the trapdoor opening in the stone house. He sensed it was from having watched Vaill give up his life the way he had. Witnessing that kind of selflessness had its effects.

A single deep breath, and he nodded to Humphrey that it was time.

Humphrey took the extender arm from its hook on his wheelchair and used the custom-made contraption to knock on the door.

Even without the listening device, Lou could hear scuffing from within. He imagined the goateed security man peering through the peephole. It was a good idea not to go for a gunfight, but now Jessup had to open the door wide enough for Lou to make his move. That would depend on Humphrey. The door opened a sliver, then a bit more.

"I need to talk with you," Humphrey said, his enunciation even weaker than usual—on purpose, Lou was certain.

"What did you say? What in the hell do you want?"

"I need to talk to you now!"

"Fucking gnome," the man muttered.

The door opened enough to emit the barrel of a pistol. Then it opened some more. Finally, it opened enough.

"What are you doing here, creep?" the man snapped. "Get back to work. You're supposed to be in—"

Lou pushed away from the wall, whirled behind

Humphrey, and threw the beaker of sulfuric acid, aiming at what he imagined would be Jessup's face. It was a perfect strike. The glass smashed against the bridge of the security guard's nose, shattering on impact, and sending him stumbling back into the room.

Immediately, there were piteous screams and the sizzle of frying skin. Jessup dropped his gun and pawed at his eyes. The air instantly turned sickly with the odor of singed hair and searing flesh. A noxious billow of greenish-yellow smoke began to fill the room.

The shrieking continued.

This was nothing Lou had wanted to do—nothing he enjoyed doing. But Red Cliff and the people within it were extremists who espoused a philosophy of pain for those less fortunate than themselves. And Cap was in serious trouble because of them.

In his years in the ER, Lou had only taken care of one acid-to-the-face injury. It was a woman who had taken out a restraining order on an abusive boyfriend. If he worked in medicine for a thousand years, Lou would never forget the sight of her face. He knew this man's eyes were burnt beyond use, and it was doubtful anyone would ever take him out of prison to give him a face transplant. But injured as he was, he would survive because his burns, though terrible, were not mortal.

Chilled by the sounds and sickened at the smell, Lou took out his Glock and aimed the weapon at Jessup's forehead. The situation was approaching unbearable. He stared down at the scorched and charred remains of what was once a human face. His gun hand began to waver as his thoughts swirled with images of all that had happened since his run in the Chattahoochee forest with Cap.

"Maybe in jail you'll find new meaning to your life," he said, holstering his weapon.

Backing from the room, he closed the door, sealing Jessup inside. Even with the heavy portal shut and a foot of stone wall between them, Lou could still hear the man's agonized moans.

"Where to now?" Humphrey asked.

"Now you go back to the lab and help Kazimi gather up all the notes and data he'll need to make a working antibiotic treatment."

"What are you going to do?" Humphrey asked.

"I'm going to find Doug Bacon and put an end to One Hundred Neighbors once and for all."

CHAPTER 54

Keeping busy and working hard is the best cure for lost faith in our society.

—LANCASTER R. HILL, SERMON AT HIGHBRIDGE BAPTIST CHURCH, NEWTOWN, GEORGIA, SEPTEMBER 21, 1933

With the map of Red Cliff in one hand and his Glock in the other, Lou made his way along the windowless stone passageways illuminated by gas lanterns. The smell of Jessup's burning flesh lingered in his nose and throat.

He passed by a series of staircases, some straight and others spiraling, but knew not to take them. His course—his true north—was to follow a snaking trail of hallways to Bacon's study. After a minute, he saw light up ahead and soon emerged through a stone antechamber into a large, greenhouse-like space—a covered courtyard with a glass ceiling. In the center of the space was a rectangular swimming pool surrounded by magnificent fountains and a rich variety of plants. Bacon's version of a program of entitlement.

Battered and exhausted, Lou circled the pool and headed deeper into Red Cliff, leaving behind the only way out he knew. It was getting close to the time he had instructed Kazimi to bolt, and try to make it to the town of Mount William—maybe five or six miles.

Humphrey had argued for the microbiologist to stay, but the debate had never been resolved. Hopefully, Kazimi would do what was right. But exactly what, Lou asked himself, was that?

The corridor narrowed. Lou felt certain he had arrived at the south end of the castle and the door to Bacon's study. Unlike his attack on Jessup's surveillance office, this time he had no specific plan except to barge in, gun ready. If Bacon was still on his video-conference, so much the better. The attendees could watch the beginning of the end of their movement. The apprehension that had dominated much of his odyssey since landing with Vaill was gone.

He was ready.

Again, Lou checked his watch. Twelve minutes gone. If things were happening the way he wanted them to, Kazimi was through the tunnel and outside the stone guardhouse, headed for town with Lou's cell phone and the number of the FBI in his pocket. There was no cell phone signal in Red Cliff. Perhaps closer to Mount William.

Wondering what he would do if the door was locked, Lou eased down on the latch. There was a soft click as the door's mechanism engaged. Adrenaline pumping, gun in hand, he opened the door slowly and stepped inside a large, oval room. Huge windows framed by burgundy velvet curtains lined the walls. Beyond them, Lou saw the moat and the stretch of lawn where Vaill had gunned down Drake. On the wall was the mammoth monitor Lou had seen through the windows. None of the men and women on the screens seemed to be looking in his direction.

Directly in front of him, facing away, was a massive,

high-backed oxblood leather desk chair on rollers. All he could see of Doug Bacon were his spit-polished black boots and his arms. His left hand, poking out from the armrest, cradled a tumbler of whiskey.

Lou aimed the gun at the back of the impressive chair.

"Okay, Bacon, it's over," he said. "Keep your hands where I can see them and turn around nice and slowly."

A few tense seconds passed before the chair swiveled. When it came to a stop, Lou could only stare, struggling to process what he was seeing. The man seated there was not the stocky fellow Lou had seen through the windows. Rather, this man was old and withered. Harris, Bacon's butler. Before Lou could react, he was startled by a voice from behind him.

"Before you move, Dr. Welcome, I'll need you to drop your gun. The other choice is I'll shoot you through the back of your head right now. The count begins at one and ends at two. One . . ."

Lou dropped his gun and raised his hands. The people on the screens in front of him had gone silent, motionless.

"Good," Bacon said in a distinct Southern drawl. "Now, then, turn around slowly . . . slowly . . . that's it."

Lou turned to see the man he knew was Doug Bacon pointing his cane at Lou's chest. The head of the cane, a resplendent, glittering gold lion's head, was flipped down, revealing the muzzle of a rifle.

"This beauty cost me over ten thousand dollars," Bacon said, addressing the videoconference attendees as much as his captive. "A master Swiss watchmaker put the mechanism together. It's a mechanical marvel. Believe it or not, the magazine actually holds five bullets. But, especially at this range, I am a deadly shot with it, so I expect if that is what I wish to do, I will only have to use up one."

These monsters are going to sit wherever they are and watch my execution, Lou thought.

"But I will add one for what I owe you for my friend, Alexander," Bacon was saying, "and one for each of the men you killed outside, and probably one for the good fellow you murdered in my surveillance room. He is dead, isn't he?"

"Define dead," Lou said.

"You should be praying, doctor, not being snide."

"I do snide better. Face it, Bacon. You've lost. All of you. You've all lost. The FBI knows who you are, and they're on their way. Whether you kill me or not, you're finished."

"I don't think so. We purposely have no cell phone signal here except for the network connected to my phone." He patted his breast pocket. "Same with radios. If you really knew anything, you would have been here with more than just the two of you. When the cause is right and just, victory is inevitable. You're finding that out."

"Is that a bit of your propaganda?" Lou asked. "Because it's crap. Hey, here's one for *you*. 'No matter how right you think you are, you're not.' Dennis Welcome. That's how he used to win arguments against me."

"I've heard enough," Bacon countered, his genteel charm all but gone. "These first couple of shots will just hurt, doctor, but be patient. I choose shoulder."

Without another word, he fired. A flash erupted from the muzzle of his gun, accompanied by a surprisingly muffled pop. Instantly, Lou felt pain explode from just above his right armpit, and also in his back. He pitched to his knees, knowing the shot had gone through and through. Blood was already flowing from the entrance hole.

"These are going to hurt you more than they hurt me, Dr. Snide. Wait, did I have that right?"

Incongruously, all Lou could think of at the moment of his death was the anatomical pathway the first bullet must have taken. He tried, but could not move his arm. Clenching his teeth, he breathed rapidly through his nose. Tears blurred his vision. But he had learned about courage and not giving up from Cap Duncan and Tim Vaill, and, anticipating a second shot, he still scanned about him for anything he could use as a weapon.

I love you, Em . . .

I . . . love . . . you . . . baby.

The Oriental rug beneath him began to swirl.

Where is my gun? Got to get my gun . . .

Lou knew he had only seconds to live.

Not eight feet away from him, Bacon raised his cane once more, this time, it seemed, at Lou's face.

"Sooner or later, you people are going to lose," Bacon said. "You're just doing it sooner."

Lou straightened up and locked his eyes on his tormentor.

"Go to hell," he said.

"You, first, sir. You first. I choose groin."

Bacon adjusted his aim lower. Lou clenched his teeth. Then, from the corner of his eye, he saw a movement from the doorway to his right, and heard a chilling scream. At virtually the same instant, Bacon pulled the trigger. Lou closed his eyes, flinching at the sound. But there was no impact . . . no pain. He looked just in time to see Ahmed Kazimi's body in flight. His arms and legs were outstretched. The bullet from Bacon's gun had struck him squarely in the chest. There was another scream, this one of agony, as Kazimi crumpled to the floor.

In the moment Kazimi had given him, using reflexes he had mastered in the ring under Cap's guidance, Lou pushed up from the floor and threw himself at Bacon. The rotund man did not have the reaction to respond. Closing the gap between them with startling quickness, Lou slammed his left fist into Bacon's doughy abdomen. The pain rifling down his right arm went virtually unnoticed. The director of One Hundred Neighbors doubled over and splayed backward, flailing as he tried to regain his balance.

"Combinations," Cap had preached. *"Always think in combinations and never rely on one punch when you can get in a second."*

Lou struck again, this time hitting Bacon with a vicious jab to the chest, followed instantly by an uppercut that connected full force with the underside of his jaw.

How's that for a fucking combination, Cap?

Bacon's head snapped back. Lou saw a white tooth shoot from the man's bloodied mouth and land on the floor. The cane tumbled away and bounced within Lou's reach like a dropped baton.

With his eyes glazed over, Bacon actually managed to stagger to his feet, blood flowing from his flattened nostrils. Pivoting now, Lou delivered an explosive kick to his face. The older man dropped like a sack of sand.

From the corner of his eye, Lou could see Harris cowering by the windows, and beside him, the screens.

Kazimi was crumpled on the floor, blood expanding from the wound to his chest.

Process.

Lou's mind calmed as it so often did in the ER.

Easy does it . . . First things first . . . Deep breath . . . Focus.

The scientist was unconscious, but still breathing, albeit shallowly. That observation was step one. Step two was ensuring that the resilient Bacon was neutralized, but not so permanently that Vaill's friends at the agency couldn't use him to dissolve the Neighbors.

Ignoring the tearing discomfort in his shoulder, but aware of increasing light-headedness, he retrieved the cane and used it to help himself over to Bacon, who was on his back, moaning and dazed. Lou stepped on the heavy man's meaty throat and retrieved the cell phone from his breast pocket. Then he fumbled with the ten-thousand-dollar cane, aiming the muzzle at the mogul's thigh, at the exact spot where the spear of Cap's femur had thrust through.

Irony. This one is for you, buddy.

"That's enough, Lou!" a voice from the doorway cried.

It was a woman's voice.

It can't be. . . .

Lou whirled. The woman standing fiercely in the doorway looked like the demure, fascinating researcher he had been attracted to from the moment they met, but her eyes were ice.

The pistol held comfortably, professionally in Vicki Banks's hand was pointed at Lou's head.

"I told you that night in the Blue Ox I was damaged goods," she said.

Lou continued to apply pressure to Bacon's throat and now the big man had begun to gag and squirm.

"Vicki. This can't be right. You're Bacon's scientist?"

"I don't belong to Bacon, I belong to the Neighbors. Our cause has given my life true meaning for the first time. I have paid them back for their confidence by discovering and developing the Janus strain. And I intend to keep paying them back. Now, move your foot, and do what you can to save this guy so he can help us if we need him. If you don't, I won't hesitate to kill you. Remember, I grew up on the streets. I've been connected to guns since I was a teen. Look at me, Lou, and you'll know I mean it. I will kill you and then go out for ice cream."

It only took Lou a second to comply and turn to Kazimi. Behind him, Doug Bacon was out cold. Off to his right, the screens continued flickering—the show of shows.

"I might seem like Scupman's lab jockey to you," Vicki said as Lou checked Kazimi's airway and pulses, and then tore open his shirt to expose a nasty wound just above his left nipple, "but I'm far more capable than I've revealed to anyone but my people. You're really very sweet, Lou. I was deeply touched by how hard you fought for your friend. I'm just sorry you're playing for the wrong side."

Kazimi was salvageable, but would not be for long. And worst of all, there was nothing Lou could do. Clearly, the bullet had missed the heart, but there was damage to any number of structures surrounding it that sooner or later would prove lethal. He tore off a strip of fabric, and for a few seconds, applied pressure. But he knew the exercise was fruitless. There was nothing to compress.

The heavy sadness in his own chest was quickly replaced by anger. He looked up at the screens.

"Do you see?" he shouted. "Do you see what kind of people you've all gotten involved with? I don't care how bright and talented you all are, or how much money you have. Everyone of you is misguided and stupid! That's right, stupid!"

"Enough!" Vicki snapped. "I have heard all I fucking care to!"

She turned her head minutely as a machinery whine came up behind her—a whirring motor. Humphrey let go an animal-like cry as he drove his wheelchair into the back of Vicki's legs. The impact was not hard, but it was startling, and firm enough to disrupt her balance.

Instantly, Lou was in motion. Bacon's cane was next to his hand. He seized it by the lower end and swung a looping backhand that would have made the Slugger proud.

Good left-handed power, Lou Welcome. You gonna hit homer to opposite field like that.

The lion's head gave him more than enough heft. Arcing in a golden blur, it smashed Vicki squarely in her jaw. There was a volley of nauseating cracks— multiple bones shattering almost at once. The force of the blow sent her spinning into the door frame. She slammed against the wood, then fell over Humphrey's heavy wheelchair, and smacked the back of her head against the other side of the doorjamb, before tumbling unconscious to the floor.

Driven by an intense rage, Lou whirled and raised the cane at Harris. "You come at me and you die!" Lou snapped, battling back a wave of light-headedness.

Behind him, Kazimi had started moaning.

At least he was alive.

Lou leveled the cane at Harris once more.

"Get some pressure on the wound right now."

"Yes, sir," Harris said. "There's an emergency medical kit under the desk. I do have some training, sir."

Bacon was moaning now. From where he stood, Lou could not tell if Vicki Banks was breathing or not. Her once-interesting face was a mass of blood.

Damaged goods. Is that what you said you were?

Fighting unsteadiness and working for every breath, Lou opened his wallet, pulled out a card, and dialed. It only took a minute for him to get connected.

"FBI, Atlanta. How may I help you?"

CHAPTER 55

Like a splinter, the longer entitlement programs
are allowed to remain in place, the more the
chance that they will begin to fester.

—LANCASTER R. HILL, MEMOIR
    (UNPUBLISHED), JUNE 1933

The first trial of the Janus therapy—code named
Phagecil for the three types of bacteriophages being
used—was about to be completed. A crowd was gathered in the Great Room awaiting the big announcement. It had been three days since Lou swung the
lion's head cane that had shattered Vicki Bank's jaw,
nose, and orbit. Under guard, she had been evaluated
at the hospital in Bangor, and then shipped to Portland,
where two teams of surgeons had begun the series of
operations that would reconstruct her face.

Kazimi was airlifted to Bangor as well, and successfully underwent seven hours of surgery. Ron
Jessup, burned beyond recognition, followed along by
ambulance. Lou expected Kazimi would be bedridden
for days, but to his astonishment, the government flew
him back to Red Cliff almost a day ago, with a tube
still in his chest, so he could continue his work with
"Mr. Miller," as the formal Muslim still insisted on
calling him. The scientists were both in wheelchairs
now, although Kazimi could walk for short distances.

Red Cliff had gone from a secluded, foreboding fortress to a compound bustling with activity. The Neighbors' helipad was getting frequent use, and street traffic into and away from the place was as steady as the surf. The Army Corps of Engineers erected a communications center almost overnight, giving everyone the cell phone service they couldn't seem to live without.

For his part, Lou had been transfused three units at a small community hospital, and then medflighted to Bangor, where tests and exploratory surgery gave him only good news. Numbness in several fingers, and weakness in his right hand along the distribution of the ulnar nerve, but nothing time shouldn't take care of. Twenty-four hours later, in a sling, he was back at Red Cliff, where he elected to stay rather than to travel back to Atlanta.

He communicated with Cap several times a day, but only for a few minutes each time. According to Dr. Win Carter, the head of Arbor General, Cap's condition was heading steadily downhill, and each minute brought Lou new fears that a treatment, assuming one was even successfully developed, could arrive too late.

Lou awaited news about the Phagecil experiment near a makeshift memorial of flowers and cards dedicated to Agent Tim Vaill that had been put together at the base of the now boarded-up window. The Coast Guard had recovered Alexander Burke's shattered corpse, largely eaten by fish and the sea, lodged between two barnacle-covered boulders near the shoreline, but Vaill's body had yet to be found.

Beth Snyder had flown to Red Cliff to meet the "saviors," as she had dubbed Lou, Kazimi, and Humphrey. When news came from the Coast Guard that they were abandoning the search for Vaill, she, Lou, and Chuck McCall held a brief vigil of silence, lit a candle, and threw it off Red Cliff into the charging waves. According to Snyder, Vaill and Maria would be memorialized at the FBI headquarters in D.C., and at all of the field offices, joining the thirty-six agents who had preceded them as Service Martyrs.

Lou was on his third cup of coffee, alone by the window farthest from the crowd, when Humphrey wheeled over. Despite the stresses of performing almost any task, Humphrey had been working around the clock, and had supervised installation of two air-conditioning units so that the temperature of the lab could be kept at below sixty—the temperature for keeping his CP under optimum control. Kazimi, who thrived in warm temperatures, showed his mettle and spirit of cooperation by wearing a parka.

Now, though, fatigue was starting to show in both men—mostly about their eyes. But soon, they hoped, their exhaustion would have proved worthwhile. Over the days before Kazimi's return, since the moment he entered the lab with a skilled assistant to begin his experiments, Humphrey had gotten the attention and encouragement lavished upon him that a lifetime of living on the fringes had failed to provide. And Lou was more than pleased to see him finally getting the recognition he deserved.

Thankfully, at least according to Humphrey, a live antibacterial treatment could be put together and tested in a matter of days. In a show of unprecedented solidarity, standing by waiting were the chiefs of antibiotic research at most of the largest pharmaceutical houses in the country, all of which had pledged to speed any breakthrough into production.

"You seem nervous, Lou," Humphrey said.

"Aren't you?"

"Little, I suppose. Been working years for this test. Phage Banks brought were in excellent condition. I've always believed myself. This first time others believe in me, too."

"I understand. I'm sure glad I believed in you, Humphrey. Cap will be excited, too. So will a lot of people for that matter."

Humphrey looked beside himself with glee. "Scupman from CDC called. He's on way here later today. Says he has place in lab for me."

"That's wonderful, Humphrey," Lou said. "Really terrific."

Before Humphrey could respond, Lou's cell phone rang. He glanced at the number and his chest tightened when he saw it was Win Carter from Arbor General. They had spoken once this morning and Cap was still listed in critical, but stable condition. *Something must have changed.*

Lou cleared his throat, took an anxious swallow, and answered the call.

"Win, what's going on?"

"Lou, I'm afraid I've got bad news to share."

Lou's knee-jerk reaction was that Cap was dead, but he quickly realized there was another possibility.

"Go on," he said, bracing himself against the back of a leather chair.

"Hank's temp shot up a few hours ago, and his pressure began to drop. Ninety systolic, then eighty. Clearly he was septic. Lou, there was nothing his surgeons could do but amputate. They tried everything they could to forestall this, but time just ran out. I'm sorry, Lou. I'm so terribly sorry, for Hank and for you."

Lou's knees became Jell-O. He braced himself more firmly against the chair.

"How is he doing now?" he asked.

"Actually, that's the good news. I just heard from his surgeon, and for the moment at least, his temp is down, his pressure is up, and his kidneys are functioning well."

Lou could barely speak. He had failed. He had let down his best friend and there was nothing he could do to change that fact.

"How high up?" he managed to ask.

The hesitation from Atlanta all but answered his question.

"They chose to go as high as they could," Carter said. "Just below the pelvis. They elected to try leaving the hip joint itself, because a prosthesis would be technically easier that way."

Prosthesis.

A lump materialized in Lou's throat. Delivering bad news had always been a part of his job, and although he never, ever enjoyed doing it, he knew he was usually effective at it, mostly by being direct and honest. He was grateful Win Carter had approached him the same way, even though the lump continued to grow.

"Thanks, Win," he said, unable to cull the hoarseness from his voice. "I appreciate all you've done. Everything."

"I just wish we could have done more."

"Me, too," Lou said, ending the call. "Me, too."

He looked around, saw McCall talking with Beth Snyder, and waved him over.

"I need to fly back to Atlanta ASAP. Can you arrange that for me?"

"Sure, Lou. Anything you need. Is everything all right?"

"No. Not in the least. They took Cap's leg."

McCall sagged.

"Oh, shit. I'm so sorry, Lou. They couldn't have put it off? Did they know what's happening here?"

"They knew. They waited as long as they could. It sounds like it was either his leg or his life. It's my fault. I let him down, Chuck. I let my closest friend down."

"Don't do that to yourself," McCall said. "You did everything you could and then some."

"I couldn't save Tim and I couldn't save Cap's leg."

"Lou . . ."

"Oh, hell. I know what you're trying to say. I'm just babbling. Listen, just help me get out of here, Chuck. Can you do that for me?"

I need a meeting and I need to go see Cap. . . .

McCall returned a sympathetic look.

"You got it, Lou. We'll warm up the chopper, and have the jet waiting for you at the airport. Goodness knows you've earned a flight in that beauty."

"Thanks. One last thing. That night you and Tim came to get me at the Blue Ox. How did you know I had been asking about the phage?"

"Scupman. He had been working for us since the beginning, passing along anything that might have been of interest regarding the Doomsday Germ. Apparently Kazimi didn't think enough of him to make him part of his team."

"But Scupman never suspected his own assistant."

McCall shook his head.

"Never a word. She was good, Lou. She was damn good at blending in. Looking like Little Bo Peep didn't hurt her any, either."

Lou sighed and wandered alone along the main passageway until he came to the French doors opening onto the cliff. In a haze, he stared unseeing across the North Atlantic. Behind him, through the windows of the Great Room, he could hear escalating commotion. It sounded as if the excitement was building.

Any minute now, he thought.

He scuffed around along the narrow, gravel walkway to the spot on the north side where Alexander Burke had filmed his good-bye message for Lola. The windblown salted air had begun stinging the moistness in his eyes, as he gazed out at the steel-gray water. His thoughts were a swirl of regret mixed with guilt. *What if I never took Cap to Atlanta? What if we skipped the morning run like he had wanted? What if my grip had held? What if I had fallen instead of him . . . ?*

"I wish it was my leg, buddy," Lou said to the sea. "I wish it was me in that hospital bed, and not you. I wish it could have been different."

From inside the Great Room a triumphant cheer erupted, followed by a steady round of applause. Not long after, McCall approached, with his hands stuffed inside his jacket pockets.

"Chopper's ready when you are."

"Thanks. That cheering mean what I think it means?"

"All the mice are alive," McCall said. "Every single last one of those sweet, furry little buggers."

Lou strained a smile.

"That's great news. I knew Humphrey could do it."

"Not just Humphrey," McCall said. "You, too, Lou. You deserve as much credit as he does."

"I guess."

McCall patted him on his good shoulder.

"Let it hurt, pal. That's all you can do right now. Just let it hurt. That's what I'm doing about Tim. And the moment you get near that beautiful kid of yours, hug her as long and as hard as she can stand it. I know I'm rambling, but I really owe you, Lou, and I really like you. And as for your friend back there in Atlanta, in a strange way, he helped save the lives of thousands of people—maybe much more than that."

"So how come I don't feel so great?" Lou asked.

"Because you're not supposed to, that's why. Time'll take care of a lot of the pain, but never all of it. Just don't forget that because of Cap, and you, and Tim, our government won't be held hostage by a bunch of wacko terrorists with twisted ideals. And thanks to you, that creep Bacon is in custody and being questioned by people who are ten times as good at their job as me and ol' Vaill."

He punctuated that remark with a grin.

Lou felt a little better.

"Maybe we'll run into each other in Atlanta," he said.

"Well, I certainly hope so. I'm gonna be there for a hundred years trying to bail myself out of the frigging report mess you've left me. The beer's gonna be on you."

"So long as it isn't at the Blue Ox. Thanks for the help getting me out of here, Chuck, and for the talk, too."

They turned and headed back to the entrance.

Another cheer burst out from within, and some champagne corks popped.

"Wish it had been sooner," McCall said.

"Yeah . . . Me, too."

"Beth Snyder wants to say good-bye before you go."

"Chuck, I really wish Tim could be here to share this."

"Who knows? Maybe he is."

"Look, I'm going to skip out without seeing anybody if that's okay with you. Tell Humphrey we'll catch up at the hospital. Tell Beth I'll be in touch."

"You got it, pal."

Lou walked around to the driveway, then across to the helipad. A few minutes later, with vivid memories of the chopper ride from beside the Chattahoochee River, he was airborne. Below him, he watched Red Cliff recede until it was little more than a speck.

Then, in a blink, it was gone.

CHAPTER 56

It is impossible to climb the ladder of success if our government has removed every last rung.

—LANCASTER R. HILL, GRAVESTONE
INSCRIPTION, ALL SAINTS CEMETERY,
MAY 7, 1945

The white van navigated the circular drive and came to a stop at the gleaming glass front entrance of Arbor General. Lou, his sling still in place, waited curbside, and as soon as he saw the driver exit the van, he came forward to help unload his passenger. Humphrey was all smiles as the power platform lowered his wheelchair to ground level. Lou came up and they shook left hands.

"Long time buddy," Humphrey said, his eyes sparkling.

He thanked his driver and motored toward the entrance. Lou fell into step alongside him.

"Three whole days," Lou replied. "But I did appreciate all the e-mails and text messages you sent. It sounds like things went as well as we could hope after I left."

"In drug companies' hands now. First batch Phagecil ready to ship. Sorry too late for Cap."

"Thanks, Humphrey. Thanks to you, it's still going to help save his life."

The automatic doors swooshed open and Lou

followed the wheelchair into Arbor General's expansive marble lobby. Having spent so much time there, he had become friendly with several of the salmon-wearing volunteers and he knew many of the security staff by first name.

Though he'd grown fond of them all, he was anxious to return to D.C., and he would, as soon as the arrangements at a top-notch rehab for Cap had been completed. He also had his old job to get back to. Filstrup had called to complain about work piling up, and the absence of a good replacement for Lou, in addition to the angry feedback he had endured from clients at the PWO. Completely out of character, he had offered him reinstatement. Of course, Lou had accepted, but not before working the man for an additional week of vacation annually for himself and also for Babs Peterbee, not retroactive, plus a nice personal donation from Filstrup to Emily's Cap Duncan Fund.

But before Lou could make any more plans, there was a very crucial piece of business that had to be completed at the hospital.

"I've heard the gag order is going to be lifted soon," he said as he and Humphrey prepared to part ways.

"Government going tell about Neighbors?"

"According to Chuck McCall and Beth Snyder, the answer is yes. Congress is worried about leaks and they want to be proactive about informing the American public about what happened, especially since it looks like Doug Bacon has handed over every member of the society. The president is preparing an address and he's going to come forward about the existence of the Neighbors and how the Doomsday Germ that's been spreading through hospitals was really a biological weapon designed by a domestic terrorist group. I hear you're one of the few people who will be publicly credited by the president for your role in this victory over terrorism."

Humphrey's thin chest puffed.

"Can't believe it," he said.

"Your life is about to change, my friend. As soon as people find out what you've done, you'll be on the cover of every major magazine and probably get an hour devoted to you on *60 Minutes*."

Humphrey's already broad smile brightened even more.

"If I have to speak, they may need rename show 'Ninety Minutes.' Good thing government cleaned my apartment. Hope they help Cassie's family."

"I believe they will," Lou said. "Chuck McCall told me that they're rushing legislation through Congress to establish the One Hundred Neighbors Victim Compensation Fund. The announcement of the fund will coincide with the president's address. I would suspect Cassie will be included."

"Terrific. She has kids not much money."

Lou didn't bother to explain how much Humphrey would be able to do for Cassie and others once the pharmaceutical companies made good on their pledges to him.

"From what I've heard, the fund will be similar to the legislation Congress passed following the 9/11 attacks," he said instead. "My daughter Emily's done a great job raising thousands of dollars for Cap, but it should be a fraction of what he'll receive from this new fund."

"Great news. You know I'll be at Arbor awhile longer."

"But not in the pharmacy."

Humphrey laughed his most wonderfully joyous laugh and applauded.

For the time being, he would continue working with a technician in his subbasement lab—a tech on loan from Sam Scupman. Soon, though, as promised, he would be moving over to the CDC. Scupman himself, the champion of bacterial power, had taken the position that simultaneously blasting the Doomsday infections with multiple killer viruses gave every reason to believe the germ would be much less of a threat to mutate.

Finally, with promises they would never lose touch with each other, Lou and Humphrey embraced and parted. Lou watched until the remarkable man and his wheelchair entered the freight elevator, and the doors glided shut behind him. Then he headed up to where Cap was waiting.

One last piece of business.

His stump wrapped up and bandaged, Cap still greeted Lou with a high five. The operation was tragic in its timing, but it had clearly saved his life.

"Good timing, doc," Cap said.

Cap's steadily improving demeanor had done more for Lou's state of mind than anything else could—except that moment when he would again get to hold Emily.

"Tell me," Lou said, adding a bit to the water already in Cap's plastic cup.

"A specialist in prosthetics just left my room. She came to talk with me about options for my new leg. Man, the technology today is really something spectacular. She even thinks I might be a candidate for this thing called targeted muscle reinnervation."

"I think I know a little about that, but fill me in."

"It's like redirecting nerves to control the prosthetic using substitute healthy muscle from somewhere else in my body," Cap said. "She has a friend at the rehab I want to go to in D.C. who does it."

"Amazing. That would be so cool."

"From what she told me, I might even be able to box again. Heck, I'd be a willing guinea pig for that alone."

"I'm ready to take you on," Lou said. "But you have to promise no kicking."

"Okay, okay, no kicking. In the meantime, I'll get fitted for a prosthetic leg when we get home. They say just a couple of more days."

"That's really great news!"

"The people from that fund they're setting up have already come to visit me. When all is said and done, I'm gonna own Stick and Move clear, with enough left over for projects in the inner city that I've only dreamed about. I'm going to start working with the disabled, too. Not just amputees, but all disabilities."

"I'd love to help. So would Emily."

"Perfect. The more I get to see that gal, the better."

Lou checked the time on the watch she had given him. "I think our friend should be here any minute," he said. "You ready?"

"More than I was when I fought Rafael Marquez."

"And how did you do in that one?"

"I knocked him out in the third. . . . Crunch!"

He cracked his knuckles for emphasis.

"Well, you don't have to wait until the third round this time."

As if on cue, without a knock, the room door opened and Ivan Puchalsky strode in, his white knee-length coat so starched it looked as if it could stand up on its own. He greeted Lou and Cap, and may or may not have noticed that he was not offered a handshake by either man.

"So," he said, "word from the nurses is that you are continuing to improve. That's excellent."

"Thanks," Cap said.

"So, Dr. Welcome, your message said it was urgent that I meet you here. I have ID rounds in a few minutes, so this really must be brief."

"Oh, it will be brief," Cap said. "I promise you that. Doctor, do you know a man named Douglas Bacon?"

Puchalsky's blank expression may have been legit.

"I'm afraid I don't," he said.

"No matter," Cap went on. "He knows you, and that's what counts. In fact, in documents signed under oath by him, he names you as one of those hospital employees scattered around the country who was recruited by the group he directed—a group calling themselves the Society of One Hundred Neighbors."

"I don't understand."

But Lou could tell now that he did.

"You were paid and paid handsomely to use your expertise in nosocomial disease," Lou said, "to slowly introduce the Janus strain, also known as the Doomsday Germ into this hospital."

"That's ridiculous. Why would I ever do something like that?"

"The list of possible reasons starts with a boatload

of money, and moves on through your suddenly mush-rooming importance in the field of hospital-based in-fection. Bacon says they had no trouble enlisting your services, either—especially when they needed you to help them cure the germ after it began mutating. So let's add immortality and worldwide fame to our list. Then we should probably include the multiple donations on record that you've made to a number of right-leaning organizations, some of which are more or less recruitment fronts for One Hundred Neighbors."

Puchalsky, his cheeks flushed, could only glare at him.

"You took my leg," Cap said with far less anger in his voice than the man deserved. "I'd like to meet the person who led you in your Hippocratic Oath, or what-ever oath doctors take wherever you came from. Now, get out of my room. I think you'll find a couple of our friends from the FBI waiting for you just outside the door. I'm looking forward to testifying against you in court."

Puchalsky looked as if he were about to spit. Then he turned on his heels and stalked out the door.

Lou could see Chuck McCall in the hall waiting for him, handcuffs dangling.

"We'll take it from here, Lou," he called out.

"You do that," Lou replied in a near whisper. "You do that." He turned to Cap. "Good thing it was your recovery program at work just then, and not mine," he said. "I would have decked him."

"And that would have brought my leg back, right?"

"Duncan, you're the best, do you know that?"

"Besides, I don't like to think of the leg that's gone. I'd rather focus on the six inches my surgeons left behind. I keep feeling the rest, though. I keep feeling the phantom limb pains. I'm told this is normal, so maybe the leg will be with me for a long time."

"Only you would think like that," Lou said. "You know, I heard there's a rowing club on the Potomac that allows amputees in their shells. How do you think we'd do as a two-man crew?"

Cap held Lou's hand in both of his.

"When are the next Olympics?" he asked.

The Boston Globe

An open letter of thanks to the nurses, doctors, and staff at White Memorial Hospital, and all those who played a part in defeating the Doomsday Germ, especially those who helped in the development of PHAGECIL.

My recent infection came close to killing me but all it did in the end was to strengthen my faith and my gratitude.

The death of my patient and friend Becca Seabury, and my own devastating illness and recovery, helped me better appreciate the gift of every single day, and the beauty of being able to care for others. I cannot wait until I am able to return to nursing again.

With all that in mind, I wish to announce my marriage, six months earlier than planned, to ANDREW GULLI of Cambridge, Massachusetts, on the day following my recent discharge from the hospital.

God Bless You All.

—Jennifer Sarah Lowe-Gulli, R.N.

Read on for an excerpt from

TRAUMA

by Michael Palmer and Daniel Palmer

Coming soon in hardcover from St. Martin's Press

CHAPTER 1

It began, innocently enough, with a fall.

Beth Stillwell, a slight, thirty-five-year-old mother of three with kind eyes and an infectious laugh, was shopping at Thrifty Dollar Store with her kids in tow. She'd been stocking up on school supplies and home staples when she lost her balance and tumbled to the grimy linoleum floor. It was bad enough to have to shop at the dollar store, something new since her separation from her philandering husband of fifteen years. It was downright humiliating to be sprawled out on their floor, her leg bent in a painful angle beneath her.

Beth wasn't hurt, but as her six-year-old daughter Emily tried to help her stand, her left leg felt weak, almost rubbery. Leaning against a shelf stocked with cheap soap, Beth took a tentative step only to have the leg nearly buckle beneath her. She kept her balance, and after another awkward step, decided she could walk on it.

The strength in Beth's left leg mostly returned, but a slight stiffness and a disconcerting drag lingered for weeks. Beth's sister told her to see a doctor. Beth said she would, but it was an empty promise. Running a licensed day care out of her Jamaica Plain home, Beth was in charge of seven kids in addition to her own, and any downtime put tremendous strain on her limited finances. She rarely had time to make a phone call. But the leg was definitely a bother, and the lingering weakness was a constant worry. She occasionally stumbled, but the last straw was losing control of her urine while in charge of toddlers who could hold their bladders better than she could. That drove her to the doctor.

An MRI confirmed a parasagittal tumor originating from the meninges with all the telltale characteristics of a typical meningioma: a brain tumor. The tumor was already big enough to compress brain tissue, interrupting the normal complex communication from neuron to neuron and causing a moderate degree of edema, swelling from the pressure on the brain's blood vessels.

Beth would need surgery to have it removed.

Dr. Carrie Bryant stood in front of the viewbox, examining Beth Stillwell's MRI. A fourth-year neurosurgical resident rotating through Boston Community Hospital (BCH), she would be assisting chief resident Dr. Fred Michelson with Beth's surgery. The tumor pressed upon the top of the brain on the right side. Carrie could see exactly why Beth's left leg had gone into a focal seizure and why she'd lost control of her urine. It was not a particularly large mass, about walnut-sized, but its location was extremely problematic. If it were to grow, Beth would develop progressive spasticity in her leg and eventually lose bladder control completely.

Carrie absently rubbed her sore quadriceps while studying Beth's films. She had set a new personal best at yesterday's sprint distance triathlon, finally breaking the elusive ten-minute-mile pace during the run, and her body was letting her know she had pushed it too hard. Her swim and bike performance were shaky per usual, and all but guaranteed a finish in the bottom quartile for her age group—but at least she was out there, battling, doing her best to get her fitness level back to where it had been.

Carrie's choice to jump right into triathlons was perhaps not the wisest, but she never did anything half measure. She enjoyed pushing her body to new limits. She'd also used the race to raise more than a thousand dollars for BCH: a tiny fraction of what was needed, but every bit helped.

BCH served the poor and uninsured. Carrie felt proud to be a part of that mission, but lack of funding was a constant frustration. In her opinion, the omnipotent budgeting committee relied too heavily on cheap labor to fill the budget gap, which explained why fourth- and fifth-year residents basically ran the show whenever they rotated through BCH. Attending physicians, those docs who had finished residency, were supposed to provide oversight, but they had too much work and too few resources to do the job.

If the constant budget shortfalls had a silver lining, it could be summed up in a single word: experience. With each BCH rotation the hours would be long, the demands exhausting, but Carrie never groaned or complained. She was getting the best opportunity to hone her skills.

Thank goodness Chambers University did its part

to fund the storied health-care institution, which had trained some of Boston's most famous doctors, including the feared but revered Dr. Stanley Metcalf, staff neurosurgeon at the iconic White Memorial Hospital. For now, the doors to BCH were open, the lights on, and people like Beth Stillwell could get exceptional medical care even without exceptional insurance.

So far, Beth had been a model patient. She'd spent two days in the hospital, and in that time Carrie had had the pleasure of meeting both her sister and her children. Carrie prepped for Beth's surgery wondering when having a family of her own would fit into her hectic life. At twenty-nine, she had thought it might happen with Ian, her boyfriend of two years, but apparently her dedication to residency did not jibe with his vision of the relationship. She should have known when Ian began referring to his apartment as Carrie's "on-call room" that their union was headed for rocky times.

At half past eleven, Carrie was on her way to scrub when Dr. Michelson stopped her in the hallway.

"Two cases of acute lead poisoning just rolled in," he announced.

Carrie smiled weakly at the dark humor: two gunshot victims needed the OR.

"We can do Miss Stillwell at five o'clock," Michelson said. It was not a request. Working at one of New England's busiest trauma hospitals meant that patients often got bumped for the crisis of the moment, and Dr. Michelson fully expected Carrie to accommodate him.

Carrie would have been fine with his request regardless. Her social calendar had been a long string of empty boxes ever since Ian called things off. During the relationship vortex, Carrie had evidently neglected her apartment as well as her friends, and it would take time to get everything back to pre-Ian levels. Carrie agreed to move Beth's surgery even though she had no real say in the matter.

The time change gave Carrie an opportunity to finish the rest of her rotations on the neurosurgical floor. She met with several different patients, and concluded her rounds with Leon Dixon, whom Dr. Metcalf had admitted as a private patient that morning. She would be assisting Dr. Metcalf with his surgery the next day.

Carrie entered Leon's hospital room after knocking, and found a handsome black man propped up in his adjustable bed, drinking water through a straw. Leon was watching *Antiques Roadshow* with his wife, who sat in a chair pushed up against the bed. They were holding hands. Leon was in his early fifties, with a kind but weathered face.

"Hi, Leon, I'm Dr. Carrie Bryant. I'll be assisting with your operation tomorrow. How you feeling today?"

"Pre—eh-eh-eh-eh."

"I'm Phyllis, Leon's wife. He's feeling pretty crappy, is what he's trying to say."

Carrie shook hands with the attractive woman who had gone from being a wife to a caregiver in a matter of weeks. The heavy makeup around Phyllis's tired eyes showed just how difficult those weeks had been. Carrie had yet to review Leon's films, but was not surprised about his speech problems; the chart said he'd presented aphasic. She doubted he'd stuttered before, but she was not going to embarrass him by asking.

"Leon, could you close your eyes and open your mouth for me?" Carrie asked.

Leon got his eyes shut, but his mouth stayed closed as well. Carrie sent a text message to Dr. Nugent in radiology. She wanted to look at his films, stat.

"He has a lot of trouble following instructions," Phyllis said as she brushed tears from her eyes. "Memory and temper problems, too."

Something is going on in Leon's left temporal lobe, Carrie thought. *Probably a tumor.*

Carrie observed other symptoms as well. The right side of Leon's face drooped slightly, and his right arm drifted down when he held out his arms in front of him with his eyes closed. His reflexes were heightened in the right arm and leg, and when Carrie scraped the sole of his right foot with the reflex hammer, his great toe extended up toward his face—a Babinski sign, indicating damage to the motor system represented on the left side of Leon's brain.

Carrie took hold of Leon's dry and calloused hand and looked him in the eye.

"Leon, we're going to do everything we can to make you feel better. I'm going to go look at your films now, and I'll see you tomorrow for your surgery." Carrie wrote her cell phone number on a piece of paper. Business cards were for after residency. "If you need anything, this is how to reach me," she said.

Carrie preferred not to cut the examination short, but a text from Dr. Robert Nugent said he'd delay his meeting for Carrie if she came now. Carrie was rushed herself. She needed to get to Beth Stillwell for her final pre-op consultation.

Dr. Nugent, a married father of two, was a compet-

itive triathlete who had finished well ahead of Carrie
in the last race they had done together. Over the years,
Carrie had learned that it paid to be friends with the
radiologists for situations just like this, and nothing
fostered camaraderie quite like the race circuit.

The radiology department was located in the bowels
of BCH, in a windowless section of the Glantz Wing,
but somehow Dr. Nugent appeared perpetually tan,
even after the brutal New England winter.

"Thanks for making some time for me, Bob," Carrie said. "Leon just materialized on my OR schedule
and I haven't gotten any background on him from
Dr. Metcalf yet."

Dr. Nugent shrugged. He knew all about Dr. Metcalf's surprise patients. "Yeah, from what I was told,
Dixon's doctor is good friends with Metcalf."

"Let me guess: Leon has no health insurance."

"Bingo."

Carrie chuckled and said, "Why am I not surprised?"

It was unusual to see a private patient at Community. Just about every patient was admitted through
the emergency department and assigned to resident
staff. Dr. Metcalf was known for his philanthropy, and
when he rotated through Community he often took on
cases he could not handle at White Memorial because
of insurance issues.

All the residents looked forward to working with
Dr. Metcalf, and Carrie's peers had expressed jealousy
more than once. Assisting Dr. Metcalf was the ultimate
test of a resident's skill, grace under the most extreme
pressure. Dr. Metcalf had earned a reputation for being
exacting and demanding, even a bully at times, but his

approach paid off. He taught technique, didn't assume total control, and was supremely patient with the less experienced surgeons. Like many world-class surgeons, Dr. Metcalf was sometimes tempestuous and always demanding, but Carrie was willing to take the bitter with the sweet if it helped with her career.

Dr. Nugent put Leon's MRI films up on the viewbox.

"It's most likely a grade three astrocytoma," he said.

The irregular mass was 1.5 by 2 centimeters in size, located deep in the left temporal lobe and associated with frondlike edema. No doubt this was the cause of Leon's aphasic speech and confused behavior.

"So Dr. Metcalf's scheduled to take this one out tomorrow," Dr. Nugent said.

"As much as he can, anyway."

Dr. Nugent agreed.

Carrie was about to ask Dr. Nugent a question when she noticed the time. She was going to be late for the final pre-op consultation with Beth. *Damn.* There were never enough hours in the day.

Carrie made it to Beth's hospital room at four thirty and found the anesthesiologist already there. By the end of Carrie's consult, Beth looked teary-eyed.

"You'll be holding your children again in no time, trust me," Carrie assured her.

Even with her head newly shaved, Beth was a strikingly beautiful woman, young and vivacious. Despite Carrie's words of comfort, Beth did not look convinced.

"Just make sure I'll be all right, Dr. Bryant," Beth said. "I have to see my kids grow up."

At quarter to five, Beth was taken from the patient holding area to OR 15. Carrie had her mask, gown, and head covering already donned, and was in the scrub room, three minutes into her timed five-minute anatomical scrub, when Dr. Michelson showed up.

"How would you feel about doing the Stillwell case on your own?" he asked. "The attending went home for the day, and I got a guy with a brain hemorrhage who's going to be ART if I don't evacuate the clot and decompress the skull."

Carrie rolled her eyes at Michelson. She was not a big fan of some of the medical slang that was tossed around, and ART, an especially callous term, was an acronym for "approaching room temperature," a.k.a. dead.

"No problem on Stillwell," Carrie said. Her heart jumped a little. She had never done an operation without the oversight of an attending or chief resident before.

Quick as the feeling came, Carrie's nerves settled. She was an excellent surgeon with confidence in her abilities, and, if the hospital grapevine were to be believed, the staff's next chief resident. It would certainly be a nice feather in her surgical cap, and helpful in securing a fellowship at the Cleveland Clinic after residency.

"Unfortunately, I'm going to need OR fifteen. Everything else is already booked," Michelson said.

Carrie nodded. Par for the course at BCH. "Beth can wait," she said.

"I checked the schedule for you. OR six or nine should be open in a couple of hours."

Carrie did some quick calculations to make sure she could handle the Stillwell operation and still be rested enough to assist Dr. Metcalf with Leon's operation in the morning. *Three to four hours, tops,* Carrie thought, *and Beth will be back in recovery.*

"No problem," Carrie said. "I'll let you scrub down and save the day."

"Thanks, Doc Bryant," Michelson said. "But you're the real lifesaver here. I don't think there's another fourth year I'd trust with this operation."

"Your faith in me inspires."

Carrie did not mention the promise she'd made to Beth during her pre-op consultation. Michelson would not have approved. If one thing was certain about surgery, it was that nothing, no matter how routine or simple it seemed, was ever 100 percent guaranteed.